THE BROKEN MIRRORS

SINALCOL

Also by Elias Khoury in English translation

Gate of the Sun
Yalo
As Though She Were Sleeping
White Masks

Elias Khoury

THE BROKEN MIRRORS

~

SINALCOL

Translated from the Arabic by
Humphrey Davies

MACLEHOSE PRESS
QUERCUS · LONDON

First published in the Arabic language as *Sīnālkūl*
by Dār al-Ādāb, Beirut, 2012
First published in Great Britain in 2015 by MacLehose Press
This paperback edition published in 2016 by

MacLehose Press
an imprint of Quercus Editions Ltd
Carmelite House
50 Victoria Embankment
London EC4Y 0DZ

An Hachette UK Company

A CIP catalogue record for this book is available
from the British Library.

ISBN (HB) 978 1 84866 982 6
ISBN (TPB) 978 0 85705 364 0
ISBN (MMP) 978 1 84866 772 3
ISBN (Ebook) 978 1 84866 773 0

10 9 8 7 6 5 4 3 2 1

Designed and typeset in Minion by Jouve (UK) Milton Keynes
Printed and bound in Great Britain by Clays Ltd, St Ives plc

CONTENTS

One departure came between us and with death,
After that first departure, another parting comes.

— al-Mutanabbi

1

Karim Shammas bent to lift his suitcase out of the boot of the black Mercedes taxi that had been taking him to Beirut airport en route back to Montpellier.

His watch said 5.30 a.m., and the Beirut dawn was tinted with darkness and dust.

It had rained the day before. The Beirut spring had arrived, carried on the sound of thunder, the thunder blending in turn into the sound of the intermittent shelling that roamed aimlessly around the city.

The man had found it impossible to sleep on his last night in Beirut. He'd drunk a lot of whisky, sat on the sofa in the living room, yawned, and waited for dawn to the rhythm of the thunder and the rain.

He'd celebrated his fortieth birthday alone. Ghazala had disappeared into her story, Muna had left to search for her future in Canada and Karim was alone at home in Beirut. Bernadette had called a couple of days earlier and asked him to come back on the fourth of January so he could celebrate the start of his fifth decade with the family. He'd told her he hadn't been able to find a seat on the plane until the morning of the following day. His French wife had cleared her throat, pretended to believe him and hung up.

He sat there alone and decided to rewrite his story. He poured a glass of whisky, placed a plate of roasted salted almonds before him, and darkness enveloped him. The electricity was cut, the light of the candle shuddered, turning objects into ghosts dancing on the walls, and Karim drank the whisky without ice, feeling his stomach burn.

He felt his life had been transformed into a shattered mirror. He'd lied a lot and they'd lied to him a lot, but his return to Beirut and his consent to his brother's hospital construction project were the mistakes that had brought his whole story out into the open and shattered it, making it hard to gather up the slivers and put flesh back onto a life that had been smashed to pieces.

He'd drunk the whisky and sat there waiting. He'd been certain she'd call but the phone remained silent and she didn't. When he thought about "her" he wasn't even sure to whom the pronoun referred. Was he still waiting after all that had happened for Ghazala, or was he waiting for Muna, who'd closed her eyes as she lay dozing beside him, then told him the story of her romance with the Italian? He saw Hend with her brown face that became longer with sorrow and her diffidence hidden behind grey eyes, and remembered a love that had been killed by fear and then turned into a family secret that no-one could mention.

He was enveloped by the sounds of the city, which seemed poised to fall into the valley of darkness – that was the image his brother's words had traced out before his eyes. He saw the city on the brink of the valley and felt everything was sliding into a bottomless abyss. Nasim had said the ship had caught fire at the Beirut docks, he'd lost all his wealth in one fell swoop, and that the hospital project was over because he was now obliged to sell it, and the flat, to pay off a part of his debts. Karim hadn't needed the news of the sunken oil tanker to know the project had fallen apart and that he'd have to return to France weighed down by disappointment and failure. Ghazala had proved to him that everything in Beirut was fragile and unsustainable, and the story of his father Nasri's death had made him realise that his brother's project had been nothing but an illusion.

He waited but without knowing for whom he was waiting. When love turns into waiting for love, a person ceases to be capable of knowing his own feelings. What did it mean, this story he'd found himself caught up in? Let no-one think it had anything to do with what people call marital infidelity: Karim had never for a moment felt he was being unfaithful to his wife. He'd had brief affairs with French and Moroccan nurses and patients but he'd never felt he was what they call "unfaithful". Maybe it was because he'd never loved his white-skinned wife, or because he did love her; he didn't know. Ghazala had been unfaithful to him with that boy with the strange name from the militias and Muna with her husband the architect who'd decided to emigrate to Canada, and Hend had betrayed him with his memories.

He was sitting in the dark, abandoned to the composition of his story, when suddenly the phone rang. He picked up the receiver and heard his wife's voice coming to him from somewhere distant and deep. It woke him from his illusory waitings. It screamed "Hello! . . . Hello!" then suddenly was cut off.

He felt hungry, flicked on his lighter, and went to the refrigerator. He opened it, then closed it again on smelling rotten apples. Everything went bad in this city that had electricity only three hours a day.

During his long stay in France he had dreamed of Lebanese apples, their perfume mixing with the smell of coffee as he inhaled the ecstasy of his childhood.

Karim had properly understood the scent of childhood only when away from his country. He could see his father, the pharmacist, holding out his hand, pouring out a spoonful of ground coffee, adding half a spoon of sugar, mixing them, and then setting about licking up the strange mixture with his tongue. He would close his eyes and sway in ecstasy at this "hand-coffee", as he called it. Then he'd open the refrigerator, take out a couple of red apples and hand them to his two boys, repeating lines of old Arabic verse by Abu Nuwas in which the Abbasid poet sings the praises of the apples of Lebanon, whose aroma is so inevitably brought to mind by the bouquet of a good wine:

Pure wine from a tun that, as it mixes with the water,
Gives off an aroma like that of the apples of Lebanon.

The fragrance of the apples would blend with that of the coffee in the pharmacist's hand and he'd tell his sons to eat an apple a day at five o'clock, for the apples of Lebanon were better than any medicine. The boys would eat their apples, the taste blending with the odour of coffee, and watch their father lick his lips, before telling them it was time for him to go to the café.

There, in that distant French city, Karim had been tormented by that vanished smell. He'd try to tell Bernadette about the scent of apples

3

mixing with that of coffee but found it indescribable. How can one describe a fragrance to someone who hasn't already smelled and savoured it? Karim discovered his failure with words when he realised that he couldn't translate that memory, or the strain produced by the nostalgia that devoured him; in the end he found that "to make love" was simply a translation of "to talk" and that when words ran out so did love.

The lover is like a translator. He transfers the words of the tongue into the words of the body, as though translating and rewriting a story. That was how it had been with Ghazala. When he'd felt the darts of love bury themselves in his back, his tongue had been untied and he'd begun to talk, recounting to her the stories of his days as a student in France and how he used to swig wine like water. He'd spoken of the endless different kinds of cheese and when she'd said she liked "white meat", which was what they called cheese in her village, he'd answered that he preferred brown and grabbed her by the wrist, but she'd slipped out of his grasp. He'd caught her but she'd kissed him on the lips and escaped to the kitchen.

He took a rotten-smelling apple from the refrigerator, felt nauseous, and threw it into the rubbish bin. He stood in the kitchen not knowing what to do. The darkness shuddered to the feeble light of the cigarette lighter, which burned his fingers, and Karim grew hungry.

He went back to the living room, drank a glass of whisky and decided to stop waiting.

He wasn't waiting for a call from Ghazala: his infatuation for her had evaporated when he'd realised he was scared of her husband. He was waiting, rather, for Muna, whom he knew wouldn't call.

He'd never told Ghazala he loved her. He'd believed, as he writhed in front of her on the bed of pleasure, that he was having sex and had paid no attention to the love that only at the end, after his fear had dissipated, had moved his tongue to speak – at which point he discovered he'd been made a fool of.

Then, without preliminaries, Muna had entered his life.

He'd met her and her husband, the architect Ahmad Dakiz, at his brother Nasim's flat, where he'd seen the plans for the hospital for the first time, heard of the plans for the reconstruction of Beirut, and listened to a fantastical story about the Frankish origins of the family from Tripoli to which the architect belonged. He'd told Muna she'd bewitched him and heard her loud laughter as she said she didn't want to hear words of love because they were all the same, and they bored her.

Karim hadn't stopped talking of love with Muna even though he knew he'd fallen in love with Ghazala – as though he were using Muna to cure himself of Ghazala, and Hend's silence to cure himself of Ghazala's clamour.

Karim didn't know how to tell the story of how this triangular relationship had taken shape in the midst of the dust of Beirut, of how his heart had been able to bear that emotional maelstrom in the midst of the storms of the renewed civil war. But now he was sitting on his own with no-one to keep him company but his glass of whisky, waiting for a phone call that would never come.

Why had he come back to Beirut?

He could admit now that he'd been stricken by homesickness the moment his brother called him about the hospital project. How, though, had he been able to mend, in an instant, the thing in his heart that had been severed ten years earlier? Bernadette had been astounded as she listened to him. "Do you think the children and I are going to go and live in the hell of Lebanon? Are you out of your mind? Or do you want to leave us and marry a Lebanese woman so you can treat her like a servant and have a boy by her? For me, *c'est fini*. No more children. My body's gone slack. Look at the stretch marks on my belly. And you, like all Oriental men, feel jealous because your brother's fathered three boys and you want a crown prince."

Bernadette was wrong. Karim hadn't returned to Lebanon with any particular purpose in mind. He'd gone because his homesickness for Beirut had left him incapable of thought, of taking the rational decision his wife was expecting.

"What do you mean, 'a rational decision'?" he'd asked her. "There's no such thing as a rational decision where the soul is involved." He'd told her that his soul hurt and that there was no pain worse than that of the soul, but she said she didn't understand him anymore and wept.

He'd told Bernadette once that he couldn't stand tears. He said her tears reminded him of his mother, who'd died when he was five. He said the only thing he could remember about her was the tears that fell from her eyes and spread over her small white face, and that when they'd taken him and his brother from the flat to sleep at the neighbours and told him his mother was dead, he'd dreamed that same night of tears. He'd seen his mother weep and drown in her tears and her tears had turned into a flood that rose higher and higher till it swallowed the bed and the room and everything.

This nightmare had returned to his dreams only in France, when he went with his wife to visit her family in Lyon, where he'd felt alone, and a stranger. He'd told his wife her family treated him as though he had the mange and that they were racists. She'd laughed and said, "That's the way they are," meaning what he took for racism was a distance that her parents maintained even with their own children; he had to let go of his febrile Oriental imagination if he wanted to become acclimatised to his new country and his new life.

That night the nightmare of the tears had returned and he felt a murderous loneliness. He'd edged up against his wife, who was sleeping by his side, intending to take her in his arms, but she'd shifted away with an involuntary movement. He'd tried to get out of bed to go to the kitchen for a drink of water but hadn't been able to find his way in the dark. He'd closed his eyes to sleep and seen his mother's eyes shocked into tears. The next morning he'd told Bernadette he wanted to go home to Montpellier.

He'd returned, carrying with him the dream of tears, not knowing why his mother had suddenly awoken in his dream. What does it mean when the dead quicken in the living? And what does it mean for us to carry the dead in our hearts, so that they become part of a life we haven't yet lived?

He hadn't told his wife what had occurred. He didn't know what had gone wrong after they married. In the beginning, meaning during the stage poets refer to as "first love", his tongue had run wild over everything. He would translate the phrase 'ala rasi and say to her submissively "sur ma tête" just to hear the ringing laugh that would emerge from Bernadette's lips. Then, suddenly, the reign of silence had begun. Or, to be more accurate, it hadn't come all at once, it had crept in bit by bit and taken over the entire terrain of his relationship with the white-skinned woman with whom he'd fallen in love at first sight when they met at the Tex Mex bar. He'd started to feel that words were betraying him, that he couldn't relax in the French language. Words, as his father used to say, are the land in which one feels at home. Sitting with his two sons at the dinner table, he'd ask them to talk. "Entertain me!" he'd say, and the brothers had to tell stories about school while their father sat, and took his ease at the banquet of telling.

He couldn't tell Bernadette "Entertain me!" He couldn't fashion his phrases into proper sentences that would make allowances for his wife's ears, those ears that couldn't stand to hear cursing in French or in Arabic. So he slid into silence, and the stirrings of infidelity began to make themselves felt in his life.

It never occurred to him that Bernadette could be unfaithful to him. He didn't know where he got this certainty, which quickly evaporated, but he didn't care. When you stop feeling jealous, love is dead, and Karim had felt no jealousy when Bernadette told him she'd gone out with a Swiss doctor who was visiting Montpellier. He'd just smiled. She flew into a fury and said that she was lying because she knew he was being unfaithful to her and that she'd wanted to make him jealous, and that he didn't love her anymore, and she wept.

Karim was sure she was lying but couldn't abide tears. He sat on the floor next to her and said he loved her and almost told her the story of his dream about tears but didn't. He felt impotence crawling all around him and heard the sound of silence.

With Ghazala, though, he used to talk, and with Muna and her strange story about her Italian friend he veritably gargled the words in his mouth. He had no idea why, in Beirut, the words poured out of him, as though the well of silence had been opened and everything had slid aside.

From the moment of his arrival in Beirut, he'd been able to see. He'd told Muna that he could see things, because back there the world was enveloped in mist. The true magic of Beirut, though, lay in the smoothness of Ghazala's skin. Who would have believed that a maid from a remote village, who lived in the Mar Elias camp, in the midst of poverty, beggary, and madness, could radiate with an astounding smoothness the like of which he had never seen in the women whom he treated for skin diseases? Then he'd discovered the secret. It was love. He'd told her about the love that lends delicacy to the body, purifies the skin, and takes the soul up into the waves of the sky. She'd laughed. And when he'd discovered the trick that had been played on him he hadn't felt thorns in the throat the way men ordinarily do when deceived. On the contrary, he'd felt that the stone of fear had been pushed off his chest. Fear is a humiliation, and once it had receded and the story had reached its appointed end, he'd become as one who dwells on the verge of tears.

Karim didn't know why he'd thought of the word "was". Seated on the Boeing 707 from Paris' Orly airport to Beirut, he'd pictured to himself the city, seeing it as it once had been, as though it was something from the past that couldn't be brought back but to which he was nevertheless going back. He hadn't said he was "going back" when he told his wife of his decision; he'd said he was going to the city to build a hospital. But he'd known he was returning to a place that no longer existed. He'd closed his eyes and seen the sentence written out before him: "Beirut was."

He'd opened his eyes inside the plane to find his wife standing in front of him, shaking him by the shoulder as if waking him from sleep. With her obliterating whiteness and small eyes, the woman had looked like Bernadette. She'd said the plane was starting its descent and asked him to put his seat back in the upright position and fasten his seat belt.

When Nasim embraced him at the airport he'd smelled zaatar and a shudder of nostalgia had seized him. Looking at his brother he recovered the mirror image that had trailed him for so long. He had been used to seeing in his twin a likeness of himself he didn't want to see, but never before had he smelled on him the scent of zaatar. Bernadette had told him, the morning after they met, that she could smell zaatar. He'd told her he hadn't eaten zaatar for ages and she replied, laughing, "You're from Lebanon. You told me you were Lebanese. That's what Lebanese smell like." He'd said to her that the true smell of Lebanon was apples. "What apples?" she answered. "It's zaatar, *thym* – you know the word? – and I love zaatar."

Two men on the threshold of their forties smelling zaatar and not crying. They'd searched for things to say but had found only ready-made words, the ones said to fill the gaps in silence. They got into the black Volvo. Nasim turned on the engine and the voice of Fairuz rang out, singing "I loved you in summer, I loved you in winter". Nasim turned to his brother who had returned; he'd bought the cassette for him, he said. "Do you still like her?" he asked, and before he could hear the reply said he didn't like her anymore. "She's become like Lebanon," said Nasim. "Everyone says they love it, and when everyone says they love you it means no-one loves you. That's how Lebanon is. Everyone loves it but no-one loves it. Like the war, none of us likes it but we all fight, and like your father, God rest his soul . . ."

"Don't talk about Father like that," said Karim.

"Why? What do you know?"

"What is it I don't know? I don't understand."

"All in good time."

What strange reception was this? Had his brother asked him to come to Lebanon so he could humiliate him and settle old scores? Karim thought the whole thing had been laid to rest once and for all when Nasim married Hend. On the phone he'd wanted to tell his brother that he'd won in the end, but he'd choked on the words.

Karim didn't want to reopen old accounts, but why in fact had he returned to Beirut?

How would Hend take his return? "In the end the dog won and bought us both," he would tell her later.

"He only bought because you sold," she'd answer.

The July sun burned the city's asphalt. Karim felt he too was burning. But he didn't ask his brother where he was taking him. He'd been certain he was going to his father's flat, but the car passed the pharmacist's shop at the bottom of the building and kept going.

"Hend's waiting for us. She's got a glass of arak and some mezze ready for you."

"I'm tired. Let me go to the flat and we can have dinner together tomorrow."

"Your mother-in-law has made kibbeh nayyeh just for you and she's waiting for you at home."

"My mother-in-law?!"

"She was your mother-in-law, now she's mine. What's the problem?"

The conversation was off to a bad start. Karim hadn't come to reopen old accounts or to see the pleasure of revenge on his younger brother's face. He'd come he knew not why, but he did want to open a new page in his life, or so at least he'd persuaded himself. While practising on the camera he'd bought by taking pictures of his two daughters he'd told his wife he wanted to devour Beirut with his eyes, to photograph it and apologise to it, to love it all over again. In his wife's eyes he'd read the words she'd kept repeating to him since their first encounter: "You're romantic and sentimental." Now the words had taken on a new meaning. In that distant past, which seemed to Karim to belong to a different time, she'd laugh and say "romantic" with the lust fluttering in her eyes. Now the word came out dry and bitter.

They'd drunk the arak and eaten the kibbeh in a silence from which they were rescued only by the racket and naughtiness of the children.

Hend said nothing. Her mother Salma, swathed in black, seemed a different woman. When Karim entered the flat and she embraced him he noted the black that covered her legs, mounting from there to cover everything else. She was wearing thick nylon stockings and the black enveloped her knees and thighs, and she looked like the widow she was.

Salma hadn't ceased wearing black since her husband had died prematurely from a clot in the brain, leaving her with a single daughter and a small sum of money that he'd put together from his work on an afforestation project in Abu Dhabi. All the same, this beautiful white-skinned woman had succeeded in making her dresses sign-posts to the shining whiteness that radiated from her thighs and wrists. A year after her husband's death she'd removed the black stockings but she had never stopped wearing black. When Karim met her for the first time, at his father's pharmacy, he was astonished by her beauty and saw the smile of triumph that was Nasri Shammas' way of proclaiming a new female conquest. When he met her later at her flat on his first visit to Hend he felt a secret frisson run through his body and compared the frankness of her gaze, with its hidden burden of desire, with the meekness in Hend's small eyes, her dainty body, and her brownness that glowed as though it had imbibed the sun.

The powdered sugar that seemed to glisten on Salma's thighs where they burst out from beneath her short dress, split above the knee, quickly vanished when the woman dispelled the young man's doubts by speaking, somewhat contemptuously, of his father's magic herbs that made plants burst with life. Karim had been convinced his father was making up his stories of passion to comfort his loneliness and stave off the advance of age – until his brother Nasim had opened a drawer and he'd seen the pictures, and been overtaken by feelings of disgust and sadness.

Why do we laugh at lovers' tales when we do the same sorts of things ourselves? Love should never be disclosed to other people because others can accept it only when they themselves are its heroes. He felt revulsion against his father but pity for himself. How and to whom was he to tell his own story with Ghazala, which had ended in something worse than a scandal? How was he to tell of his conflicting feelings, of his heart that kept changing course and taking him off to he knew not where?

He thought of that line of ancient verse and smiled.

Suddenly, with the return of the electricity, the flat burst into light. He heard the hum of the refrigerator, saw himself sitting on the couch holding an empty glass of whisky, and realised he was ridiculous. He refilled his glass and said out loud,

M-a-n is so called for his a-m-n-esia,
The heart for its constant inconstancy.

The electricity! It was enough for the electricity to come back for the nightmare of black thoughts to be swept aside. Karim decided to view his life as comedy. Nothing was worth tormenting oneself over because the true nature of things was unclear. He felt a sudden affection for his father, had a vision of him lying in the middle of the living room, and laughed at the meaninglessness of meanings.

He'd told Muna that the sorrows of separation were meaningless. He'd kissed her on her lips, which were wet with water, and laughed as he slept with her for the last time. He'd said they had to make their last time more beautiful than the first. He reminded her how shy and afraid she'd been and that the language of the body was wordless. He told her that their affair must not end in the dumbness with which it had started and made love to her before she had time to dry her body, pulling the towel off her and taking her laughing.

Muna had arrived without warning. It was 7 a.m. when Karim opened the door and saw her standing there hesitantly, wearing her morning exercise clothes, which were stained with sweat.

"I came to say goodbye. We're leaving for Canada in a week."

She went into the living room. Karim left her and went into the kitchen, put the coffee-maker on the flame, and heard the shower being turned on in the bathroom.

She stood there, wearing the white towel that covered her body and left only her thin white legs visible, and said she was sad.

He hadn't asked why she was sad but had laughed and approached her and said that her wet body was the best way to say goodbye.

He turned on all the lights in the flat and went to the kitchen, where he took a handful of zaatar, scattered it over a piece of dry bread, and devoured it.

"It's all because I drank a lot without eating anything. It's over. That story is finished and tomorrow, in France, there won't be a story, there mustn't be a story," he thought to himself.

He'd stretched out on the couch, started to feel the creeping numbness that comes before sleep, shaken himself awake in a panic, set the alarm for 4.30 a.m., and sunk into a deep sleep.

Karim Shammas bent to lift his suitcase out of the boot of the black Mercedes taxi that had been taking him to Beirut airport en route back to Montpellier.

The sky lit up and the whistling started. The driver ducked to protect himself from the mortar shells that had begun to fall on the airport road. Suddenly the car turned. Karim heard the screeching of the tyres and felt everything shake. He closed his eyes and prepared for death. He heard the driver shout that he was going back to Beirut. He opened his eyes and asked him to keep going and get him to the airport. Suddenly the car stopped and he heard the driver's voice say through the screeching of the tyres that he couldn't. "If you want to go on, sir, find yourself another car. I've got children and I want to go home."

Karim had a vision of himself as another person. He got out of the car, bent over the boot, lifted out his suitcase, set off down the middle of the dusty, garbage-strewn road, and thought he'd reached the end of the world.

This was how his Beirut adventure ended, with a ringing in his ears and the feeling that he was supporting himself on his shadow. When he caught sight of the Beirut airport building, with its ruined façade, he looked back and wept.

2

When Karim Shammas agreed to return to Beirut for the hospital construction project put to him by his brother Nasim, he didn't know that the civil war, which had come to an end in Lebanon, would begin anew within him.

"The war will never end," Mrs Salma had said to him when she saw him in front of his father's pharmacy on Zahret el-Ehsan Street in Beirut. He'd seen the woman, who covered her head with a black silk scarf, coming out of the pharmacy and had made up his mind to run but instead had remained rooted to the spot.

The woman, who was in her fifties, approached him, gave him a contemptuous look, and asked him why he was going to France and leaving his fiancée behind.

He said he'd never been officially engaged to Hend, was tired of the war, and couldn't take it anymore. "I'll come back when the war's over," he said.

"The war will never end because it's inside us," said the woman. She folded her arms over her chest, bowed her head, and went her way.

And Salma was right.

The Pretty Widow, as his father called her, had said the war would never end and had entreated him to remain in Beirut. He didn't remember exactly what she'd said. Had she asked why he was leaving his fiancée, or why he wasn't taking her with him?

Hend had told him she didn't want him. She hadn't said exactly that, but she'd said she'd never go abroad and leave her mother alone in Beirut.

The problem had begun a long time before, as the love that had lasted four years began to evaporate.

"To be honest, I have no idea who you are. How can I live with a man I know nothing about?"

"But you know everything!"

"Everything means nothing," she said.

And Hend was right: everything had turned into nothing. He'd reached Montpellier, joined the university and its associated hospital, and the picture of her that he'd placed on the table next to his bed had become a burden. He decided to put it in a drawer, where it stayed. When he finished his studies and moved from the dormitory to his new flat, he'd left the picture in the drawer by mistake. On remembering it a week later he'd felt an obscure nostalgia which was swallowed up in a roar of laughter.

Bernadette had told him he used his loud laugh to hide his shyness and weakness, but he hadn't understood. He'd thought his resounding laugh was an expression of his strong personality. That was what he'd felt during the only battle he'd fought in, at Nahr el-Bared Camp near Tripoli, when he was nineteen. He'd been in a trench opposite the mound occupied by the Lebanese army, holding a Kalashnikov, with Nabil Abu el-Halaqa lying on his stomach next to him, holding one of those big belt-fed machine guns that they call a Degtyaryov, to cover his comrade. Suddenly the bullets flew. This was nothing like the training course that Karim had taken, which had lasted fewer than ten days and hadn't taught him how to identify the source of fire or draw up a plan to confront a possible attack on his position. Instead, he'd found himself firing wildly and laughing out loud and not noticing that his colleague's gun had fallen silent. When the firing stopped as suddenly as it had started he'd turned to his comrade and found him sitting bent over, moaning with pain. When Nabil announced to him that he hadn't been able to hold on and that he'd had to empty his bowels, Karim burst out laughing again. "You mean you shat yourself, you coward? Get up, get up! I can smell it." But Nabil, shaking with fear, said he didn't dare leave the trench and was so afraid of the snipers he'd had to shit right where he was.

"The smell's everywhere!" yelled Karim. "At least cover it over, you arsehole. Cats are better than you," and he burst out laughing.

Nabil would die years later in the battles for the commercial souks, his comrades recounting that he'd died because of his reckless courage – while Karim, after the experience at Nahr el-Bared, hadn't dared to take any but a symbolic part in the fighting. That, though, is another story.

Instead of replying to his French wife that he was laughing because he didn't care and if you don't care nothing can frighten or embarrass you, he burst out laughing and said nothing.

Everything had turned into nothing. Hend had entered a hidden space called forgetting and only re-awoken the day his brother Nasim phoned to tell him he'd married her but hadn't invited Karim to the wedding because Hend had refused to allow any celebrations. "She wouldn't even agree to invite her mother and your father." He hadn't roared with laughter that day. That day, he'd felt choked and a strange feeling had come upon him from he knew not where: it was as if Nasim had stolen his life from him; as though, by staying there in Beirut, he'd taken the city from him.

On top of that the political choices of the two brothers had intervened: the younger had become sole inheritor of the flat and pharmacy, while it had become impossible for Karim to return to the east side of Beirut where the Phalangists ruled. Then, after the savage assassination of Khaled Nabulsi, he'd found he couldn't breathe. The air had been cut off in Beirut and he'd felt he was breathing not air but thorns, so he'd decided to emigrate and never come back. Everything inside him had died and he no longer cared. He'd phoned Hend, who had come and sat before him in silence at Uncle Sam's, close to the American University in Beirut, listening to his sudden decision and saying she wouldn't go with him because she couldn't leave her mother.

Her mother Salma, however, had a different perspective. She'd looked at him with contempt and said the war would never end because it came from inside of them.

Where did she get such eloquence? And who was this woman who had so nearly been his mother-in-law?

Hend said her mother wanted her and her son-in-law to live at home with her because she couldn't bear to live alone.

"But it's still too soon," Karim had said.

"I know, I know. My mother's a bit childish. She abandoned me when

I was young and now she wants to cling to me for the rest of her life. Obviously I don't want that, but I haven't the heart."

"We haven't agreed to get married yet," said Karim.

"We haven't agreed? You're right, we haven't talked about it but, you know, I love you and you love me."

She had told him she loved him and wanted him just when what he called "the oil of desire" had started to run out. Beirut had disappeared under the shelling and this girl had taken the thread of chastity in her hand, as though something had awoken inside her and turned her into something like a wife. Which was the real Hend? When he'd held her in his arms for the first time, she'd trembled like a small bird. They were at her flat, and her mother wasn't there. It was the eve of Good Friday, the voice of Fairuz was warbling from the radio "Let Your Son's death be life for those who seek it", and Hend was listening, on the verge of tears. He sat down next to her saying nothing but listening to the requiem for Christ. He lit a cigarette, felt the singer's voice covering him in blue velvet, and had a vision of himself bending over Hend and taking her. She flowed like water, and Fairuz's velvet blended with Hend's face, which was covered in dew. He held her to him and everything inside him shuddered.

They were sitting now in the same café, drinking orange juice while she talked to him about her mother and he couldn't understand how she could say "I haven't the heart" after all the stories she'd told him about her childhood at the half-time boarding school, and her unshakeable feeling that her mother was living somewhere else.

He took hold of her hand and she looked around as she withdrew it. "You mustn't! Any moment someone will see us." Why hadn't she said they mustn't in the past, when, uncaring, she'd looked for opportunities to be alone with him, even discovering dark side streets where he found himself clasped, as he walked with her, by her dainty body, which embraced him and pulled on him and only released him after the final shudder?

He'd told her he was leaving and had taken her hand, which she withdrew without speaking, so he understood that she understood that their love was gone. But he was wrong. He'd discovered his mistake here, in Beirut, when he heard her say her husband had never forgiven her "even though I was a virgin, as you know. Every time he sleeps with me I feel as though there's something in his eyes he wants to say but doesn't."

"But he knows," said Karim.

"Did you tell him?" she asked.

"Kind of, but it's not important."

That first day, he'd taken her hand and she hadn't withdrawn it or said "You mustn't." She'd let her hand flow and he'd listened to the voice of Fairuz and thought memories were like tears.

Why had she spoken of her mother? Who was this woman whom he had to meet at his brother's flat the moment he arrived in Beirut?

Hend had told him her mother's story many times, but each time he was amazed. He found it difficult to believe this story of a woman in the village of Kherbet el-Raheb in the Akkar district who'd left her husband and three children and run away to Beirut to marry the agricultural engineer Sami Naqqash. Salma's story was full of mystery. She'd met the engineer when he came to work on land reclamation in Akkar and had lost her head – that was what she had told her daughter. "He spoke to me and I lost my head. I, poor thing, was just a child. I was twenty-one and he was forty. Tall, his head shining with white hair. Dark-skinned, with a bewitching smile and laughing eyes. He saw me walking on the road. I was carrying Mokhtar, my baby son, may God make his life easy, and he stopped and looked at me and smiled. I felt as though I'd been paralysed. Then I understood that that's what love is. No, I didn't sleep with him or let him kiss me but he used to hold my hand and I could feel his heart beating against my fingers and my heart felt as though it was going to fly away. I fell in love with him and was like a mad woman and I followed him to Beirut and we got married."

Salma didn't tell her only daughter the details of this adventure, which had caught the imagination of the people of Kherbet el-Raheb and been transformed into a rustic legend called "Salma and Sami". Nor had she spoken of how it had ended with her husband – who'd sworn he'd kill her – sitting with the agricultural engineer in the Gemmeizeh Café in Beirut, drawing up with him the contract of settlement which eventually made Salma's divorce, and marriage to her lover, possible.

*

The story went that Salma was the most beautiful young woman in the village. She was the fourth and last daughter of Salim Mokhtar, who worked as a hired hand in the wheat fields of Sheikh Deyab Abd el-Karim. Her beauty manifested itself in the milky whiteness of her complexion, which caused the young men of the village to swarm like hornets round her father's house.

Salma was born nine years after her mother had stopped having children. When his wife got pregnant, Salim Mokhtar was sure God had decided to have mercy on him and give him a son who would keep his name alive; he'd named the boy Salah and sat down in front of his wife's belly to wait for him.

The midwife didn't dare come out of the room, which was swallowed up by the steam that rose from the basins of hot water. Even the child cloaked itself in the surrounding silence. The man heard the first sign of life in the form of a weak crying, quickly stifled. "No!" he cried. "It's a girl? Salah has turned out a girl?" He left the house and only came back three months later, having slept in the fields and eaten green plants and earth. In the end, though, he did return and he fell captive to the beautiful child who gleamed with a whiteness the like of which none had seen, and once her three sisters had married their cousins he took to speaking of her as his only daughter. Abu Salah was never seen now without his daughter Salma, whom he addressed as though she were a boy called Salah, and he never tired of playing with her or supervising her school-work, so much so that people thought he must have gone slightly mad.

Having completed her studies at the village school, Salma decided to go to the proper school in the town of Halba, which amounted to breaking every tradition of the village – traditions that forbade the education of girls or, when they allowed it, required that the girl not advance beyond the school under the village oak.

Salim Mokhtar put all these social practices behind him with a single leap and took to walking five kilometres every morning to take his daughter to school and doing the same in the afternoon to bring her back home.

People said the man was in love with his daughter and had fallen victim to her grey eyes, the purity of her white skin, and the magic of her smile. His wife said it was madness: the girl ought to stay at home, help her mother, and wait for a groom. "You're crazy, Abu Salah. Who lets his daughter go to school like a boy? What are people going to say about you and me?"

But the man paid no attention and told everyone who asked that the world had changed and women weren't part of the furniture, that he'd made up his mind and no-one had the right to object.

Salma went to school for two years. Then along came the groom and the groom was the son of the owner of the land on which all the inhabitants of the village worked as labourers, so her father couldn't refuse.

When he told her she wept and he wept at her weeping and said to her, "As you wish, my daughter. I am prepared to leave the village and go and work as a porter in the port of Tripoli for your sake, but please don't cry." But Salma wouldn't stop weeping. Her father said he'd go to Sheikh Deyab and make his excuses but she shouted at him "No!" and said she consented to the match.

Hend had never seen her mother's village, which lay far away in the middle of a valley next to the Great Southern River, which ran, exhaling the perfume of water, along the edge of Kherbet el-Raheb, so she couldn't furnish her story with sign posts. She told Karim she'd forgotten the details because memory needs a place, time erases memories, and people only come across their memories in the crevices of places.

The story, however, took an unexpected turn and ended in a series of tragedies that engraved themselves deeply in the memory of the people of the village.

Salma had suddenly choked back her tears, told her father she would marry the man, and gone to her wedding as if to a funeral. Her mother couldn't understand Salma's hesitation over an offer of marriage that had fallen upon her from the sky. The groom was a youth of twenty-five and she was fifteen. The groom was the only son of a man who owned the lands of seven villages. The daughter of a poor labourer, she would be transformed into a lady whom all the women in the village would fall over one another to serve. She would live in a big house of stone and leave their house of mud.

The story goes that the man was patient with Salma till patience itself could be patient no more. The first night he cut his hand to allow those waiting to cheer at the sight of a sheet spotted with virgin blood. On the second he approached her and she covered her face with her hands so that her tears wouldn't fall on the ground and he slept next to her and didn't touch her. The third he took her hand and felt such a killing coldness that he pulled back. The fourth he said it wouldn't do and she said, "Leave it till tomorrow." The fifth she said she was sick and the sixth he asked her what she wanted and she said she wanted to go to school. He said she was asking the impossible and promised to bring Shaykh Hafez to teach her at home, but she said she wanted to study mathematics and science, so he laughed and said, "We'll see." The seventh night he took her by force. She wept and pleaded with him but he ripped off her clothes and flung her to the ground and opened her. That night a lot of blood flowed because Qasem Abd el-Karim couldn't stop. Two days later, sitting next to her on the bed, he told her he'd tasted the sweetest honey in the world and that though a man didn't usually apologise to a wife, he was going to. He said this and more and she bowed her head and covered herself in her tears. He said he wanted to weep because he loved her but that that would be unbecoming, and he left the room.

When Salma disappeared Qasem couldn't believe she'd gone off with another man. She'd lived with him six years and had had three boys by him, and then suddenly she'd vanished as though she'd never been. She disappeared, and so did all her belongings. She took everything: the clothes and the small mirror and the face towel that she perfumed with rose water. And when the report arrived that she was living with the agricultural engineer, the unsuccessful crime was committed.

Abu Salah wept and wailed before his feudal master, saying he'd kill the woman himself because she had sullied his honour, but his master looked at him with contempt and said, "No, it's nothing to do with you. She's ours. She was ours alive and she'll be ours dead."

Karim told Hend he didn't believe the bit in the story about the mistake. The husband had come, carrying a gun. He knocked on the door and the engineer opened it. The man fired, then went into the bedroom where Salma lay trembling, shot her and left.

"But he didn't kill anyone," said Hend. "Father was hit in the leg and my mother wasn't hurt. The victim was my grandmother, Father's mother, who was visiting her son to beg him to send the woman back to her husband, because she could smell blood."

"It seems the blood my grandmother smelled was her own," said Hend. The story ended with reconciliation, the dropping of the court case, and Salma's marriage to her beloved.

The engineer died four years later of a clot in the brain and the first husband died too, killed during the peasant uprising in Akkar, and Salma had to swallow all these bitter pills at one go.

"I don't know how to say this, but I never forgave her," said Hend. "I lived all on my own. She put me in the Zahret el-Ehsan school as a half-boarder. I lived with the orphans who walk in funeral processions to collect donations and only went home at night. I'd come home my eyes half closed and when I opened them again I'd find my mother had taken me back to school."

"Childhood memories aren't the story," said Karim. "Childhoods are just scraps of memories that we patch together later to make up our story when we're grown."

The first time Hend told him the story and said how her mother had put her in the boarding school so she could live her life the way she wanted and work in the office of Samir Yunes, the lawyer, he assumed that the woman, who was still a girl, had abandoned her daughter to be free to pursue her romantic involvement with "Uncle Samir", as Hend called the lawyer. But the second time Hend told the story, she told it differently. She said her mother had gone to the lawyer to recover her rights to her three children and that she, Hend, had been jealous of her three brothers, whose pictures she'd never seen, that her mother had spent all her time finding people to intervene with Sheikh Deyab Abd el-Karim to allow her to see the boys, and that she'd tried to get in touch with her father to help him. The latter had told the young lawyer from Tripoli, whom Maître Samir had sent to see him, that his daughter was dead, that he was condemned to live in shame, and that he hadn't seen his grand-children since the day she'd run off with the engineer, because he no longer dared leave his house.

Hend said her mother had suffered greatly. She'd gone to everyone, had behaved like a mother bereaved, and had refused for the rest of her life to stop wearing her mourning clothes. When Uncle Samir asked her once, as he ate lunch at their flat, why she didn't stop wearing mourning – seeing that the man had died five years earlier and it was enough – she said she wore black for herself, because she couldn't see her children.

Hend said her mother had spent her life chasing a mirage, while she had spent her childhood jealous of her three brothers.

"My mother never stopped talking about them. The tears would run down her cheeks even though she wasn't crying, and she'd talk of the three white moons, so beautiful that their light dazzled people, and she'd give me strange looks as though I was the one keeping her from them. I'd feel, I don't know . . . I'd feel as though the night had stuck to my skin and I'd hate myself because I wasn't white like my mother or the three moons."

The third time she told him how her mother suffered and how she was forced to work in the lawyer's office from dawn till dusk to make an honest living. "The money she inherited from my father ran out and she had no choice. My mother had learned how to type and went to the lawyer who'd been kind to her from the beginning and had tried to help her get her boys back. She worked for him for the rest of her life and became more than a secretary and if it hadn't been for him, God rest his soul, we would have died of hunger."

"He died too? Your mother must have salt on her thighs, as they say."

"Don't talk like that. My mother was a respectable woman."

"But you told me he bought you the flat – just like that, for charity's sake?"

"I don't know, but I do know that Uncle Samir left us something too and my mother used to say that his wife was mad and kept having nervous breakdowns and the man lived an awful life even though he had the golden touch when it came to money."

The fourth time she told him how much her mother loved her. "I know I'm her whole life. That's why I don't have the heart to leave her and why I agreed when she told me she wanted me and my husband to live with her."

The fifth time Hend showed her exasperation. "I don't know what she does at that old pharmacist's place. I can't understand her. She clings to me as though she loves me but I know she never has."

" 'That pharmacist' is my father," said Karim.

"I know he's your father. You've never told me anything about him. I've told you everything about my mother."

"There's nothing to tell," he answered.

Salma had been everywhere. Karim met her for the first time when she was forty-five. He saw her coming out of the pharmacy with her short black dress that revealed the whiteness of her thighs and gave an indication of the possibilities of her firmly projecting breasts. He went into the pharmacy smiling and Nasri said to him, "See the red plums? At forty a woman's like a ripe plum and I love plums!"

Karim Shammas found the woman everywhere he looked. When he discovered she was Hend's mother he felt afraid, but it was too late to go back and he came to think there was a gap of silence that could not be bridged. He kept the secret to himself and avoided visiting Hend in her home so that he wouldn't be reminded of that savage flash he'd once seen in her mother's eyes. He hadn't talked about it even to his twin brother, so how could he speak of it with Hend? Mothers are off limits.

"Thank God my mother died when I was little," he'd said once to Hend.

"Doesn't everyone love their mother?" Hend had asked in disbelief.

"No, not that. I meant something else," he replied.

"What did you mean?" she asked.

"No, well, how can I put it? Maybe it was better that way because she didn't have to put up with Father any longer."

"Why? Did Uncle Nasri give her a hard time?"

"No but his eye was very 'white'."

"What does it mean, 'his eye was white'?"

The discussion ended in silence. He took her hand, kissed it and said nothing. How was he supposed to tell a daughter about her mother when mothers were wrapped in the cotton wool of sanctity? How was he to tell her about the amazing potion his father had concocted from wild plants to make women his victims?

When Karim joined the medical school at the American University of Beirut, the secrets of the Shefa Pharmacy started to reveal themselves to him. Contempt for his father and hatred for his insatiable sexual appetite grew within him. His father said he'd understand things when he grew older and refused to let him enter the laboratory. "It's the secrets of the profession, my son, and you refused to do pharmacy. Your brother, who was no good at school, knows more about pharmacy than you. One day, when you're older, you'll understand."

Nasri Shammas was fifty when the incomprehensible obsession struck him. His sex life had more or less settled down after his wife's death. He'd refused to remarry "because", he used to say, "of the boys", and he believed that one marriage was enough for him and there was no need for a second round of sexual dissatisfaction. He took care of his needs with prostitutes. Once a week he'd go to a brothel in that celebrated street of prostitutes named after the greatest of Arab poets, al-Mutanabbi. Once, he told Nasim the hardest thing one could do was love a prostitute. "When that happens everything turns into a mirage. You're thirsty and you drink thirst. You drink to quench your thirst and you find yourself thirsty again." Nasim didn't ask what the story, which everyone knew about, was, because the man had become such an idiot he'd invited Sawsan to the flat. The smell of scandal had spread through the neighbourhood and the twins had felt ashamed.

As Karim had listened to his brother haltingly recount Hend's version of his father's death, he'd said he could see the woman in their flat in front of him and remember how nauseous he'd felt.

The brothers had come home from school to find their father sitting in front of a woman. They pulled back to get away from the strange smell but Nasri ordered them to come forward and shake hands with Tante Sawsan, as he called her.

The brothers never mentioned the matter again, as though it had been erased, and Nasim's tears and Karim's silence and sudden dumbness along with it. When Karim listened to the story of his father's death, though, the smell came back, he could see before his eyes the bulging thighs, red-painted lips and long violet-coloured nails, and he believed the story.

"You mean Father didn't slip, the way you told me over the phone?" asked Karim. And when he found out that his father hadn't died quickly but had been taken to the hospital where the doctors had diagnosed a small crack in the skull and internal bleeding caused by his fall, he'd felt afraid. Nasri took six days to die and opened his eyes only once, for a few moments.

"I was standing next to him, holding his hand, and he opened his eyes. He saw me, his hand let go of mine, and he closed them again. Then two days later he died."

"Did he recognise you?" asked Karim.

"I don't know," his brother replied.

"Maybe he thought you were me," said Karim.

It was a habit of Nasri's deliberately to get the names of the two brothers wrong. He'd call out to one of them using the other's name and when the boy got angry the father would roar with laughter and apologise and say it was going to be hard for women in the future.

When his brother called to tell him of their father's death, Karim had been struck dumb. He replaced the receiver and put his head between his hands, preparing to weep, but the tears hadn't flowed. A lump had stuck in his throat and choked him and he'd felt he was being throttled. Against habit, he went home at noon. Bernadette asked what was wrong and he didn't answer. He stood up, opened a bottle of wine, started drinking, and told his wife he was hungry. He ate a huge amount of spaghetti and basil and drank two bottles of red wine. Eating the spaghetti he thought of ox cheek. Talal, a Lebanese youth who had come to France to study cinema, had told him about this amazing dish when they were in some bar. He said that a friend of his father's from Damascus who was living in Paris, and who called himself Zeryab, cooked the tastiest French dishes and had invited him to taste ox cheek. He said the flesh melted in the mouth even as the tongue savoured the fragrance of the spices. Karim ate the spaghetti and thought of ox cheek; in fact, he might go so far as to say now that at that moment he'd seen the ox in front of him and had been ready to attack it, to rip it to pieces. That was the day he discovered that death stimulates the appetite. He told his wife that Man is a cruel and trivial being because he believes he can overcome death by eating. Then he burst into tears and told Bernadette he didn't believe Nasri was dead because the man could never die; how was he to explain to her that he'd been convinced his father would never die because he had no soul? All his life he'd felt quite comfortable with this idea, which had struck him long ago – only for him to discover its fragility at the moment of the old man's death.

The brothers were sure their father would never die: he'd told them as much himself. Karim didn't know when his father had spoken those words, but he knew they were a part of his life, as though he'd been born with them. In all probability Nasri had said to his sons what he had to reassure them. The boys had been terrified by the death of the father of a boy at school. They hadn't talked about it but had been unable to sleep; their dreams had become more like waking fantasies and they'd stopped being able to recount what they dreamed.

They used to tell their father their dreams to entertain him. Nasri believed that sleep was a person's window onto the soul, so he trained his sons to remember their dreams and the boys were expected to make up shared dreams. Things got mixed up in Karim's mind because he no longer knew how dreams ought to be told. Usually, his brother began and he interrupted Nasim to tell his own stories, but soon he'd find himself following the course of his brother's dream. Did the twins see the same dreams?

Though, in fact, they weren't twins. It was their father who'd turned them into twins and imposed on them the illusion that they resembled one another in everything, leaving in so doing his fingerprints on every aspect of their future lives.

The two children were terrified when the father of one of the students at the Frères school died unexpectedly of a heart attack. They came home from school with the signs of panic sketched in their eyes, but Nasri noticed nothing. He was sitting in the living room sipping coffee and smoking, and sitting next to him was Tante Sawsan. The woman's nails were painted a bright violet and there were smears of lipstick on the butt of her cigarette. Her voice was loud and hard and her eyes looked droopy because the mascara had run. Nasri was looking at her, his smile swaying to the swaying of her face as he sank into the thick smoke from her cigarette. He saw his sons were in the flat though he hadn't noticed their arrival. He asked them to come up to the woman, who kissed them, leaving on them a smell of sweat mixed with a cloying perfume. When the boys had arrived home at 4 p.m. they'd been surprised to see movement in the living room. Usually the flat was empty, their father at the shop, the windows closed, and there'd be a smell of the disinfectants with which the pharmacist cleaned the flat for fear of germs. That sunny spring day in April, however, they'd found the windows open and smelled a strange smell. Their father went off with the woman, leaving them on their own, and when he returned at 9 p.m. the flat was in darkness and the boys were in bed. He heard a strange sound in their room, went in on tiptoe without turning on the light, and found them crying. He went up to them and they pretended to be asleep. He shook them and tried to wake them up, and their crying stopped. But they never showed they were awake. The next morning, as they were eating fried eggs, he asked them what they'd been dreaming about, but they didn't answer. When he insisted and looked at Nasim, who as a child had provided the weak point through which the pharmacist could force himself into the life of his sons, the boy burst into tears and asked his father not to die.

That morning Nasri promised his sons he wouldn't die. He told them he would stay with them and never leave them.

"We don't want that woman who was with you yesterday," said Nasim, crying.

"O.K.," said Nasri. "Forgive me. I was abandoned for a moment. God abandoned me and put me in the way of that whore."

"What's a whore?" asked Nasim.

"You're still young. Shut up and don't ask questions!" yelled Karim.

The boys decided to believe Nasri but Sawsan's shadow continued to haunt the flat, even creeping into their dreams, and the name of the woman with the violet nails stayed with them a long time.

When Nasim told his brother about the first time he had sex with a prostitute in the souk, he said he'd "sawsanned" to the singing of Mohamed Abd el-Wahhab emerging from a large wooden wireless set on the prostitute's bedside table; she'd opened her legs, yawned, and fallen into a doze.

"Was her name really Sawsan?" asked Karim.

"Sawsan's something else. I'm telling you how I got on. I was sawsanning her and everything was going fine but when I told her how nice sawsanning was she started to laugh and you know what happens if someone laughs and you're inside them."

"I don't know and I don't want to know," said Karim.

"You're an idiot and you always will be an idiot about women. The only way to learn, you ass, is from whores, because if you don't start practising now the women will laugh at you and you'll have a headache all your life from the horns."

When Nasim had told his brother he was an idiot he was referring to his relationship with Hend. Nasim took back his words when he found his brother was having an affair with the brown-skinned girl. In truth, though, there was nothing to take back as matters hadn't gone any further between them than smiles when she'd come to the pharmacist's with her mother. Nasim had said to his brother jokingly that perhaps she'd love both of them at the same time, then noticed the anger on his brother's face and said, "No, I was just joking, don't take it so hard. But I have to take you to the souk so you can get some practice on the women there."

Karim couldn't get Sawsan out of his mind. He saw the image of his father mixed up with weird sexual dreams. Karim hadn't admitted to his brother that the first ejaculation of his life had been a result of one of those dreams, but Nasim had known with a twin's intuition that Sawsan's nights moistened his brother's too with the smell of manhood.

Nasri had told his sons not to be afraid as he was never going to die. Karim believed his father, and the business became linked to a strange conceptualisation that had taken shape in his mind via some process he couldn't understand. He grew convinced his father wouldn't die because the man had no soul. His father, with his white hair, was a mass of taut nerves and muscles. The pharmacist continued to run and swim up to his death at the age of seventy-six: he was thin and had firm muscles – unlike his sons who tended to be slightly overweight and had problems with their health. Karim got stomach aches and Nasim carried from his childhood the burden of asthma, which, he reckoned, was the result of genetic factors inherited from their mother, who passed on to them the whiteness of her skin, her straight back, and her poor health. The dark-skinned father with the crown of white hair would look at his sons in sorrow and ask himself what relation they bore to him: "It's like you weren't my children. I swear I have no idea where your mother got you from." Nasim overcame the asthma when he was twelve and started to swim, but poor health continued to dog his elder brother.

Karim had told his brother that their father had no soul and would, therefore, never die, since, for a person to die, the soul has to leave the body. Nasri, in contrast, was a body without a soul, one that held itself together on its own, as uniform in its consistency as something cast out of brown mud and then baked in the sun.

When Karim had picked up the receiver in Montpellier and heard his brother's voice recounting the news, he'd seen, as clearly as though it were taking place before his eyes, a strange scene: his father falling to the ground and breaking up into pieces like a child's doll, the limbs and various parts all becoming detached. He'd knelt down to pick up the pieces and put them together again, and every time he touched a piece it had turned into sticky clay. Had the dream come from the sense of exile and loneliness he'd felt when his brother told him their father had died and that there was no need to come to Beirut because they'd already buried him? Or was it a fantasy, a picture created by the poor connection and the crackling that had obscured his brother's voice?

"Why didn't you tell me so that I could come to the burial?" Karim had asked angrily.

"I couldn't get a line. Have you forgotten where we are? It's the war's fault. Anyway, don't take on. We all die someday. What matters is that the man didn't suffer."

Karim now understood why his brother's voice had been neutral, even indifferent. Now, in the Beirut to which the dermatologist had returned, leaving France to smell once more the scent of ground coffee mixed with apples, he understood that the father who had slipped in his son Nasim's living room had committed his last crime at the moment of his death, and that the man had lived his whole life for Sawsan.

Sawsan was the name the brothers gave to having sex, and the woman with the dirty violet fingernails occupied a large area of the private language that they hadn't stopped using. When Karim decided to emigrate, his brother had asked, "What are we going to tell Hend about Sawsan?" and Karim had given him an angry look and asked him not to mix Hend up in things of that kind.

"What, you haven't done any Sawsan together?"

"Of course not. Are you crazy?"

"You mean you love her without having . . . ?"

"It's none of your business."

"You must be lying. You can't think I'm so stupid I'd believe you."

He hadn't got as far as Sawsan with Hend. Throughout the four years, they'd played around at the edges of sex, which was why he didn't feel guilty when he decided to go to France. He'd spoken to Bernadette of fear. He'd told her that the war had taught him that fear makes an empty space in one's heart. He'd told her that the fear which hits you in the knees is only a beginning and not to be compared with the deep fear that grips the ribcage and makes holes in the heart.

He hadn't been able to explain to Hend the fear that had made him lose all his feelings for her and everything else in Beirut, and think of nothing but escape. He'd wanted to leave so that he could find his heart again and learn to breathe once more.

He'd told his French wife he was going to Beirut just to take a look, promising he'd leave the final decision to her. Bernadette didn't believe him. She said he was a liar, like all Lebanese. She also said that she'd been amazed to discover that the Lebanese lie without realising they're lying: they lie and believe themselves, and then proceed to act in accordance with their lies. She said she couldn't tell fact from fiction in her husband's stories and then was even more taken aback by his reaction. He'd laughed and said, "You're right *mais c'est pas grave.*" How was he to explain to her that nothing was *grave* except the grave, meaning death, and that the rest was "all soap"? When she heard his translations of Lebanese proverbs she'd scowl and get angry and ask him not to talk to her about soap or speak of "slipping people up".

She'd been right to do so. He'd kept going on about soap till his father had slipped and died and now he had no choice but to go back to France. He thought of telling her, when he got back to his home there, that it was the soap that had decided everything, and he smiled. Then he seemed to see her scowl, which devoured her face until there was nothing of it left but her long reddish nose.

Nasri Shammas, to whom the title "Dr" had attached itself because of the remedies he put together in his pharmacy and which he claimed to have invented, hadn't slipped: someone had made him slip. Hend told him this, but Nasim thought he was responsible. Nasim was astounded when he found out that Hend had told his brother and cursed at his wife for it. "Don't believe her, she's a whore!" he'd told his brother, and he'd screamed in his wife's face and cursed her out. "All women are whores. That's what Nasri used to say and she's just like the rest of them."

When Hend heard the word on her husband's lips she left the flat saying she'd never come back. It was night, and raining. Karim tried to catch up with the woman to persuade her not to leave but he stopped in his tracks when he heard his brother's voice say in threatening tones, "You too, you want to screw my wife for me? Stay where you are and don't you move."

Nasim's voice sounded like those of the militiamen, and in his finger, raised in warning, Karim had seen a phantom gun poised to shoot.

After everything that had happened Karim had decided to go and see the older woman, for Hend's sake, but what was he supposed to say and where would he find the words? Should he apologise to Salma because he'd fled Beirut out of fear for his life and of the fate the war would bring? Or should he use as his excuse the destiny that had decreed Hend remain in the family as his twin brother Nasim's wife? Should he try to justify the brutality with which his brother dealt with his wife or get to the bottom of the truth, which would otherwise remain forever unknown?

When he visited her on the last day of his Beirut trip, he'd felt as though he'd been struck dumb. He'd sat down like an idiot and had no idea what to say.

Hend had gone back to her husband and had no need of his words, but she'd become another woman. She would live the rest of her life with a husband who no longer resembled the Nasim who had consoled her after her fiancé's departure and then made her broken heart an offer it could not refuse.

3

Karim hadn't felt sad at missing his father's funeral as he'd decided, from the moment of his arrival in Montpellier, to forget Beirut and the war and devote himself to rebuilding his life. But he had felt a chasm open up inside him, that "valley that forms inside a person's guts to teach him that he's the slave of time", as Nasri used to say when flown with wine. The pharmacist drank red wine in inordinate quantities and his tears would run down his cheeks as he listened to Umm Kulthoum singing about waiting for love. He'd answer his sons' questioning looks at these lachrymose moments by saying that Umm Kulthoum's voice opened up the bottomless chasm that exists inside us all. Karim saw his father cry only at moments of ecstasy, when the Egyptian singer's voice became a great womb that expanded to embrace all desires and sorrows. Wine and tears, these were the waters of life, Nasri would say as he devoured raw sheep's flesh. He'd put together little morsels of raw sheep's liver for his sons and decorate them with mint and onions, and he'd drink and wipe away the tears of ecstasy.

Deep in his soul, Nasri believed himself to be a philosopher because he'd discovered the secret of desire. This business of the secret came about after the incident with Sawsan and because of his sense of guilt when faced with his sons' tear-drenched dreams, which had made him decide to change his life, giving up his weekly visits to Beirut's street of prostitutes, cutting his ties to the woman with the violet nails, and devoting himself to developing his talents as a maker of potions and blender of herbs.

This new chapter in Nasri's emotional life revolved around his shop and took bizarre forms that drove his first-born son, who was studying medicine at the American University in Beirut, to feel alienated from everything. It was a story never told, but all its elements were present in the minds of the two brothers, as though they knew all its details, and as though it had been told to them complete. No story is real that isn't born of silence, whispers, and fidgets.

Nasri Shammas was celebrated for his brilliance as a pharmacist. The fame of the Shefa Pharmacy took wing after he discovered a cure for skin burns. The preparation was just a kind of heavy, sticky, black ointment but it took Nasri Shammas' name to the heights once the Beirut fire brigade endorsed it as the one and only treatment for the burns their men sometimes suffered. Nasri never disclosed the secret of this black ointment and he continued to make pharmaceutical discoveries, including a potion he sold as a cure for house plants, from which he made a fortune. He told everyone there were no chemicals in this Green Potion because he'd concocted it from a combination of herbs, and that the miraculous powers it possessed could bring dead plants back to life and make living plants flourish amazingly. The Green Potion was his means of worming his way into women's hearts. He refused to go to people's houses; those wanting his remedy had to bring their plants to his pharmacy, where he would mix the required amounts. And the potions he prepared produced magical results.

The first time Salma came to his pharmacy it was because of a basil plant that was refusing to grow, the second over a wilting jasmine. The white-skinned widow had found her sole consolation in the world of plants. Her balcony, which looked out over the Beidoun Mosque in the lower part of Beirut's Ashrafieh district, was full of them. She planted Damascus rose bushes, claiming that their smell reminded her of the three sons she had left behind in their distant village when, compelled by her heart, she had come to Beirut. Love, though, has no logic: she had come because of a desire that had filled her heart only to find that same heart ground to powder by the longing for another kind of love. Once she'd told her daughter she was an ass. "I'm an ass. I left three men for the sake of one and look what happened to me! The man died and left me with a girl and now I live like I'm dead."

Why did Salma always lie to herself? Hend discovered the secret of her lies only when she got married and began herself to live the lie of a hankering for a love that had vanished and was now forbidden to her. She'd told her husband, as she warned him against her mother, that the woman was a liar. Salma didn't make up stories, as many do, as a veil to conceal her life; rather, she put together tragic scenarios in whose shadows she could live and so give her life meaning. She wept for her children and wore mourning for her husband, but she lived out a long affair with the lawyer in whose office she worked. It came to an end only when he proposed to her that they change to being friends, saying that he couldn't anymore, that he had to remember his age, and that it was over. This was the beginning of the desert. The lawyer was seventy-one and Salma had just turned forty-five. She was terrified by the thought of the end and what they call, in literary Arabic, "the age of despair". It was then that the pharmacist's shop opened its doors to her and she tasted, in the herbal preparations that he made, an unquenchable desire.

The relationship remained a secret because the pharmacist was implacable with his women – no emotions and no melodrama; plants and pleasure, and that was it. No calls, no love letters. When the Damascus rose had reached more than a metre, he decided it was time for Salma to enter the trap. He told her her eyes were sad and that her radiant white face was under threat of losing its bloom. He told her that the age of despair didn't begin at forty. "It's long after that. That's just an illusion. Your despair, madam, is psychological and I have the answer." He said he had a herbal potion that would give her back her lustre and keep the dullness from her eyes. "Maybe it's because I don't sleep well at night," she said. He disappeared for a few minutes and returned bearing a small flask.

"Is it like the Green Potion for the roses?" she asked.

"Take it and put a teaspoonful in a cup of hot tea before you go to bed and then see how well you sleep."

He said if she put a teaspoonful of the herbal liquid into her cup of tea in the evening and drank it before sleeping, she would wake up a new woman. "Drink it, come back here tomorrow evening at five, and tell me."

Salma hesitated before agreeing. Then she took the small bottle and left, only to find herself the next morning just as the old pharmacist had said. Everything in her was bursting open and desire was plunging from her lips to her breasts. In the midst of the biting chills of March she took a cold shower and ended up hotter than before. Everything in her was alight, she felt she was another woman, and she found herself, without knowing how or why, on her way to the pharmacy. She remembered the man had told her to come at five in the evening but she was in front of his shop door at ten in the morning. He saw her, made a sign to her with his finger to go away, and held up the five fingers of his hand to remind her of their appointment. Salma's face flushed red with embarrassment and shame and she left, having decided never to return. She felt humiliated before this older man who was always swallowing his saliva and gargling with water and spitting it out because his salivary glands had dried up. Despite this, she found herself counting the minutes; time hardened over her eyes and refused to move. She took a hot shower, stood contemplating her naked body before the mirror, and was swept by an irresistible lust. She was aware of her body as she never had been before. She approached the mirror to allow her body to embrace its image and saw desire dangling like bunches of light and darkness. She told the old pharmacist, who was greedily licking her breasts with his tongue, that the waters of his flask had watered both the image and the shadow of the image as the two merged and parted, and that she'd discovered the other woman who lived inside her. "Tell me, Doctor. What's that called?"

At a quarter to five Salma had found herself walking once more in the direction of the pharmacy where the man was waiting for her. He took her hand and led her into the back room. She smelled perfumes, herbs, and medicines, felt dizzy, and put out her hand to steady herself against the wall. The pharmacist took her by the arm and sat her down on the couch and began to devour her. She told him, "Take me," and he answered that he was going to eat her and started devouring her breasts. She tried to ask him about the mirror and how she'd seen the image merging with its shadow but he told her to stop talking. "No talking!" he yelled at her, so she stopped talking and went inside herself, where everything was overflowing. Slowly, darkness spread over the man and the woman lying on the bed of lust and they became like two shadows.

And when the rite of love that the pharmacist refused to call love had ended, Salma put on her clothes and got ready to leave. She refused, however, to take the little bottle. "That's it, Nasri. Hend and Nasim are about to get married and you still want to fool around? That's it, my dear. I'm getting old and soon I'll be a grandmother. Plus you're never satisfied. Tell me: you give me that medicine, but what do you take yourself? How can your body stand it at your age? Anyway, I'm done with it. I'm tired of this body of mine that doesn't feel like it's mine anymore."

He told her he'd thought about it and maybe she was right, "but what does 'right' mean? There is no right in this world." He said too that his medicine had proved that the body had no limits. "Desire is like time: it's always there because it repeats itself endlessly."

She asked him about the other days of the week and he scowled and said there were no other days and asked her not to mention the subject again.

After two months of their meetings, which took place regularly every Tuesday at five, she told him she wouldn't be sticking to the time he'd set and would arrive whenever she felt like it because she'd begun to feel jealous. He told her sharply that the game of love and jealousy ill became one who had reached the last stage of life's journey, and that if she was looking for love she'd have to find it elsewhere "because I don't have any room left in my heart."

Did Salma break the agreement and arrive some other day to find the shop's doors closed? Did she feel jealous, or was it that she'd had enough of the "love potion" game? Or did the relationship go on for years, as Karim believed?

No-one but Salma knew the true story and she told it to no-one. She told her daughter, whose heart Karim had broken by leaving for France forever, to accept Nasim's offer of marriage. She said life had taught her that "it's all the same. What matters is for the woman to know how to make her soul hover above her body when she's making love. Love, my dear, isn't feelings. Love is practice."

How had this woman, who had abandoned her village and her children for another man, come by such a capacity to philosophise? Is it true that once she went to Nasri without taking the potion and that when the man realised the woman wasn't intoxicated with desire but was watching him, everything in him went soft and he couldn't perform anymore? That he put his clothes on in a hurry and said "It's over"?

But it wasn't over because Salma kept up her relationship with Nasri for the sake of her plants. The strange thing is that she didn't feel the man had tricked her. She told him once she was grateful to him for his amazing potion, which had made her savour the taste of the lees, and he'd smiled and said nothing. The relationship would take another turn, however, when Nasri found himself obliged to accompany his son Nasim on a visit to Salma in her flat to ask for the hand of her only daughter.

When Karim had heard the news of his father's death, he'd drunk two bottles of red wine, then sat in the living room with a glass of cognac before him, swaying in ecstasy to the voice of Umm Kulthoum resounding through the flat as she sang to the music of Sheikh Zakariya Ahmad, "I wait for you." Bernadette had asked him to turn down the volume "because we're living in a civilised country called France"; he'd cursed her *sotto voce* in Arabic. He'd felt the chasm opening inside him and heard Nasri's voice, coated with wine, declaring that Man was an idiotic creature incapable of understanding that his death as an individual was of no importance except as a marker of time.

Had Salma's relationship with his father made him feel an aversion to Hend so that he had to escape from Lebanon and never go back?

When Karim left for Montpellier, he was afraid, because of the savagery with which his friend Khaled Nabulsi had died. Had Nabulsi been his friend? He'd hardly known him and had no idea why Khaled had chosen him, of all people, to tell him of how he'd seen death in the General's eyes. He'd seen death and died. What did death look like? Does everyone see his death before he dies?

Karim set off for the past, only to discover that he could no longer visit it. Things happen in a deluge and pile up one on top of the other. The father dies as a result of slipping on the living-room floor at Nasim's flat, and the man's image holds sway over his son's imagination in a southern French city, where the father holds up his glass of red wine and announces he never drinks water. The pharmacist's medical theory in this regard rested on a curious supposition. When asked at the café why he never drank his glass of iced water before starting on the Turkish coffee, he answered that he never went near water because it was bad for one's health. "A man's blood is full of iron and what happens if you put water on iron? The iron turns to rust. That's why I only drink the juice of the grape. Wine doesn't rust and it stops everything else from rusting."

The man who had come up with the rust theory began his day by drinking a litre of cold water: in the early morning one's sun still hadn't risen, the soul was in a limbo between life and death, the blood was cold, and you had to drink water to clean the body out. In the morning, and only in the morning, water didn't oxidise the blood. The morning was for water, the rest of the day and the night were for wine. The only exception was Sunday, when Nasri would get up early to buy mutton and prepare the kibbeh nayyeh, the tabbouleh and the grill. He'd set up the arak table too, as alcohol worked as an antidote to the poison of the water and turned it white as milk. The only thing that went with raw meat was alcohol that had been distilled by fire, which made it purer than water.

Sunday was arak day. The father would sit at the head of the table and get drunk, talking of women in their role as the chemistry of the world. He would eat and talk and discuss mutton, which had to be eaten raw, for the sheep, by virtue of its not needing fire, had become a symbol. It was the last marker that tied a person to his past and reminded him of the taste of the beginning.

The sons didn't understand the connection between chemistry and flesh, were disgusted by the smell of the blood in the raw liver, and would eat the kibbeh only after it had been dipped in olive oil, which absorbed the taste. In France, though, the flavour of things would change.

Two months after his marriage, on a Sunday, while Karim was waiting for his wife Bernadette to finish putting on her make-up so that they could go to the Place de la Comédie and eat lunch at one of the restaurants there, he'd felt a desire for kibbeh nayyeh and a glass of arak, and to tell his wife about the chemistry of women. The Lebanese doctor hadn't drunk a drop of arak since his arrival in the French city, having turned instead to French wine, in which he'd discovered the flavour of life, becoming an expert on the different kinds, and how to match them to the dishes of French cuisine, which he'd adopted, claiming it was the greatest in the world. But once he found himself in his own home, and with the woman to whom he was married, he'd felt things weren't right without arak on Sundays. He told his wife, as they ate their *coq au vin*, that the following week he'd invite her to eat a Lebanese lunch that he'd prepare at home. The nurse looked at him uncomprehendingly with her blue eyes. Karim had avoided talking about his country and had refused her invitation to the city's Lebanese restaurant, saying Lebanese food was heavy on the stomach and reminded him of things he'd decided to forget. He'd kept in touch with the taste of his country only through his Turkish coffee which, after his marriage, he would also stop drinking, substituting for it espresso.

She'd asked him what was going on and he told her about his father's Sunday ceremonies. The woman smiled and said her father had warned her that this homesickness would soon appear.

"What did he say?" he asked her.

She told him her father had said that when a man marries he returns to his family and his homeland.

"But he wants to forget Lebanon. He's more French than you are," she'd responded. "Plus I don't mind. I married a Lebanese and I want him to be a bit Lebanese. It's better."

She said her father had warned her against Oriental men. They bullied their wives and beat them.

"And did you believe him?" asked Karim.

"Of course not," she answered.

"You were wrong. You should have believed him," he said and burst out laughing as he saw how her face changed, her lower lip falling, a sign of her annoyance. He put out his hand, touched her lip, and felt desire. She'd known since their first encounter that when he put his hand out to touch her lower lip it meant he wanted her right then, after which remaining in the bar or restaurant where they were was out of the question.

She said they hadn't yet eaten. "Wait a little. Plus you know I don't like making love in the afternoon."

"I'm not a bully and I'll never beat you, but it's how things are," he'd told her, saying the problem was one of language. The Arabs call the father or husband "the master of the house" and he'd discovered that in Hebrew the word *baal* was used for "husband" – the very word used in classical Arabic. In the ancient Phoenician-Canaanite language the word meant "lord" but was also the name of their chief god, which meant, in other words, that the husband was a *baal*, i.e. was a god.

She looked at him with her sky-blue eyes and said she didn't like that kind of humour. They finished their meal in silence and when they went home he didn't try to have sex with her during their siesta but lay next to her like an angel.

The following Sunday morning Bernadette awoke to a clattering in the kitchen and found her husband fine-chopping parsley and tomatoes and mixing minced meat with onion, the dishes piling up in the sink. She went to help him but he asked her to leave as her presence would spoil the surprise. He said he'd make her a *café au lait* and bring it to her in the living room.

At 1 p.m. the surprise had turned into a table covered with vegetables, the tabbouleh and kibbeh nayyeh at their centre. He poured the arak and they drank. She said the Ricard tasted different. "Ricard!" he said angrily. "Like Ricard," she said. At this he explained to her that arak was the essence of white grapes, that it was mixed with aniseed while being distilled, and that it was the most sublime product of the Ottoman Empire at its height and not to be compared to the aniseed liquor from which Ricard was made. He made her a plate of tabbouleh and she ate and said the salad was nice but there was something in it that tasted strange. He explained to her, as he gave her a piece of the large tomato that he had hollowed out and filled with salt, spices, ice, and arak, that the people of Lebanon sprinkled arak over the tabbouleh, which was not a salad as she thought, but God's *juneina* or garden, being all the vegetables produced by the earth mixed with cracked wheat. He explained that the word *juneina* was the diminutive of *janna*, meaning Paradise, because the paradise that God had promised Man was an endless garden whose vegetables, fruit, and waters were never depleted.

Bernadette ate of God's garden, feeling the burning taste of the arak, and her tongue had just started to get used to the flavour of the arak that permeated the parsley when the time came for the kibbeh nayyeh. He presented her with a plate decorated with mint and white onion, and she had barely inserted her fork into the dish when she heard him say there was no need for a fork. The kibbeh was eaten with bread, using the hand. She placed a morsel in her mouth and tried to get used to its strange taste, closing her eyes to concentrate on appreciating the kibbeh, then asked him what it was. He tried to explain to her that kibbeh was a mixture of mutton, onions, cracked wheat, salt, and spices and resembled steak tartare.

"Now I understand," she said.

She jumped up and ran to the kitchen, returning with a raw egg, and before the astounded Karim could say or do anything, she'd broken the egg into a small dish and beaten it with her fork preparatory to putting it on top of the dish of kibbeh.

Karim snatched the dish from his wife's hand and the raw egg spilled onto the table.

"What are you doing?" he yelled in Arabic.

"*C'est du steak tartare, non?*"

"Absolutely *non*! Now look what you've done."

The Frenchwoman burst out laughing and took a napkin to remove the traces of egg from the table, which gave off a cloying smell. He took the plate of kibbeh and threw it into the garbage, trying to explain to her that egg made everything *zinikh*. When he searched for an equivalent of the word *zinikh* in French he couldn't find one – not *odeur âcre*, not *pourriture*, certainly not *relent acide*. How was he to explain to her the meaning of *zinikh*? He resorted to the dictionary but found nothing and contented himself with saying "*C'est un odeur désagréable.*"

She said she understood nothing and that his conduct did not resemble that of the civilised man she had married. He tried to placate her, saying it wasn't his fault but that of the French language for not including the word *zinikh*.

Time, however, would change everything. Bernadette ended up making tabbouleh, kibbeh, and all the different casseroles. She didn't sprinkle arak over the tabbouleh because she discovered that the custom had died out in Lebanon and that Nasri hammas was the last Lebanese to sprinkle arak over the "vegetable garden", as the two small boys had called tabbouleh, which became an almost daily dish. But the issue of language grew in importance: it reached its peak after his brother informed Karim that he'd married Hend, and Karim became afflicted, when talking to his wife, with the habit of coughing through his words.

Dr Karim Shammas had met Nurse Bernadette César at the Tex Mex bar. The Lebanese doctor was drunk. He had drunk too many beers and tequilas to count. He had no idea how the blonde with blue eyes found her way into his bed. In the morning he got a surprise when she told him she worked as a nurse at the Hôpital Saint Bernard, where he did.

He told her he hadn't noticed her, perhaps because the white nurse's uniform was like a veil, and was seeing her now as though for the first time.

"You and the nurses!" she said.

"Me?"

How had he failed to notice the presence of this woman, for whom he'd been looking? Since arriving in France he'd found himself incapable of approaching any blue-eyed blonde. All the women he'd met were brunettes.

Later he'd tell Bernadette that he'd left Beirut to escape the sun, which tanned the earth, the trees, and the women and turned them brown.

"Aren't the leaves of the trees over there green?" she'd asked incredulously.

"Not exactly. You know, it's just a way of speaking, *c'est le sens de la parole*," he said. He saw the confusion in her eyes and tried to explain that "when we Lebanese say 'it's just a way of speaking' it means we don't have that particular meaning in mind, or that the meaning doesn't have a meaning." He laughed out loud and asked her to forget about it.

Karim had discovered Montpellier's Tex Mex bar by chance. He was walking down a dark street and the name caught his fancy. He went in and drank a beer. Suddenly his eyes caught Sophie's. The tall well-fleshed woman was standing behind the bar and laughing, the drunks gathered around her. He could see her large firm breasts gleaming through the opening of her blouse. He went up to the bar and found himself beneath the huge bosoms and within range of the loud chortling. Sophie turned towards him and yelled, "A new customer! He has to try the tequila with salt." The clamouring and murmuring around the bar increased and Karim had the feeling he wasn't following what was being said. He stood there waiting for his glass of tequila. The woman undid the buttons of her yellow blouse and, with lightning speed, her breasts popped out. She took the bottle of tequila, doused her cleavage, and sprinkled a little salt on it while simultaneously seizing Karim's head. The Lebanese doctor found himself following the droplets with their intoxicating bouquet on their downward course and gobbling at her cleavage. He felt the woman press his head between her huge breasts and that the world was spinning.

She pulled his head out and poured again, and the faces and lips leapt forward. Karim saw his face among those of the others. He tried to gather up the drops with his tongue and the dizziness started. He pulled back and his eyes met those of a French girl with a dainty face smiling at him and nodding her head. He couldn't remember what they said but in the morning, when he saw the girl in his bed and found out she was the Nurse Bernadette who worked with him at the hospital, he felt a bit sheepish. He lit his first cigarette of the morning and contemplated the beauty which had been hidden from his eyes throughout the previous months by a nurse's uniform. She asked him why he'd said the night before that his name was Sinalcol. "You made me laugh," she said. "You were lapping up the tequila and claiming your name was Sinalcol? *C'était sympa.*" She explained to him that *sin alcohol* was Spanish and meant "alcohol-free". He said he couldn't remember, and that it was the name of a friend of his so he hadn't thought about what it meant.

He said he didn't know the man: "It was just my idea that he was my friend because he was like a ghost. The war had created a ghost whom no-one ever met. Maybe the man didn't exist but he became a name and I thought of him as my friend because he fascinated me."

"How could he fascinate you when you hadn't met him?" she asked.

"His name fascinated me," he answered. "It's a long story. I'll tell you about it someday."

He heard her say, "You Lebanese!" and ask him where he kept the coffee because she needed a cup of *café au lait.*

He leapt out of bed, trotted to the kitchen, and put the little holder in which he boiled the water for his coffee on the stove, explaining to the

French nurse that he didn't drink French *café au lait* in the morning, he drank Turkish coffee.

"You're Turkish?" she said wonderingly. "I thought you were Lebanese."

He said Turkish coffee was Lebanese coffee too and that it was a *spécialité libanaise*. She laughed and didn't understand.

As time passed Karim would forget the taste of Turkish coffee because Bernadette hated it and it was only with Ghazala, the maid who brought the taste of things back to his tongue, that he would rediscover its strong flavour and the jolt to the heart that accompanied the first morning sips of it.

When Karim left Beirut for France his consciousness had been wrapped in fog. All he could remember now of the first months of his stay in Montpellier was the sense of loss that made him accept everything. He was like someone who wanted to forget who he was, forget how things had pulled the carpet from under his feet. He told Bernadette later that he had lost the taste of things and wanted to marry her so he could recover his soul.

The French nurse had been taken by surprise by the offer of marriage made by the eccentric Lebanese doctor six months after they met. She'd told him she was afraid and would prefer it if they could go to Lebanon so she could meet his family before accepting the offer.

He turned his face away and said no. "Not Lebanon. I'll never go to Lebanon, not now and not after a hundred years. Refuse if you like but you'll never go to Lebanon."

Bernadette hadn't been able to believe her ears when she heard Karim say he was going to Lebanon to build a dermatology hospital in Beirut. She told him he'd changed a lot. "You're not the man I married."

"And you're not the woman," he said and burst out laughing.

He'd told Nasim when recounting what he'd done in France that he'd discovered his other face there. "It's as though I'm not me. It's as though over there I was someone else."

"And now, have you gone back to being you?" Nasim had asked.

"No," Karim had responded. "Now I've become a third person."

There, in France, Karim had put on the face of the doctor he was to become. He'd found himself one of a circle of physicians around Professor Didier Struffe, a French doctor of Russian origin who was professor of dermatology at the University of Montpellier. Alongside a group of outstanding French students, Karim passed the *concours internat* exam, being the only foreigner to do so. At his first meeting with his White Russian professor he'd said that he'd wanted to study psychology but been afraid to. He told his professor, while informing him of his decision to study dermatology, that he'd been afraid of himself. "Faced with a patient whose soul has disintegrated you must yourself possess an unshakeably well-grounded personality, and I don't."

Professor Struffe had astonished him by speaking of the skin as the person's alter ego. "I am my skin," he would say as he explained to his students that the skin was the most important part of the body. "The skin's most important function is to mediate between the person and the external temperature. Without skin we would be naked before death," he said in his first class. "Did you know that the skin of someone weighing seventy kilograms weighs fourteen kilograms and has a surface area of two square metres?" He spoke of the human skin as though it was a work of art, drawing for his students a picture of an organ that contained within itself all other organs, and of a consciousness that extended over the entirety of the human body.

The skin of pleasure and the skin of pain. A skin that defines the limits of the body and a skin that connects it to others. A skin that sweats and a skin that blushes. A skin that protects a person and a skin that makes him vulnerable. The professor said a person could live without the four senses of sight, hearing, smell, and taste, but he could not live without the sense of touch because one who loses his skin loses his life.

Karim Shammas said to his Russian professor: "I get it. No blood and no madness. We're in the presence of touch and the seductions of the fingers."

He entered the empire of the skin, the relationships between epidermis, dermis, and hypodermis. He told Bernadette, whose belly had started to show stretch marks after the birth of their second daughter, "It's the dermis, my dear. The fibres have begun to break up and the white skin is the problem. Your white skin has begun to split. I can treat it with ointments or by laser, as you wish."

The enchantment of skin diseases lies in the fact that treating them is like dealing with an artistic phenomenon, which is to say it's like music. The doctor has to discover the rhythm of his patient's body, and when he does so the problem is solved, and treating it with ointments is almost like looking for ways in which it can be seduced. Of course, there are diseases that were once resistant to treatment, such as syphilis, which penicillin came along and put an end to. A residue of such diseases continues to exist, and these made Karim's skin crawl. There was, for example, "cockscomb disease" – in French *V.P.H.* – a kind of wart in the area of the testes or penis which now, thanks to antibiotics, can be treated.

The world constructed by the White Russian professor saved Karim. Later he would tell Muna, as he licked her white, wet thigh, that he could read her via the relationship of his hand to her skin, read the topography of her soul and the intricacies of love.

She said she'd come to say goodbye to him, not listen to a lecture on medicine.

He said he wasn't lecturing but recounting his feelings and discovering that we can only read love at the end. The poets were wrong when they wrote of the combustion at the beginning of love because that was only an illusion ignited by illusion. The reality could be read at the end, at the moment of loss, and only those who lost were capable of discovering its meanings.

"Cut the philosophy," she'd said and busied herself drying her wet body.

Karim stopped talking. He felt he had no right to speak, for when you discover that the game has been played to its end, only silence suits the moment.

Only the body speaks; that was what his studies in Montpellier had taught him. Within the fingers and palm of the hand is contained the whole world.

He told his Russian professor the story of the Spiritual Fluids on which Dr Dahesh had built his entire school and the students laughed along with the professor, who'd said, "This isn't a class in magic and legerdemain."

Karim didn't believe those cock-and-bull stories himself, he'd only wanted to provide support for the "I = my skin" idea propounded by his professor. His father's brief conversion to the Daheshism that had become widespread among Lebanese doctors during the 1950s had led the pharmacist to learn the art of legerdemain. What had caught Karim's attention, though, were his father's memories of the most important dermatologist in Beirut, Dr Marcel Khineisar, who was a follower of the Daheshian School – founded by an Assyrian from Bethlehem – that had dominated Beirut's social and political life in that decade. Dr Dahesh's theory stated that one's skin flowed, and that he could cause a person to be present in more than one place. This in turn had driven his father and many other doctors and pharmacists of his ilk to believe in magic as the highest form of religion.

Karim had wanted to say that the magic of the human skin reminded him of flowing, that a person flows from the tips of his fingers, and that to cure his patients all the successful physician has to do is receive that outflow and bring them to a discovery of the balance that puts paid to all disease.

Nasri, who had discovered the best ointment for treating burns, thought the only disease for which there was no cure was death. "Death is a disease. It's the only disease whose sole cure is desire. When desire is present, death vanishes and when it ceases to exist the only choice left is surrender."

"What does it mean that I am going back tomorrow to France?" Karim asked himself as he opened his eyes to the sound of the Beirut thunder and listened to the sloosh of the rain that had enveloped the city.

He saw the ghost of his father approach him, heard the rustle of the loose clothes that Nasri used to insist on wearing to hide his small paunch. He saw the woman's hand push his father, saw his father fall to the ground, and beheld black, sticky blood.

He opened his eyes to the sound of the alarm clock, shaved quickly, and descended the long dark staircase to the entrance of the building where the taxi was waiting for him.

4

Muna came to Pinocchio's wearing a green dress and everything about her undulated. Thirty was exploding within her svelte figure, her long thin visage hid a diaphanous veil of sorrow, and her glasses, which covered a part of her face, established a distance between her and the world.

Karim had no idea how things had reached this point. He'd met her at his brother's flat. She'd come to the dinner party with her husband the architect Ahmad Dakiz. The architect had talked at length of the project to build the hospital, which he was designing, while his wife had sat and said nothing throughout. A few minutes before the evening ended she turned to Karim, asked him about life in France, and expressed her astonishment at the physician's decision to return to Lebanon. "Who comes back?" she asked, and when Karim answered that a person needs his roots she burst out laughing. "Ahmad, tell them about your roots and your crusader forefathers!"

Ahmad had recounted snippets of an incredible story and everyone had broken into laughter.

"You mean you're a crusader *and* a Muslim?" Karim said laughing.

Muna didn't laugh, though. She said she wanted to emigrate to Canada. "My husband wasn't able to take me to France because the French are looking for their roots too but now we're going to Canada. That's a country that's pulled out its roots, which may be better."

She asked Karim about stretch marks and said she wanted to visit him at his clinic because she was worried about a small problem.

"Where's the problem?" he asked her.

"It's not a big deal. Just some marks on my belly from the children. When should I come to the clinic?"

"I don't actually have a clinic in Beirut," he said, and gave her his phone number.

Karim didn't want anything from the woman, who had seemed to him drained. Her white complexion was drained, her beauty was drained, plus the way she twisted her lips when speaking Arabic, after the fashion of francophone Lebanese educated in foreign mission schools, made him furious.

Here in Beirut he'd discovered that he'd never stopped loving Hend, who had become his brother's wife. But he didn't know what to do with that love, which had become a nightmare.

He'd told her he hadn't left her because he'd stopped loving her but because he was afraid, and when you're afraid all you feel is fear.

She'd said she didn't believe him but it didn't matter anymore because she felt she had to get away from this family and didn't know how.

She said she wasn't stupid like her mother. "My mother ran after love and you know what happened. They all died. She loved four men and all died, one after the other. I don't know if she loved your father but I know she killed all the men she loved and when it was your father's turn I had to take care of it for her."

Hend turned around and asked him if he still loved her.

Now, when he recalled the question, he felt that the whole thing had been unreal, more like a dream. Was it reasonable for the woman to ask him about love while talking of murder?

Muna had phoned him to make an appointment so he'd invited her to dinner at a restaurant.

"Dinner? No, impossible. Have you forgotten I'm married?"

"And I'm married too," he answered, laughing.

They agreed on lunch at Pinocchio's, where they ate pizza and drank wine.

As he'd expected she didn't asked him about stretch marks. They talked about everything, meaning about nothing, and in her eyes he saw a certain glow that came from nowhere and revealed to him in her drained whiteness flashes of light escaping from her eyes and lips.

Muna was reaching out to him. She was sitting opposite him in the restaurant, bending forward and extending her left hand, which she placed, empty, on the table.

He took hold of her upturned hand.

"What are you doing?" she asked.

"I'm holding your hand," he answered.

"Why?" she said.

"Ask your hand," he answered.

He told her, as he lifted the palm of her hand and placed it on his ear before kissing it, that he listened to hands. "Fingers are the gauge of beauty," he said.

"And the eyes?" she asked.

He saw the translucent honey colour shining in hers.

"Your eyes are beautiful," he said. "I meant at first to specialise in the eye but in France my professor taught me that the skin is the person, and today I've discovered the fingers."

"But the eye is more poetic," she said.

"There's nothing poetic about medicine except talking about it. Actually, I was lying to you," he said. "In fact at the beginning I had it in mind to specialise in psychiatry but I couldn't go through with it. I felt I was going mad. One madman can't treat another."

She withdrew her hand from his and said, laughing, that she loved mad people.

He took her back to her flat in his car and as she got out she said that next time she'd consult him as a doctor.

Karim saw himself sliding. There was the Beirut heat, and this woman Muna who was bursting with the colour green. Karim didn't know what colour he liked best. When his French wife asked him about colours he'd answer that he didn't care. That day, though, he discovered he loved green. The colour appeared in the form of a short dress that reached down to white knees and enfolded a delicate greenness from which flowed undulations that enveloped her calves.

When Muna came, Karim was living the fever of Ghazala but he didn't dare place his relationship with the maid in the category of love. Was it reasonable to be in love with a maid? He'd convinced himself she was just a form of sawsanning. True, she wasn't a prostitute and had nothing in common with the way that violet-fingernailed woman had looked, but it was just a sexual relationship with no more distant horizons.

Muna contacted him five days later and asked for an appointment. He suggested the same restaurant and she responded that she wanted to meet for a professional consultation, which would be impossible in a restaurant.

"How about coming to our place? Ahmad would love to see you too."

"Who's Ahmad?" he asked her.

She burst out laughing and he suggested the meeting be at his flat at 12.30 on Friday. He suggested Friday because Ghazala didn't come that day, and before ending the call he asked her to wear a green dress.

On entering the flat she asked him why he liked green.

She was wearing an orange skirt and a thin white blouse. She said her green dress was at the cleaner's.

He said he'd changed his mind and now he liked orange. He opened the bottle of chilled white wine, poured two glasses, and said green reminded him of the Green Woman he used to see in his dreams when he was small.

When Karim told Muna the story of the Green Woman he was struck by the unexpectedness of the memory. He said memory was scary: it woke when it pleased, dropped in as though out of nowhere, and had no rules. He told her about the Iraqi poet he used to meet in a bar in Montpellier. "I'd only meet him when we were drunk and all he'd talk to me about was the poems he hadn't yet written. Once I asked him to read me something he'd written recently. He responded that he'd given up writing because every time he went near the blank paper he'd be deluged with memories from he knew not where of his childhood in el-Amarah in Iraq, and these hidden memories scared him and were turning him into a poet who lived poetry instead of writing it."

"Literature's different. No, that's not normal – poets imagine their memories," she said. She also said she was very fond of poetry and knew all Mahmoud Darwish's poems about Rita by heart.

He said he used to think the same, "but it seems memory works in mysterious ways and when it gives up its secrets a person becomes a slave to his past, which he hadn't known was his."

They drank the bottle of wine and he listened to her as she recited some lines about Rita. He took her in his arms and heard her whisper incomprehensible words. He embraced her and she seemed shy. She got into bed in her clothes. He lay down next to her, naked, lifted the coverlet and saw that she was naked. He moved close to her and felt a blind strangeness: two strange bodies that couldn't find a rhythm swimming in the darkness of desire, a strangeness wouldn't be broken until the last day, when Muna came to him to say goodbye and he took her with the water falling from her body and felt sorrow, because he sensed that the end of their relationship had been the moment when it began.

They'd made love as though searching for love. On the last day, he told her that in the beginning they'd been like two blind people and her modesty had been like a veil that prevented him from seeing. When Muna gasped, and he heard a moaning that broke through the barrier of silence, his water burst forth copiously and he took her lips in a long kiss. As he floated above the darkness of his eyes he held tight to her waist to stop himself from drowning.

She pushed him back a little and said she needed air. He retreated, lit a cigarette and sat facing her on the bed. Muna covered her white nakedness with the white sheet, raised her right hand to wave away the smoke of his cigarette and the sheet slipped off her shoulder and her breast appeared, a hanging white pomegranate. He bent over and took the nipple in his mouth and she covered her chest with the sheet but he didn't pull back. He pushed his face into the darkness of the white and heard her little gasp before she took his face in her hands and pushed it away.

She said the moment she saw him at his brother's flat, she'd decided he was the one. "You know, you and your brother look a lot like one another. Nasim's been a friend of my husband's for a long time and your brother's always been making signs to show that he wants me. I thought he was a drag and would say to myself, 'What does he think he's doing? I'm his friend's wife!' Then when I saw you, I said it's you."

"Meaning you fell in love with me."

"You're as much of a drag as your brother. Who said anything about love? Go on, tell me about green."

"But the green was love."

"You mean you fell in love with a woman who wore only green?"

"A Green Woman. How can I put it? There was no love, just something strange."

He told her that the strange thing was how the Green Woman had leapt out from his memory, as though she'd been sleeping there.

He lifted the sheet she'd covered herself with and she pulled away as though panic-stricken and pulled the sheet up to her neck.

"What are you doing?" she asked.

"I want to examine you. Drop the sheet and let me work."

"Right. I'd forgotten you're a doctor."

She closed her eyes and held still. Karim saw a thin white thread bursting out from below the whiteness of her belly, which flowed as though it were a mirror. He wanted to tell her that he didn't like white skin because it crumbled beneath his eyes and that brown skin, which mirrored the hues of wheat, resisted being pulled apart because it was thicker. The whiteness of Muna's skin, however, seemed to him different from any that he'd seen as a doctor in France. He massaged the thin thread with his finger and told Muna that the stretching wasn't important because it didn't affect her beauty, but he could prescribe her an ointment if she wanted.

"Are you speaking as a doctor or as something else?"

"As a doctor, naturally. If I wanted to speak as something else I'd have to become a poet, faced with such beauty," he said.

"Please, cut that out. So the ointment will get rid of the white thread?"

"Not completely. The human body is made to withstand the marks of time and for sure it'll go back to the way it was."

He told her he'd write down the name of the ointment for her and she would have to apply it once a day, after bathing, for ten days. "Then we'll see."

Muna tried to cover herself but the doctor took the sheet in both hands. "Can anyone cover the sea?"

"What a horrible comparison!" Muna said. "If any of my students wrote a simile like that he'd get a zero."

The doctor laughed. He said that when he saw her body he'd been reminded of the story of the "White Mediterranean Sea" and the Palestinian teacher at A.U.B. who insisted that his students use the right names. "That sea," the teacher used to say, pointing out of the window, "we used to call the White Sea until the Westerners imposed the term 'Mediterranean' on us. We give our seas the names of colours because our eyes always see them as coloured. That's why the names of our seas are the White, the Red, and the Black. Only the Dead Sea has no colour, because it's dead." Karim said they'd laughed at the teacher and he'd only understood what he meant when he saw her body enveloped in its whiteness and beheld before him nothing but the sea.

"An unpleasant simile. I'm putting a cross against that line," she said, putting on her glasses and covering herself. At that moment, Karim reignited. He couldn't work out what had happened to him with this woman because he hated women who wore glasses and he no longer liked white, but in this city he'd found himself set on fire by things he thought he hated. The glasses made him lose control and he found himself holding Muna to him once more.

"No, that's enough. Once is enough. Tell me the story from the beginning and then we'll see."

Karim had discovered that real words, meaning words that fill the mouth and impart the taste of fruit, come only after making love. "That was the secret of the Arabs," he told Bernadette during the days of their first love. He told her that the secret of *The One Thousand and One Nights* lay in this, that Scheherazade never opened her mouth until they had made love. She filled three years' worth of nights with words and when the love ended the story ended. She'd told the mad king, "That's it", and brought the three sons she'd borne to plead for her, or so she could threaten him with them.

No, he hadn't put it like that. In fact, at the time he'd said the opposite of what he thought now. He'd said then that love made the story endless because "one thousand and one nights" doesn't imply a set number of nights: the number opens, rather, infinite doors. The stories might go on forever, and the love too.

Karim lit a cigarette and began to cough. He ran to the refrigerator and returned with a bottle of ice-cold water.

"Eduardo was like that," said Muna.

"Who's Eduardo?"

"It doesn't matter. Let me go and make tea."

She wrapped herself in the white sheet and went to the kitchen, so he went after her.

"Please, I don't like men who come into the kitchen. Wait for me in the bedroom."

She returned with two glasses of tea and lay down on the bed. Karim sat next to her and started to narrate.

"Once upon a time a long while ago (first we'll tell a story and then to bed we'll go) there was a woman . . ."

"Not like that. I don't want a story from *The Thousand and One Nights*. I want your story with the Green Woman."

Karim said that stories had to begin somewhere, which is why our ancestors had used the past imperfect tense, because everything was born imperfect and would die imperfect, but he didn't want to tell that story now because the colour green no longer mattered, so he was going to tell her another story.

In the form in which the scene leaked from Karim's memory, it seemed ridiculous: a woman lying on the bed, her eyes shining behind her spectacles, and a naked forty-year-old man, his white skin shining with sweat that added colour to the hair on his chest, sitting at the end of a bed holding a glass of tea in his left hand and a filterless Gauloise in his right, puffing cigarette smoke into the air and telling the story of a green woman.

He said the woman was called Majda and she used to come to their flat once a week to clean. But she wasn't a maid, or didn't behave like one. She would arrive in a hurry and leave in a hurry. She was said to have had three children but they'd all died at birth, "and I don't know . . . We knew she was married to a man called Abu Sultan and that this Abu Sultan didn't work. Then, when Majda disappeared, we discovered the truth.

"She was the only woman Father didn't view as a sex object. He was a strange man. A pharmacist, and cultured, and he read a lot. He'd made a special niche for himself in his little community, which was limited to his friends at the Gemmeizeh Café where he went every day to play backgammon. All the same he became – how can I put it? – he became another person when he laid eyes on a woman of any kind whatsoever. He used to say each age possesses its own special magic. But he talked of Majda with respect, didn't lounge about in front of her, and watched his language. She was pretty. A strange woman. She didn't speak a word. She'd come in the morning, do the laundry and the cleaning as if there was no-one else there, then gather up her stuff and go home."

Majda disappeared twice over. The first time was when she got pregnant, the second when she gave birth to her baby in a welter of haemorrhaging and blood.

The story goes that Majda suffered a great deal at her husband's hands and that he didn't work. He'd beat her to pocket the money she brought back from working as a maid in people's houses. Then he discovered his path in life: he manufactured a sort of hump for himself and became a beggar. He'd go off every day to the area of Ras Beirut, where no-one knew him, and work all day. Back home he would shrug off his hump, snatch his wife's money, and set off to get drunk and consort with prostitutes.

"Am I boring you?" asked Karim.

"Not at all," said Muna, yawning. "But where's the story? I mean what's the topic and what happened to make you fall in love with the maid?"

"That's not what the story's about. It has nothing to do with me. I mean, I didn't fall in love with her but I got scared.

"Majda lived with her husband in a shack located at the beginning of the Zaroub el-Haramiyeh settlement, an area considered in those days to lie outside the confines of the city even though it was close to el-Burj Square. The inhabitants were the unemployed and every kind of vagabond, thief, and beggar. The wooden shacks were roofed with corrugated iron sheets that gave no protection from the cold in winter or the heat in summer. Still, the inhabitants found in it a refuge from homelessness. You had only to pay three lira a month to Wajih, one of the men working for Hajj Murad, a Beirut gang leader, for him to allow you to build yourself a wooden shack. Wajih, who was in his early thirties, wore a red tarbush like his boss Hajj Murad and imposed charges on the inhabitants of the shacks. These he called rents, the individual amounts being determined by his mood and his estimate of how much you could pay.

"The issue was that Wajih could never see eye to eye with Abu Sultan, who refused to pay the charges on the grounds that he was too poor and who would make a scene, weeping and wailing, on the street. Even when he found himself a steady job as a beggar it changed nothing, till it reached the point at which the shack was to be demolished.

"Wajih told Majda that were it not for his belief that she was a holy woman and his being a god-fearing man, he would have burned the shack with man and wife inside. 'Like you know, lady, we fear only the Good Lord in His Heaven but what can I say? You made me feel as though my hand was paralysed.'

"Was Majda a saint, as Wajih claimed, and as many others came to believe after seeing repeated green apparitions of her next to the ruins of the shack?

"I honestly don't know. What everyone does know is that Majda almost died. She went into labour at four in the afternoon. It was winter, she felt paralysed, she saw the blood and started screaming. The people of the neighbourhood came running and didn't know what to do. After a short while the midwife – her name was Imm Saad – came, yelled that the cloying smell would kill her, and began tearing sheets into strips and placing them on Majda's belly, helped by others. The shack filled with the smell of blood – the bedding, the pillows, their belongings. The midwife yelled that she could do nothing – 'Call the Red Cross, the woman's going to die before our eyes!' – and the blood never stopped. Majda was at death's door. The ambulance arrived and took her to the hospital and she gave birth to a boy after a difficult operation.

"Once the woman had been taken to the hospital, the neighbourhood women volunteered to clean the shack. They took out the furniture and scrubbed the floor. No-one knows how it happened but the furniture got thrown onto the rubbish tip at the end of the lane.

"When Abu Sultan reached his house at 9 p.m., drunk as usual, he was surprised by what he saw; and when people told him what had happened to his wife and how they had cleaned out the house and that the woman was now in the Hôtel Dieu hospital, all he asked was about the contents of the house.

"'Where's the stuff?' he screamed.

"'God will replace it for you, neighbour,' said one of the aged women who had hurried to the shack on hearing the man's screams, thinking something bad must have happened to Majda. 'There was nothing worth keeping – bedding and rugs. It's not a problem, we'll get you more. Go to the hospital now and check on your wife.'

"'Where's the stuff?' Abu Sultan asked again, moaning like a wounded animal.

"'I think they threw it on the tip at the beginning of the street,' said the woman.

"Abu Sultan ran and the men and women of the area ran after him, everyone fearing the man had lost his wits because his wife had died. They ran till they found themselves at the rubbish tip, where the man waded into the blood-soaked things and a cloying stench filled the air.

"The story goes that the Beirut rain fell in ropes that stormy autumn evening and that Abu Sultan drowned in blood. He was searching for something like a madman and the people around him kept trying to calm his rage, advising him to put his trust in God, but he paid them no attention and spoke to no-one. He stuck his head into the mound of rubbish and sank into it.

"Everyone said it rained blood that evening.

"They said they saw Abu Sultan raise his blood-smeared face from the mound of rubbish, hugging a pillow and dancing.

"They said the man burst out laughing as he danced with the pillow, screaming that he'd found his life's savings.

"They said he lifted the pillow, which was stuffed with money, and ran in the direction of his shack, which he doused in paraffin and set fire to; and that he danced before the columns of flame, which rose upwards, challenging the rain. Then he disappeared. He took the pillow, soaked in blood and water, and left behind him the ruins of his shack, a woman on her own, and a child."

Was the money in the pillowcase ruined? Or did the man manage to dry the banknotes out and use them to start life anew elsewhere? Did he use the money with which he'd stuffed the pillowcase to find work or did he spend it on drink before returning to his old profession as a beggar and marry another woman to support him with the money she earned as a maid?

"No-one knows what really happened," Nasri told his two boys when they asked him about the Green Woman. He said he'd never seen her again after the incident, "but people talk a lot. People need saints and victims and fill their lives with them and Majda was a victim who asked for nothing because she was a saint. It's best when the saint is the victim. Then the story's the way it should be. I know Abu Sultan and I know it wasn't like that. He was a decent fellow and he worked at the petrol station at Hajj Murad's place washing cars and in the neighbourhood they called him 'Wadia the petrol station chap'; and his name wasn't Abu Sultan. I don't know where 'Abu Sultan' came from. Well, maybe it was from his first wife who they say stole his money and ran off to Egypt with an Egyptian building guard. She was a widow and her name was Imm Sultan, I know that. Then Abu Sultan was hit by a lorry at the petrol station and crippled and Hajj Murad fired him without giving him a penny in compensation. I don't know how Majda put up with him. It's wrong to tell tales. He used to beat her a lot. I know because I used to treat the poor woman. Then I realised he was beating her because he had a problem and I got rid of the problem with a potion that I'd invented. I don't know what to call it – a complex about women had turned into a practical problem with his wife – but I do know that everything was fine and there's no call for all this gossip."

Nasri's words failed to convince his sons, who thought his story about Majda was of a piece with the ones about fairies and afreets that he told them. They named her "the Green Fairy" and saw her looming out of the ropes of rain and waving to them from afar.

What happened to Majda is wrapped in mystery. The woman didn't return to the neighbourhood. She left the hospital with her infant and people only saw her after that in her green apparitions – a Green Woman who appeared only after sunset, standing in the shadows and looking into the distance, bending over the remains of her shack and waving to people with her little green pocketbook, then vanishing into the dark.

Karim said he'd seen the Green Woman once in his life. "I was with my brother Nasim. He said to me, 'Come on, let's go and see the Green Fairy!' It was five in the afternoon, raining, and we got soaked. I told my brother, 'Forget it. We'll get sick standing out under the rain like this,' but he wouldn't agree. He said I was a coward. That was what he thought of me even then. So we waited and when it started to get dark we saw her. She was like a ghost or something and I started shivering with fear and the cold. She looked at me, raised her hand as though she was pointing at me, or as though she was asking me to go to her. I wanted to run home but I was rooted to the spot and couldn't move. I screamed but no sound came out. I grabbed hold of Nasim and heard him say 'Let's go closer.' I saw him bend over, pick up a stone, and throw it at the woman but it seemed as though the stone just flew and never landed on the ground and the woman disappeared."

Karim said that when he thought of his encounter with the Green Woman he saw a stone flying and not landing, as though the Green Woman had turned into a tree, and he didn't know how he got back home, all wet with the rain and the darkness and the fear.

Had he told Muna that story? She'd asked him about the story of the Green Woman and he'd smiled and said he loved her green skirt. She'd said she was tired and wanted to sleep and had turned her back and begun to breathe deeply. Then suddenly she'd sat up in bed and said she had to go home: "Ahmad will be waiting for me now." She ran to the bathroom and closed the door behind her and he heard the sound of the shower. He went up to the bathroom door and opened it. She yelled at him from behind the plastic curtain, telling him to go out and shut the door: "I don't like anyone to watch me when I'm showering." He shut the door, went back to the bed, closed his eyes, and slept.

Muna left the flat while Karim was dozing. He opened his eyes and saw that the sun had coloured everything green. The green sky was falling through the window onto his bed. He rubbed his eyes thoroughly to get the green shadows out of them. Had it been a dream? Had he seen the Green Woman beckoning to him to approach while he dreamed? What had his father been doing there?

The Green Woman pushed Nasri and the man fell to the ground. Black blood ran from his forehead, and he died next to the sodden remains of the shack and the fire.

This dream would pursue the doctor throughout the six months he spent in Beirut. He decided not to believe Hend's story. Could it really be true? Could Nasri have been murdered? And was the story of his father having fallen into a coma, as related to him by his brother, just a half-lie intended to cover the blood that had been spilled?

All Karim could remember about his mother was her fear of blood. Even during her long illness she had trembled at the sight of blood on her sons' knees and screamed, "O Lord, save us from the blood!" The disease had ravaged the woman until all that was left of her were her shining brown eyes. Her body had grown emaciated and she'd ended up the size of a little girl, but the brilliance of her eyes, which lasted until she died, concealed the life she hadn't lived.

Karim remembered his father yelling at the priest, who had sat down at the dining table to prepare the announcement of her death and had written, "The late lamented Laure Tibshirani, wife of Nasri Shammas, departed this life having performed in full her religious obligations, etc."

"No!" Nasri had screamed. "She didn't depart this life!" and the priest had said, "You're right, Mr Nasri. We should write, 'passed into the mercy of the Almighty'." "No!" said Nasri. "She didn't depart and she didn't pass. Life departed from her. The pity of it! Those eyes of hers kept on shining even after she was dead. She didn't depart and she didn't pass. The pity of it, Laure!"

Karim didn't remember what they wrote in the announcement because he was too young and didn't understand that the clichés written at the important moments of people's lives aren't just clichés. They are complex figures of speech possessing a status in people's souls so emotive it makes tears fall from their eyes. He did remember his mother's eyes, though. The father had led his sons towards the bed of their dead mother, whom cancer had transformed into something more like a small child, and ordered them to look into her eyes, which shone with a brilliance like that of water: "You mustn't forget your mother's eyes, the way they stayed open gazing at life even after death." The father went forward, placed his hand over his wife's eyes and closed them. At that moment, everything went white. All Karim could remember was the white that filled his eyes. It wasn't a fainting fit because the child didn't fall to the ground. He remained rigid where he was and didn't move. The milky white surrounded him from all sides. Nasri led his sons to the living room, which was crammed full of people, and there they heard the wailing and they cried. Karim said that the tears that fell from his eyes opened them, and he saw the people and felt the need to hide.

When Karim attempted to remind his brother of the story he was surprised to find that Nasim didn't remember the open eyes. Nasim said he hadn't seen anything: "I saw something small and white on a white sheet. Are you sure Father closed her eyes? Why, did she die with her eyes open too?"

Karim was aware from his experience as a doctor that lots of people die with their eyes open and that it has nothing to do with the dead person's psychological state; it's a purely physiological matter connected to the circumstances of the moment of death. But at that moment he saw his father lying on the ground, the blood running out of him, his eyes open onto the abyss of death.

5

They were twins, or so they believed. Karim was born on 4 January, 1950, Nasim on 22 December of the same year. This was a cause of pride to the pharmacist Nasri Shammas and a compensation to him for the fact that his wife Laure had been incapable of bearing more children. The boys were alike in every way and never left each other's side.

Nasri Shammas, owner of Beirut's Shefa Pharmacy, spent most of his spare time at the Gemmeizeh Café, where he never stopped recounting his heroic deeds and telling of his ability to father two children in a single year. He would smoke his daily nargileh, play backgammon, and tell stories. The boys only discovered why their father insisted on taking them each day to the café, where they were bored, when they found out that their mother was ill.

Two white-skinned boys who looked so much like each other they could have been twins. The elder, Karim, was introverted while the younger was jolly and sociable, but they never left each other's side. After their mother's death they turned into a single person, or so it seemed to most people. Nasim, the sturdy one, defended his brother at school and stopped the bigger boys from hitting him while Karim did the studying for both of them. He trained his younger brother till their handwriting ended up looking the same and the teachers couldn't tell the difference. This game of one person with two heads appealed to their father. When he asked one of them to tell him a dream he'd dreamed he'd interrupt and ask the other son to finish it for him, so that the boys came to believe they were one soul with two bodies.

They slept in one large bed but when they turned nine Nasri decided the time had come for each to sleep by himself. They refused but the stubborn father exchanged the wide bed the boys had inherited from their mother for two beds, which he put in the same room. Karim and

Nasim rebelled and took to sneakily sleeping together in one of the beds, so that the father had to carry one of them to the second bed at midnight, though when he got up in the morning he'd find them both sleeping in one.

They lived alone with their father, without relatives. Nasri, who was an only child, had no contact with his distant cousins. His wife Laure was from a large family but the fates had willed that her family should distance themselves from the two boys. When she died everyone expected Nasri would marry Laure's younger sister. Marta was three years younger than her sister but "the doors of destiny had failed to open before her", as they say. True, she was short and not beautiful, but the family decided to believe that the reason she had failed to marry was her devotion to her sick sister and the care she took of her sister's two boys. Nasri thought it was all over for him and didn't argue when his father-in-law visited him and opened the conversation by talking about the need for decency, saying Laure's sister would make the best mother for the boys. Nasri just asked for a bit of time, arguing he couldn't marry until a year after his wife's death. The whole family thought this a logical arrangement and things seemed to be heading in the right direction, but they hadn't reckoned with the boys going mad.

Nasri told Laure's father that the boys had gone mad and that he wanted him to talk to them in his capacity as their grandfather.

Abdo Tibshirani was sixty-five years old. The dignity of white hair covered his head and thick moustaches adorned his broad white face – a man who knew life inside out. He had a shop in Souq el-Efrenj where he sold the best kinds of fruit. He'd seen his three sons married and believed nothing could make up for the pain of the loss of his daughter Laure but the marriage of her sister. And now his son-in-law had come along to make a mess of his white hairs.

Abdo placed a hand on his moustache and looked at Nasri with his bulbous eyes: "You think you can make a fool of these moustaches of mine?" he whispered. "You want me to believe a story like that *and* demean myself by negotiating with those brats?"

Nasri tried to tell him what had happened but the man refused to

65

listen. "We've set the date for the wedding and I don't want to hear any more such nonsense from you."

Abdo closed his eyes; when the elderly man closed his eyes it meant that the conversation was over, for neither his wife nor his sons dared talk in the presence of this pantomime of sleep, during which he became another person. The whispered speech that was his means of communicating with his sons would turn into a yell, the calm that filled his face would turn into an angry flush, and in that condition he would think nothing of beating his sons or his wife. Nasri saw the closed eyes, but instead of leaving he made himself comfortable on the couch and closed his eyes too.

Two men with eyes closed, as though in a duel with the darkness, neither daring to open his eyes lest he find himself in a confrontation with no escape.

The first man opened his eyes, looked at Nasri, and whispered, "Get up, son-in-law, there's a good fellow. Go back to your boys and sort things out for the best."

"Honestly, Uncle, I'd like to," said Nasri, his eyes still closed. Then he opened them, looked into the older man's eyes, and said the boys were the problem. He tried to explain, and the older man closed his eyes again and gestured with his hand for him to stop talking. But this time Nasri didn't stop talking, so Abdo shook himself, jumped up from his chair, and started cursing, at which Nasri left the house.

The break didn't come about because of the curses that rained down on the widowed pharmacist's head but because Nasri committed a sin unforgivable in the Tibshirani family's eyes: he tried to use Abd el-Nour Yaziji as a go-between. Abd el-Nour was the neighbourhood butcher. His left leg had been severed in an accident he'd suffered as a young man when he jumped off a tram to avoid paying the five-piastre fare and found himself in a welter of blood beneath its wheels. He survived with one leg, moved around with a stick, and acquired a reputation as a good man by reason of his kindness to the poor, becoming, with the passing of time, a kind of headman for the neighbourhood, making peace among its people and arbitrating its disputes. Everyone was confident that the only thing this forty-year-old man wanted from an ephemeral world was that it provide for his modest needs.

Abd el-Nour had never married. He told anyone who asked that he'd taken a vow of chastity following his painful accident, and that he'd meant to become a monk in any case, except he'd been prevented by his fear for and love of his ageing mother. This wasn't the whole truth, naturally, but it was – as Nasri was wont to put it – a close relative. It was rumoured, though God alone knew if this was true, that he'd gone to the monastery of Mar Elias Shouweya in Dhour el-Shoueir to become a monk, but that the head of the monastery had turned him down on account of his lost leg. As the head of the monastery pointed out, affliction by reason of impairment or physical disability was not admitted as a valid reason for donning a monk's habit. "Go, Abd el-Nour," the Greek head of the monastery had said, "and be a monk in society."

The "societal monk" had not, as he claimed, forgotten the things of this world, and it was this that led to a complete break between the butcher and the pharmacist. "People are deep. No-one knows what's inside them till they produce what's inside them, and the butcher was hiding in his clothes," said Nasri to his sons as he told them the story of how the family had cut its ties with both him and its grandsons.

Nasim remembered the story only vaguely. He remembered that it was he who had started the rebellion but didn't remember the details. Karim, who was six, had burst into tears when his father informed him that Marta was going to be his mother. He remembered first crying and then starting to play along with his brother's craziness. Nasim climbed onto his bed and started jumping up and down as he cried, and Karim started jumping up and down with him. Then the younger brother picked up his pillow and started jumping with it and they started throwing the pillows, screaming all the time.

Nasri tried to understand what was going on but was deafened by the boys' jumping and screaming.

"O.K.! I won't marry Marta and you won't have another mother."

Suddenly things calmed down, the storm blew over, and the twins sat down jammed up against one another on the edge of the bed, where their tears blended with unending laughter.

"I won't get married, but tell me why," said Nasri.

All he could hear was the sound of the children as they choked on their tears and wiped their noses with their sleeves. He looked at Karim and asked him but instead of answering Karim looked at his younger brother.

"What is it, Nasim, sweetheart? What's the matter?"

When the father heard what the matter was, he burst out laughing.

"You don't want me to marry Marta because she's got big ears? That's what the matter is? If that's all, then I am going to marry."

This time the children exploded with anger and started throwing the pillows at Nasri, who heard Nasim say, "If she comes to the flat, we'll run away", and Karim echo him: "It's us or Big Ears!"

Nasri hadn't noticed how large were the earlobes that hung down from Marta's head. In fact, he hadn't looked at his intended bride as a female. When he married Laure her sister hadn't attracted his attention at all and with time, and especially with his wife's long illness, he'd come to see her as comic. She'd come to the flat like a whirlwind, go to her sister's room, and immediately take hold of the patient's wrist to see if she had a pulse, then check that she had had her medicine. Next she'd turn her attention to what needed doing in the flat. She'd wash the clothes, clean, and cook. She rejected Nasri's idea of getting a maid and said a maid would turn everything upside down and be a bad influence on the children. Marta became a dictator. The only time Nasri had to himself was early in the morning when he met his sons at the breakfast table while Marta closed the patient's door and bathed her.

Nasri thought of her as a free maid while the boys thought of her as the phantom of death. What Nasri didn't know was that Marta used her ears to scare the boys. The young woman, who had passed thirty without finding a groom, believed that by making a display of her wealth and wearing her jewellery she might attract the awaited suitor. To this end she filled her wrists with bracelets and hung an odd kind of heavy gold earring from her ears. What Marta hadn't realised was that the earrings would stretch her earlobes, and to a comical degree. Was it because the young woman noticed the distortion that she took to wrapping a black silk shawl round herself, which she kept pulled above her neck to cover her ears? Or did she wear the shawl because of chronic neck pain? No-one knew. But Karim and Nasim were filled with terror every time their aunt took hold of a big bronze key and threatened to unlock her ears and put them inside if she heard a peep out of them.

Big ears like caves, dangling earlobes, a key, a woman, and darkness. Karim didn't know whether the story about the earlobes was real or if he'd made it up when in Montpellier he saw an exhibition on Nepal to which the French professor had taken them to show them that human skin has been used as a cosmetic device at all periods and in all cultures. When, during his visit to Beirut, he'd tried to get corroboration from his brother's memories, Nasim appeared to remember nothing but the jumping up and down on the bed, the throwing of pillows and the crying. He couldn't even remember what his aunt looked like.

"I've forgotten my mother. All I can remember is the photo of her that Father hung at home, as though she'd turned into a picture. When you forget the voice of someone who's died it's over, and I can't remember my mother's voice. You want me to remember the ears of a woman whose name I wouldn't even have thought of if it weren't for you?"

The issue wasn't the two brothers' memories or the woman's ears. It was that the butcher-monk had had his eyes set on Marta, and instead of acting in good faith as an intermediary had told everyone what was going on. All the women of the neighbourhood came to know that Nasri's boys didn't want him to marry, and that the man wasn't going to break his sons' hearts just to solve the marriage problems of the Tibshirani girl with the long ears.

At this point in the story Nasri's involvement in the matter comes to an end because Abdo Tibshirani threw him out of his house when he paid him a visit at the suggestion of the butcher who claimed to be acting as a mediator.

It all ended up with the butcher marrying the Tibshirani girl, after the man with the missing leg succeeded in staunching the young woman's tears and conquering her heart with sweet words. This compelled Abdo to agree to his daughter's marriage because Marta threatened to commit suicide if she didn't marry the butcher.

When Nasri learned of the marriage he realised that the source of the story that had made the rounds had been the butcher, and he went to him and congratulated him, laughing. But the butcher thought he was visiting him to make fun of him, so he threatened the pharmacist with his cleaver and told him never to mention Marta again.

"The world's a great mystery," Nasri told his sons as he related to them the story of how the Tibshirani clan had exited their small family's life forever.

"The only thing he got out of his monkishness was the one line from the Gospel, 'Marta, Marta, thou art troubled about many things; but one thing is needful.' He sweet-talked the girl with that one thing till he got to do one to her himself," he told the boys, laughing.

In this tripartite family so nearly cut off from the rest of the world the two children lived alone, growing in closeness to one another and in isolation from the rest.

The twinning relationship that had bound the boys to one another began to come apart at school. Karim differed from his younger brother in everything. Nasim was the "sly one", as Brother Eugène, headmaster of the Frères School, called him, and the sly one was naughty, lazy, and a bully. The clever boy, on the other hand, was shy, sad, and a loner.

The clever boy did all his brother's homework, coached him, and performed miracles to make sure he passed and wasn't held back a year: Nasim couldn't bear the thought that he and his brother might be in different classes. The first real crisis between the brothers occurred when Nasim failed First Intermediary and Brother Eugène decided to make him repeat the year.

"What's going on between you and Brother Eugène?" Nasim asked his brother derisively.

Nasim said he was going to leave school. "I'm sick of priests and the smell of incense and I can't take the Jesuits and their whisperings anymore."

Nasri agreed with his son. He went to see Brother Eugène and said he'd never agree to the twins being in separate classes.

Brother Eugène tried to convince the man that he was ruining his son's future.

"Karim *est un génie*, I mean your son's a genius, and you'll ruin his future like this. If Nasim doesn't want to repeat, it's up to him, and you. You can move him to any other school, but for Karim it would be a terrible thing to do. We want him."

Nasri said that when he heard the words "We want him" he was struck with fear and decided to move both boys to another school, whatever the cost. "When those priests set their eyes on a boy, they get him."

"What do you mean, 'They get him'?" asked Nasim.

"I mean they sweet-talk him till they make a priest of him."

"But I don't want to become a priest," said Karim. "I want to study to be a doctor."

"No, you're going to study pharmacy. Who else am I going to leave the shop to?"

"What about me?" asked Nasim.

"You're going to study pharmacy too."

"But I'm not convinced we have to change schools," said Karim.

"I told you, I'm afraid of the priests."

"But I told you that I'm not going to become a priest, whatever happens."

"I'm afraid of something else," said the father.

"I don't understand," said Karim.

"I do," said Nasim and burst out laughing.

"Shut up, boy!" Nasri yelled, and left the flat.

Two days later Brother Eugène came to their flat and informed Nasri that the school administration had agreed Nasim could move on to Second Intermediary on condition that he gave an undertaking he would apply himself to his studies.

And that was how it was. Nasim gave the undertaking, but an exposure that would come close to ruining his life lay in wait for him. And when Nasim tried to escape the scandal two years later by running away from home, it was he, with his father's connivance, who cooked up the business of the souk to save his elder brother from falling prey to the machinations of the Jesuit priest.

Did Nasri engineer the incident?

Many years later Nasim would tell his brother that his father had asked him to take his elder brother to the souk so he wouldn't have to wonder anymore. He said their father knew Nasim went there but he'd turned a blind eye. "I remember I was coming back from there one time. It was a Saturday evening and it was summer and hot. Father came up to me and said, 'So how were the sports, you little prick?' and laughed. He put his hand on my shoulder and said, 'Good health to you! That's how men are supposed to be.'

"I answered that I'd been at the club doing sports.

"Father burst into laughter and said, 'Do you take me for an idiot? I saw you there! I was coming out from Uzun the Turk's. I can see you're a connoisseur like your father. But you have to tell me, boy, because we can't have father and son going to the same places. That would be wrong.'

"'You're right,' I said. 'That would be wrong,' and I burst out laughing.

"'Take your brother,' he told me, 'He's blind and doesn't know anything. Take him before the priests get their claws into him and we lose him forever.'"

"You mean Father was worried about something?"

"Why? Was there something?" asked Nasim.

"No. I mean, like all the boys," said Karim.

"You mean he fucked you?"

"Of course not! I mean, something not far off."

Karim never told anyone what "not far off" meant. He'd put the whole thing out of his mind, as though it had never been, and when his brother insisted on knowing the details his response was just to give a small smile so that he didn't have to say anything. "I mean it was nothing. Just talk, that was all. Stuff about the Greek philosophers and how they used to interact with their students through intimate relationships."

"So did he make a Greek philosopher out of you or not?"

"Of course not! What a thing to say!"

"I'm going to make an honest-to-goodness philosopher out of you and I'm going to use a Greek lady professor too!"

Nasim said that "if it weren't for Madam Athena's patience and experience we would have been shafted." He said he'd asked Uzun the Turk for advice and she'd suggested the Greek because "a case like your brother's needs a woman with real experience or the kid will be lost."

"And when I took you to Madam Athena's and saw how you turned red as a beetroot and your voice stopped coming out, I was dying of fear. But the lady was terrific. She was patient as an angel with you and everything went O.K."

The big parting of the ways between the two brothers began when they were both sixteen. At first they were like stand-ins for one another: that was how Karim explained his relationship with his brother to Bernadette. Nasim would live out his naughtiness and tell his brother about it and Karim would live out his life of books and take his brother into the worlds of the heroes of novels. "We were like one person divided into two," he said, "till I discovered that I wasn't living my own life. That happened when Nasim came and told me he'd been to the souk and slept with a prostitute. He advised me to stop masturbating and said, laughing, that the entrance to life was via the vagina and that women possessed something insatiable and the only person who could give it the water it needed was a real man, and he invited me to go with him but I was afraid. At the beginning I made out it wasn't allowed and said it was a sin and dishonourable for a man to buy something beyond price. I said that love couldn't be bought or sold. My brother laughed and explained that he wasn't talking about love but about sex: 'That's one thing and this is another, old man.' I could do nothing faced with a woman of forty. I saw her there in front of me, naked, with her big breasts and her curves. She came up to me, took my hand, and put it on her breast, and I felt paralysed and broke into a cold sweat. The sweat spread, making patches on my clothes, and I wanted to get out of the place. The sweat covered my eyes like tears. The sweat was salty like tears but its salt was sharp-tasting. At that point the Greek woman took me by the hand and led me into the bathroom. She filled the tub with hot water topped with soap bubbles that smelled of orange blossom. She ordered me to take off my clothes and she put me in the water. She closed my eyes and I felt as though the mountain that had been crushing my chest had been lifted off me and the buoyancy of the water got to work – a silken hand massaged my body and I rose upwards to embrace desire. I don't know what happened but later I found myself in the bed, drinking in the gasps of that woman who made me taste the flavour of life."

He told Bernadette, the first time he slept with her after they were married, that he wanted to drink the air she breathed. She didn't understand. "Drink the air! What kind of metaphor is that?"

He tried to explain to her that words must enclose meaning so that the meaning can keep its meaning, and that in spoken Arabic they don't say "I want to smoke a cigarette" but "I want to drink a cigarette" so the tobacco melts in the mouth and imparts to it the flavour of the plant.

"All that smoking imparts to the mouth is a nasty smell and in the meantime it destroys your lungs," she said. "Also, I don't like having to play with water every time we make love. Love's one thing and taking a shower is another."

He'd told her the story of the Greek woman and that was his great mistake. Lovers only become aware of their mistakes when it's too late. In the early days, though, buoyed by the water of desire, they rush into reckless talk and tell stories that shouldn't be told. Stories aren't to be thrown around without regard for their significance, or they become absurd. He told Bernadette of the family's decision to take him to the prostitutes' quarter because of their fear of the priest's fondness for him, and he talked to her about the woman whom he'd persisted in seeing until the end, meaning until she told him "That's it, son. I'm old enough to be your mother. And it won't do anymore, I'm very sick." Two days later they took the woman to the hospital because of a clot on the lungs and she died there a week later.

"*Tu es un homosexuel latent*," said Bernadette.

"That's what Father and my brother thought, but it's not true."

Karim told Bernadette that he used to visit her twice a day during that last week.

"So you were in love with her."

"That week, she used to call me 'son' and I called her 'mother'."

"It looks as though until I rescued you from your drunkenness at the bar and brought you back to your place you'd never made love to anyone but prostitutes."

He hadn't told her about Hend out of fear that he'd find himself caught up in the story of Salma, and he was right not to: had he told her,

Bernadette would have thought he was going to Beirut because of his former sweetheart and never have believed he was going to look for Sinalcol.

In any case, his French wife didn't believe the business about Sinalcol. What Karim had told her when, drunk in the bar, he'd given himself that name, wasn't the truth. In fact, he'd adopted the mocking nickname given him by the youths of Tripoli because, in the character of that mysterious man whom he'd never met, he'd seen his double and his mirror.

When Karim emerged from the Greek bath and found his brother waiting for him, he was dumbstruck: he discovered that his brother resembled him only in being a larger, coarser, version of himself. The same features, a circular whiteness forming the face, a large nose, thick lips, honey-coloured eyes, but Nasim was taller, his chest muscles rippled under his shirt because he swam, his nose was slightly crooked and larger than his brother's, and his little pot belly, which would get larger with time, gave him a touch of manliness that Karim lacked. The fundamental difference between the two brothers lay in their eyebrows. Karim's were long and thin, his brother's short and thick.

"Like a woman's," his brother said.

"What pretty eyebrows!" Brother Eugène had said as he put his hand on his clever student's head and brought his fingers down to the full lips.

"Do you pluck your eyebrows?" the Greek madam had asked, once she'd succeeded in untying his tongue.

Karim came to hate his eyebrows and wanted them to change so that people would stop telling him his face was pretty as a girl's. His brother told him that the best way to make hair grow was to put chicken droppings on it. The boy, who then ten at the time, believed his brother and took to slipping into the garden of the sisters Marie and Angèle Shartouni every evening, entering the coop and looking for chicken droppings to put on his eyebrows before going to sleep.

When the sisters came to the pharmacy and complained that Karim was stealing eggs from their coop, the father roared with laughter and said, "That's impossible! My son hates eggs. I force him to eat eggs in the morning against his will and now you come along and tell me he's stealing your hens' eggs! My dear ladies, we give eggs away!"

At first Nasri couldn't understand the reason for the bad smell given off by his older son. He went into the sleeping boys' room and the smell hit him in the face. He bent over Karim and smelled shit. He shook him hard but the young boy refused to open his eyes, so he turned on the light and screamed. Nasim woke up at the noise but Karim turned over, pretending to be asleep.

"What's that smell?" yelled the father.

Nasim burst out laughing and told his father the story.

"Get up, you idiot. I thought you were more intelligent than that. Your younger brother's pulled a trick on you and made you put shit on your eyebrows. Ride the rooster and see where it takes you!"

The next morning Nasri explained to his elder son that long thin eyebrows were a sign of beauty: "Don't you believe any of that stuff, my boy! Women pluck their hair and go through hell to make their eyebrows nice. Princes have eyebrows like that and you're a prince and the son of a prince."

"But what does 'ride the rooster' mean?" asked Karim.

"You'll find out for yourself soon enough, when you grow up."

It was only later, in Montpellier, that Karim would become convinced of what his father had said, when Bernadette told him on the morning of their first encounter that his eyebrows were beautiful and that when she'd seen him beneath the tequila woman's breasts it was his long eyebrows, soaked with alcohol and salt, that had bewitched her.

The two spinster sisters wouldn't drink the pharmacist's potion until years later, when the story of their hysteria came to be on the lips and tongues of all, and they were the rooster that Nasri rode, compelling him to give them a stupefying potion to put an end to a scandal that destroyed his reputation.

Salma's story wasn't as straightforward as Nasri would have told it, had he told it, but once Salma withdrew from his life the man, who had been feeling his age and that his body was beginning to betray him, collapsed.

The scandal of the two elderly women wasn't the cause because it was still in his power to turn their tragedy into a joke. Indeed, the man treated even the Lebanese civil war as a comic phenomenon. When the discussions that took place at the Gemmeizeh Café among the backgammon players grew heated, he used the word "comedy" again and again to describe his country. "Lebanon is death's comedy. There isn't another people in the world that has turned everything it holds holy into farce the way we have. Even death makes us laugh now. Laugh, brothers, because nothing ever ends in this country. Whatever goes comes back and if it doesn't its ghost comes back. Laugh so I can have a laugh too!"

The story of the two spinster sisters would have made for good comedy but it cost Nasri his mocking wit and was the beginning of his descent into melancholy, where he would remain until he died.

The problem the twins had with their father was that throughout his life the man never stopped proclaiming his good opinion of himself, and it was the brothers' duty to listen to his theories and show their astonishment at them so that he didn't get upset and start scowling.

After the Greek bath that proved to the father that his first-born son had escaped the perils of the priests he began to expatiate at the breakfast table on matters of sex and the erotic sciences and boast of his being one of the leading experts on the chemistry of the relationship between body and soul.

He'd devour two fried eggs every morning because he'd found a permanent cure for cholesterol in the herbs that he distilled in his alembic. Nasri had made the breakfast table, on which he'd set out labneh, cheese, olives, and innumerable kinds of jam, the main locus for the exercise of his authority over his sons, starting with his theory that from the medical point of view breakfast ought to be the main meal of the day for anyone who wanted to keep healthy.

Surrounded by his boys' dislike of the smell of fried eggs and their unwillingness to eat, he would turn this morning encounter into a playing field for his ideas and those essential lessons, drawn from his life experience, from which he wanted his sons to benefit.

Karim decided to ignore his father's lessons, which he considered banal. He'd succeeded in training himself to shut his ears and listen to the silence. It was no use just to think about other things during his father's lectures: Nasri was a master at jumping from one topic to another to pique his sons' curiosity. As a result, Karim had discovered what he called "secret cotton wool". As soon as his father began to speak, he'd plant invisible cotton wool in his ears to block out the sound. To the rhythm of the silence he'd eat the labneh dipped in oil and entertain himself by observing his father's inaudible enthusiasms.

All the same, what had stuck in his ears was enough to make him hate himself in France, especially when he began to hear the echo of his father's voice in his own and see how he had involuntarily adopted many of his father's rituals and theories.

When Hend told him how his father had died and his brother later angrily corrected her version, he'd understood that both versions were lies, but the subject didn't interest him. He'd felt he was in danger of becoming a dupe like his mother, and that even in death his father was capable of devouring everyone around him.

It wasn't true that he'd left Hend after seeing the contents of the drawer that his younger brother had opened onto hell. On the eve of his departure for France he'd thought it was the reason, but now, back in Beirut and listening to the story of his father's death, he was no longer certain of anything. As soon as he'd arrived in Beirut, at the moment he'd found himself in his brother's home eating kibbeh nayyeh and seen Salma swathed in black, the pictures in the drawer and the window onto his father's sex life with which they had provided him, with the Shefa Pharmacy as backdrop, had come back. He could see himself at that moment, standing next to his brother, who had managed to steal the key to the secret drawer, and the drawer opening before his eyes to reveal those terrible pictures in which Salma appeared in unbelievable positions. The pictures were part of an album that brought together a number of the women who had fallen victim to Nasri's amazing Green Potion.

"Just look at Salma! What a fucking beauty! If I'd been in your place, I'd have had the mother and daughter together," said Nasim, laughing.

Karim's throat was dry and he couldn't respond. He tried to swallow but could find no saliva in his mouth. He could feel thorns sprouting in his gullet as he set upon the pictures, trying to tear them up.

His brother pushed him away from the drawer and said, "You're a fool. All that intelligence and medicine and multiplication and division, but you're still an idiot, pretending like you didn't know. Everyone used to see Mrs Salma going to the pharmacist's all hot to trot and coming out glowing. What's the big deal? I just wanted you to have a laugh. Now you've seen what that shit does to women – but I want to ask him how he persuaded them to be photographed. Can you imagine the scene? What a mess! There's Salma . . ."

"Shut up! You and your father are both shits. I want to get out of this house."

"Do you think Hend knows about her mother's thing with the pharmacist?"

"Don't even say Hend's name."

The drawer with the pictures had pursued him since his arrival in Beirut. True, he'd opened the drawer and found it empty, but he hadn't dared ask his brother what had happened to the album.

Now, though, he found himself uncertain of everything. Had things reached a point where the old man had drunk the same green liquid that was his means of access to women's bodies?

When Karim had left Muna in bed on that final morning of farewell and gone to the kitchen to make breakfast, she'd followed him, wrapped in her towel, to tell him she was in a hurry because Ahmad was waiting for her at home, and he'd responded, "No, you can't leave until you've tasted the most delicious breakfast in the world." He made a Spanish omelette out of fried eggs, labneh, and pine nuts. "This was Father's favourite breakfast," he said, "but I was an ass and I used to think, stupid as I was, that I hated the taste of eggs with labneh. Then I grew up and realised that eggs with labneh are the best food in the world. In France, whenever I slept with a woman, I'd taste labneh and pine nuts on my tongue, but they don't have labneh there." He said the French had three hundred types of cheese and even so they didn't know the most delicious thing in the world, and how "when we dunk the labneh in the oil we smell life. Life smells green, like olive oil."

"I didn't realise you were so in love with your stomach. I would have cooked you fattet makdous," she said. "Granny's from Aleppo and for her Aleppo is fattet makdous and kufta with cherries."

"Cherries with meat! The most important thing, mind, is to put pine nuts in the omelette."

As she got up in a hurry to get dressed and go, she said she'd loved the breakfast.

"Shall I teach you to make it? It's very easy."

"No. I'd rather keep the omelette as a memory."

When she came back to the kitchen, where Karim was washing the frying pan, he turned and saw her standing in front of the door, waiting for him.

He went up to kiss her and she pulled back, said she was late, and left.

He made a pot of coffee and sat down alone. He lit a cigarette and heard Nasri's voice stealing into his ears, breaking through the barriers of cotton wool and talking of women.

"Was my mother like that?" asked Nasim.

"Don't you dare to speak your mother's name! The mother is a sacred being, my son. I'm not talking about mothers, I'm talking about women."

"But mothers are women too," said Nasim.

His father nodded and didn't reply. Then he suddenly pushed his plate aside, stood up from his chair and said that talking to his son was a waste of time.

The father left the breakfast table and desisted from all further talk about women. Now his voice came back to Karim, who had pretended to hear nothing.

"A woman is the essence of desire. Men are just a small detail in the world of love, which has no limits. That's why I'm amazed when men come to me and ask for restoratives, because they won't do any good. The real man is the one who makes the woman feel he's a man, end of story."

"How exactly?" asked Nasim.

"What I mean, my dear son, is that, when we speak of love we're speaking of something magical and the magic is all in the hands of the woman. If she wants you, you'll do fine and if she doesn't want you, nothing will work, because men are nothing."

Nasri tried to explain to his son that he wasn't talking about the urges of early adolescence, when desire is blind and random. He was talking about love when it became the warmth of the heart and nourishment of the soul. At that point, it could only be through, and for, the woman.

Nasim tried to ask him about prostitutes: "But with them it doesn't make any difference to me and it's not like what you say but things work fine all the same." The father answered that that was something temporary and linked to being young. Youth was life's little trick "because it dupes us into thinking that its exuberance is life itself when it's only an excess of life that we have to rid ourselves of so that we can enjoy life".

I was created for friendship; should I return to youth again,
I would take leave of my grey hairs with pain in my heart, weeping.

"Prostitutes," he said, "are needed to take life's overflow, meaning needed by men who've been emptied of life."

"But you told me you went there, and you weren't a teenager."

"That was just a passing mood but now it's over. Love comes to me, and when it comes I let it come."

"You mean you're this old and you don't take restoratives?"

"Never. Absolutely not."

Nasri claimed to his son that Sawsan's visit to the flat had been a mistake but he was lying. He'd known the first time that he slept with her that she was the one, this was the woman he wanted. He'd had sex with lots of prostitutes before and had felt empty after the encounter, like a vessel whose water had been poured out onto the ground, as though the woman he was sleeping with wanted him to get it over with quickly and go. This Sawsan, though, made him feel a desire not demeaned at the moment of its ending. He took to visiting her twice a week and spending a lot of time talking with her. She told him her story and he told her his and in the end he couldn't leave her. One stormy Saturday night, with the rain pelting down, he entered her room in the souk and began to talk. He ordered a bottle of wine and said that that night he wanted her *skarsa*, meaning his for the whole night, and was ready to pay. That was the night of his insane decision. He slept wrapped around her fragile white body and whispered that he wanted to marry her. She laughed, patted him on the back, and told him to go to sleep. He sat up in the bed, lit a cigarette, said he wasn't joking, and repeated his invitation. She said she didn't believe him and it was impossible. He told her he'd made his mind up and was inviting her to come to his home on Monday to meet his sons. Things didn't work out well though. Sawsan made the mistake of coming the way she was, with her fingernails painted violet, in her short dress that showed off her thighs, and with mascara smudges around her eyes.

Nasri told her he couldn't, for the boys' sake. She said she'd expected as much. He said he loved her and would never stop loving her.

It all fell apart though. Sawsan changed and turned back into a prostitute like the rest and the fire was extinguished. With the extinction of Sawsan's eyes and her body Nasri realised his love wouldn't be able to rescue him from the abyss of his sense of worthlessness and impotence. When Sawsan dropped the reins of desire, love fell by the wayside and the man could no longer save the situation. What confused him was that Sawsan's phantom never stopped making him burn with desire and longing, but when he went to her and got close to the indifferent body lying on the bed he was extinguished and felt impotent. At first Sawsan would try but her mechanical efforts were no use. Then she'd burst into laughter and say, "You'd better change, sweetie. It looks like it's over. The spark's gone. It's a good thing we didn't get married because it would have been a mess."

He tried to tell her he didn't know what was going on but he wanted her. When he started to lose confidence in himself he decided he'd change and it was O.K., but his thirst for the woman's body only got worse, and it was this that would lead him to come up with the Green Potion.

Nasri didn't tell his children what had happened with Sawsan. The prostitute's visit became taboo, never to be talked about, as though it had never happened. Despite this Nasim had a different opinion and he used Sawsan – who never left his memory and in whom he saw a means to get out of his inability to settle down at school – to justify his flight from home.

"Did you sleep with Sawsan?" Karim asked him.

"I told you, it was her that got me work at the shawarma and bean restaurant, with Boss Nakhleh Kafouri."

"So you slept with her."

"But it wasn't important. She told me I reminded her of Nasri and she believed my story and got me work and it was fine."

Nasim's flight, which lasted a week, changed Karim's life because he still felt so guilty three years later that he felt compelled to impersonate his brother in the government exams, and if he hadn't, Nasim would never have got into the Faculty of Pharmacy at Beirut's Jesuit university.

Sawsan turned the family's life upside down and transformed Nasri into a wolf – which is how Karim described his father when he told Bernadette about the man's loneliness, wolfishness, and alienation.

The Greek experience changed Karim greatly. After it he decided to keep clear of his brother's way of life because he'd discovered that Nasim wasn't his mirror, and he constructed his own emotional life. When his Greek instructress got sick he stopped going to the souk and started secret affairs with girls, which reached their peak with his love for Hend. Even that, which he'd hoped would remain a secret, almost turned into scandal. Nasim came to him and said he fancied Salma's only daughter. The brothers always used indirect language when speaking of their father's relationship with the widow who was always coming to the chemist's to buy treatments for her house plants.

When Nasim mentioned Hend to his brother, Karim turned pale and said nothing. "It looks like there's something going on I don't know about," said Nasim and he turned to his brother, patted him on his shoulder, and told him it didn't matter. "Don't get upset. There are more girls than you can shake a stick at. It's good I didn't get any more involved with her than that."

Karim didn't ask his brother how deeply he had been involved with her, just as he didn't ask Hend, and he forgot about the whole thing.

Fate, however, had something else in mind.

It was only when he was back in Beirut that Karim heard the story of how his father, the pharmacist Nasri Shammas, had died, and it was Hend who told him.

Nasim and Hend had come to see him on New Year's morning, bringing a breakfast of manaqish and kenafeh-with-cheese. They'd begun eating when the phone rang. Nasim picked up the receiver, his face turned pale, and he said he had to leave.

Hend stood up to go with her husband, Nasim asked her to stay, and left. Karim and Hend finished their breakfast in silence, he gazing into space, she looking at the ground. The sound of chewing rang in his ears and he felt he'd lost the power of speech.

He was afraid Hend would revisit the story of their former love, as she had when she'd visited him during the first days of his stay in Beirut. Ghazala had been mopping the living-room floor and Karim was wearing his pyjamas, sitting at his desk sipping coffee and feeling an irresistible desire for the woman. He dressed quickly and received his brother's wife in the living room, from which the large carpet that covered the now damp tiles had been removed, leaving everything gleaming with water.

They went to Paul's restaurant nearby and Hend began to talk. He wanted the meeting to end quickly, before Ghazala could leave. Listening to Hend it seemed to him he was seeing his life through the veil of tears that covered the face of this woman who drank not one drop from the cup of espresso that had been placed in front of her. But his desire for Ghazala had taken such control of him that he was unable to concentrate, and this gave her an impression he hadn't intended to convey.

When he got up to pay the bill and leave, Hend put out her hand and took hold of his. He left it in her soft outstretched hand and no longer knew in what direction desire was taking him.

Hend didn't speak on that occasion of the love that had fallen into oblivion, she spoke of her disappointment. She asked him if he knew his brother well because she'd discovered after they got married that she didn't. She said she'd been surprised to find that, after a month of marriage, the man had changed utterly and she'd felt she'd fallen into a trap.

"At first he was like you. I swear he was like you down to the last detail. He'd soften his voice and hang his head when he spoke of love as though he was you. I felt as though I'd known him for ages. I don't know how I came to accept his invitation to a cup of coffee. He said there was something important he wanted to talk to me about and I felt a kind of drowsiness come over me. From the first moment I felt as though the love story I'd lived with you might go on. I felt as though God was maybe going to pull me up from the bottom of the well into which you'd shoved me, and I couldn't refuse. He made me an offer I couldn't refuse, and I accepted."

Karim said it was nothing to do with him. "You're one of the family now and you should think of me as your brother."

"My brother!" she said and smiled bitterly.

She spoke, and Karim felt as though he wasn't there. A white cloud covered his eyes and he felt as though he had cataracts. He saw Nasri in front of him, describing the milky whiteness that had invaded his eyes. He called it "the blue water" and said he hated that name and didn't know why people had come up with a name that didn't refer to anything real: the blue was just an illusion because all one sees is white. And he said if the operation wasn't a success he'd commit suicide. He asked Nasim to put a poison pill in his drawer: "Afterwards you can say what you like, but blindness means suicide. Nasri isn't going to live a single second as a blind man. Got it, you arseholes?"

Nasri was sixty years old when the milky colour started to take over his left eye. He realised from the first moment that he was going to have to face it and there was no alternative to an operation. This man, who had spent his whole life treating people and prescribing treatments and who had conducted himself before his patients like a god, was terror-struck by the idea of having to undergo surgery. He'd treated himself with herbs, diets, and combinations of medicines, and these, he was convinced, suited his body, but he'd never got involved with two things: the eyes and diseases of the prostate. Faced by cases of this sort he'd stand in front of his patients like an idiot, raise his thick white-streaked eyebrows, and advise a visit to the doctor. The pharmacist, who despised doctors and said they were no more than fungi growing on the tips of the tree of chemistry fashioned by pharmacists, would, when faced with the mysteries of the eye and before the terrible spectre of the emasculating diseases of the prostate, lose his cunning, swallow his words, and advise his patients to visit a doctor.

But he couldn't swallow his eldest son's decision to study medicine and he never forgave him. "You, the one I've been depending on to complete me and complete my mission, you, the clever one Brother Eugène used to adore because you were so exceptionally intelligent when it came to maths and chemistry – you want to abandon me? Who am I going to leave the pharmacist's to? Your dumb brother who's a dunce at everything? I swear I'll never forgive you. You're not my son."

"But, Father, pharmacists can't work without doctors."

"That's what they want you to think but you know it's just piffle."

When Nasri uttered these words he wasn't telling the truth. In fact he thought this son of his, so clever at school, was a fool when it came to the practicalities of life and believed his younger brother, sharp as a tack, could take his herbal mission forward properly. He just wished he could merge his two sons into one. "It's like I'd been sliced into two halves," he told his adolescent sons as they discussed how Karim would present himself using the name of his younger brother at the entrance examinations for the Faculty of Pharmacy at the Jesuit university.

Nasri's dreams about his two sons were ambiguous and confused but the image he wanted to remember – even though he wasn't certain he'd actually seen it in a dream – was that of a youth with one body and two heads. The features of the two faces were so close as to be identical; the problem lay in the eyes. The eyes were closed and surrounded by circles of darkness. Faced with this dream, Nasri found himself unable to wake, even though he knew this double visage only visited him just as dawn was breaking; all he had to do was open his eyes for the image, which hurt them and made him feel incapable of rising from his bed, to dissolve.

Nasri told Salma his greatest disappointment was his two boys. They were drinking coffee on the balcony of his son Nasim, who had married Hend. The house plants he'd given his son were bright, large, and green. He talked to her of basil because he knew she was fond of it and used it in innumerable dishes.

"See that basil, Salma? It's all my own work!" he said, laughing.

"Your son will kill you if you pull that dirty trick on Hend. Be careful!"

"Don't worry, Salma. Does anyone kill his own? I go personally once a week and apply the potion. Those games are over now. But it was kind of a nice game and I can still taste it on my tongue."

The woman shut down her face and Nasri saw the sorrow and realised she had locked a door and there was nothing he could say. He wanted to tell her that he'd repudiated those days, that what was left of the era of the green fluid was the memory of what he'd had with her, and that now he wanted her as the companion of his last days, as his sweetheart. Nasri had no idea from where such salvation and tenderness had suddenly descended upon him but he was honest to the point of embarrassment in talking about it. All he would ever remember of this meeting was that word; he'd felt the *embarrassment* of salvation and discovered that his love and affection for his sick wife still slept in some secret part of his soul, and that Salma could now occupy that place. Salma was fated never to believe him, not because he was lying but because he was incapable of believing himself and because there were dozens of reasons to make her doubt his words, especially after the scandal of the two elderly spinsters.

Salma had told Nasim it wouldn't do. The woman had no idea where she'd found the courage to say this. First she spoke to her daughter and asked her to ask her husband to take his father in hand. Hend's answer was that she wouldn't get between her husband and his father.

"I've got enough problems, Mother."

"Why? Your husband too?"

"Please. Don't make me say anything, it'll be better for us both."

Salma found herself talking to her son-in-law Nasim. She knew he knew what had happened between her and his father but she screwed up her courage and spoke. The man's face turned pale and he left his flat in a fury and didn't return that night. Did Nasim really not know about the business with the two sisters, which was common knowledge? Or was he just pretending in front of his mother-in-law? Or was he angry at the impudence of this woman who knew he knew what had happened between her and his father but had the effrontery to talk of virtue?

The morning of the next day he phoned his wife, told her to stop worrying and asked her not to ask him what had happened but to ask her mother.

Nasri was sitting on the balcony contemplating the green leaves and watching his three little grandsons, Nadim, Nasri, and Bashir, who were playing under their grandmother's supervision. He hated his grandsons. Well, that wasn't the right word, but he felt slighted because Nasim hadn't given his eldest son his grandfather's name. He hadn't said anything, not having given his own eldest son his father's name. He'd been right, though. How could he have named his eldest son Georges after the man who'd squandered the family's wealth and spent his life at the gambling table, compelling his eldest son to go to work when he was twelve so he could guarantee his school fees? "But I'm not Georges. I'm his opposite. I didn't die of diabetes like Father, I dedicated my life to those bastards and didn't remarry when their mother died." Suddenly he saw Nasim's finger approaching his face. Salma had withdrawn with the children indoors and Nasri found himself looking into his son's face, sclerotic with fury, and at his wagging index finger.

He was struck dumb that day and saw the spectre of the end. He could find nothing to say because he felt as though the wall with which he'd fenced off his life had collapsed. He believed a person built a wall around himself and this wall fell apart at the moment of death, when one could no longer control oneself and therefore lost all dignity, the smell spreading everywhere. On his son's finger, pregnant with threat, he smelled his demise and he felt the need to get to the bathroom as he could no longer hold himself in.

Nasri ran to the bathroom but lost his way and saw everything wreathed in milky white, as though "the blue water" had returned to fill his eyes. He wanted to tell his son everything but couldn't speak. The words rained down as tears and he went staggering towards the bathroom, closed the door, and instead of urinating wept and smelled the smell of his tears.

From that moment, Nasri decided to cut off all contact with his son. He shut himself up in his flat, stopped going to the shop, and remained alone, waiting for the angel of death.

His defeat was not on account of Nasim's finger. He was used to his son's abuse and when the Prodigal Son, as he called him, had hit him, he'd taken a decision and thrown him out of the pharmacy. Nasri's defeat bore, rather, the name of Salma. He'd always refused to confess to the woman that he loved her. Her loving him was love enough as far as he was concerned. But it wasn't just a game of seduction and a green potion. What Salma had never told the foolish pharmacist was that what he'd thought was no more than sexual desire resulting from his magic potion was love, or something like it.

But Salma had lost her faith in love because of Nasri's stupidity and never used the word again. Once, in fact, she chided her daughter, who'd come to her in tears over her husband's bad behaviour, and said she was so sick of the miseries of love that she'd rather she never had to use the word again because it had no meaning.

"But Mother, you abandoned the whole world and your heart suffered agonies over your sons because of love!"

"I was an ass and maybe I still am but there's no need for you to be like your mother."

Salma's love for the foolish pharmacist, who never saw life from any perspective other than that of hunger, dried up: in his feverish love-making with her he used only words connected with food and he made sounds like someone smacking his lips while eating, not those of some-one enjoying the pleasures of love. And when she despaired of his love she threw a flask of the magic potion in his face, went rigid on the couch in the back room of the pharmacy that they used as a bed, and watched him fall apart.

He had come to her with words of love after the scandal of the Shartouni sisters. Salma had taken the women to the hospital and told the doctor the reason for the nervous attack that had made them go out naked into the street. The doctor said a case should be brought against the pharmacist, his licence revoked and the fellow thrown in gaol, but Salma refused to give him his name.

Nasri told Hend he was done for and had lost his will to live. He said Nasim had murdered him "and it's not the first time but this time I can't take it anymore. I've put up with a lot, my daughter, as you know."

He began telling the same story, about how he'd thrown him out of the pharmacy because Nasim had turned it into a hashish den. "He's not a pharmacist. You know how he got into the pharmacy faculty at the

Jesuit university – I'm sure he must have told you – and he didn't do well. His brother couldn't take the exams for him anymore. The teachers know the students there and there's no messing around."

She said she knew the story because he'd told it to her numerous times; she'd come as an honest broker and wanted to invite him to Nasri's birthday party. "It's amazing how the boy's growing up to look like you, he's just like the young Nasri!"

"And him?" Nasri asked.

"He's agreed. Just like nothing ever happened."

And so it was, and what had been ended up as though it never had.

Karim said he couldn't make head or tail of the story. They were sitting on their own, chewing their food in silence and waiting for Nasim to come back, when Hend said Nasri had neither slipped nor fallen.

"I don't know what happened but he seemed restless. He'd sit and stand and take a sip from his coffee cup and get up and open the windows. I said, 'Uncle, it's cold.' He said he was hot. I was afraid his blood pressure might have gone up. I asked him if he'd taken his medicine. He said he'd taken it but he seemed excited. His movements weren't normal. He stood up and said he wanted to go. He pulled a cassette out of his pocket and said he wanted to play it to me. I don't know what happened – he tripped on the chair and was going to fall. I ran and took hold of him. He stood up and grabbed on to me. I tried to get out of his grip but couldn't. I yelled at him to let go. His hands were like vice and he kept pulling me towards him. It seems I kicked him and he fell and his head started bleeding and he passed out. I phoned Nasim. He came and took him to the hospital and said, 'Don't say a word, I don't want anyone to know what happened.' And then he died."

"So it was you?"

She nodded.

Karim tried to speak but a cough devoured his throat. He tried to tell Hend she'd been the hand of justice. He tried to say that justice was the great Satanic intervention in human life. Satan was the inventor of justice because of all creatures Satan alone could be just: he was both oppressed and oppressor, for justice was the other name of vengeance. His coughing obscured much of what he said and instead of speaking he choked on his words. He tried to tell her . . . he would try to speak, the coughing would get worse and Hend sat before him, her lips shining with the sugar syrup she'd eaten with the kenafeh, looking at the ground in silence. As his coughing got worse, she ran to the kitchen and came back with a glass of water.

This was what Hend told her mother when she went to live with her, after she decided she could bear no more humiliation in her conjugal home. When the coughing fit had passed Karim lit a cigarette and said what she'd done was called just, but he hated justice because the just in Lebanon were the criminals, given that there was no scale by which to measure life or justice.

He asked her why she'd told him.

"I don't know," she said. "I thought someone should know."

"But my brother knows. You told me he asked you not to tell anyone."

"I felt you specifically should know because you're the real killer."

"Me?!"

"Of course you. Who else? You're the one who put me in that situation. You took off without telling me anything and left me stuck with this family."

"Please don't talk like that. It makes me feel like I'm living in a melodrama."

"But melodramas express the truth."

"Maybe, but they oughtn't to be turned into stories. So it was you?"

"I didn't say that, but maybe. I don't know what was happening to him. There was nothing I could do. I didn't mean to push him. Perhaps I didn't push him. I don't know what happened. I asked Nasim and he told me, 'Drop it. It looks like he'd been smoking hashish and there's no point creating a scandal.' Why did your father take drugs?"

"I don't know. Maybe you should ask your mother."

"My mother! What's it got to do with my mother?"

At that moment Nasim arrived. His face was black with fury and sorrow. He looked at his brother and told him that things had got difficult and he'd call on him the next day and give him the bad news. Hend got up and left with her husband.

91

Hend told her husband she'd told his brother about his father's death, and that was a mistake. Her mistake was not in the saying but in the timing, as Karim tried to explain when he phoned her to say goodbye.

"No, Doctor!" said Hend. "No, it had nothing to do with the timing. Does any self-respecting man tell his wife she's a whore and the daughter of a whore in front of their children?"

Karim tried to explain to her that insults shouldn't be taken at face value and told her about his friend the Iraqi poet whom he'd met in Montpellier and who, whenever he got drunk, would delight in Lebanese insults because they were the most refined form of metonymy.

"What does 'metonymy' mean?"

"It means making comparisons. How can I put it? It means saying one thing and meaning another. You package the words in images and the image becomes the point and the words lose their meanings."

Karim didn't tell Hend what had taken place during his meeting with his brother and the direct approach, devoid of any of the rules of metonymy, that Nasim had used to describe his father. He limited himself to offering advice, because a woman has no place if not next to her husband and her children.

6

Karim hadn't gone back to Beirut to search for his father's killers or to take revenge on them. Such a story wasn't right for him and wasn't like him. Karim had read something similar about a man who went back from France in search of his father's killers that was written by Maroun Baghdadi and published in the *al-Nahar* Supplement after the young Lebanese director's death. Maroun was a beautiful man and could seduce any woman; that was how Karim had seen him when he met him in Montpellier. He recalled that he'd watched his film *Little Wars* at a private showing at the university, after which the Lebanese student who'd talked to him about his ox-cheek feast in Paris had invited him to a restaurant in the Place de la Comédie. There the students hovered around the director, who told them of his project for a new film he was making about mutual forgiveness and said he was looking for a writer to help him with the screenplay. At the time, it had occurred to Karim that he might write the screenplay, but he'd been afraid of looking ridiculous so gave it no more thought.

The ghost of the Lebanese director filled his imagination once more when he read fragments of the story of his horrible death following his fall into the stairwell of the building in which he was living in Beirut, close to the Tabaris roundabout, as he prepared to shoot his new movie.

Karim told his wife that his friend Maroun's death had transformed him into a hero because, basically, Maroun was confused about whether to be a hero or a director. The hero's role had selected him for killing, and the story he'd written had devoured him.

He was taken aback to hear Bernadette asking him about the blonde woman.

"What woman?" Karim asked.

"I was told a mysterious woman was with him the night he died and I wouldn't rule out foul play."

"Where do you get all this information?"

She said she'd become more Lebanese than he and knew the Lebanese news in detail while all he cared about was eating tabbouleh.

He told her such thoughts came from her reading of crime novels and that Lebanon wasn't right for crime novels.

She said that was precisely Lebanon's problem, because when crime novels become a possibility it means the country has succeeded in separating crime from its social environment, but "you people live crime without realising".

She asked him why he'd used the word "friend" when talking of Maroun Baghdadi. "Was he really your friend?"

Karim said he'd met Maroun twice in Beirut at the flat of a man called Danny, where they used to discuss Marxism, and that Maroun hadn't been interested in such discussions. He'd kept joking around and flirting with the girls. Then he met him in Montpellier and had been sure that Maroun wouldn't recognise him, which was in fact what happened because the director was preoccupied with a beautiful black girl who'd come with Talal, the Lebanese student who'd invited him to the restaurant.

"So he wasn't your friend," said Bernadette.

"He was sort of a friend," he replied.

"Everything's 'sort of' with you. I can't make you out anymore. You say you love Lebanon but you won't let us visit it, tremble when you talk about your brother, and don't want us to get to know your family. Your father died and you didn't go to Beirut. I don't know you."

He told her no-one knew anyone. "You think I know myself to start with that I should open for you the gateways to knowledge? No-one knows himself because an individual is a forest covered with a tent and the tent is all secrets and the secrets are attached to one's skin."

"But you're a skin doctor," she said.

He told her the secret of the medical profession was the patients. It was up to the patient to be convinced that the doctor knows; only then could the doctor practise his profession. "In other words the doctor is an assumption not an absolute truth. If you believe him, you'll be cured. If you don't, there's nothing he can do."

Bernadette said he was talking about magic, not medicine: "But you're a failed magician, the proof being that your magic hasn't worked on me for a long time."

He tried to tell her about Nasri, who'd played around with chemistry till it killed him. The old man must certainly have taken his own Green Potion and sat waiting at the shop, but his latest victim – let's call her Najat – never came, or never took the potion. He waited a long time and when he got sick of waiting he went to Salma's flat, but Salma wasn't at home, or didn't open the door, so he found himself making his way to his son's flat to die.

Did Nasri try to rape Hend, or did he appear so strange that he scared the woman into kicking him to the ground, with the result that seven days later he died?

Karim had thought the story of the search for his father's killers didn't concern him and wasn't what had brought him to Lebanon, and that he ought to forget the whole thing. The hospital project had been an appropriate occasion for him to return to the scene of that crime of his of which no-one knew anything, and in which he'd participated unknowingly – or at least unaware of the devastating impact of his failure to act decisively, which had compelled Khaled Nabulsi to leave him to go to meet his end in Tripoli. But Khaled would have gone in any case. The man had seen his death as inescapable and gone to it and the whole thing had nothing to do with Karim.

Khaled was authentic and the authentic have no choice but to die. He, on the other hand, was the imaginary Sinalcol, just a ghost who didn't exist and who left no footprints on the ground. That was why he'd decided to be a brother to the real Sinalcol.

He'd said he was looking for Sinalcol and had convinced himself he was. The name pleased Muna, who laughed a lot as she drank white wine with him and listened to the story of what he called his "spiritual twin" who had passed through the ancient quarters of Tripoli like a ghost, then disappeared leaving neither track nor sign.

"Are you serious, his name was Sinalcol?" Muna asked.

"That's what they say but how should I know? Danny told me about him when we went to work with the Qubbeh neighbourhood group in Tripoli, and then Khaled Nabulsi, God have mercy on his remains, tried to kill him because he'd earned himself a bad reputation, which reflected poorly on the Revolution, but he failed. Then Khaled died and I went to France and took Sinalcol with me."

"Who were Danny and Khaled?"

"They were my comrades in arms."

"Where are they now?"

"One's dead and the other's living as though he were dead," said Karim.

"And Sinalcol?" she asked.

"I don't know. Maybe he's dead too but I haven't heard anything about him. I'm going to Tripoli soon to ask about him."

"So no-one's left alive except you. It's the scallywags who make old bones!" she said.

"No, I'm alive because I took off. Death passed close by me but by a miracle I escaped."

He'd wanted to tell her he hadn't returned to Lebanon because of the hospital but to look for Sinalcol, and for what remained of what he'd lived through in Tripoli during the war. It had been his greatest experience of life and of death and in that city he'd discovered that life has no meaning and that people invent meanings to be able to accept the idea of their death.

Still, he'd said nothing to this woman who'd come to him from he knew not where, and with whom he'd started a relationship designed to make him forget the wound through which the story of his fling with Ghazala had bled away. Now, sitting with Muna, he could feel the tingle of blood flowing through his veins once more but he was just distracting himself with a relationship which Muna had given him to understand could never be anything but ephemeral from a love story that had inspired in him embarrassingly simple-minded emotions. In transitory relationships you have to lie: they're like a story you have to write and whose features you have to draw, not one in which you can play the hero. Heroes are stupid or, let's say, they believe, and when you believe you take a beating. He was a hero with Ghazala. He'd believed the passion, only to discover that he'd been taken for the biggest ride of his life. With Muna, though, things were clear and didn't need thinking about: he had to talk to fill the gaps in the imagination created by desire. This didn't mean he was against love. On the contrary, ever since he'd begun to feel that his marriage was slipping away from him and taking on a form that had room only for repetition, he'd been living in hope of a new great love. That was how he'd lived his ephemeral relationships in the distant French city. But when Ghazala's story ended he'd realised that love was the victim of contradictory expectations, or a misunderstanding based on two different points of view.

He'd left Hend because he hadn't been able to tell her about the fear that had unstrung his joints after the killing of Khaled Nabulsi, and because he'd become aware that their love, which he'd thought would last forever, had been wiped out in a single instant. It was only during his coughing fit, as he listened to his brother telling him over the phone that he'd married Hend, that he'd rediscovered the choking feeling that used to fill his throat whenever she left him to go back home.

"You told me Sinalcol was from Tripoli, right?"

. . .

"I must tell Ahmad. It's got to be *lingua franca*."

"What?"

"*Lingua franca*."

"What does that mean?"

"It's the language of the last remaining crusaders. Someday Ahmad can tell you about his grandfather and father. I can't tell stories."

"Forget about *lingua franca* and all that crap. When we were young there was a fizzy drink called 'Sinalco', a patriotic imitation of Cola, and I remember it was good. It tasted a bit like tamarind, and I don't know why it disappeared. Probably the company went broke."

"And the factory was in Tripoli, right?"

"I don't know."

"The company doesn't matter," said Muna, "I'm talking about the man. If he was from Tripoli he must have taken the word from there and not had the soda pop company in mind. Soon you'll hear the true story and you'll see I'm right."

Muna put on her glasses and looked at him as a teacher might at her students. She asked him to stop talking about the subject because it wasn't his field of specialisation. Her voice had the condescension and arrogance of women teachers' voices, so he could find nothing to say except that she treated him like a schoolteacher, that she was incapable of forgetting her profession, and "God help your husband!"

Later Karim would go to Tripoli, hear the story from Ahmad, drink lemonade with ice cream in front of the Dakiz Mosque, meet Mr Abd el-Malek, Ahmad's father, and hear from him the strangest tale imaginable. He'd discover through the man's secret language that war, which he'd believed from Danny's teaching to be "the engine of history", used people so that it could grind them up and treated them as means to an end, for history was just a wild beast with an unquenchable thirst for the blood of its victims.

What he didn't know was what was happening to him now and why he felt this incurable fragility, and why he found himself stuck once more in that old feeling that he was part of another man, or formed, along with that other, a single individual with two heads.

At primary school his favourite game with his brother had been what they called "the four eyes game". They'd stand back to back and watch the school playground from in front and behind. They didn't need to exchange information because what one of them saw would be transmitted wordlessly to the other's consciousness. Nasim had invented the game and it was his means of defending his brother, who, because of his weak build, was constantly getting beaten up. This way the younger brother could put a stop to the attacks to which his brother was subject. Karim's continual persecution by a boy called Michel Aql had to do with the lady teacher, whom Michel accused him of being in love with, saying that that was why Karim did better than him in French. This Michel was the leader of a gang of boys and challenged Karim for first place in the class and always failed. Karim's crime was that he was soft on his teacher, Madam Olga Naddaf, who did indeed return his affection, with tenderness and concern. She was a woman in her early thirties, white and full without being fat, with wide black eyes, a small tip-tilted nose, lips as thin as if drawn with a pen, a brow that radiated light, and always dressed in white. The students called her Madam Bride because she wore white to school every day, as though she owned white dresses for every season.

For a whole year the French teacher dwelt in Karim's eyes. The boy wished she would take off her glasses so he could see himself in the mirrors of her eyes. When Muna told him her husband used the word "mirrors" to refer to glasses, he burst out laughing. She said this term, and many like it, were part of the secret lexicon of the Dakiz family. "The eyes are the mirrors of the soul," he told her. "You're distorting the language. The Tunisians also call glasses mirrors." He told her he'd found this out in Paris when by coincidence he met the Watermelon, as he used to call her after he'd forgotten her name.

Why did memories rain down on him in Beirut, and what did it mean when things which forgetfulness had secreted away kept popping up again from some hidden place of whose very existence he had been unaware?

Now it was the Watermelon, reappearing like a ghost. Karim found himself incapable of understanding the relationship between past and present. It was as though memory gave everything a ghostlike cast; as though, rather than remembering himself, he was seeing another person who resembled him.

When he met her in Paris she'd asked after his father who, she recounted, had turned up the morning of the day after they'd all had lunch together. She said his father had been waiting for her in the foyer of the hotel, had caught sight of her, and walked with her to the dining room where they'd had breakfast together. She'd said she was in a hurry because she had to catch a flight. He'd said he would escort her to the airport. He'd gone upstairs with her to her room on the excuse of helping her to pack her bags, and slept with her.

This had been at the beginning of Karim's relationship with politics.

He'd entered the American University in Beirut to study medicine and the storm in his head had begun. There he met young members of the Fatah movement and his relationship with the organisations of the Lebanese Left that called for armed struggle started.

The Tunisian woman was thirty. Brown and full, with shining eyes and a laughing, radiant face. He'd met her at a conference in support of the Palestinian cause organised by the student council at A.U.B. She was working for a Tunisian underground paper put out by the Trotskyites called *Perspectif*. She gave a lecture on the Tunisian fighters during the 1948 war and mentioned a man from Sfax whose oral witness she said she had recorded and was going to publish in a book. She said he'd gone from Tunisia to Palestine on foot via Libya and the Sinai Desert. She said the Egyptian army had arrested him in Falouja and the man had spent four years in Egyptian prisons before being released and making his way back to his country. The Tunisian woman had held the audience spellbound. Karim didn't know how he found himself next to her. It was 8 p.m. and the darkness of the humid June evening was advancing down Bliss Street. She asked him to show her to a restaurant and they walked for innumerable hours on the Corniche after buying falafel sandwiches. He told her she was a free woman and she laughed. "What does free mean?" she asked. He said it meant being emancipated like the women of Europe. She said it was the Revolution that had emancipated her. By the time they got to the Intercontinental Hotel in the Rawsheh district he'd taken her hand. When they reached the hotel entrance and it seemed that Karim was determined to go up with her to her room she said she was tired and he was still too young for such things.

He invited her to lunch the next day. She said she would accept his invitation on condition that he took her to his family home because she wanted to eat home-cooked Lebanese food, and "don't forget, we're cousins: we're both descendants of Elissa the Phoenician." He didn't dare tell her no-one cooked in his house because his mother was dead. He decided not to tell his father, who didn't eat at home in the middle of the day anyway, and to get his brother out of the way so he could be alone with the woman, who was ten years older than him.

He gave himself away, though, when he asked his father about the best restaurant from which to buy food cooked in the traditional way. The game was up and the Tunisian woman found herself surrounded by three men. Karim recalled her saying she'd found herself in front of three copies of one man and that Nasri had roared with laughter, boasting to her that he'd fathered two sons in one year.

"Am I like my father?" he'd asked before leaving her room at the hotel.

"You will be when you're older," she'd said, laughing.

The banquet Nasri had prepared was magnificent – vine leaves with trotters and kibbeh labaniyyeh, as well as starters, with tabbouleh in pride of place.

The father presided over the show. He cracked jokes, told stories, and filled the dining room with undulations of desire.

He said he'd cooked everything with his own hands and that he hated restaurant food because the flavour of things disappeared.

"Food is history, *mademoiselle*! A spiritual chemistry to be perfected only by those who know that matter can be transformed into spirit."

"You're a cook?" she asked. "Karim didn't tell me his father was a cook."

"I'm a pharmacist, I know how to mix things," he replied, and he began telling her about his pharmacy and his inventions and the special green liquid that set plants ablaze with life.

Karim and his brother tried to get a word in but Nasri had the conversation on the end of a fine thread which only slipped from his hand when Karim spoke of the Fedayeen bases in the south. At that, Nasri's face clouded over. He left the dining room and returned bearing a bowl of red watermelon.

"I love *dalla'*!" she said.

She described how they called watermelon *dalla'* in her country. Nasri regained control of the conversation by praising *dalla'* and saying the word came from *dala'*, meaning coquettishness, and that he wished he'd had a daughter so he could call her Dala'.

"No, sir, I don't think so. The word must be Berber originally," she said. "The *dala'* you're talking about is something else. It's an Egyptian word –" and she roared with laughter.

"Words are like the stones of a monument," said Nasri, "or like fossil-ised fish. But the difference between the word and the stone is that the word is a spirit and the spirit doesn't disappear. It lives even if it loses its memory."

When the Tunisian woman got up to go and Karim stood up to leave with her, the father leapt up and said, "I'll take you in my car." Karim sat in the back while his father drove, the woman sitting next to him. Karim beheld that day how his father laid down a carpet of words to cover the road over which the tyres of the Peugeot 304 were gliding.

When they arrived in front of the hotel, Nasri turned off the engine and kept on talking and the girl remained immobile. Karim got out, opened the front door, and stretched out his hand; the girl got out, utter-ing words of thanks.

"Come on. Get in, lad!" said Nasri.

"See you later," replied Karim. He slammed the door and went into the hotel with the girl.

"You slept with him on the same sheets?"

"Your father's a sweetie. There's a man for you."

She asked him how his father was and said he'd sent her lots of mes-sages and that he was the romantic type. She hadn't answered his messages, though, because when she got back to Paris she'd decided to marry her French boyfriend and was now the mother of three boys. She said her eldest son looked a lot like Nasri; she thought she'd got pregnant in Beirut but wasn't sure, and that anyway she'd named her son Victor in honour of Nasri.

"You mean I have a Tunisian brother?"

"No, French. My former husband was French. Now I'm living with a Tunisian here in Paris, but my boys are French."

Why hadn't she agreed to let him sleep with her? She'd let him come up to her room, then said she was tired and sleepy because she'd drunk a lot of wine. She lay down on the bed fully dressed. Karim lay down next to her. He kissed her but she turned her face away. She said she wanted to sleep, turned her back on him, and dozed off. Karim left the room on tiptoe, bearing the taste of *dalla'* on his lips, only to discover years later that his father had stolen from him both the woman and the *dalla'*.

This son-devouring father was behind the problem that led to his split with his brother. Madam Bride had nothing to do with it, she was just a fragrance – that was how Karim decided to remember her. The fragrance vanished a year after she started working at the school. It was said that the maths teacher, Nabil Moussa, had married her and taken her off with him to America. Karim had hated the teacher, with his thick moustache, small eyes and extremely brown skin. Now he understood that the man had won his teacher's heart and his kindness to Karim looked more like pity. No doubt Madam Bride had told her friend about her twelve-year-old suitor, but instead of making him feel jealous of his rival she'd made him feel pity. Thus was a further layer of sorrow added to Karim's face.

The day he went to school and discovered that a new teacher had taken her place he was overcome with depression. He'd wanted to tell her he'd read *L'Étranger* by Albert Camus for her sake, and that from the first line, when the French writer announces his mother's death, he'd felt as though it was he who was writing the novel. The same feeling would stay with him throughout his life: he'd read, and once the words had become embedded in his eyes he'd be transformed from reader into writer, which was what convinced him he could never become one. Every time he got drunk with the Iraqi poet in Montpellier and began reciting passages that he'd learned by heart from Arabic, French, and Russian novels, his drinking companion would look at him suspiciously and tell him he was mad: "People usually learn poetry by heart but you learn prose. You're crazy, I swear." He didn't say he'd committed the prose to heart because of a woman the taste of whose kiss on his cheek on the last day of the school term, and how his face had been stained with red and he'd felt the tears spreading in his eyes, he could never forget. The same day the man with the moustaches had pinched his cheek, laughing as he advised him to get some exercise during the summer and not waste all his time reading: "Olga tells me you read a lot. You're too young still for reading. Go and play and be happy. The days that pass don't come back."

Could Karim describe what the lady teacher did as a betrayal? He couldn't claim he hadn't understood the meaning of the word "love" and when he came, many years later, to memorise the poem "He Weeps and Laughs" and got to the line that says

A heart habituated to pleasures while young
Like a rose bud opened by the touch of the breeze

he felt that al-Akhtal al-Saghir had written the verse for him.

He saw Madam Olga's white thighs gleaming through her skirt in front of him and felt pins and needles in his lips.

"What kind of shitty love is that?" Nasim had asked him. "You've got the whole school laughing at us."

"What business is it of yours what I do?" answered Karim.

"Everyone gets us mixed up. Even the teacher herself can't tell the difference between us. I swear if you weren't my brother and like my own soul and more, I'd have stuck it in her."

"Don't talk that way about the *mademoiselle*! She was the best teacher."

"You're an idiot. All the students saw how Mr Nabil used to go with her to the classroom at the lunch break and smooch with her. You believed that story they told us about how she'd married him and gone off with him to America? Brother Eugène caught them at it and threw them out of the school. They didn't get married or anything. She's a whore. She put one over you and made you her patsy and made us look like idiots and if I hadn't been there Michel and his gang would have made mincemeat of you."

Olga wasn't the issue that created the first fissures in the twinned relationship between the two brothers. The real rift came about because of Nasri, who discovered that Nasim was no good at school.

The father discovered that Brother Eugène had been telling the truth: Nasim had a real problem with his studies, it was something to which all the teachers drew attention. He found reading difficult and seemed to understand nothing in class. The surprise came though with the exam marks, when the boy got Outstanding in everything. He almost rivalled his brother, as to whose intelligence all the teachers were agreed.

"Perhaps the boy has a psychological problem and needs treatment. Maybe he gets confused with the teachers because he's shy. Really, it's very odd. The boy's a little devil. There must be something not right. I suggest he see a psychiatrist."

"A psychiatrist! Are you saying my son's crazy? No, *Mon Frère*, we don't have any of that nonsense in our family! The boy's fine and his marks are good and praise God both boys are turning out to be smart. Did you know, *Mon Frère*, that I didn't get married because of these boys? I look at them and can't believe it, and now you come and talk to me about psychological problems? Out of the question!"

When the father left the school the veil fell from his eyes. He realised that the boys were hiding something and that what the Jesuit had said was true. From the very beginning he dismissed any possibility of a psychological problem since, in his opinion, that just couldn't be, and he dealt with the matter himself. The morning of the next day he decided not to take the boys to the shop with him early as he usually did in the summer, wanting them to smell curative herbs from their earliest days so that they could go on with his work after he was gone; he gave them Tuesdays off, allowing them to stay home to give him a chance to attend to his private affairs.

That day, their egg breakfast over, instead of getting up and telling them to get dressed he asked the boys to fetch their school books. The examination began and Nasri discovered the deception. Nasim read with difficulty, as though he were spelling out the letters.

"What kind of a farce is this?" yelled Nasri.

And the man listened to the strangest confession he'd ever heard. The two boys were one person. The first was for lessons and the second for being naughty. He also discovered that he was now paying the price for his child-raising methods, since he'd never bothered to teach his boys himself but had left it to the older one.

"What else could I do?" asked Karim. "Do you really want me to let my brother fail at school?"

"It would be better for him to fail and re-do the year and learn something, but this way we're making him half illiterate, plus he's a year younger than you. I put you in the same class so you wouldn't be separated and this is the result. Brother Eugène was right. He told me, 'Your son Nasim has a psychological problem,' though in fact it looks like you, the dumb elder brother, are the one with the problem."

"I can't survive if my brother isn't with me in the classroom," said Karim.

"Nor me," said Nasim.

And so the journey of torment began. Apparently the father wasn't the only one to have noticed the problem and the new school year was transformed into a kind of festival of persecution that encompassed both home and school. At school the new maths teacher, Maxim Sininian, discovered that Nasim hadn't grasped a thing, while at home the task of teaching the son was taken on by the father, who went about it savagely, and this situation came to an end only with Nasim's disappearance.

Karim was sixteen when he woke up to find that his brother had left home. He informed his father, who was shaving while listening as usual to the B.B.C. news in Arabic on a transistor radio he'd put in the bathroom. Then began the search and the torment, which lasted a week, during which they went all over Lebanon and looked everywhere except in the place where Nasim had taken refuge.

Years later Nasim told his brother he'd felt as though his heart had burst and he couldn't take it anymore. The whole world was falling apart and all he could see was blackness, so he ran to Sawsan, who adopted him, and he called her Suzanne. "Do you know what it means if a woman adopts you? You sleep with her and she behaves like she's your mother. She found me work at the bean and shawarma restaurant at the end of Mutanabbi Street. I worked from five in the morning and went back to her at the end of the evening dog tired and she'd give me a bath and feed me and put me to sleep. Do you know what it's like to stand next to a shawarma spit that's turning in front of the fire all day long? The sweat came out all over my body and I'd be preparing sandwiches and dishes for the women who'd be coming from the souk dying of hunger, and with every drop of sweat I felt like Nasri was being pulled out from under my skin and I felt I was free. Sunday morning I woke up early as usual and began getting dressed to go to work. Suzanne grabbed me and told me, 'Go back to sleep. It's Sunday and Sunday is the Lord's Day. Sleep and in a little we'll get up together and go to church.'"

"But we don't go to church," he told her.

"From now on you're going to go. Sunday's set aside for the smell of incense, the light of candles, and a plate of kenafeh-with-cheese. Go back to sleep and then we'll talk."

Nasim went back to sleep and woke at 8.30 a.m. to a kiss on the brow from Suzanne. He took a shower, got dressed, and they went to church, where he discovered incense.

He told his brother that mass was the most beautiful thing – angelic voices, a metropolitan wearing a crown, and white beards puffed up with the perfumes of incense. From that day on Nasim was regular in his attendance at mass and imposed on the family the tradition of eating kenafeh-with-cheese for breakfast on Sundays.

"At the end of the mass, she led me by the hand and made me stand behind her in the line till I received communion. I drank a drop of sweet red wine mixed with a little crumbled bread from a little spoon carried by the priest and felt I was drunk. Afterwards we went to el-Burj Square and ate kenafeh at Buhsali's. She told me, 'You're to eat kenafeh here every Sunday, got it? Now you've sweated your father out of your system and it's time for you to go home. Don't tell anyone where you were. That's your secret and your secret has to become a part of you. If you tell your secret, you'll get it in the neck. The secret has to stay with you and me.'"

"So you learned holiness from a prostitute!" Karim said, laughing.

"I'm not talking about holiness, I'm talking about the taste of life. That's what it tastes like – Suzanne and kenafeh and the mass, not that teacher of yours who put one over you and made all the students laugh at us."

Nasim went back home on Sunday at twelve noon. He opened the door and went into the bedroom. His brother caught up with him and started yelling and asking him where he'd been. Nasri came in, told Karim to shut up, hugged his son, wept, and didn't ask a single question. The father behaved as though nothing had happened and ran to get the table ready. Nasim said he wasn't hungry because he'd eaten kenafeh-with-cheese.

The father went out and returned bearing a platter of kenafeh and from that day on kenafeh became a part of Sunday breakfast and remained so until Nasri died.

Nasim didn't tell the story of his week away from home. He kept the secret to himself and let no-one in on what had happened. What he told Karim was the synopsis but, as we know, the relation between the actual story and its synopses isn't always exact. He never told how he'd arrived at the souk that Sunday morning to find the street empty and the houses shut. When he asked the guard of the building where she worked about Suzanne, the man chased him off. "Go away, arsehole, and don't let me see you here again! It's Sunday and Sunday morning there's no work. You think the women are machines? They're human beings just like you and me. Plus we don't take kids. Don't let me see your face again and get out of here before I give you a hiding."

Nasim had had no other option. He'd decided he couldn't go on living through the torture parties by day and the insults he received from his father during the evening tutoring. He'd felt his head wasn't working properly and that all he wanted to do was sleep. The letters following one another over the pages just looked like lines of ants; he was incapable of deciphering what they stood for, and when with his father's help he succeeded he found he was incapable of memorising them. The words slipped about in front of him and his eyes would become swollen with drowsiness. It was an endless daily torment accompanied by insults and beatings. Nasri had never before actually beaten his sons. When he became incandescent with anger and felt the need to beat the boys, he'd leave the flat and not come back until he'd smoked a narghile at the café. He'd fill his head and chest with Persian tobacco, which cools hot heads, and return to the flat, where he'd tell them, smiling that implacable smile of his from the corner of his lower lip, that he would never beat them because they were orphans. All the same it seems that when he found out about his younger son's laziness the Devil got into him, and the gurgling of the narghile no longer sufficed to calm his fury. Karim never believed his father hadn't known the truth about his younger son's academic situation. He felt Nasri had been aware of the problem but had shrugged it off. Then he discovered, from practising medicine, that parents see in their children only what they want to because love is blind, and Nasri had dealt with his younger son like a blind man. Nasim's body became covered in pimples, the light in his eye died, and he ended up almost unable to move. His naughtiness at school ceased completely and the boy was transformed into a pitiful rag.

The blind love that Nasri harboured for his boys was transformed into something like an aversion. He came to hate himself in his sons: instead of seeing himself split into two halves, as he had supposed, he began to see them as mirrors of his failure and loneliness. The oppression was all directed at Nasim but Karim too was close to feeling afraid and losing his balance.

Karim began to lose weight. The pharmacist father diagnosed his son as anaemic and took to giving him fish oil and forcing him to eat raw sheep's liver.

The one was divided into two and home became a hell. Nasim despaired of life and made up his mind to kill himself. Not a chink opened in the solid wall before him so he ran away from the flat at eight on a Sunday morning, only to find himself alone in front of Suzanne's closed door.

All he could remember was her name, so he decided it was her. He went to her because no-one had gone to him. He'd decided to go away and never return, so he found himself standing at the end of the street not knowing what to do.

When he saw her he recognised her by her shoulders. He didn't see her face when she came through the doorway of the building where she lived but he saw her straight shoulders and ran to her. Suzanne found him in front of her, recognised him immediately, and asked what the matter was. He uttered broken words from which she gathered that his father had thrown him out of the house. Instead of continuing on her errand to wherever it was she was going she took him by the hand and went back into the house. "He's a relative," she told the guard, whose eyebrows had shaped themselves into exclamation marks.

He sat down on the couch in the small living room attached to her bedroom. She made him a cup of tea, lit a cigarette, and told him to tell her his story.

He spoke but did so without telling because he didn't know how to tell stories. When his brother asked him about Suzanne on his return from France, he told him not to ask what had happened because he didn't know how to tell it. "Till now I still can't talk about what happened. All I know is she asked me to tell her my story and I didn't know what to say, so she pulled the words out of me and put them together differently and in the end it was her that told me what had happened. Please, I've forgotten about it and I don't want to talk about it."

Nasim said he'd forgotten, but he had forgotten nothing. It was that week which made him what he became. He returned home and the persecution stopped, but his life had been turned upside down and he started to feel an obscure hatred for his brother.

The story he'd told Hend about his father refusing to allow him to be held back a year at school and deciding to take his sons out wasn't true. It was one of Nasim's tricks to convince himself that separation from his brother had been impossible. He'd failed years more than once and endured the coercion that followed, and all he wanted was to make it as far as the school-leaving exam class because he knew his brother would take the exam for him. The business about transferring from one school to another happened after Brother Eugène decided to expel Nasim. The boy was moved about among a number of schools, eventually finding refuge in one called Pioneer Secondary which specialised in lazy students with rich parents. There Nasim managed to get as far as the school-leaving certificate exam, which he passed because his brother went disguised as him. Karim continued the swapping game when he took the Faculty of Pharmacy entrance exams at the Jesuit university in his brother's place and passed. That, however, was where the charade ended, with Nasim bluffing his way to being a pharmacist, meaning that he never took a university degree but just started practising the profession with his father.

When the civil war broke out in April 1975 Karim was a student at A.U.B., living in West Beirut. His relationship with the Left was taking root. He was in the process of becoming an activist in a small Lebanese organisation set up by Fatah called the Socialist Revolution Movement. Nasim was living in East Beirut and had begun to have dealings with youths who referred to themselves as "the Organisation" before this was incorporated into the Phalanges.

The civil war wasn't the main reason for the split between the two brothers. That had happened the day Nasim disappeared and then returned to the flat a week later a different person. Everything changed. True, they went on with their game, which reached its climax when Nasim married Hend, but they knew it had ended and that the "four eyes" were now only shadows fashioned by memory.

Nasim turned to sports and became a champion swimmer. His muscles bulged and he spent a lot of his time at the sports club. Karim, on the other hand, grew thinner and more introverted, finding his tongue only at the university where he discovered that ideas could be transformed into material force, and where he embraced the belief that men could make history.

Nasim became a make-believe pharmacist and only stopped working with his father when Nasri discovered his son wasn't merely selling the narcotic pills from the shop but taking them himself. He would vanish for days, then return in a filthy state, seemingly drunk, throw his rifle down in the corner of his room and sleep as though in a deep coma.

Nasri fired his son, telling him he was destroying his father's reputation. "I, boy, invent real medicines and you want to turn the shop into a hashish den?"

That day Nasim raised his hand against his father. He was on the verge of striking him but held back at the last moment. He gathered up his things and left, and only went home again when he was wounded in the war. When this happened Nasim gritted his teeth and told Nasri he ought to kill him but wasn't going to. "Do you know why I'm not going to kill you? Because you aren't worth the loss of a bullet. God protect you though, because I may kill you at any moment."

Listening to Maroun Baghdadi telling the plot of the film for which he was seeking a writer, Karim thought his own story with his brother would make a good basis for it. He said he'd like to suggest a different plot line: the man returns from France not to look for his father's killers but to get back the woman his brother stole from him. He said the story of the search for the killer and of getting caught up in the maze of the sectarian conflict would result in just another traditional film. It would be better to stay away from the trap of a sectarian reading as the war had divided the individual into two halves, with the first half killing the second, and the father would end up being the victim. In his version, fathers and sons would equally be victims.

The director smiled and said he didn't like didactic films, he wanted the truth the way it was. "Sectarianism? Why not? It's how we are, after all. The father has died and the son is coming not to take revenge but to find out."

"Where's the justice?" someone asked him.

"I'm not looking for justice. Let's forget justice and reality and look for the crime. I'm trying to say we're all criminals."

"Criminals and victims," said Karim.

"No, not victims," said Maroun. "No-one in this war deserves to be called a victim, just a criminal. That's why justice doesn't concern me: it makes it look as though there's an oppressor and an oppressed. I want to say that all Lebanese are oppressors."

"But we were defending the Palestinians and the Palestinians are oppressed," said Talal.

"Palestine's another story," answered the director. "That bit I can understand."

The director said he understood. But Karim was convinced this beautiful slim young man was like the victims, and that Danny was right when he told Maroun he wouldn't live to see the end of the war because he could see death inscribed on his forehead.

Maroun had laughed and said they'd all be dead by the time the war ended because it was going to be a war without end.

7

Karim hadn't known that the fates would make his brother the last witness to his own relationship with Beirut. Relations between the brothers had ended with the outbreak of the war. From 13 April, 1975, which became the official date of the start of the Lebanese Civil War, the brothers found themselves in opposing camps. Karim left the Gemmeizeh district – which had become part of what would come to be known as East Beirut – the following morning and only went back once, a year after the Hundred Days War of 1978, during which it had been shelled continuously by the Syrian army, which had entered Lebanon in 1976 on the pretext of imposing peace on that small nation torn apart and divided among its different sects. Karim went back then to make sure his father and brother were alright and to consult them on the possibility of his going abroad to complete his specialist studies in Montpellier.

His father had understood that he would never return.

And Hend had understood that he would never return.

Only Nasim had said he'd be waiting for him.

"Wherever you go, you can't go anywhere. You'll come back here because this is where the whole thing is."

"I lost. I don't have anywhere anymore," said Karim.

"And we lost too. This is where the losers meet," said Nasim.

"You lost? You've risen to the heights, God protect you from envy. You've gone from being a hoodlum to being a businessman!"

Nasim said he didn't want to get into a sterile discussion with his brother. "Everyone made his masks. I just can't believe you became a fighter. You're an intellectual and a doctor and intellectuals are cowards and you're going abroad now because you're a coward, no more no less, and I'm not with you to protect you. Admit you're a coward and forget the philosophy and then I'll respect you. You know you've been my ideal all my life and I'm like everyone else, I hate my ideal as much as I love it. Don't let the hatred win. Go where you like but please, no philosophy and no sermons!"

When Karim went back to the flat in Gemmeizeh, everything had changed. Even the smell had changed. The smell of the quarter, a mixture of jasmine and the incandescence of burnt coffee, had disappeared, its place taken by a smell like the burning of rotten garbage.

"That smell comes from the Normandie tip. They keep filling the sea with landfill made from rubbish. It extends the surface area of Beirut and the rubbish of the past gets mixed up with the rubbish of the present. A city that uses rubbish to devour the sea and grow, that's Beirut," said Nasim.

Three years were all it had taken to destroy his memories. Karim saw how his father had changed from a man into an old man. Nasri was sixty-four. He had known how to fine-tune his health to the rhythm of his desires, so where had this old age come from all of a sudden? He would eat fatty meats and then flush them out with two days of a milk diet. He would smoke a narghile and not inhale. He'd enjoyed sex in a disciplined way and without excess. He'd walked a full hour every day to burn off his fat and cholesterol.

Karim had no idea what had happened to the man. Was it the war? Fear of the unknown that life might bring? Nasri hadn't been afraid of the war because he had no respect for it. He'd told Karim on the phone that he wasn't afraid. "Come whenever you like, boy. You're afraid of the barricades? Fuck the barricades and those that man them! They don't scare anyone because they're just kids playing around. Wait for me at the Museum crossing and I'll come and get you."

How could he convince his father that the war was not a game but "the engine of history", as Danny used to say, citing Karl Marx?

"Why? You think you know your Marx? If you knew Marx you'd stay out of it. Does any of you know what Marx said about the Lebanese in the war of 1860? He called them 'the savage tribes of Lebanon'. That's what Marx wrote about you, you arseholes. And what kind of a family is this anyway? One thinks he's a communist and the other's a Phalangist and a Fascist. All we need is for one of you to kill the other and we'll be a parable. Come back here and set your brother straight for me. I'll work it out with the Phalanges and we'll get you into the Jesuit university and you can work with me in the shop."

When Karim finally came to say goodbye to his father he found himself alienated from everything. The district had been scarred by shelling, the people traumatised. Nasri said he'd retrieved his double-barrelled shotgun from the store room and everyone was terrified.

"I felt as though everything had been laid bare. We were at the mercy of the bullets and I couldn't think of any solution except to get the gun out of the store room and not die till I'd killed one of them."

"Are you going to go out and fight, Father?"

"I didn't say I was going to go out and fight, I said I wanted to defend myself. The fact is I was scared to death but when I took hold of the gun I felt myself stop trembling. That was when I understood the fighters. It's funny really. A fighter goes to fight and he's dying of fear. So, to stop being afraid, he shoots someone. It's like the merry-go-round children play on."

He spoke of the murder of Michel Hajji. "His father, Seroufim, God rest his soul, was my only competitor. We used to meet at Hajj Niqoula Ghamiqah the barber's. He was an old man with white hair and I was young, and he was a great pharmacist and I was rising like a rocket. He used a strange expression to say he wanted to cut his hair: he'd tell the hajj, 'I want to cut my head.' I don't know why he talked that way. He told me, 'Your future's all before you, Nasri. What do you say we go into partnership? That way you can be a mentor to Michel and help him.' God rest his soul and ours."

Nasri had been saddened by Michel Hajji's death fighting in front of his pharmacy. He said he feared for his son Nasim. "True, he's a dog, but blood's thicker than water, my boy."

Nasri had expelled his younger son from the shop after he'd turned it into a hashish den, "but Nasim's done well. I don't know what he does for a living but it looks like he's made it to the top."

"Imagine! He said he wanted to kill me. He raised his hand at me and then he couldn't find anyone but me to take care of him. He came to me with a wound in his thigh. The bullet was lodged in the flesh and we couldn't go to the hospital. I operated without anaesthetic, I had no other option. I anaesthetised it with some ice from the shop refrigerator and he started bellowing like an ox and cursing me and saying he wanted to kill me. I had the scalpel in my hand. I told him, 'Shut up! I could kill you right now', but no-one kills his son. When he got better he claimed he was lame and went back home saying I'd deliberately messed up his leg and uttering threats and warnings. No, no, I don't want to see him. Damn him and damn you along with him. I don't have children. I'm an orphan."

Karim laughed as he tried to persuade his father that a father who had lost his children wasn't called an orphan.

Nasri wasn't serious about refusing to be reconciled with his son. Karim read in his eyes the shadows of humiliation. "There are only two things in this world, my boy, that can humiliate a man – children and love. I escaped from the humiliation of love and then you and your brother came along to humiliate me over again."

Karim told his brother it was shameful for him to humiliate his father and that he'd take him to the flat. "You drop in and say hello to him and have lunch with us and that's the end of it."

"But he's the one who humiliated me," said Nasim. "It was the Hundred Days War, the last I took part in. Then I said, 'That's it! I've had enough! We die and the thugs are as happy as larks,' so I decided to become a thug and be happy too. I worked at the port, import–export, and God began to look kindly on my efforts. But your father has a narrow outlook, he can't accept the idea that I've left the pharmacy. He threw me out and he's waiting for me to come back like a dog, but I'm not going back."

Karim tried to persuade his younger brother that reconciliation with their father didn't mean going back to working at the pharmacy. It just meant making up so that he wouldn't feel lonely.

Karim didn't believe the story his brother had told him about their father trying to kill him when taking the bullet out of his thigh. "That's all bullshit, my dear brother. When are you going to stop telling lies?"

"I swear to God it's not bullshit! When the shelling stopped I went to the doctor. I was dragging my leg on the ground. He examined me and said 'It's probably a split tendon' and advised me to have it massaged. He said I might be lame for about three months till the tendon grew back. Father must have done it deliberately. He knows more than a doctor. He wanted to lame me but I'll show him. The war will be long, and one day I'm going to kill him."

"You want to kill Father?" Karim asked in amazement.

"And you too. I know why you've come. Of course, you want money from Father so you can go to France. He won't give you a penny. If you want money ask me and I'll give it to you."

"You want to kill me?"

Karim had got up to leave, certain his brother was demented, when Nasim launched himself at him, seized him in his arms, and kissed him. He asked him not to be angry and said he'd only been joking.

"What kind of a stupid joke is that? Please, don't make jokes like that with me or with Father."

"Fine. Do you want money?" asked Nasim.

"A little, around three thousand lira."

"You'll have them tomorrow."

"No. I won't take tainted money."

At this Nasim jumped to his feet and started swearing. "Tainted? All money's tainted. If people weren't thieves they wouldn't have invented money. People invented money so they could steal. Do you know anyone with money who isn't a crook? You believe Father invented medicines and made his money by honest means? Father's a conman. He stole the burn medicine from Seroufim Hajji. Michel, who died a martyr, God rest his soul, told me. He said his father didn't want to talk about it because Nasri had threatened him. Hajji's from Antioch and has no family to back him up and Father fooled him and made him think he could have him killed."

"To be honest, brother," said Karim, "I don't believe a word you say. I haven't been able to understand anything you've said since the time you disappeared that week and went to Sawsan, the one you call Suzanne. It feels to me as though whatever you say you're bullshitting. Even when you're telling the truth I feel you're lying. God help the woman who marries you, I don't know how she'll be able to deal with your lies."

*

Karim couldn't believe what his brother had said about his father. Nasim wasn't a liar in the way his brother claimed, but he did try to fit in with life. He deceived everyone and was deceived by everyone. Everyone treated him like an animal so he had no choice but to become one. He behaved like a wolf when he could, a fox when he found himself hemmed in, and a ewe lamb when he had to save himself from being destroyed. He rose with the waves and slept beneath them.

Nasim had told his brother only fragments of the story of his blind flight that winter morning. He'd intended never to return home because suddenly home had collapsed and the game had ended. He hadn't known where he was going. His world was narrow and allowed him no room. He'd left the flat without a penny in his pocket and walked along Gemmeizeh Street. That cold winter Sunday morning the Beirut streets were empty and it was raining heavily. He paused in front of old Abu Fu'ad's barber shop. The man, who was over seventy, was bent over arranging the newspapers he sold. Nasim noticed on the front page of *al-Nahar* a picture of Abd el-Nasser addressing the crowds. He didn't read the headline. He looked at the huge throng waiting for a word from the Leader's mouth and felt as though his own was full of stones: when Abu Fu'ad asked him what was wrong and where he was going in all that rain, Nasim didn't reply. He wanted to speak but the words refused to emerge from his mouth, so he swallowed them and moved on. Later, with Suzanne, he would learn to spit words. That amazing woman used the word "spit" to mean "speak". She told him that lying was the spittle that made everything stick together. "Don't you tell anyone you came to me. If they ask you, and I'm sure they will, don't say anything. Spit and lie. That'll teach your father a lesson. How could anyone with a gorgeous boy like you behave like that?! You're a real man, that's why your father gives you a hard time. Screw him and the school and the Frères. You think if the Frère had fucked you like he fucked your brother your father would be happy?"

Nasim was surprised his father hadn't asked him where he'd spent that week. He'd hugged him to his chest and kissed him. When he heard his son say he'd had kenafeh for breakfast he'd gone to Buhsali's central Beirut branch and bought a platter of kenafeh-with-cheese. Nasim had eaten again because he hadn't been able to say no to his father's sad eyes. Karim asked his brother where he'd been but Nasri had rebuked his elder son and told him not to ask. "For this my son was dead, and is alive again; he was lost and is found," said Nasri, repeating what the Gospel says about the Prodigal Son, and the second day he told him not to go to school. He took him instead to a dermatologist whose name he couldn't remember but who had fair hair. The father whispered to the doctor and then Nasim went into the inner room of the clinic on his own. The doctor asked Nasim to take off his trousers and expose his lower half. He examined him in front and behind.

"It looks like you've slept a lot with women," said the doctor.

He patted him on the back of the neck and told him to get dressed. Then they went out together to the waiting room where Nasri was waiting, standing up.

"The boy's in great shape and clean," said the doctor.

Nasim never got the chance to spit the way Suzanne had taught him. He went back to school but the persecution stopped. All the same he had to face his feelings of inferiority regarding his brother and lead a wandering life from one school to the next, so he chose to excel at sports and spit on the world of his father and his brother.

"Father shafted me. What a hard-hearted bastard! Not once did he ask me where I'd been and he died without my telling him. Not long ago, he was at my place and we were drinking and Hend went into the kitchen or somewhere – never once has Hend sat with us when Father's come to the flat, she pretends she's busy and disappears. I said to him, 'Father, don't you want to know where I disappeared to when I left home for a whole week? It's been on my mind to tell you.' He lifted his glass and sucked a small sip from it. Till the end of his life Father always sucked at his wine and arak and every time he saw me belch he'd give me a hard time. 'Alcohol is a spirit, my boy,' he'd say. 'The spirit can't be drunk, it has to be sucked up. It's a sin to gulp at it. Man is spirit and alcohol is spirit and when spirits meet they meet transparently. Alcohol isn't water and it isn't food. Alcohol is spirituous matter that cannot be experienced in material form.'"

"God rest his soul, he loved to philosophise to us," said Karim.

"But he wasn't philosophising then. I felt he was talking from the heart and I believed him. Father changed a lot after the scandal with the two sisters. He became spiritual and all he'd talk about was the poetry of Ibn Arabi. It seems he went back to the teachings of Dr Dahesh."

"Father became a human being?" Karim asked in surprise.

"If you'd seen him the last three years you wouldn't have known him."

"So why . . . ?" Karim swallowed his question and fell silent.

Nasim behaved as though he hadn't heard the truncated question and went on with his story.

"As I was saying, he said he didn't want to hear because the subject pained him. 'But it's a nice story,' I told him. He said he didn't need stories anymore and anyway he knew everything. 'Did she tell you?' I asked. 'What "she"?' he answered. 'Since you know, you must know who I'm talking about,' I said. He pushed the plate away from him and buggered off."

"But Father did know," said Karim.

"You told him?" asked Nasim.

"Of course I told him. Every time he looked at me I could see the question in his eyes and I couldn't help it."

"But you swore to me and said we were twins and twins don't betray each other!"

"I swear I couldn't help it."

"Now I understand why Suzanne did to me what she did. You're a traitor, a Jesuit, and an ape! You're the one I should have killed."

Nasim had never mentioned what Suzanne had done. He'd decided long before to wipe the humiliation from his memory. He'd gone to Suzanne a month after his return home. She'd told him to keep away for a whole month, she didn't want to see him till he'd spat out all the words in his heart. "Come back and see me in a month, on Sunday the tenth of January, and we'll go to church together and take communion and then you can come back here."

"Sunday! But you don't work on Sunday and I'll be wanting to . . ."

"You're an idiot. With you it's not called work, it's called affection."

On Sunday, 10 January, Nasim left the flat. Nasri was getting dressed so he could go and buy kenafeh-with-cheese when he heard his son say he was invited to breakfast at a friend's and would be late getting back.

His father went on getting dressed as though he'd heard nothing and Nasim left the flat without objection from his father.

Suzanne was walking to church with her women friends. When she saw him standing waiting for her at the entrance to the souk she turned her eyes away and kept going. He caught up with her. She turned round and said, "What have you come here for? Go back to your father."

"But I came because we had a date."

"Go back to your father and leave me alone. Who makes a date with a prostitute? I'm a prostitute, sonny, and you're from a respectable family. Leave me alone, please!"

"But I love you!"

"Don't use that word with me. I've heard it a lot already and when I believed it I turned into a cum-rag. Ask your father and he'll tell you. And you too, you're hardly out of the egg and already up to no good. Leave me alone! You're all liars."

"Us?"

"Right, you. All of you. All men are liars. You and your father and all your kind. You're the real prostitutes. For us it's work. We have to prostitute ourselves to live, but who's forcing you? Money, respect, dignity and you whore yourselves like streetwalkers. Leave me alone and go say hi to your father for me. If I see you here again I'll break your leg."

Laughter rose around Suzanne, who continued on her way to church.

Nasim's heart broke that day. He felt a pain in his ribs and couldn't inhale. He felt as though his ribs had pierced his chest wall and that his throat was on fire. He'd bent his neck and couldn't raise his head again. The woman he loved had made him a laughing-stock and murdered him with her mocking laugh.

He told Hend when he asked her to marry him that he knew she had a broken heart and that he wasn't offering to mend it for her. In fact, he was offering to join the breaks in his to those in hers. He said Fate had broken his heart too and he wanted her so that he could taste the flavour of the beginning of things once more, because all he could taste now was the end.

Suddenly this rough-spoken man had become a mass of tenderness, but Hend hesitated all the same. She told her mother she was afraid of him

121

because he was so like his brother. She said he was Karim but with coarser features. "It's as though I've lived this moment before and heard these words, as though real isn't real."

Her mother smiled and said all men resembled one another in the end and marriage was a cup all women had to drink. "You have to marry, daughter."

"But I don't love Nasim, Mother."

"The one you don't love you come to love, and the one you love you come to hate. That's life."

"Alright, but why?"

"Don't make things complicated. See how it goes. It's better than sitting at home like a care on the heart. Plus, at least you'll get a child."

Hend worked as a secretary in the office of the ophthalmologist Said Haddad. Her mother had found her the job after the family's financial situation had become unbearable but Hend had been planning a different future for herself. She'd finished her degree in political science at the Lebanese University and wanted to find work befitting her aspirations. She dismissed the idea of trying to join the diplomatic corps because Mrs Salma had said she'd rather live with war than with the humiliation of life abroad. So Hend worked for an advertising company but after three months found herself incapable of coming up endlessly with slogans for washing powders. She thought of working for a government department but they weren't taking on new employees, not to mention that to get a position you needed the backing of one of the country's political leaders, none of whom she knew. In the end she agreed to work as a secretary at the ophthalmologist's where she discovered a world of slavery she hadn't believed still existed in this day and age. Her work was limited to recording the appointments of the patients and taking them in to see the doctor. True, she feared for her sight when faced with the horrible eye diseases she saw and with the idea of blindness that was ever present in the clinic, but in the end she got used to it and ceased to see, discovering that what mankind strives for is to not see. This is the secret of life: to get so used to things that you don't see them; then when you do lose your sight you discover the enormity of your loss – or so Nasri told her when he spoke to her of his horror of "the blue water", or cataracts, which devour the eye with their milky whiteness. Listening to her account of the world that she'd discovered in the ophthalmologist's clinic, Nasri had said things became important only when you lost them, "and I've lost everything or I'm about to. That's why everything now is important to me."

Nasim could understand nothing of what she was trying to tell him. She was announcing to her husband her categorical objection to the presence of a Sri Lankan or Asian maid in the house and Nasim was trying to persuade her to agree and provide a new model for how to treat maids, but she refused.

She tried to tell her husband about the world she'd seen at the ophthalmologist's clinic but he wouldn't listen. He claimed he was listening but in fact he was thinking about other things. Her problem with the man was that from the very beginning he'd refused to listen to her. He'd just kept nodding his head, so she'd found no way out of agreeing to the marriage.

He'd told her about his broken heart but hadn't mentioned Suzanne. He'd said his heart had been broken when the Jesuit had discovered his high marks were the result of deception, and he'd felt as though he'd been abandoned in the middle of the double world he inhabited with his brother.

"Karim did nothing. He saw how Father was torturing me and he just watched. I felt he was happy and enjoyed watching, like when kids take pleasure in torturing a lizard or a kitten and then I got it that he's not my twin and the idea of one person with four eyes was an illusion. The discovery of the illusion broke my heart and I ran away from home, maybe Karim told you."

"No, he didn't tell me. Karim never talked about you or your father. Where did you go?" she asked.

"It doesn't matter," he said. "There was a woman who took pity on me. She was a distant relative and she found me work in a restaurant."

"And then?"

"Then Father came to the restaurant and started crying in front of everyone. I was embarrassed and went back home."

"You slept at her place?"

"Of course. What, you think I should have slept on the street?"

"And was she pretty?"

"She was old enough to be my mother. She said, 'You're an orphan and I want to adopt you.'"

"And why did you go back with your father?"

"I don't know," he replied. "I didn't really think. I just saw him crying and went with him and found myself back home."

Nasim felt she didn't believe him but he went on with his lie. He couldn't retreat because he'd decided not to tell anyone about Suzanne. He'd promised her and he wouldn't go back on his word. When she'd repulsed him like that on the day he'd gone to visit her as agreed, he'd felt as though the air around him had been cut off, that he was surrounded by walls. He'd gone back to the flat and found his father waiting for him in front of a table resplendent with kibbeh nayyeh and local arak, the platter of kenafeh in the middle.

It hadn't occurred to Nasim that Karim could have given his secret away to his father. He thought Suzanne must have done it herself, because she was a prostitute and one couldn't trust a woman of that sort, and it was his mistake. When his brother confessed his betrayal to him, he felt the need to kill. He'd already discovered during the war that people possess only one instinct, which is to kill, and all other instincts branch out from that. You kill to eat, you kill to dominate, you kill to kill. The urge to kill had flashed out suddenly like lightning as he listened to his brother. Blood flashes in the eyes of killers – he'd seen it in his comrades' eyes – and when his blood had flowed, close to the Salam football ground in Ashrafieh, he'd been scared of both the blood and the eyes. He'd run to his father's flat shaking with fear and collapsed the instant he reached the door, his knees no longer able to support him.

Listening to his brother's confession, he'd felt the blood flash in his eyes. He said he'd kill him, lit a cigarette, dragged the smoke deep down his lungs to disperse the ghosts of killing, closed his eyes, and said he was joking. But he wasn't telling the truth then either.

Hend had told him his brother's phantom hadn't left her for the past four years and she thought it would be difficult for her to love another man.

"Can you agree to marry a woman who has loved another man?"

He smiled and didn't answer. He said he'd loved her since he first set eyes on her and hadn't stopped loving her even when she was going out with his brother. He said he'd retired from the field because he couldn't be involved in a rivalry with his twin, but now he would compete with her heart. "Your heart can't refuse my love because I love you from my heart."

Hend decided that the man didn't hear and discovered that other people don't hear either; that it's easier to see than to hear, because listening requires a kind of collusion with others. And she accepted him. She accepted him because she loved him, or so she thought. The whole thing seemed unreal to her, as though she was living in a dream and had rediscovered with Nasim something of the undulations that she had felt when in love with his older brother.

She said she didn't want a Sri Lankan maid because she couldn't forget the tears of the woman called Meena, who was in her early twenties, plump, lively, and full of the love of life. She would come every day to the clinic at 3 p.m. and give the doctor's food to Hend, who would take it to the side room where Dr Said would devour it in minutes before getting back to work.

Dr Said, who was sixty-five, was one of those rare doctors who believe in medicine. Usually doctors order their patients not to smoke and impose a special diet on them because of cholesterol and blood pressure but don't themselves stop smoking or devouring fatty foods or developing pot bellies. Dr Said was different. He followed his own advice because he didn't want to die. He told Hend he was a doctor and knew why people died, so he was going to close all doors in the face of death and live until he was fed up with life.

Hend couldn't understand how someone who had passed sixty could not be fed up with life. What was he waiting for, now that all waiting had ended? She'd got fed up before making it to twenty-five. Beirut was the city of boredom and despair, she told the doctor, "because the war keeps repeating itself endlessly and I'm sick of war."

The doctor told her he couldn't understand why she talked that way. "War's like life. Everything in life repeats itself but it's renewed or gives the impression of renewal. This is the secret of the seasons of nature, and the war too renews itself and its people and its slogans, as though it sums up all time. Modernity mixes in it with backwardness and to its rhythms we discover the meaning of history."

"I'm sick of myself," said Hend.

"There's the mistake," responded the doctor. "The secret of mankind is love. War gives us the illusion of history and the seasons give us the illusion of nature renewing itself, but love makes us live what is unique. We believe we're living something special and exciting that no-one but us has ever lived. It seems you're not in love, my dear, even though you're a cute little thing."

"Please, Doctor! No love, no worries!"

"You're wrong, Hend. Love and you'll see."

"But first I have to find Mr Right."

"What are you talking about?" said the doctor. "Love love and you'll see it can make anyone a Mr Right."

And that was how it was. Hend found herself loving love. Husky voices enchanted her and shining eyes intoxicated her. She was like someone sailing seas filled with surprises and discovered that her relationship with Karim had been practice for the love that awaited her.

In Nasim's disappointment at life she saw her own, in his troubles with his father an echo of her own interrupted childhood, and in his feelings of loneliness something of her own despair and frustration after her sad experience with Meena. She learned from him not to ask. When she asked him about his work he said he didn't want her to bother about such things and all she had to do was welcome his soul and his love and forget everything. Hend washed her new world in the waters of the sea. Nasim rented a chalet at the Beach Club pool which looked out over the Bay of Jounieh and sank with his beloved into the saltiness of the sea. He was a champion swimmer and she felt intoxicated whenever the water covered her brown body, which flashed in the sun.

Hend was amazed when Nasim didn't try to sleep with her during the long chalet days. He would sip kisses from her lips and play around with her but went no further. Hend had no objections, but she wasn't going to initiate matters. She was afraid of the savage look that drew itself over his eyes when he grew angry.

When they were on the verge of getting married he asked where she'd like to spend their honeymoon. He proposed going to the island of Crete, in Greece, but she refused. "The honeymoon will be at the chalet in Jounieh," she said.

He asked her why and she said she'd waited for the honey a long time at the chalet and wanted it nowhere else.

And when he slept with her for the first time he was overcome with amazement.

"So you're still a virgin!" he said wonderingly as he kissed her on her small brown breasts. He asked her about "him" but she didn't reply. He tried to speak but she silenced him by placing her hand over his mouth.

Once they were married Karim's name had disappeared from circulation. Nasim started referring to his brother in the third person, as "him". Hend understood that this "him" referred to her former lover. She didn't notice that things had changed fundamentally because she was busy with her pregnancy and the psychological and biological transformations that swept over her during the first three months. It was only after the birth of her first son Nadim that she discovered the man she was living with was a mere shadow of the man who had loved her at the chalet in Jounieh. She told him he'd changed. He said it was she who had changed. He didn't like to be asked where he was going or where he was travelling to or whom he spent his evenings with in Beirut. He said it was work and that they'd agreed she would have nothing to do with the subject. And when she asked him about the source of his growing wealth, he told her it would be better if she just spent the money and didn't ask how it was obtained. She asked him why he betrayed her with other women and he was furious. The savage look she feared came into his eyes and he told her never to ask him that question again.

Nasim had never told his wife, whom he loved, the secret reason for his refusal to make love to her during the year of passion in the chalet. She'd supposed he was avoiding it because he thought she'd slept with his brother and didn't want to open up a distance in their relationship.

That was true, but only in part. The truth was that he was bidding farewell to his old world with all its prostitutes, and in his innocent sex with Hend he'd found a way to cleanse himself. Then when he discovered Hend was still a virgin he was overcome by a kind of reverence towards her: he got up, went down on his knees before the bed on which she lay naked, and made the sign of the cross. Hend burst out laughing. "Do you think you're in church?" she asked. "You're a saint," he said. "Forget the saints and the fancy talk, he was a coward, that's all." He closed her mouth with his hand and asked her not to speak because her words were spoiling the aesthetic quality of the moment.

Nasim had decided to abandon the world of prostitutes and its depravity. He had severed his ties to the past and steeped himself in a love the like of which he hadn't tasted since his few days with Suzanne.

But without his knowing how or why he found life leading him by the nose. He justified things to himself at the beginning by saying it was part of his work. Work as a smuggler couldn't go right without the accessories. He told himself these were the necessities of his work and that no-one living in the night of the city and the alleyways of its wars could keep such a life at a distance.

This is not what he told Hend, because he was certain she'd think he was lying, and in fact he was. Or perhaps "lying" isn't appropriate, but Nasim didn't know how the title "liar" had attached itself to him. When your father, your teachers, and everyone else around you decides you are a liar you become one even when you're trying to tell the truth, because you don't believe yourself.

In one of her fits of anger she told him he'd never loved her and just wanted to take over his brother's bequest so he could prove to himself he was better than him and take a revenge proportionate to his childhood torments. Nasim had felt then that the woman wanted to break his heart. He couldn't answer because the words stuck in his throat. He remembered that he was supposed to spit the words, the way Suzanne had taught him, but refused to do so because he didn't want to give up on the woman.

He looked at her with defeated eyes and asked if she'd married him for love.

"Of course," she replied.

He felt she wasn't telling the truth but contented himself with her assertion. "If that's so then let's just love one another and don't ask about what I do at work or outside the house."

"But I want to understand what I mean to you."

"You're my wife, the mother of my children, and my life. Please don't let's get philosophical. I haven't changed. This is how I am, but that doesn't mean I don't love you."

"You're unfaithful to me and you love me? I don't understand."

"I'm not unfaithful."

"Why are you like that?"

"Why is there a war?" he replied.

He said, "Why is there a war?" and felt as though the voice was not his own, as though it was the voice of the man who had murdered his dreams and those of his comrades. Nasim had never had a chance to experience the intoxication of victory. The leader of the Phalangist militias had been elected president of the republic to the whine of the Israeli bombs that had set Beirut on fire, but then Bashir Gemayel had been killed in a huge explosion on 14 September, 1982. It was the Feast of the Cross. It had rained water and dust and Nasim remembered being afflicted with a kind of blindness. The dust had covered his face and eyes and he'd felt as though the world had come to an end.

But it had not. The killer had been detained and had stood before the interrogator, but instead of answering the question "Why did you kill Bashir?" he'd asked, "Why is there a war?"

From this Nasim had learned to answer one question with another. When you live in Beirut, or any other city in the Arab world, you have to adapt to the absence of answers and the discovery that every question leads to another question.

He'd said to Hend, "Why is there a war?" not because he didn't know the answer to her question but because that was the correct answer.

"What has the war got to do with our private lives?" she asked but didn't wait for an answer; she jumped directly to the conclusion and decided he'd deceived her.

She never said she was shocked when she discovered Nasim wasn't the twin she'd been waiting for, that he only resembled Karim superficially, and that she was going to have to live her whole life with her vanished illusion.

But Nasim heard what she hadn't said – or so she imagined when she saw the lopsided smile that sketched itself on his lower lip. He'd never claimed he was a copy. In fact, when his brother was mentioned in his presence, he'd say only one word: "coward". When his father complained that there was no news from his son and wondered how come he never asked how he was doing in the midst of the hell of war in Beirut, Nasim had said, "Your son's a dog and a coward. He ran away and he's making himself out to be a big shot because he married a blonde and speaks French."

"Anything but a Sri Lankan maid!" said Hend.

Nasim tried to persuade her, and Salma tried, but it was no use.

It was Salma who'd suggested the idea of the maid to Nasim. She'd said she was getting old and couldn't manage any longer.

"You persuade your daughter! The woman's driving me insane with those ideas of hers that she gets from God knows where."

This was how Ghazala made her entrance into the family's story. It was Imm Fu'ad who suggested Ghazala, but Hend decided to treat Ghazala as a friend and refused to allow her to work in the house like a maid. Imm Fu'ad had worked in Nasri's flat after Majdeh disappeared. To the boys she was just an elderly woman. She came three times a week, cleaned the house, did the wash, made the food, and disappeared. She was rarely seen. She came in the morning after everyone had left the flat and departed at 1 p.m., before they got back. She was the ghostly guardian who took care of everything without becoming part of their life. Nasri wanted to keep her outside the family. The Trinity, as he called himself plus the boys, had to remain independent and without external ties: "I didn't not marry just to have some strange woman come and share my children with me." He told his sons no-one must be allowed to break their circle. "One day you'll get married but don't ever let women come between us. You and your wife are your household but here it's us three till God sees fit to take us."

Nasri was unaware of what would in fact befall the Trinity. Time doesn't teach; it just kills and destroys. When Nasim came to tell him of his decision to marry Hend, Nasri started to shake with rage. The only words he could find to say to his second son were "Beware and again beware!" In Nasim's decision to marry Hend he saw something approaching a violation of taboos. "Even Cain and Abel weren't like that. Beware, my son!" But his rage was mixed with sorrow and he mumbled words his son couldn't make out.

When Karim had gone abroad his father had felt relief, for the business with Hend and her mother had to be excised from the family; carnal passions had to be kept outside the home. Salma was a carnal passion, and she had left. Nasri had suffered greatly at the ending of the relationship that had connected him to this white-skinned woman, and the bitterness would continue to dog him; and when, one day, he tried to go back to her he would discover he'd run headlong into a wall of illusion.

When Hend conceived her second child Nasim decided it was time to bring a maid into the house. He made all the arrangements without consulting his wife. He went to an office that imported Sri Lankan maids, where he discovered that such offices were a gold mine and the trade was a profit-maker on all fronts. He thought of expanding his own operations and opening an office of the same sort alongside his other commercial activities.

Two days before the woman reached Beirut he told his wife to get ready to welcome the maid. He was proud of himself because he'd managed an arrangement with the director of the employment office that was a good deal by any standards: he'd hired a forty-year-old woman who spoke Arabic well, having worked previously in Dubai, and who was the mother of four children.

Nasim was taken aback by Hend's categorical refusal.

"No way," said Hend. "It's a slave trade." Nasim tried to calm her down and Nasri intervened to say that the story of the Sri Lankan maids was very similar to that of the Lebanese at the beginning of their migration to America. It had begun, he said, at the end of the nineteenth century, with women. His mother's aunt was a case in point: she'd left her husband and three children in their village in Amioun, migrated to Boston, "and then she got the whole family out and was within an inch of getting my mother out. What sort of work do you think these Lebanese women did in America? Were they university teachers? Obviously not. They were maids. They went and they worked and they slaved and they made it and now the maids' grandsons and grand-daughters bring over servants and are all stuck up. One day, in about a hundred years, Sri Lankan women will start bringing over servants from other countries, and so it goes, it's the way of the world. Don't fret over it, my dear."

Hend refused to stop fretting and said no. How could she tell them that she couldn't forget Meena's face and her round belly?

"Meena messed up your mind," said Salma. "Who leaves a job over some Sri Lankan woman? And anyway, who can prove George is the boy's father? They're all prostitutes, my girl. I'm not saying anything but you know that migration and poverty break families down and they're women without countries or families. Prostitution becomes normal. It's always the same with the first generation of immigrants."

"So the Lebanese are all prostitutes?"

"What kind of talk is that, my girl? Is that how we talk now?"

"Well, all the Lebanese are immigrants. The ones who didn't migrate overseas migrated from their villages to Beirut."

"I didn't say it was so," said Salma. "I said it was possible."

"Take yourself, my dear Madam Salma. You ran away from the village with a man who wasn't your husband, so you can be sure that everyone says about you what you're saying about others."

"What sort of person talks to their mother like this?"

"And that's not all. I know and everyone else knows, so we'd better not say anything and let sleeping dogs lie."

Hend hadn't told her husband how her view of the world had changed because of Meena. She'd joined the Association for the Defence of Human Rights, which brought together activists, male and female, in defence of female foreign domestic workers in Lebanon. They'd put together an amazing amount of information on the ill treatment of Sri Lankan, Ethiopian, and Philippine women in Lebanon.

Still, Hend felt that she'd been at fault and it was too late because she'd been unable to do anything about it.

"It's idiocy," said Nasim as he looked at the picture of a child with a white complexion that Hend had taken out of her pocket book.

Hend was ready to admit that she'd been an idiot but she could never forgive George or his father, Dr Said Haddad.

The friendship between Hend and Meena had developed in the normal way. The Sri Lankan girl came each day carrying the doctor's meal, and when he finished she'd pick up the empty tiffin box and go back. The friendship grew in waiting and silence. The girl spoke little and when she did tried to pronounce the English and Arabic words properly, not the way people here in Lebanon think Sri Lankans speak.

Hend asked her which city she was from and she said Colombo.

She asked why she was working as a maid in Lebanon and the girl smiled and didn't know how to reply.

With Meena's daily visits to the clinic, though, Hend came to understand that the girl had been unable to complete her studies at teachers' college because of her father, who suffered from partial paralysis. This had forced him to stop working in his small fabric shop and she'd had to come to Lebanon because her mother, brothers, and sisters had found themselves with no-one to provide for them.

"I decided to study Arabic, madam."

"My name is Hend. Don't call me madam."

"Yes-madam," said Meena and burst out laughing.

In Meena Hend discovered the mystery of the east. Listening to her story of the mountain on whose summit Adam had left his footprints she'd said to her, "The real east is there. We're not in the east, we're in the middle, which is why we live in a state of confusion over our identity. You're the real east." And she said she'd like to visit India and Ceylon.

"We're not east either, madam. Whole world become West, all of us imitating all of us, which is why sun sets and you don't know where it's going to rise."

Through Meena Hend discovered a world fenced about with secrets and bitter experiences. She began to notice the theatre of balcony friendships and how the maids who lived at the backs of buildings with closed doors went out onto balconies where they communicated in sign language for fear that their mistresses might notice, because they were forbidden to speak.

"What about you?"

"I'm different. Mr George not let Madam take passport and close door and he say this not humane. Meena's a human being. If she wants to leave work she can go but of course Meena not leave. When it was war with Israel we stayed in the flat. The doctor not able to leave work. Then suicides begin. Mr George say to the doctor we must go. We went to Brummana. Brummana very nice. I wished we stayed."

In 1982 people left Beirut to escape the Israeli invasion and left the maids behind in locked flats, thinking they wouldn't be away long. However, the siege and shelling of Beirut lasted three whole months, resulting in a tragedy when five maids killed themselves by throwing themselves off balconies before the fighters could force the doors to the flats.

Meena spent a large part of the war in Brummana because Mr George said life in Beirut had become intolerable.

"Who's this Mr George?" Hend asked.

Meena's long neck swayed and a smile sketched itself on her lips before she answered that he was the doctor's only son: he had studied law and was a gentleman.

When Meena phoned Hend and asked her to meet her outside the clinic, Hend invited her to meet her at Chez Jean in Ashrafieh. Hend arrived at 8 p.m. to find Meena standing on the pavement outside the café, waiting for her. Meena said she'd arrived early but the waiter had thrown her out. "This is a respectable establishment," he'd said. "We don't let in your kind."

"Don't be upset," Hend had said. "Walk home with me."

At home Meena had told her story. She said she'd come to say goodbye because she was going back to her country and wanted to ask her about that ten thousand dollars that the doctor had offered her, and to tell her that she was at a loss and didn't know what to do.

"We have to take them to court. Are you certain that George is the baby's father?"

"*Yes-madam.*"

"Don't keep saying 'madam' and stop talking in Sri Lankan, please!"

Meena smiled and said that the Sri Lankan women called that way of talking "Lebanese", and the way their mistresses talked to them made them laugh.

Meena told her story. Hend listened and could scarcely believe her ears. She said it was an old story and it would be better to get rid of the baby. She looked at Meena, saw the small foetus curled up inside her belly, and told the girl she was a donkey. "Why did you let him make a fool of you and sleep with you?"

In the summer of 1982, as Beirut, moaning with thirst and flowing with blood, writhed beneath the Israeli shelling, Meena discovered the virtues of pomegranates and lived in a sort of coma until a pomegranate seed turned into a foetus in the guts of the girl from Colombo.

The story didn't resemble those of the maids who are raped in Egyptian films. Meena insisted she hadn't been raped and that now she was paying the price but that she felt humiliated because George hadn't just abandoned her, he'd run away. The mistress said he'd gone to America to pursue his studies at Harvard University.

"I left the flat yesterday and went to live with my friend Mali in Sadd el-Bushriyeh."

"We'll bring a case and force them to acknowledge the child," said Hend.

Hend had only convinced Meena with difficulty of the necessity of staying in Beirut and bringing a court case against George because the girl didn't want anything, or didn't know what she wanted.

"The bastard left you and ran off. He has to pay the price."

Hend didn't know how Meena had found out that George hadn't run away, that he'd wanted her up to the last moment but could do nothing because he was afraid his father might die. They'd quarrelled, George saying he didn't know what he was supposed to do and the father yelling that the maid must be forced to get an abortion. Suddenly Dr Said had fainted and fallen to the floor. He was taken to the hospital, where the doctor diagnosed a stroke and said Dr Said would have to take care of his health.

The doctor in charge of the case looked at George and said, "Your father's an old man and you have to keep an eye on him. The worst thing for someone with a heart problem is getting upset. Be careful no-one lets that happen."

Meena said love had taken her by surprise. The Sri Lankan girl who had found herself compelled to work as a maid in Lebanon had arrived in Beirut without any idea of what it meant to live in a city torn apart by war.

She'd gathered that it was better to go to Lebanon than to the Gulf States. The domestic workers' contractor in Colombo had said Lebanon was better even with the war, and when she asked about the war she was told it was like the war of the Tamil Tigers in her own country. From this she understood that Beirut was like Colombo – the war affected only its most far-flung splinters. But they'd lied to her: the war was in the heart of Beirut, and the Lebanese may well treat their maids worse.

Meena arrived at Beirut airport to find that maids were treated like cattle. No sooner had she got off the plane than the Sri Lankan women were told to gather and put in a closed room. A soldier came, took everyone's passports, and told them not to talk. She found herself in a small room like a prison cell where she remained for about two hours. Then an officer carrying a cane in his hand came and started reading out names. When a young woman heard her name she followed the motion of the officer's cane and went to stand in front of the door to the room. In the end the officer had read out the names of all the women in the room and led them outside, where they found three contractors waiting for them, two men and a lady, waving their passports. Meena stood there not knowing what to do. She looked at the officer and asked him about her passport; his answer was a blow with his cane on the back of her neck and a loud laugh. She stopped in her tracks and he gave her another blow with the stick and said something in Arabic. Meena looked at him as though stunned and burst into tears. She saw a man waving a passport and running towards her. He grabbed her hand and took her out to the baggage area. She took her suitcase and found herself stuffed with other maids into a pick-up which took them to an office.

She spent her first night in a closed room resembling the one at the airport and in the morning the white-haired man opened the door and she heard her name. She went out of the room, which had filled with the smell of sweat, and breathed air for the first time. And her mistress was waiting for her.

The man had asked for her passport and pointed to her mistress, who nodded her head and said, "*Yalla, yalla!*" It was the first Arabic word she learned. The mistress spoke to her in a strange kind of English which had no trace of verbs, so that she'd say "*passport with me*" and gesture with her hand towards her chest. Meena answered that she wanted to keep her passport but the mistress insisted on speaking to her in that strange language, saying the conditions of the contract stipulated that the passport stay with her; she would give it back to Meena when the contract was over and she wanted to go back to her country. She made a gesture like a bird beating its wings to clarify the idea.

The bizarre world that Meena had entered quickly started to fall into place. The mistress continued to treat her with arrogance, but the doctor was kind and so was his son. She discovered that things weren't as bad as they seemed because she was lucky compared to the friends from whom she learned the language of the balconies.

Meena learned Arabic from the television and began leaving the flat daily to take food to the doctor, and she built herself a world out of waiting. She made a hundred dollars a month, seventy of which she sent to her family and the rest of which she saved, spending nothing on herself. She supposed that after five years, when she'd be twenty-four, she'd return to her country with about 1,500 dollars. She'd join the teachers' college again, study for three years, graduate as a teacher of English, and get married.

In five years her brother would be twenty and he'd have to find work and take over responsibility for the family. She'd decided therefore to go on studying English in Beirut and to learn Arabic too.

She told Hend her situation was different and she meant it.

The difference she was referring to wasn't attributable simply to the doctor's kindness and sympathy but because she'd been able to impose her presence on the family. She became the household's "little mistress", as George called her. She cooked all the Lebanese dishes, cleaned the flat, and took care of everyone. Even the mistress came to like her, though she insisted on continuing to talk Sri Lankan English with her while holding her nose, which had shrunk following unsuccessful cosmetic surgery, up high, as though she smelled something bad.

Meena couldn't recall George being present in her life at all. The young man would leave the flat in the morning and not get back until night. Meena rarely saw him in the flat. Dr Said joked with her about how beautiful she was and would say she'd arrived ten years too late. "If you'd come ten years ago I would have been in trouble, but now *no*. The engine's kaput and gone rusty, my dear, and it's all down to age and the madam."

Meena had imposed her presence and felt as though her loneliness in this strange city and her dealings with the Lebanese, who behaved as though they were the most refined nation in the world even though they spent all their time cutting each other's throats, were the desert she must cross in order to discover herself, as her blind grandmother had taught her.

She met other girls from her country only on Sunday, when she went to the church of St Francis. Meena wasn't a Christian but church was her only way of meeting colleagues. She was convinced that prayer meant contemplation of the self, that the Buddha was manifest everywhere, and that she would find repose in the burning candles fragrant with incense.

Each Sunday she returned to the flat feeling sad after having listened to stories of oppression, torment, and even rape. She felt she'd fallen into a trap and there was nothing she could do about it. At church she also met a group of young Lebanese men and women who would come from time to time and ask how the maids were, promising them help. Meena realised there was a barrier inside every Lebanese person that prevented all empathy and recognition of the other. Hatred exists everywhere and she remembered the terror she'd felt in Colombo. The same terror, the same war.

Meena knew all this and felt it deep inside her, so what had happened to put her in this quandary?

Hend said Dr Said had put on a show for his son. "You think you can tell me anything about him? I know him inside out, he's the biggest play actor in the world. All the time he's putting on an act for his patients and pretending to be sicker than they are when actually he's as healthy as a monkey."

"*No-Madam*, I know him. I just don't know why he did that."

"What *I* want to know," said Hend, "is why *you* did that."

The sun was setting behind the pine trees and Meena was standing alone on the balcony of the Brummana house. She could see a bo-tree in the midst of the forest. She could hear the tree speak in the wind that blew through its branches. She felt like going down from the balcony to the tree and asking it to rid her ears of the sound of lamentation that filled the skies of Beirut. She saw her grandmother sitting beneath the holy tree looking at her and making sounds that Meena couldn't hear. Her grandmother had said that the sound of the wind in the bo-tree leaves was the voice of the dead. "The dead never leave us. They talk to us through the sounds of the branches, they care about us, and they teach us what to do."

Meena heard the voices of the dead and saw the water. She didn't understand what had happened to her in Lebanon. She'd felt lonely, as though she'd gone deaf. Arabic, which she had tried to learn, was intractable and closed, and the English she used to know had begun to fade away into that strange linguistic mix her mistress used in her dealings with her. So she sought refuge in water. She spent so much time washing and scrubbing the house that she made the mistress angry. It was true that the building where Dr Said lived had an electric generator and an artesian well but the mistress lived in a state of constant terror at the idea of the city running out of water. Meena therefore exploited the times when the mistress was out of the house to shower and play with water, especially on the large wide balcony.

The obsession with cleanliness, with twice-daily showers, and with picking everything up to wash made Dr Said laugh. He saw in it repressed desires and told his wife to leave the girl alone, saying "when the well runs dry we'll decide what to do."

This woman of water and soap hated Lebanese food and found herself without a sense of taste. She'd learned to cook all the different Lebanese dishes but for herself she cooked her own food, mixed with spices, hot pepper, and the flavour of life. She couldn't fathom the attitude of her mistress, who, as soon as she smelled the food that Meena was preparing in a corner of the large kitchen, would hold her nose and open the windows, screaming, "*Windows! Open windows!*" in the maid's face.

When the doctor decided to go up to Brummana to escape the inferno of the Israeli invasion, Meena felt a terrible sense of estrangement. Something had changed in these Lebanese who had fled the sound of shells in Beirut for the mountain resort, which soon was teeming with people. She no longer liked leaving the house because the comments people made on the streets were full of racism, and in the eyes of the young men she could read hatred and rapine.

She told Khawaja George she was afraid.

In Brummana she'd begun to get to know George, the doctor's only son, who kept to the house, read the newspapers, and smoked incessantly.

She'd thought she was alone in the house when she was surprised to find George entering the kitchen, carrying some pomegranates.

"What's that strange smell?" said George.

"I'm cooking, mister."

"It smells like Indian food and I like Indian food."

He asked her to put a little of the food on a plate for him and said it tasted good.

He gave her the pomegranates and asked her to seed them.

"Be careful you don't let a single seed fall on the floor because every pomegranate contains within it one of the seeds of the pomegranates of paradise," he said. He said the people of that country had once worshipped the god of love, whose name was Ramoun and who lived in the pomegranate trees.

She finished seeding the pomegranate, put the red seeds into a glass bowl, and took it out to the balcony where he was sitting.

"That day, he saw me," said Meena. She told Hend that she'd felt how his eyes had seen her and that he'd put his hand on her cheek and told her she was beautiful.

"And after that you slept with him?" asked Hend. "God, what a silly goose!"

"*No-Madam.* After, nothing."

She said he'd asked her what perfume she used and she'd smiled and answered that she wore water perfume. She asked him if he could smell the water and he replied that water didn't have a smell and burst out laughing. Meena laughed too and said the scent of water could be detected only on people's bodies, and that the only real scent was the scent of people. She said her grandmother had told her people were created from mud and water, and that their original smell was the smell of soil moistened with rain.

Meena said everything had happened at the Feast of the Cross. The Feast of the Cross that fell on 14 September, 1982, arrived weighed down with the rain of sorrow. On that day Bashir Gemayel, leader of the Christian militia allied with Israel, who had become president of the Republic of Lebanon, was killed. Brummana looked haggard and black. People stood in the roads, stunned. She heard Dr Said tell his son that he'd been expecting this outcome. George wept as he said that the dream was dead.

Three days later Lebanon was full of corpses. After seeing the pictures of the massacre on the television Meena said she wished she was blind because all she could see in front of her was dead bodies. The doctor had carried a copy of *al-Safir* and was beside himself. The pictures of the massacre at the Palestinian camps of Shatila and Sabra filled the front page of the newspaper, and that evening the whole family watched the news. Meena was sitting on the floor in a corner of the living room trying to understand what the television was saying, and when she started to understand some of the words that traced themselves over the bloated corpses she got up and ran to her room, where she burst into tears and started banging her head against the wall. George fidgeted in his chair and wanted to get up and go after her but Dr Said was the first to enter her room and see the blood. The doctor took the woman in his arms, embracing her flowing tears. George reached the room and didn't understand when he saw blood on his father's shirt. He went over to them, led Meena by the hand to the bathroom, and washed the cuts on her head. The cuts weren't serious, just grazes.

George spoke to her but she didn't answer. She left him and went to her room.

That night George knocked on Meena's door. She knew it was him but she hesitated. When she opened it he hugged her to his chest. The smell of alcohol wafted from his mouth and he looked like a lost child. He pulled her towards the bed. She said no, then yielded to his kisses.

Meena couldn't remember what happened after that. She said George talked but she didn't understand exactly what he was trying to say. She said he was angry because she hadn't told him she was a virgin but he put his head on her neck and held her to himself for a long time before leaving her room at two in the morning.

Meena said she didn't blame George. "It was my fault," she said.

"That was it?" asked Hend.

Meena nodded her head.

"So you only slept with him once?"

The girl was silent and didn't answer.

"You slept with him a lot. I bet he made a fool of you and told you he loved you."

"*No, madam.* No fool. He never say the word but he say I make him crazy and he wish."

"He wished what?"

"I don't know," said Meena. "I'm mistake. I loved him and I still love him but it's over."

Three and a half months later Meena went to the doctor to be sure her misgivings were right and that the interruption of her period was not due to psychological tension, as the social worker whom she met at the church had told her. She wasn't unhappy. She immediately decided to get rid of the foetus and went back to the house.

She didn't tell George she was pregnant, she just told him straightaway that she'd decided to get rid of the foetus and wanted his help in finding a doctor to carry out the abortion. George didn't open his mouth. He put his head in his hands and said, "It's wrong." She asked him to get her an early appointment with the doctor, left him in the living room, and went to her room. She heard his footsteps outside the door but he didn't knock. She closed her eyes and tried to sleep.

Two days later George came to her room at night and she was waiting for him. He sat on the edge of the bed and said he loved her. She said this wasn't the time for being emotional and asked him about the doctor. He said he'd made her an appointment with a doctor who worked at the

Greek Orthodox hospital and he'd take her there the day after next at 9 a.m. "No," she said, "I'm going to go alone. You shouldn't have to go through that," and she asked him the doctor's name.

At Dr Salim Hamid's clinic the surprise that no-one had expected occurred. The doctor was kind but after he finished the examination he said he was sorry but couldn't perform the operation because the foetus was in the fourth month and it would be murder and a sin. "I can't. I apologise. Go to someone else, maybe they'll do it, but not me."

At that moment Meena decided to keep the child. She returned to the flat exhausted and nauseous. She heard the mistress scream, "Where were you?" while telling her to get lunch ready because Dr Said had invited some of his friends over, but she didn't answer. She went to her room and closed her eyes.

She spoke only to George, who came home late, confident that the doctor would have performed the abortion. When he heard his mother yelling to say the maid was refusing to come out of her room he told her to calm down and went to her. Meena told him she was going to keep the baby, whatever happened.

"Be patient. Maybe I can find another doctor to do the abortion."

"I don't want to kill the child, I'm going to keep it. I know I should have been careful. I don't know what happened, I felt very queasy but I didn't take care of things. It's my responsibility, it's nothing to do with you. It's my child and I won't let anyone kill it."

This was the turning point that led to the bitterness. Had he said he could do nothing, had he washed his hands of the whole business, she would have understood and been understanding, but instead he sat next to her on the bed.

And when George left the room he found his parents waiting for him in the living room. He told them Meena was pregnant. He didn't know what he was supposed to do. It was his fault.

The family was seized by a fit of madness. There were screams and threats. The mistress swore she would kill herself and the father said an abortion was the only solution because if she didn't get one it would be a death sentence for the whole family. He tried to convince Meena to accept the principle of an abortion but was taken aback by her adamant refusal.

When Dr Said suffered a stroke, however, everything changed. George disappeared into the hospital with his father because he refused to leave him even for an instant, and when the patient came home George was no longer with him.

The mistress passed the information on to the maid. "George has gone to Harvard and he'll be there for four years. You'll have to get your things together and go. We've had nothing but trouble from you."

Dr Said tried to convince Meena to go through with an abortion. He said he knew all the doctors and would take her to the best.

Meena refused, and Dr Said's last offer was $10,000 provided she left Lebanon immediately.

"Tomorrow I don't want to see your face," the mistress said.

"Tomorrow evening I'll bring you the money and the ticket and you'll leave the day after," said Dr Said.

"Never! No way!" said Hend. "You can stay with me if you don't have a place to sleep and tomorrow I'll go to the association. We'll hire a lawyer, bring a case, and smash them to pulp."

Later Meena would write to Hend to tell her she'd been wrong. "The decision to bring a case was a mistake and there was no need for it."

Meena returned to her employers' flat. She got her things together without saying a word of farewell. From then on things moved fast. The lawyer from the Association for the Defence of Human Rights brought a case against Advocate George Haddad and his father Dr Said Haddad and Dr Said brought a case against the maid, accusing her of defaming him and his son. Meena was summoned to the Palace of Justice where the judge issued a decision that she be detained pending interrogation. Two days later Hend went with the lawyer to visit Meena at Roumieh Prison, only to discover that a decision had been issued by General Security for her deportation; she'd been deported from Lebanon the next day on board Air Lanka flight 420, destination Colombo via Dubai.

The story didn't end there. Hend left her job at the clinic and had a nervous breakdown. Meena for her part wrote a letter to Hend six months later in which she told her she'd given birth to a beautiful boy and had wanted to call him Ramoun but everyone there referred to him as Baby Lebanon, and she was going to marry a young man who worked as a tuk-tuk driver; everyone there loved the boy; she was sad only for her heart and because George would never see his son.

Meena contented herself with sending a picture of the boy to Hend who, though Meena had asked for nothing, took the picture to Dr Said's clinic. The moment he saw her he put his hand over his heart and doubled up, groping for a chair.

"Cut the play-acting," yelled Hend. "Do you take me for an idiot?"

The doctor took his hand off his chest, stood up straight, and in a shaky voice ordered Hend to get out of the clinic.

What Meena's letter hadn't said was that when she was being led in handcuffs to the plane she'd caught sight of a ghost standing in the distance, watching her. Meena was sure the ghost was George.

Hend gave an implacable "no" to the presence of a Sri Lankan maid in her house. "I don't want a maid, Sri Lankan or anything else. I don't want anyone to help me with the housework. Aren't I already a maid myself? What for? What don't I already have? I've got nothing to do all day except sit at home and wait. At least this way I keep myself occupied."

Hend hated herself. She went to the offices of the human rights N.G.O. and resigned. She told May Nashawati, the president, that she hated herself and hated N.G.O.s. "I'm a liar and you're liars. I believed myself when I was browbeating the doctor and reassuring Meena but it's impossible to work in a society based on lies and crime. Our role was to paper over the lie with a worse lie to quieten our consciences, and look at the disaster."

Hend was crushed when she left the association's headquarters. She felt as though her voice had been strangled and she could no longer walk. She felt dizzy and nauseous.

"The doctor must be telling everyone I'm a fool now," she told her mother when she got home, but Salma had no mercy on her daughter. She reminded her of what she'd told her when Hend had returned, so proud of herself, to recount the events of her last meeting with the doctor.

Hend had entered the doctor's office and said she wanted a word with him.

Dr Said looked up from the papers in front of him. "Nothing wrong, I hope, my dear?"

"I've come to tell you I've decided to leave the job because I can't work with you after what's happened."

"Why? What's happened?"

"Meena!" she said.

"What?" replied the doctor, in a shaky voice.

"I'm a member of the Association for the Defence of Human Rights and we've hired Advocate Iskandar Lahham to take on the case."

"You?"

"That's why I can't go on working for you. I won't work for racists who have no mercy and exploit people."

Hend turned to go. The doctor leapt up and grabbed her by the wrist. "No, I won't let you go till you've heard what I have to say."

"I'll hear it in court," she said. "It's my fault for believing you were ill. I believed you and worried about you and then I realised it was all a show put on to kill Meena and the child in her belly and blackmail your son and force him to go abroad."

The doctor stood up, trembling, put his hand on his heart, and said in a croak that he'd never forgive her. "You're like a daughter to me, Hend. Why are you talking to me like this?"

All Hend could remember of what she would refer to as "the doctor's ravings" were the words "the black child". The word "black" emerged from between his lips and she saw tar smeared over his tongue and mouth and felt disgusted. He was pretending to bewail his bad luck because he had only that one son: "It would mean ruin, my dear. How could he live in Beirut with a woman of that type? We'd be a laughing-stock. And anyway what did I do to God that I should have a black grandson?"

Hend told her mother that when she heard the word "black" she turned on her heel and slammed the door behind her.

"But the doctor's right. I'd have done the same in his place," Salma had said. "Suppose it had been you. I would have died."

Hend went home that day with her shoulders drooping, despondent and filled with sorrow, but Salma showed no mercy, even reproaching her for losing a job over a stupid point of principle that was no use to anyone. "A maid's a maid and always will be, that's how I see things."

It was in the midst of this sorrow, amounting almost to a nervous breakdown, that the relationship between Hend and Nasim began gradually to slide. Nasim laid out before her a carpet of words. She told him she felt as though she was sliding on soap. "Your words are like soap, and I'm going to start slipping."

"Slip away and don't worry about it. I'll catch you."

"But it's soap and the soap's not real."

"Come, don't be scared of my words or the soap."

"What should I be scared of?" she asked.

"Be scared that I'm unfaithful, though I could never be unfaithful."

He spoke to her of the betrayals that surrounded him on every side and said with her he felt safe.

"But I think it's hard to love you, I don't know why."

"Nothing's hard," he said and invited her to go swimming with him at the chalet, and she went.

Hend hadn't known how to tell Nasim how it had been between her and his brother. She said she couldn't talk about the subject because it made her feel unfaithful. "It's as though I were betraying him, even though it was he who left me."

Nasim told her not to feel guilty as he was the guilty party, if there was a guilty party.

She said no more – not because she was convinced of his point of view but because love stories seem ridiculous to those who didn't live them.

Nasim was holding a bunch of white Maghdousheh grapes. He asked her whether she liked grapes and said laughingly that grapes were the fruit of love.

She took a grape from the bunch and said she'd thought pomegranates were the fruit of love.

"That was a long time ago," he said, and explained to her how low pomegranates had fallen. "In the old days pomegranates stood for a woman's breasts and when a lover spoke words of love to his beloved he would liken her breasts to pomegranate fruit. Do you know what we mean today when we say 'pomegranate'? A pomegranate is a hand grenade. See how the pomegranate has fallen from the throne of love and become part of the war? Also, in the old days, my dear Madam Hend, pomegranates were considered the acme of fruit, whereas now they've

disappeared from people's tables and they use the juice to make pomegranate treacle, and pomegranate treacle is something sour to go with
small fried birds."

He said pomegranates were finished and the only people who gave
them any respect were a few romantics who wept false tears of love.

"But I know a love story that happened because of pome-granates."

"The lover must have been a liar or a con man and the girl a
nincompoop."

"You're right," said Hend. She took the bunch of grapes with its shiny
white spheres and started to devour them.

The story of the Sri Lankan maid ended with Nasim selling the maid
he'd brought to Beirut to his friend and partner Antoine Sebai, a deal on
which he made a thousand dollars, at which point it occurred to him that
this was an easy and amusing trade. In the end, though, he decided to
keep out of it lest the last remaining thread connecting him with his wife
be broken. Hend refused to agree to let even Ghazala come more than
once a week. Then, after six months, she decided to dispense with her
services altogether.

Why could Hend no longer understand his language?

He told her she'd known everything from the beginning, during the
days at the chalet, and been happy with his lifestyle. He'd told her everything without telling her anything but she'd understood what he was up
to, of that Nasim was certain. If not, then what did it mean when a
woman told you she loved you?

Nasim was certain of one thing – that he wanted this woman, whatever
the cost. He'd made major changes in his life for her sake and divorced
cocaine. How to explain to someone who's never tried sniffing the white
powder what it means to abandon your nose and lose your appetite and
feel as though you're as heavy as a stone and unable to move your limbs,
and then be frozen like a statue, waiting for the desire to evaporate, by
which time you've turned into something as stiff as a plank of wood?

Cocaine was king of the tables in those days. It was manufactured in
Wadi el-Shirbin, a remote village on the slopes of Sannine. Antoine Sebai,
who headed the militia in Beirut, asked Nasim to join him as pharmacist.
They brought in experts from Colombia and Turkey and started making

cocaine and heroin. God looked kindly on their efforts: cocaine was a guest at young people's tables throughout the war. Nasim, despite amassing a large fortune from his activities, decided to pull out after the killing of Antoine, who was found incinerated in his car. Nasim realised then that he couldn't challenge the big fish, and that the drugs game was directly tied to the militia's leadership.

Nasim bent with the wind because he'd learned that the civil war was a bending game, and once you start bending it becomes a way of life. Nasim wasn't a coward, but he'd discovered early on that the game wasn't worth dying for. He'd seen death in his own blood when he bled, and then the news of Michel Hajji's death had come and paralysed his capacity for thought. He'd been lying in bed at his father's flat when Robert Hayek had arrived soaking from the rain and brought the news. Nasim had been struck speechless. He pulled himself together and went, dragging his injured leg behind him, to the Greek Orthodox hospital where the body, shredded by bullets and wrapped in a white sheet, had been deposited in the morgue. Nasim looked at Michel's face and found it unrecognisable. The features had been almost erased, as though all dead people look alike. He bent over his friend's brow and kissed it and was taken aback by the smell of death and the taste of sponge.

Nasim had asked, "Are you sure this is Michel?" and not waited for an answer.

"That's not him," he said, retreating, fighting to overcome an insistent urge to vomit. He bent over next to the wall to be sick but couldn't. His guts were torn up and he emitted croaking sounds. Robert went over to him and patted him on the back. "Let's get out of here," he said. Nasim followed without objecting, saying nothing and feeling fear. He couldn't explain clearly to Hend what lay behind this fear. How could he tell her he'd been afraid of the body because he hadn't been able to recognise it? How could he explain why he'd found himself unable to go on fighting? Robert promised he'd get him into the B.G. Squad, the elite Phalangist military force that was later to become the scourge of the civil war. Nasim was proud of the proposal because it would prove his ability and talents to everyone beyond doubt. Before Michel's corpse, however, his strength collapsed. He saw himself laid out in the cold locker and imagined Nasri standing in front of the body, wanting to vomit, and he felt the humiliation of death.

"The humiliation of death, my dear sweet Hend," he said, "is the very essence of humiliation. That's why when a person wants to die he has to get away from people and surrender himself to nature and die alone and not let anyone see his corpse. But the humiliation of death catches up with everyone and no-one can escape it because we have to be buried and that's where the tragedy lies."

Hend looked at him in astonishment. Where did such talk, which had no context, come from? She told him she was used to not understanding when he spoke, so she expected nothing from him, but she did want to know exactly what he did for a living.

Was Hend afraid of Nasim as she claimed to his face? Or did she feel pity for him, as she told her mother?

"A man, my dear, is nothing to be afraid of. Men are to be pitied. Poor things, forced all the time to prove that they're men!"

In this woman Nasim saw the new beginning for which he'd been waiting. He told her he'd always loved her and he hadn't been lying because from the very first time he met her, at the entrance to the pharmacy, he'd been conscious of the frisson of mystery that radiated from her dainty brown face and slim body. Hend was not short, as her stooped walk might give one to believe, but somehow, with her flat-heeled mules and simple long dress whose colour she was always changing but of which the cut was always the same, with her knees that she clasped to her chest when she sat at her ease and her wandering glances which never came to rest on anything in particular, she resembled a creature that slid over things. He'd stood next to her on the pavement and made her laugh. He didn't remember what he'd said or why she'd laughed but she'd said he was "sweet, and funny", so he decided it was her. He invited her to a coffee and she said she couldn't because she was waiting for her mother who had dropped by the pharmacist's to buy the famous plant potion. He asked for her phone number and she smiled without answering. Then, when he'd seen the love in his brother's eyes, Nasim had gone back on his decision and made up his mind not to get into a conflict from which he would emerge, as usual, the loser.

The story wasn't just one of hare-brained revenge, as Nasri claimed when announcing his adamant opposition to the marriage.

"You're going to come with me to ask for her hand whether you like it or not and don't you dare play the arsehole the way you have all your life."

"I'm against this marriage," screamed Nasri.

"You'll do what I tell you or you know what'll happen."

"Nothing happened," Nasim told Hend. "He came and paid you all a visit like a good boy and asked your mother for your hand."

"But why was your father so absolutely against the marriage? It was terrible, how his jaw dropped, as though he couldn't speak. Even though my thing with your brother was old and well in the past."

"He said it was because Karim and I were going to end up like Cain and Abel."

"What a thing to say! You mean he was plotting for you to kill one another?"

"No, what he was afraid of was that I'd kill my brother. He thought of me as Cain. That's what he screamed as he pulled the bullet out of my leg. He said, 'If you think you're Cain, I'll kill you before you can kill you brother.'"

What had seemed like a passing misunderstanding between Hend and her husband because of her refusal to allow a maid into their house quickly opened up all the other wounds that she'd thought had healed in the course of the love story she'd lived with Nasim during the year of the chalet, which she thought of as "the year of the grapes". She had no idea where Nasim managed to find grapes at all four seasons of the year; it was something of a miracle in a city closed off by civil war. He told her he imported the grapes from South America especially for her. "Here it's winter and there it's summer. I can bring summer in wintertime. That's the philosophy of trade, and this is love, which makes a summer of all our days."

At the chalet they swam at all four seasons and all four seasons had the same name – "the mending of hearts". Over these seasons, fashioned from the grapes of desire, Hend learned to love herself. The waves of the sea turned into intermeshing mirrors reflecting her face and body, and

Nasim's eyes, which looked at her with rapture, were transformed into windows onto her broken soul.

Following Meena's deportation, everything had looked ugly. She couldn't bear to look in the mirror. She came to see her face as a mask she couldn't take off. She hated her short hair, which fell over her eyes in front and filled them with shadows, and she no longer loved her dainty body or her way of walking with such short steps that an onlooker might have thought she was about to fall over. Hend decided she wanted to get rid of her name, her eyes, and her hair, and that she was capable of dying.

"You're right," she told him. "The two broken hearts have met. Come, let us get married."

They married at that crucial moment that Nasim had designated "walking the knife's edge". His withdrawal from the world of drugs had left a taste like sawdust in his mouth. He'd found himself alone, stripped of the protection Antoine had guaranteed. The climate which had created the impression that white powder could cover over blood, and that the blending of red and white made money flow like water, had dissipated.

It is hardly true, as novelists say, that wars create a climate of solidarity among people. Wars turn a person into an isolated being, a monster living among monsters, listening only to the howling of the wolves surrounding him on every side. Nasim lived in loneliness and fear. The illusion of the cocaine laboratory had dissolved, all his projects had collapsed, and he found himself having to start from zero. And at zero he met Hend and saw her afresh. He told her that, when she appeared in front of him, he'd felt as though the mist had cleared. Everything had appeared as though covered with a sort of milky colour and he'd thought that cataracts, "the blue water", had come to him early – as though his father's curse had afflicted him with premature blindness. Hend laughed and said the Arabs called it "the white water" while the Greeks had named it "the yellow water", but what he was claiming was unfounded because when working at the ophthalmologist's clinic she'd often seen the mark of the disease on people's pupils and there was nothing like that in his eyes.

At the beginning he'd played the "blue water" game with her. He'd felt alone, life seemed meaningless, and the phantom of his twin brother, who had become a doctor in France, had appeared before him. So he decided to play at love with this timid brown girl whose skin shone in the sun and revealed glimpses of a beauty filled with diffidence. Revenge on his successful brother was no longer on his mind, or so at least he believed and so he tried to explain to her when the angry mask drew itself on his face in reaction to her hurtful words.

Love had come in the midst of the fever of work. Nasim had re-established himself using the money made from his former trade, and within two years had turned himself into a timber, iron, and petrol merchant. He imported building materials and laughed up his sleeve. He hated the war yet wanted it to go on because it was his only source of livelihood. He smuggled and made money and lived like a king.

He told Hend he loved her but that his work required her indulgence. No, he didn't work in prostitution, as she had accused him of doing. All that had happened was that he'd gone to the souk while the shells were falling and rescued Suzanne and put her in a flat in the Badawi district, on the edges of Ashrafieh, and started supporting her financially – as any son with a mother whom he had found only after a long absence would have done.

But Hend didn't want to understand. She spent her time at home with books. He had no idea from where this reading fever had come to her nor why she read only depressing novels. He told her Kafka had nothing to do with them. "What kind of a story is that that you've read three times now? All we need is to start turning into cockroaches!"

"But we are cockroaches and we don't know it. Perhaps if we did we'd find a way out of the situation."

When Nasim wanted to summarise the crisis in his relationship with the woman, he'd say the problem was one of choosing between life and death. "I love life and all you can see is death. I want to live and go out and get drunk and dance and you want to stay at home. I want to love you and you want me to be fed up with you and everything else."

Hend refused to go out with her husband to the nightspots that had sprouted like mushrooms at a seaside resort called Maameltein. Just once, because he insisted, she went with him and listened to a young male singer performing Umm Kulthoum songs in a voice with a light coating of huskiness, but she'd felt the place was like a cabaret and that the women were behaving like whores. The dancing started to the rhythm of "You Are My Life" but it wasn't Oriental dancing. Men and women took over the dance floor and swayed back and forth arbitrarily without moving from their places and their laughter rang through the space. Then, when the singer began singing about Ramallah, a kind of fire ran through the dancing throng and they started yelling the words along with the young singer. At this point Nasim grabbed her hand to pull her onto the dance floor, but she yanked it back and said she wanted to go home because she was about to choke.

On the way back she said she was amazed at how such people could sing about Ramallah and Palestine while the blood of Shatila and Sabra had yet dry. Nasim threw his cigar out of the window and told her she hated life. "I swear I don't understand you. What do you expect us to do? People want to live and dance and sing. Ramallah, Shramallah – do you think anyone cares what they're singing? The people were drunk and wanting to live."

"That's the drunkenness of death," she said.

She hadn't been able to tell the women from the whores, she said. It was as though the borders of things had broken down and the men had turned into pimps for their wives. "What's that about? Who could live like that?"

He said it was the war. "War's like that and we have to live."

"No. You're like that and I won't accept that way of life."

But Hend couldn't find another. She felt disgust at the charitable associations that took care of the wounded and disabled because she saw in them the ghost of the Association for the Defence of Human Rights that had done nothing for Meena. At the same time she refused to enter her husband's world, which she saw as a mirror of the disintegration of Lebanese society, and she could no longer find anything to say to her mother, who saw in her son-in-law Nasim the man she'd never managed to find.

"The most important thing in men is generosity, my dear. Your husband's well off, he's doing well. Why are you always making a long face? Why can't you understand that this is your lot in life?"

Karim had no idea why Hend had told him the story of his father's death. He hadn't understood exactly what had happened: had she pushed him, or had he fallen as she tried to escape his grasp? Could it really be that Nasri had tried it on with her too? If that were so, why had Nasim said Nasri had changed a lot during his last days, exciting only pity and grief?

"It was almost like he was my son but, how can I put it, it was like someone who has a cripple, God forbid, for a son: he feels sorry for him and he loves him. You love your son whatever he is, after all he's your son, but with your father it's difficult, I swear it's difficult. You can't not feel pity for him but where are you supposed to get the love from? Love has to be new, like Brother Eugène used to teach us at school, and that was why Christ became a baby, so we'd love him. There's no love without the beginning."

Nasim recounted how Nasri's body had become much thinner, his skin turning black and becoming covered with spots. If you looked at him from behind you might think you were looking at a wide pair of trousers with a man hidden inside, but when you looked at him from in front you were faced with a phantom wreathed in black. Nasri had insisted on dyeing his hair, for the whiteness, whose praises he'd sung while life still coursed through his body, had come to seem hateful. When Nasim mocked his black hair, which looked like a wig, he told him white was the mark of death and he could stand the colour no longer because it was the colour of blindness.

After the finger that his son had held up to his face – as though about to poke his eye out – Nasri had waged a battle with headaches against which all manner of herbal medicines proved ineffective. Then suddenly his eye problems had begun; the left eye, on which a cataract operation had been performed, began to dim even while the right flooded with white, and terror and silence prevailed. Dr Said, the best-known ophthalmologist in Beirut, proposed cleaning the left eye using electric shock therapy and operating on the right. He explained to his patient that the procedure involved a certain risk: the lens that had been placed in the left eye was scratched and could not be replaced; as for the right eye, it was difficult to predict the degree of success of any operation because it wasn't just a matter of the lens but also of a torn and broken cornea.

From that moment on Nasri lived in a state of melancholia from which he never emerged. He had no-one left to consult or complain to about his cares. The man discovered he had no friends and was alone.

"This is old age," Nasri told Salma. "Old age is discovering that you're alone in the world, that you have no friends you can consult or whose advice you can ask as you confront your fate." He'd gone to Salma as one lost, wanting to tell her that he'd discovered he loved her and wanted her to be the companion of his last days. He knew the visit would avail him nothing because he'd left it too late, and that he would never be able to soften the woman's heart, which had fossilised with sorrow, but he went to her having no idea why.

She'd screamed, as she wept, that it was her fault. She was standing with Nasim and Hend by the bed in the hospital. An oxygen mask covered Nasri's face and nose. Salma said it was her fault because she'd never told Nasim the truth.

"What truth, Mother-in-law? The man tripped in front of me and fell down! His oil had run out, as we say. The doctor had told me it was only a matter of days."

"Fell in front of you or didn't fall in front of you, I don't know. What I do know is that Nasri came to see me a week ago and told me the truth and the truth was that he was nearly blind. He'd refused the cataract operation for his right eye and only saw shapes with his left. I ought to have told you but I said nothing, I don't know why. Every time I came by to tell you I'd forget. The man fell because he was blind and we let him die."

"Blind?" screamed Hend.

Had Nasri really been blind? Why had he waited three years to tell the truth about his condition and how had he managed, living amongst the white shadows that consumed his eyes?

Nasim thought his father had probably come under the influence of a dermatologist who was a follower of Daheshism. This man seemed to have pulled the wool over his eyes with the wonder-working of that Palestinian of the Assyrian sect who had been born in Bethlehem and, on moving to Beirut, declared himself the prophet of a religious movement that combined Christianity with Islam. Nasim knew nothing about Salim Moussa Ashi and his school, which had dominated the Lebanese political scene in the forties and fifties of the twentieth century, before the two brothers were born. Nor in fact was the pharmacist Nasri interested in the matter. In his youth he'd been an enemy of all things spiritual, reading atheistical books and parading his admiration for a Lebanese physician and thinker called George Hanna who had created turmoil in Beirut with a little book entitled *Uproar in the Upper Sixth*. Nasri was a disciple of Dr Hanna's but refused to join the Bolsheviks because he didn't believe mankind bore within itself any singular nature that was good. "You've convinced us, Doctor, that mankind is descended from the apes. Well and good. We believe you. Now how do you expect us to believe that the ape which became a man forgot his animal nature and became all good? What's all this nonsense about conflicts ceasing if we assure mankind its basic needs? An animal, and with an imagination – how do you expect it to be content with its needs? Human need never ends." In a heated discussion that took place at the pharmacist's he told Dr Hanna he didn't understand how an atheistical party could be intent on popularising religious ideas under the guise of fighting religion. "Man isn't the flat plain you think he is," he told Dr Hanna. "Man is a tangled forest and when you take away the unconscious it means you're founding a new church and that, my dear doctor, won't do."

What had happened to the Nasri who'd believed that man was a chemical formula? How could he have allowed the dermatologist, Dr Khineisar, to brainwash him into believing in the spirituality of magic, that man possessed more than a body, and that Christianity and Islam might be a single religion, or two faces of the same religion?

Karim had had no idea of the radical change that had come over his father in recent years. His relationship with him had been limited to a seasonal phone call lasting no more than two minutes, during which the father would restrict himself to asking after his two grand-daughters and refuse to answer any question about himself. "Don't ask me 'How are you?' What do you want me to say? Can anyone say of himself that he's well when he can no longer savour life? Can you explain to me, my dear doctor, why the taste of things has gone? Whether I'm eating kenafeh or I'm eating shit, it all tastes the same to me. When you can tell me that I'll answer your question. Please, drop the questions and reassure me that Nadine and Lara speak Arabic. Don't you dare not teach them Arabic, my boy, or they won't be your daughters anymore. Men aren't the sons of their fathers and mothers, they're the sons of the language they speak. That's why we call it the mother tongue. Our true mother is the language. Tell me you speak Arabic with them."

How could Karim explain to his father that that was impossible? How indeed could he tell him that they hated Lebanese food and refused to say at school that they were Lebanese and spoke Arabic? That when they pronounced the name of the family they did so with a French accent, so that "Shammas" came out as "Shammah"; and that they pretended they were from Lyon, their mother's city?

Nasri had wanted to end his life with Salma. None of them knew – though Salma did know – that he loved her and that the game with the Green Potion had been simply a beginning, but that the woman had been afraid of him. Throwing the flask of Green Potion in his face, she'd told him he understood nothing. "You think I come here to you because of this but you don't understand and you don't want to understand that life isn't about a lot of ballyhoo and a few moans and lying. Life's about love and companionship and tenderness."

When he told her about his eyes and the white that was turning into shadows and covering everything with pale yellow she smiled and told him to stop playing games with her. "That's enough, Nasri. Gimmicks like that won't work anymore, with me or anyone else. Anyway, what we need now is a veil to draw over our sins. To make a decent end you have to ask the Lord of Worlds for decorousness, may God grant it to both you and us. Tell me, do you see yellow or green?"

When she looked at his eyes wandering over the distance she realised the man wasn't lying but still found herself unable to believe him. "You know what your problem is, Nasri? Your problem is that I used to be afraid of you and maybe I still am but when you're afraid, my dear, you can't believe. That's why I can't believe you, and your boys too never believed you even for an instant."

"But I lived like that for the boys' sake!"

Nasri didn't know how those words came to slip out from his lips because that wasn't how he saw his life, though in fact he no longer knew how to read it. His past seemed very far away and his story seemed unfamiliar, as though the man who'd lived his life was some other person, or persons. It was as though things would have passed in a flash and the twinkling of an eye but for this accursed body.

"You talk like that because I've grown old. You're right, Salma, but the older the body becomes the smaller the soul feels itself to be. I spit on you, mankind! How you disgust me! One ends up as a child again in an old man's body. God, how hard it is!"

Nasri didn't try to convince Salma to overcome her fear of him because he didn't in fact know what had driven him to go to her. He told her that what's gone never comes back and she was right to fear him: "No-one's more frightening than one who's frightened." He said he'd been afraid of love, so he'd squandered it in play, he'd been afraid of life so he'd smashed it and he'd been afraid for his children, so he'd lost them.

She asked him how he spent his days, half blind. She advised him to employ a maid to help him and see to his needs, to which he muttered that he'd sworn no woman would enter his house after the death of his wife "and it would be stupid to break my oath just to bring a maid. I wish, Salma . . . but I know it's not possible because Nasim would kill us both. Maybe it's better like this. And then there's God, and God helps me."

"What? You've started believing in God?"

He didn't say anything but stood, picked up his crutch, and left, humming a tune by Abd el-Wahhab.

Nasri was alone now – that was what he'd wanted to tell Karim on the phone when he asked him to come and see him in Beirut before he died. "I just want to see the girls. Do you really want me to die without having seen Nadine and Lara?" He didn't say, though, that in his last days he had discovered the existence of God.

Nasri wasn't prepared to explain his relations with God. The man who had spent his life mocking religion – so much so that he despised the Bolsheviks as the proselytisers of a new one – found God in the midst of the blindness that enveloped him in whiteness. His god wasn't the wooden doll that his friend Saroufeem, the pharmacist, had given him as a present when he returned from Paris. The man had brought with him a small African mask carved on an oblong piece of wood about twenty centimetres in length. The mask was made of ebony and its wide eyes seemed to open onto an abyss. The pharmacist told him that he'd happened upon it on the Boulevard Saint-Germain and had bought it from a black female vendor standing behind a stall full of such masks. The vendor had enchanted him with her African costume and the tattoos that covered her hands. The woman, who resembled the work she sold, had told the Lebanese pharmacist that her small carvings were the faces of gods. She'd tried to explain, in halting French, that he could turn the mask he'd buy into a personal god for his own private use.

"But how does the mask become a god?" he asked her.

"The moment you believe in it, the spirit of one of your ancestors occupies it and it becomes a god."

Saroufeem said he'd bought the mask for Nasri.

The idea of a personal god pleased Nasri immensely, especially over the period when he became aware of the danger to Karim from Brother Eugène, for Karim was outstanding not only academically but in religion classes too. This scared Nasri, who knew that nothing is more conducive to illicit sexual relations than a religious atmosphere, in which the smell of incense blends with that of desire and prayers become whispers that lead people into the darkness of the soul.

Nasri announced the birth of his personal god at the lunch table. He raised his glass, poured a little of the wine on the ground, drank a toast to the ancestors, held the black mask in front of him, lifted it up, and looked at Karim, declaring as he did so that this god was better than all the other gods because it only became real when you believed in it: "We can pray to it and we can insult it. We can worship it when we want and we can hit it when we want and it will stay with us and never leave us the way the other gods do their followers." He kissed the forehead of the god, to whom he had given the name Hubal-bubble, and told his sons that the African tradition from which this black god hailed required that sons worship the god of their fathers; when the father died they had to bury the god with him, at which point each son had to find his own personal god before whom to bow down.

"If Brother Eugène asks you about God, tell him we worship our own special god and have nothing to do with his god that died on the cross. Our god doesn't die and he belongs to nobody but us. We love him and we hate him and we entreat him and when he doesn't answer our prayers we ignore him. There is no sin in our religion and no regret. Our god makes mistakes like us and we don't punish him because he doesn't punish us but we can do with him as we please."

Nasim roared with laughter, took the black face from his father's hands, kissed it, then spat on it. Then he turned to his brother and told him to kiss the god's forehead. "What did you say his name is?"

"This is farcical," said Karim and got up to leave. His father grabbed him by the wrist and forced him to sit.

Hubal-bubble was thenceforth a guest at the dining table, where Nasri and Nasim found him a source of material for jokes at the expense of the Jesuit priests and of Karim's faith in the god whom the Jesuits worshipped at the school, and in whose name they compelled pupils to recite prayers each morning.

Then, all of a sudden, Hubal-bubble disappeared.

Nasri was certain Karim had thrown Hubal-bubble in the rubbish but he was wrong. Hubal-bubble was the gift Nasim wanted to give Suzanne when he went to see her on his date with her. He'd worked out a whole scenario of worship and even made up a prayer to be recited before they had sex. He imagined Suzanne taking off her clothes in the room and looking at him out of the corner of her eye. He saw her creamy white breasts bursting out and felt dizzy. But instead of jumping up and taking her in his arms he'd take Hubal-bubble in his hand and place him on her head. He would ask her to kneel, he'd kneel beside her himself, and he'd recite the prayer, then ask her to repeat after him the words, in which he spoke of the human body as incense for the gods.

But Suzanne had mocked him and thrown him out.

She'd left him standing on the pavement and spoken words that had made wounds in his heart which healed only when he married Hend.

And when Hend had shut the door to herself in his face, he'd felt the need for Hubal-bubble and regretted having thrown the wooden god onto the rubbish tip in Mutanabbi Street.

Nasri hadn't asked his sons about the black mask. Hubal-bubble disappeared and his story along with him. Instead, the elderly man, now partially blind, had closed the pharmacy because he could no longer work and had overcome his loneliness with music. He'd discovered his god through the songs of Mohamed Abd el-Wahhab, and dispelled the gloom with the ecstasy of rhythm.

He was sitting in Nasim's flat trying to tell Hend about the comfort that music spreads and poetry fashions. He told her she must teach the children to play instruments. He said God was the rhythm of the world and that the world fashioned its rhythms through music. He recited lines of verse that Abd el-Wahhab had set to music and said that a single line of verse summed up all the prayers that mankind had composed to glorify their gods.

"Listen!" he said:

My lord, when my soul was in his hand,
Destroyed it, may his hand forever rest unharmed!

He stood up and asked for the tape recorder so he could play her the ballad called "The One You Have Made to Suffer". His foot tripped on the edge of the carpet and he tipped forward, hands outstretched. Hend recoiled but the man could not stop his forward trajectory, and it looked as though he was going to fall on top of her. She tried to free herself from his hands by pushing them away and he fell to the floor.

No-one had had any idea that Nasri was nearly blind. Nasim had assumed his father's personal dirtiness was a result of old age. Only Salma knew but she told no-one.

"Oh my God!" screamed Hend. "You mean I killed him without realising what I was doing?"

"I'm the one who killed him," said Salma, weeping.

"No-one killed him," said Nasim. "His oil ran out so he died. Weird you'd believe his stories after everything he did to you. God have mercy on his soul and ours, full stop. I don't want to hear about this business again from anyone!"

8

Karim had had to explain matters to Hend and make her understand why he'd turned his back on their four-year relationship. He'd said love had ended when he was left with no alternative but to emigrate to France. But he'd lied; or, let us say, he'd tried to tell her the truth without actually telling it, meaning he'd tried to be kind so as not to hurt her feelings.

Stories don't end, they go to sleep, and what sleeps may wake at any moment, or never wake at all.

By adding new stories Beirut had awakened all stories. Karim would lose his new gamble because in fact he hadn't gambled. He'd found himself on his way back to Beirut, so he'd gone back.

Karim had thought Hend's story had ended when he met Jamal at the Baissour camp in Tyre in 1976, but it hadn't. It had taken another course and become a sort of safe haven for the young man who felt the civil war was shaking the foundations of everything meaningful to his existence. Jamal wasn't a love story, she was an attempt to climb the ropes of the impossible, to catch the flashes of lightning that fell from her eyes as she looked upon things Karim was incapable of seeing.

He'd never dared tell anyone the truth of his feelings for Jamal. How could he, when he was so unsure of everything? Had he loved her? Or had he believed he'd loved her only when he read fragments from her diaries?

Reading Jamal's diaries after her death, Karim discovered that words bear many meanings. As he gathered up his sorrows and tried to write the story of the Palestinian girl who had led a suicide mission on the coastal road between Haifa and Tel Aviv, he'd fashioned himself a love story out of a rubble of words, and through these, as phrases strewn over tattered pages, Jamal had entered his memory.

Strange are the dead! They occupy the gaps in our imagination and become like ghosts playing with our memories. Karim told himself the reason was that moment of loss which he'd continued to relive since the phone call from his brother inviting him back to Beirut for a hospital construction project.

He'd agreed and beheld before him the dead.

He'd seen Nasri falling to the floor, his eyes opening onto the death that had petrified within them.

He'd seen Khaled, his eyes rubbed out by death, falling like a mighty boulder under the hail of bullets that ripped his body to pieces.

He'd seen Jamal's eyes like two points of light on the ship of death. She'd left before him the fragments of words which he designated "diaries"; she had departed without turning to look back.

He'd seen and not seen; he'd felt unable to resist the lure of a city which had turned into a mysterious smell that emanated from time to time from his memory, making him dizzy.

He told Bernadette that the smell of memory made him dizzy.

Bernadette hadn't been able to understand why the man had decided to return to Beirut for the sake of a project that would never be realised.

She'd told him his project was impossible: "The hospital will never be built and the girls and I will never go to Beirut."

Bernadette said she should have realised from the time of their wedding night that he was a man who lived in the imagination and fashioned truths from his illusions.

She spoke of his coughing, which never stopped when he was in bed, and the noises he made while asleep, as though he were talking classical Arabic.

Why did the doors of hell open at the end, and what did "the end" mean?

Things had started to take a different turn when Nasim had phoned his brother to inform him he was marrying Hend. Before Karim could come out with the word "Congratulations!" he heard the name and the words turned to lumps in his throat and he started to cough. Later he'd discover that words die when a person chokes on them. The cough that would never stop had begun that day. The Lebanese doctor went to a French throat specialist, only to discover that what he had wasn't an ailment but what they call "psychosomatic". He didn't know how to tell

Bernadette about this psychological disease that had come to an end only when he'd returned to Beirut. In fact, the problem manifested itself only at home, where he became incapable of talking with his wife and daughters. The moment he opened his mouth to speak the cough would begin, the words would turn to stone, and he'd feel he was choking.

He had no idea what had happened. Bernadette and the little girls, Nadine and Lara, filled his life. He'd decided to forget that other country. He'd buried his body in the Frenchwoman's white body and had forgotten everything. He'd even begun dreaming in French. During the first days of their love he told her she was his homeland. Bernadette couldn't understand the obsession of this Arab, whose appetite for her body never waned, with homelands. He'd make love to her as though clinging to her for safety, feeling her body with his fingertips and not closing his eyes the way men do when making love to a woman, and when he was done he'd sit naked on the bed, listen to the songs of Fairuz, and grow melancholy.

In Beirut Bernadette disappeared from the screen of his consciousness as though she'd been erased. There, amid the ruins of the city, he felt as though his French life had been just a dream and that by returning to his city he was rediscovering the young man he'd left behind to wander, lost, through Beirut's corridors of fear.

Grudgingly, Bernadette had agreed. She'd said she knew him well and that the six months he was going to spend in Beirut would only add new disappointment to his life.

She'd said she understood him and knew his heart would burn with longing for Nadine and Lara; he'd discover again how much he loved them and wouldn't be able to live without them.

Bernadette was right, for this woman with the blue eyes wreathed in love and tenderness knew how to read his feelings.

She loved him when love came and treated him like a child when she sensed he was lost in his new land. She was harsh with him when he went too far in derision of his former life. She had extended towards him a bridge that would allow him to make peace with himself.

She told him that that was love.

Love isn't desire, that comes and goes. Love is the warmth of safety, the enjoyment of secret understandings, the pleasure of discovering life through the eyes of children.

She left her job at the hospital to devote her time to the house and her two daughters, and decided to be nothing but the wife of this man who excited her with his contradictions. She loved in him his vacillation between an illusory manliness to which he pretended and a shy femininity that overwhelmed him whenever he came face to face with life's difficulties and upsets.

In Beirut Bernadette was erased but the longing for his little ones grew in his guts. He would get up from sleep to the sound of their crying and, on finding himself in Beirut, go sadly back to bed, resolving to call them early the following morning before they went to school.

But in that accursed city the telephones did not work.

And when the project had fallen apart altogether, to the rhythm of Radwan's voice and his threats, he'd felt that all he wanted was to return to Montpellier to embrace his white-skinned wife and breathe in the smell of their first love.

On their wedding night Bernadette was overcome with astonishment as she listened to a strange request from her husband.

They'd signed the marriage contract in the town hall, in the presence of a coterie of French friends, and then they'd all gone on to Palavas-les-Flots, where a banquet of that royal fish, the sea bream, grilled inside a mountain of salt, had been laid out, bottles of champagne had been opened and white wine had sparkled to the rhythm of the waves.

Karim drank a lot that night, as bridegrooms always do. He danced and ate and said he wanted to become one with the "White Sea", which from the restaurant balcony looked grey. He took Bernadette's hand and led her to the beach.

They ran and laughed and rolled on the firm sand of Palavas and he pulled her by the hand and told her that he wanted to swim.

She told him he was crazy and she loved his craziness because it made her laugh. Bernadette's chortling grew louder as she watched Karim approach the cold water, take off his shoes, and enter the sea in his clothes. She watched him shiver with cold and told him to come back, but he continued. Then she saw a high wave that was rolling forward, bringing with it a cold spray that reached the beach, and she screamed with fear and sat down on the sand. He, though, instead of disappearing into the wave, started running so as to beat it to the shore, his clothes soaked.

"Did you see? I beat the wave!"

She ordered him back to the restaurant, where she wrapped him in her long coat and said they had to go home before he caught a cold, but Karim refused. He opened a new bottle of champagne and raised his glass in a toast to his new country, France, the taste of whose sea he had sampled that day, and with the body of whose most beautiful woman he had been baptised.

"You're crazy," she said on their way back.

Karim had said he didn't want to go home because he'd reserved a room in the hotel.

"Why the hotel?" she asked.

"For the honeymoon," he said.

"But we've been living in the same house for a year and we don't need all that nonsense," she said.

"But a marriage isn't complete without the hotel," he said.

Bernadette was exhausted but Karim insisted it wouldn't do. Getting married meant having sex. And when she said she couldn't because she was having her period, his eyes gleamed: he said that was even better because "that way I'll feel as though I've opened you up".

"How vulgar! What do you mean, 'opened me up'? What could be uglier than 'opening up'? Thank God it wasn't you who did that because I would have hated you for the rest of my life."

Karim laughed and didn't reply. He said he was cold and needed her body to feel warm and continued steering the little Renault towards the Hôtel Royal.

The next morning he said apologetically that it had just been a *caprice*; he used the French word but was thinking of the Arabic word *nazwa* – from the verb *naza*, meaning "to leap" – which is only used figuratively, to mean "rampant desire".

The word *caprice*, however, doesn't have that sense, being simply a neutral expression indicating unexpected desire. He'd said the French word, with a cough, because he couldn't think of another, then leapt onto his French wife and made love to her, coughing and shuddering.

What, though, had happened to Bernadette?

After six years of marriage and giving birth to two children, the French nurse had become fed up with him and his desire, to the point that he'd begun to feel that desire had abandoned him and the magical whiteness of the Frenchwoman's body had begun to crack and turn to yellow.

The coughing rescued him from his failure in the matrimonial bed. He had no idea what had happened. He would approach Bernadette, take her in his arms, feel his desire starting to crest and then, suddenly, before he'd taken her, he'd collapse into nothingness, and the cough would rack him. The woman would get up to make him a cup of balm-mint and the grief would spread over her face before she returned to her sleep and her loneliness.

He didn't tell her that his cough was different now. At the hotel he'd slept with her without bathing or removing the traces of sand and the taste of salt from his body. It was as though he were still eating fish. He'd slip into her and with her and sway above the ropes of flame that shot from his eyes and never stop coughing.

"You'll get sick," she said.

The man didn't care if he got sick. He was like someone swimming, borne upwards by the ecstasy, then falling into the depths, then rising again.

Bernadette told him the following morning that she loved him but didn't want that to happen again.

"Making love during one's period isn't healthy, as you know."

"I don't know anything," he said, wresting the cup of *café au lait* from her hand and making love to her again.

"But you're a doctor and you do know."

"Medicine's for the hospital but with you I'm a chronic patient."

The chronic illness became a reality, even with Nadine and Lara. Can a person lose the ability to talk to his children and be afflicted by a kind of dumbness concealed beneath a cough? Karim was enchanted with his two daughters. Nadine was five and Lara three. He told his wife he was now husband to three women and wanted a fourth to feel that the love was complete.

"You're joking," said Bernadette. "I know you want a boy."

He said "No" and he wasn't lying. He felt it was his duty to found a line of women so he could free himself entirely from the burdens of the heavy past that he'd carried with him from Lebanon. The idea of having a son who would grow up to resemble his grandfather terrified him.

"I don't want a boy. I want to fill the earth with beautiful girls."

She said he had to be reconciled with his twin brother to smooth the way for a reconciliation with his father.

He said he'd come to France to forget he was one of an illusory pair of twins that had devoured his life and prevented him from learning how to live, and all he wanted of his father was that he be erased from his memory.

Bernadette didn't believe him despite the fact that she enjoyed the relationship he'd succeeded in establishing with his daughters, which allowed him to treat them as friends and spend all his spare time playing with them.

Suddenly, however, things were turned upside down.

The upheaval started not with the decision to go to Lebanon, as his wife believed, or wanted to believe, but with Karim hearing Hend's name from his brother's lips when he announced on the phone that she'd become his wife.

It seems Nasim had hidden the fact of his marriage from his brother for four years and when his new wife's name happened to cross his lips he pretended to be amazed that his brother didn't know.

"I phoned and told you. It just seems you didn't believe me or didn't want to believe me."

"Impossible," said Karim, overcome by a fit of coughing.

That was the day the coughing and throat-clearing began. Words started to weigh heavily within the mouth of the Lebanese doctor, and intermittent fits of coughing, which turned into chronic coughing in the marital bed, swept over him.

The girls sensed the change and started to distance themselves. No-one is quicker at picking up the vibrations of love than children. When he'd been fully preoccupied with them they'd refused to go to sleep without his kisses. When he was forced to stay late at the hospital the girls would be waiting for him in the living room; he'd come home and find them asleep on the couch there, and he'd take off his shoes, run to them barefoot, and carry them to their beds with kisses. Their smiles of contentment were all he needed to feel intoxicated.

From those kisses he had learned the meaning of intoxication. He'd realised that the Arabs were mistaken in attributing the power to enrapture solely to the voice of Umm Kulthoum, even though it made those who sank into it stagger as though drunk.

He told her his father had never got drunk on the smiles of his sons. He was an egotist interested only in his own little pleasures. "I learned rapture here in France. A smile from one of the girls is enough to lift me to heaven, where I stagger with the drunkenness of love."

Where had it come from, though, this miserable cough? It had turned into a kind of rope knotted tightly round his throat, making him speechless and alienating him from the little world he'd built for himself in France to curl up inside when seeking protection from his memories.

Nadine and Lara could feel the man withdrawing, so they started to do the same. With the intuition of children, they picked up on what Bernadette failed to understand until she heard Karim deciding to go to Beirut to build a hospital.

"It's insanity," she said. "What's happening to you? Don't you realise you'll destroy all of our lives with this decision?"

He had never lied to Bernadette – as she claimed he had when she heard his decision to go to Lebanon – in their entire married life.

He told her she'd misunderstood him, as she had in the past when she'd misread his motives for cutting off all ties with his country.

Bernadette could hardly believe what happened to the man after they got married: he suddenly turned into a Frenchman and began making efforts to secure a transfer to Paris.

He told her that one could become a true Frenchman only in the environs of Paris. There they spoke proper French, rasped their *r*s, and sucked on the word *oui* as though drinking it.

Bernadette said she hated Paris and living in large cities, which was why she'd left Lyon and chosen to live in Montpellier, a small city that looked out over the Mediterranean. She said she'd first thought of Marseille, whose seaside esplanade had enchanted her, but then she'd felt the city wasn't French enough and living there would be like living in some city on the North African coast.

But Marseille is Beirut. He said he didn't like Marseille because its esplanade was like the one in Beirut, and when he'd visited it he'd smelled the smell of civil war.

She said she'd fallen in love with him because he was Lebanese and had something of the perfume of the Orient about him.

The woman hadn't understood what it meant for the dead to come alive in the living, and Karim was incapable of explaining it to her.

His problems with the dead had begun in Beirut. He'd gone to France to escape them, but they had suddenly awoken, as though they'd been sleeping all along inside his soul.

Do the dead sleep inside our souls? And when do we become aware of their having woken?

Had Nasri woken them when he died, besieged by white, or was it because Karim had made the mistake of calling himself Sinalcol when he met Bernadette in the bar? Bernadette had laughed as she explained to the Lebanese doctor what the word meant in Spanish. Karim laughed too because he'd thought the name could be the hook with which to catch the blonde French nurse who made him feel as though he had at last arrived in France.

Bernadette, though, hadn't given up the game of calling her husband by the name of Sinalcol when he was making love to her, as though it had become their spur to desire.

And when Karim had yelled at her, in the midst of his coughing, to stop using the name, Bernadette had understood that the spell was broken.

But was Sinalcol dead?

Had his disappearance following the entry of the Syrian army into Tripoli been an announcement of his death? Does disappearance equal death?

Karim knew that more than seventeen thousand Lebanese had disappeared during the war as a result of abductions carried out by militias at the flying sectarian checkpoints, and he knew that in Lebanon, most of the time, to be abducted meant to die.

Still, Sinalcol's disappearance did not necessarily mean that he was dead. He could have emigrated to America or Brazil and disappeared there, as had done many Lebanese war criminals who are now business-men all over the world.

Karim didn't know the man's real name, but Sinalcol had become the phantom that exemplified the Lebanese civil war in the country's north-ern capital in the years 1975 and 1976. Then, after the Syrian army's invasion of the city, no-one saw him and no-one knew what had hap-pened to him. He was described as keeping his face covered with a red chequered scarf, moving through the darkness of the night and picking out a small number of commercial establishments on whose metal doors he would write the word "Sinalcol" in red chalk. The next night he'd go past the same shops and collect the protection money that their owners had put into the small cardboard boxes that he'd left the night before. Defaulters would find the doors to their shops dynamited.

Sinalcol never stole. He'd blow off the metal door and go his way. The owner would arrive to find his goods untouched and realise he had bet-ter pay up at once or . . . and so on and so forth.

Sinalcol became the talk of the city and stories were made up about him. Khaled tried to kill him but failed, and that was yet another story . . .

When Bernadette asked him to describe Sinalcol to her, he found him-self at a loss for words. He could find no French word for *shabbeeh*, a term the language of the common people of Lebanon had come up with as way to explain certain acts, such as robbery, extortion, and murder at checkpoints based on the religion specified on a person's identity card, as being due to the civil war; so he said something Bernadette couldn't understand – he said he was a *fantômiseur*.

He'd wanted to make an attributive from the word *fantôme* and all he could come up with was a term that made things even more obscure. Never having seen him, he didn't know how to describe the man. In response to her insistence, however, he'd begun describing him, only to discover that he was describing his brother.

"Amazing! Did Sinalcol really look so much like you?" she asked.

It was Danny's fault. This tall blond man, who had studied philosophy in Paris and returned to Lebanon to make the revolution he'd tasted on the streets of the Quartier Latin, had been his window onto the world of the civil war.

Karim had cared nothing about the civil war. He was the opposite of his brother. How could one care about a war among religious sects when one felt no allegiance to any sect or religion?

He'd told Nasri he hated this country for committing suicide every hundred years and felt no allegiance to it. The man nodded in agreement but said war wouldn't break out again. "A bit of faking around like in 1958 and then the Americans will come and sort it out."

After the Americans had come and gone and not sorted it out, Nasri had uttered his famous aphorism: "This war has come to drag all wars into the mud. After the Lebanese war there won't be any respectable wars anywhere."

Karim found he'd become a part of the war involuntarily, even though he never actually fought. He claimed to have taken part in the fighting but he hadn't. His war had been limited to two training courses, the first at the Nahr el-Bared camp close to Tripoli, where he'd found himself involved without realising it in clashes that broke out between the Lebanese army and the Fedayeen, and the second in a village near Tyre where he met Jamal. In both instances Danny had been behind it.

Danny should have died, the way heroes are supposed to, but he stayed alive and returned to his job teaching philosophy at the French Lycée in Beirut, and after his divorce he disappeared from the scene.

Why had Karim's life been turned upside down when he met Danny at the American University in Beirut?

On his return to Beirut Karim phoned Danny and they went together to the Sporting Club restaurant where they drank arak and ate fried fish. Danny seemed to have aged. He walked with a limp as a result of an injury to a spinal disc that had forced him to undergo two unsuccessful operations, and now he walked bent to the right.

Karim could sum up the Lebanese civil war in two names: Sinalcol and Khaled Nabulsi. He had no idea exactly how the fates had led him to Tripoli, but the proximate cause was Danny, the tall philosophy teacher who was the leader of a Fatah student cell.

Danny deserves a novel to himself and remained lodged in Karim's imagination as a character of fantasy. He told Bernadette that people who become a part of ourselves lose their reality and become like the heroes of novels, of whom we remember only the shining image, which becomes a vessel for a human condition that loses its meaning when separated from their names.

Had Karim returned to Lebanon to put a red rose on Khaled's grave or to search for Sinalcol, as he claimed? Or had he concocted the story to justify a return that had no cause other than a mysterious nostalgia for a past which Karim knew in his depths had gone, and which would never come back?

Karim had phoned Danny because he was the last friend he had left in Beirut. He wanted to ask him about Khaled and Radwan and the rest of their friends.

Karim had no idea why he'd fashioned a story for himself when there was no story to fashion. His relationship to the war didn't call for any such implacable sense of belonging. But when he found himself alone in France he'd made a mirror of the war to superimpose upon the mirror of the story of his family, a story which invoked in him nothing but feelings of loneliness and humiliation.

Karim had smiled on seeing the panic that traced itself on Bernadette's face as he described to her the business of "the mirror of war".

She said she could no longer understand why he'd placed that thick wall between himself and his father and brother. She said that at first she'd believed it had to do with the trauma of war, and she hadn't asked for details because she respected his sorrow and his silence.

He'd told her only of his mother and her eyes, opened onto death, a few fragments about his confusing relationship with his twin brother, and his story with the Greek prostitute who'd taught him the meaning of sex. He'd said she should read him as a blank page bearing a few nearly meaningless scrawls, and that he was starting his life anew, as though he hadn't had one before meeting her.

But that day he came to her, stifling his cough, to tell her he was going to Beirut not just to build a hospital but because he wanted to see what had happened to the mirror of the Lebanese war that he had superimposed upon the mirror of his own life.

He'd been unable to explain to his wife the meaning of the expression, which seemed just a hollow metaphor, like those repeated by the heroes who occupy the screen in French films about the Second World War.

Karim was convinced that his metaphor was as hollow as his life, for he was sure of nothing. His memory presented itself in the form of black spots out of which emerged the phantom of a man who looked like him and in whom truth was mixed up with its lookalikes, so that he resembled a man stumbling over his own shadow.

After two months' residence in Beirut, though, he'd decided to reopen his old accounts and recover the shadows of that past. It was Muna and her husband Ahmad Dakiz who led him back to the ledgers of his time in Tripoli, where, in the middle of the crusader castle of Saint-Gilles, all the ghosts of the past had emerged, and Danny had reappeared.

Danny didn't know literary Arabic well but insisted on speaking it, employing classical turns of phrase to assert the depth of his attachment to his country. He'd been born in Abidjan to a family that had migrated from the village of Beit Shabab in Mount Lebanon. His father had worked as a cloth merchant there and died, poor and sick, of fever. Danny had spoken of his father and mother only once, when he recounted how he'd returned with his two sisters from Paris, where they were studying, to attend their father's funeral. There they discovered that their mother had decided to return to Lebanon and was asking Danny to cut short his education in order to dispose of his father's possessions. Danny had interrupted his study of philosophy, only to discover that his father had been penniless and that he would have to flee his creditors or find himself in prison.

"Lebanese capitalism is a decadent phenomenon and the proof thereof is my father. In Africa, if you don't work in smuggling and fraud, you die a pauper. The rich in Africa are naught but a handful of thieves, the lot of them! Verily, they are like the comprador class in Lebanon."

This was the first time Karim had heard the word "comprador". He was too embarrassed to ask what it meant and look stupid, and in the end he got used to using it without knowing what it meant, after which he understood it, or imagined he did. It ceased to matter: once in France, he swallowed dozens of words whose meanings he imagined he understood because he used them in his daily life.

Danny never spoke of his mother, so Karim sketched a scenario in his own mind according to which the woman had returned to Beit Shabab to live in her house there. When he asked Danny about the political situation in the village, though, the tall man had looked at him in surprise; he said he'd only visited the place once and didn't care for the countryside.

Once Danny had disappeared for a whole week without anyone knowing where he was, and when he reappeared there was something broken about his eyes which his wife Sahar interpreted to Karim as due to depression: his mother had died alone in an old persons' home, suffering from dementia.

Danny seemed to Karim more like the hero of Albert Camus' novel *L'Étranger* than the revolutionary leader he was trying to be.

He was, though, a man of extraordinary charisma. Was the charisma a consequence of his height, his fair hair, and his eyes, which were always red as a result of his frequent late nights? Of the long white scarf he used to wrap around his neck, winter and summer? Of his detailed knowledge of the texts of Marx and Lenin? Of his being the first Lebanese intellectual to join the Fedayeen and fight in southern Lebanon? Or of his beautiful wife Sahar, who worked as an architect with the Alami Company in Beirut, supported the household and their only daughter, and asked nothing of Danny except that he never stop loving her?

Karim fell under the man's spell when he attended the first political meeting at Danny's flat in Tall el-Khayyat. In response to Danny's call for the foundation of a Marxist organisation within the Fatah movement he could think of nothing to say but "Yes". He hesitated, however, when it came to taking part in military activities.

He said he'd never killed a sparrow so how could he kill a human being?

He said he agreed that violence was the way of the revolution but he was a doctor and the revolution needed his knowledge, not his blood.

"You're just talking so you don't have to talk," said Danny, and he persuaded Karim to join a week-long military training course at the Nahr el-Bared camp close to Tripoli. It was there that Karim's life began to shape itself into elusive shadows.

This way of putting it isn't quite accurate, because the idea of shadows had occurred to Karim only after his return to Beirut, when the darkness of the city blended with the darkness of his soul on the last night of waiting. At that moment he discovered that all that remained of him, and to him, was a collection of obscure images derived from a life that traced itself like black shadows on the demolished walls of the city.

When Hend asked him why he'd come back to Beirut he said he had no idea.

"Do you believe this story about the hospital?"

He answered that the architect had finished working on the plans and things were moving along fast.

"But your brother's changed a lot. It's as though you know nothing, or you know and don't want to know."

He said he'd come back because he didn't know what he was supposed to do with his life, and that back there things seemed to have lost all taste and meaning.

"You mean you've come looking for meaning in a city where everything's meaningless?"

She told him that the meaning of things was within, and she felt that what lay within her was coming apart. "You didn't have to come. What do you want with us and our tangled stories? Go back to your house and your wife and daughters! There's nothing here. Even the memories no longer exist. People here grind their memories underfoot."

Had he phoned Danny so that he could grind his memories underfoot?

When he called him, Danny's voice had sounded unsure, as though he didn't recognise him. Then the voice had regained its composure, suggesting lunch at the Sporting Club swimming pool.

They'd drunk arak but the words had failed to take shape and had scattered in scraps over the table. Danny had spoken at length about his illnesses and the two difficult surgical procedures he'd had performed on his spine. When Karim asked him about Sahar he was overwhelmed with gloom and said he knew nothing about her except that she was living in Brussels.

"And your daughter Suha?"

"Suha got married," he said, "and is living in Montreal."

"Who's the groom?"

He lifted his hand in a way that indicated he neither knew nor cared.

"Did she marry a Lebanese?" asked Karim.

"No," replied Danny without a further word.

Silence and sea and waves. The words melted and vanished. Danny was like a sheet of copper. The daily swim that the doctor had imposed on him had had its effect on his face and skin colour. All that was left of him was his fair hair, some of which had fallen out, outlining a sort of bald patch covered with tufts, and his front teeth, stained black with French tobacco; a man who had decided to bury his memories and live without a memory.

He asked him about the boys and Danny said he didn't see any of them. He asked him about Radwan.

He asked and he asked but Danny's silence rose like a thick pall that could be dispelled only by the chewing of food and the drinking of arak.

When he asked him about Sinalcol, Danny burst out laughing. "Aren't you Sinalcol? Have you forgotten what the boys used to call you? Comrade Doctor Sinalcol! And behind your back they'd say 'Look at those intellectuals! They come just so they can play the Sinalcol over us!'"

"That's something you came up with," said Karim. "You're the one that took to calling me Sinalcol in front of the boys and so the name stuck and all because I refused your order to kill the guy."

"Now you're Sinalcol again, like in the old days," said Danny.

Karim hated this name they'd stuck on him, erasing the *nom de guerre* he had chosen for himself. 'I'm Salem!' he used to say. 'Please, brothers! No-one is to call me Sinalcol!'"

The name Sinalcol had stuck to Karim against his will. He'd done everything in his power to expunge it but names are like eye colours: they're difficult to change. During his first years in Montpellier he was much disturbed by a recurrent dream in which he saw himself walking down a long deserted street, a mask covering his face, then standing in front of a shop door and writing the name Sinalcol on it in chalk and running away, as though pursued.

And then, when Bernadette asked him his name, he'd answered in his moment of drunkenness that it was Sinalcol!

"Do you still remember, Karim, what I always used to say though nobody believed me? Now all of you can see with your own eyes how right I was."

"You're always right, Danny."

"My name's Faris, not Danny. Danny was the *nom de guerre* I used in the days of the Fedayeen. Now it's over. Danny's dead and it's Faris sitting in front of you. Though really I don't know what to call myself. When I hear the students calling me Mr Faris, I split my sides laughing. Imagine the insult to one's dignity when one doesn't know what one's name is any longer! As I used to say, 'The bastards ride boats and the heroes have to swim back.'"

"Is it true what they say about Maroun, that he had a tall blonde girl with him and she disappeared?" asked Karim.

"It's not important," answered Danny. "Maroun came to see me before he started shooting the film and told me the storyline. I told him, 'That's stupid. We can't make a film about forgiveness because the war isn't over. First the war has to end and then we can write about it.' But that wasn't the problem. The problem was that everything was wrong. Poor fellow, he embodied the Lebanese lie in his name and then paid for it with his life. His name was all wrong. He was called Maroun but he wasn't a Maronite, and he was from the Baghdadi family but he wasn't an Iraqi. That's the philosophy of the Lebanese war – the names are borrowed but the deaths of those who bear them are all too real."

Karim said Maroun's death was a symbolic expression of the extinction of the revolutionary generation in Lebanon. "I met him in France and he told me about the film and I could see death in his eyes," said Karim.

"Don't say that!" said Danny. "You know well that anyone who sees death dies, because his death is traced in the eyes of the murderer, and you know who I'm talking about."

What a bizarre lunch! Karim had wanted his meeting with Danny to put together what had been broken and had found himself faced with a man who hunched over his terrible back pains as he walked, broke instead of joined, and painted what was present in the colours of absence.

"The war would have broken out with or without us and it kept going without us, so I regret nothing. Or at least I'm sorry about one thing, which is that instead of devoting myself to writing a book of philosophy I became a fighter, and once you've written with bullets it's hard to write with a pen. I'm working now on a study that proves that none of the literary types who wrote about war did any serious fighting. They were basically adventurers who stayed on the margins. Neither Hemingway nor Malraux fought in the Spanish War. Malraux fought with the French resistance to Nazi occupation, it's true, but after that he stopped writing so he could become a minister. My study will deconstruct the myth of the writer fighting or being committed to the struggle. That's rubbish. Lorca wasn't a hero and Neruda wasn't a resistance fighter. As for Nazim Hikmet, who reduced his readers to tears with his poems about his Munevver when he was in prison, as soon as he was released he got rid of her and married a Russian nurse."

"But!" said Karim.

"No buts! Am I right or am I wrong?" Danny responded.

He reverted to the celebrated expression he used to use to put an end to any discussion at cell meetings, when he'd ask, "Am I right or am I wrong?" so his listeners had no choice but to say "right" because the tone of "or am I wrong?" left no room for "wrong".

"But Saint-Exupéry," said Karim.

"You're right, but Saint-Exupéry wrote *The Little Prince* and didn't write about war. Plus I'm not talking about that kind of writer, I'm talking about the revolutionary writers."

"Right," said Karim.

"The problem," said Danny, "is that heroes don't collapse in the face of death, they collapse in the face of writing. This is the great illusion. They want to become writers, or find someone to write about them, which is what I shall refer to in my study as 'the folly of immortality'. They believe that writing is a way to stay alive after death, which is nonsense."

"Right," said Karim, "but you're a hero. I don't understand why you want to become a writer."

Danny explained to Karim that the problem of heroes was called retirement. Withdrawal from the struggle was equivalent to death, "which is why you, my friend, may consider me dead."

Karim had wanted to ask his friend about the mystery of his

disappearance immediately after the killing of Khaled, but did not. What use were questions after all these years? Danny was the reason, Karim had told himself when he decided to flee Lebanon. Danny was the guide who'd led Karim to Nahr el-Bared, introduced him to Khaled and the boys of the Qubbeh district, and thrust him into the midst of the maelstrom of terror that had led to his decision to go to France.

Those days appeared in Karim's memory as black patches. The medical student at the American University of Beirut had fallen under the spell of the appearance of Malak Malak at Tall el-Zaatar Camp following his arrest immediately after killing two deans at A.U.B. It was claimed that Danny had masterminded Malak's escape from Roumieh Prison and was waiting for him at Hammana when he withdrew with fighters fleeing the camp following its fall in 1976, in one of the Lebanese civil war's biggest massacres.

Karim hadn't been particularly interested in politics. The famous A.U.B. students' strike of 1974 had meant little to him. He'd taken part in the strike, which had erupted because of an increase in tuition fees, just as he'd participated in the sit-in at the Assembly Hall when students occupied the A.U.B. buildings, but he hadn't felt involved and had remained on the margins of the movement. That was why Karim wasn't one of the 103 students expelled from the university when the strike ended.

The strike was a proclamation that the Palestinian resistance and its left-wing Lebanese allies had become an axis of political life in Lebanon. "He who holds the university holds Beirut," said Danny to the circle of students he directed. It never crossed anyone's mind that the university administration would call in the Lebanese police to break into the buildings and put an end to the strike, and then expel all the strike leaders.

The strike had had to be defeated so that it could achieve victory through blood. Malak Malak, a fourth-year student at the Faculty of Engineering, from a Christian Palestinian family from the area of Haifa which had joined the flood of refugees in 1948, was the hero of the story.

After trying to complete his studies in Iraq, where he was subjected to arrest and torture at the hands of the Iraqi intelligence services who attempted to force him into collaborating with them, Malak succeeded in escaping and returning to Lebanon, becoming the killer of the two deans Nujeimi and Ghusn, and saving by this insane act the future of all his fellows.

Malak's crime, the blood that flowed, the collapse of the university's administration, and its consent to the return of the expelled students all formed the final chapter of symbolic violence that paved the way for the transformation of Beirut into an arena of blood.

Danny didn't hide his pride in having helped Malak to escape from Roumieh Prison and in advising him to take refuge in Tall el-Zaatar camp. To Danny the incident was a declaration that revolutionary violence had become the sole language through which change could be achieved.

"You've changed a lot," said Karim.

"We've grown old," answered Danny.

"What news of Malak?" asked Karim.

"What Malak?" asked Danny.

It was obvious that Danny had forgotten Malak and his story. Everyone had forgotten the tall dark-skinned young man who had escaped from Roumieh Prison to become a fighter in Tall el-Zaatar before disappearing. Even the story of the killing of the deans of Engineering and of Students at A.U.B. had died and became part of the unsaid.

And Malak had said nothing.

His girlfriend Hala said he'd changed a lot in Iraq. She said he'd told her only scraps of his bitter experience there, contenting himself with saying that death was preferable to prison. When she asked him to tell her what had happened he gave her a copy of Abd el-Rahman Munif's novel *East of the Mediterranean*.

"Read this novel if you want to know the Arab world," he said.

"A man who had entered the darkness of silence," said Hala. "I didn't know him anymore, it was as though he'd become another man. Does that other person live inside us, only to emerge suddenly from we know not where and perform acts that would never have occurred to us?"

The Lebanese interrogator who had detained Hala as part of his attempt to uncover Malak's partners in crime was impressed by the young woman's ability to avoid answering his questions.

"I'm not avoiding them," she said. "It's the truth. The night of the crime we drank a cappuccino at the Café Express on Hamra and he told me he didn't love me anymore because love was over and that he was going to Johnny's to play cards. He said playing tarneeb was better than wasting his time with a girl like me who didn't understand anything he said anymore, and he turned and left."

. . .

"No, he didn't say anything about killing the professors at the university and he was in a good mood. He may have been talking to me and telling me things from a place I couldn't reach. Maybe he was right. After his expulsion from the university and his travel to Iraq and imprisonment and torture there maybe he'd found a solution in a language I don't know, the language that's inside one's soul and that we can't measure in words because it's fashioned without words."

"What are you studying at the university, *mademoiselle*?"

"Philosophy," she said.

"I must say I've never come across a case like you. Just between you and me, I didn't understand a word you said except what everyone knows about him being arrested in Iraq. That must have been something alright! What imaginations they have! I used to hear stuff about imprisonment in Iraq and couldn't believe it. Perhaps we should learn a thing or two from them. But that's not what matters now. What matters is that I didn't understand a word you said, perhaps because you were talking to me in philosophical language."

"No, officer, that wasn't the language of philosophy, that was the language of crime," she said.

"You're talking about the philosophy of crime, right? The new generation, God help us! You've been no use to us. Get out of here and good riddance."

Hala hadn't been talking about the philosophy of crime. She'd been talking about the war that had made her feel she'd lost her balance. She'd fallen in love with her fellow student, a Palestinian, only to find herself covered in blood. She'd rebelled against her conservative Beirut Sunni environment and told her father, Hajj Yahya Fakhani, that she was going to marry Malak in spite of everything. She said he'd graduate in a year and they'd go to Cyprus and have a civil wedding like everyone else.

Her father threatened to kill her.

She paid no attention. The strike took place and everything went to hell. Malak was expelled along with the others. He left to continue his civil engineering studies in Iraq, then cut them short and returned to Beirut. But the man who returned wasn't the Malak she knew. It was as though he'd left his laughter and endless jokes in Baghdad and come back wearing a new face.

He'd become laconic, dissatisfied with everything. In response to her insistence, he'd told her what happened, how they'd asked him to work with Iraqi intelligence, how he'd been detained a number of times for short periods, and the kinds of torture to which he'd been subjected.

He said he'd discovered in the prisons of Iraq that a person can become separated from his body and had been astonished to find himself praying to the Virgin and asking for her help.

"I'm telling you, people are dogs. They forget themselves and their masks when faced with disaster and go back to being like Granma and Granpa, sunk in superstition."

He said he'd sunk into superstition, and if he hadn't believed that his grandmother was praying for him he would have fallen apart and become one of their intelligence agents.

"Do you still love me?" Hala asked.

"How should I know what love means? For God's sake, stop asking questions like that!"

The man disappeared, it became difficult to get in touch with him, and Hala had to go to Johnny's flat to look for him. There she found him hunched over a game of cards, the cigarette never leaving his lips. He saw her, threw the cards down, and they left together to sit in the Café Express, where Malak could find nothing to say to the girl whom he'd promised he would one day marry and, on the liberation of Haifa, take to the Abbas Effendi Garden on Carmel.

Their love was over, Malak said. It was over because after his experience in Iraq he could no longer talk. He said he'd discovered that a person has inside him words that have no language, and she wouldn't be able to grasp the meanings of those words because she hadn't lived the experience with him.

She said she loved him and understood his pain but "this isn't right, my darling. Let's get married and then we can see what to do."

He looked at her with empty eyes, as though her words had slipped past his ears.

Hala decided not to contact him again but wait until the psychological crisis through which he was stumbling had passed. Then she was taken aback to see pictures of him in handcuffs filling the front pages of the newspapers and to hear of his double crime.

She went to the home of his friend Johnny, a Jordanian-Palestinian student who'd also been expelled from the university, to find out what had happened. She knocked for a long time on the door of the flat on the third floor of the Fleihan Building on Abd el-Aziz Street, but it stayed closed. She descended the stairway of the dark building and found policemen waiting for her and spent the night at the Hbeish police station before the officer released her as immaterial to the investigation.

Hala wasn't committed to the struggle like the other members of their university coterie. She was a student of philosophy at the Lebanese University and didn't feel she could associate herself with the political atmosphere that prevailed in the Beirut universities. But she was in love and willing to do anything for the Palestinian who had occupied her heart and hurt it. She told him that her love for him made her feel a pain in the heart and that she would stay with him and put up with his way of life even though she didn't believe that this struggle would lead anywhere. All the same, she hadn't expected the byways of that struggle to lead her beloved to madness.

She told Johnny when she met him that Malak was different from them all because he'd taken his convictions to their conclusion, whereas they spent their time elaborating statements condemning the crime, this being part of the deal that allowed them to return to the university.

Johnny said, hiding a scowl, that Malak was insane. "It was an insane act. The organisation had nothing to do with it and we condemned it because assassination is an act to be condemned."

"If you're against assassination can you explain to me why you used the crime so you could all return to the university while Malak is in prison and they're going to sentence him to death?"

Johnny tried to explain to her that politics was like that; she wasn't committed to political action and couldn't be expected to understand its complexities and she shouldn't worry "because there's nothing that can't be fixed".

Hala disappeared from the scene. Danny, who told the boys of Hala's detention and release, said the girl had nothing to do with anything. "I don't know how Malak could have been her boyfriend and promised to marry her. A conservative girl in the full meaning of the word who had nothing to do with the political struggle. I don't know what he saw in her. It's not enough for a girl to have brown skin and green eyes for one to take her as one's life companion."

"Politics is like that," Danny had said, stressing the difference between mass struggle and assassination. Karim couldn't think what to say. He didn't say that the statement was tendentious nonsense, though that was what had occurred to him. He felt lost because sometimes he fought with the boys and was a part of the civil war, but he didn't know how to tell his comrades that playing with the fire of wars like this could lead only to the abyss. In fact, he did say this to Danny once when they were drinking vodka. Sahar was there, filling the flat with her vivacity and beauty – a svelte woman with pencilled eyebrows, honey-coloured eyes, and a loving smile that never left her lips. With her was her daughter Suha, who was seven, and whom everyone who saw her thought was a miniature of her mother. They were like two sisters competing for the heart of one man, and Danny relished this double love.

Karim said that playing with the sectarian fires of Lebanon and reviving the bloody scores of the civil war of 1860 would mean an end to all revolutionary thinking and a return to the dark ages.

Danny smiled contemptuously as he tried to explain to his hesitant comrade that, unlike Nevsky Prospekt, revolution doesn't go in a straight line and that Lenin had known, as he led the world's first socialist revolution, that it would have to get its feet dirty in the mud of history.

"But Nevsky Prospekt's in Petrograd, not Beirut," answered Karim.

"True," said Danny, "but revolution here is the same as revolution there."

"But here there are only sects, and sects are scary," said Karim.

"True and not true," said Danny. "Don't forget the classes and the class struggle. But you're right, the sects are a big danger and the only thing that can deal with and neutralise that danger is a cohesive revolutionary vanguard."

"But where's the vanguard?" asked Karim.

"We're the vanguard," said Danny. "You saw Malak's heroic action and how he forced the university to reinstate all the expelled students. That was vanguard stuff."

"But you just said we were against assassinations!"

"Against them in principle, that's true, but on occasion they are necessary. We're against military coups, but the October Revolution obliged Lenin to carry out a kind of military coup. Revolution, my friend, doesn't go in a straight line like Nevsky Prospekt . . ."

Karim had nodded as though he understood and agreed but he didn't. Before Danny, he found his will paralysed. The philosophy professor was capable of deploying an irresistible logic. He was a man full of ideas and ambitions who led a student cell at A.U.B., and, at the same time, the Qubbeh district group in Tripoli, which was made up of thugs, the unemployed, and agricultural workers, and who went home to drink Vodka Martinis while listening to classical music.

Danny said he'd wanted to be a musician and that when he was young he'd learned to play the piano; he'd stopped when he began taking an interest in maths and philosophy. "Then came the struggle, comrades, and the struggle taught me that the true philosophy and the greater music are praxis."

When Karim had asked Danny about Malak he'd said he knew nothing about him. He said he'd arranged his escape from Roumieh Prison, "where Malak had made his blankets into a rope and descended from the prison window to find our comrades waiting for him. He wasn't alone. It doesn't matter that Mustafa Qaddour, one of Tripoli's Republic of the Wanted, was with him, what matters is that the boys showed him the way to Tall el-Zaatar, which I know they got to only after major difficulties and after being fired on by the besieged camp's defenders. Malak shouted, 'Don't fire, I'm Malak!' It seems one of the boys had heard his story, and

187

from that moment he disappeared. The fact is I don't know. Atef, Abu Iyad's assistant, advised him to go abroad because he was on the wanted list and the revolution couldn't protect him. I think he went to East Germany and there the Stasi enlisted him and we heard unbelievable stories and that they did an operation and changed the way his face looked. Honestly I don't know. Maybe he's in Beirut right now but we wouldn't recognise him if we saw him."

"And Hala?" asked Karim.

"Who's Hala?"

"His girlfriend."

"I don't know," said Danny. "Or yes, my wife Sahar said she was teaching philosophy at the Good Shepherd School and lives like an old maid."

"I'd like to see her," said Karim.

"Don't waste your time. She has only one story to tell and it's not believable. I think she made it up to give some meaning to her life. Malak supposedly phoned her after a long time and made a date with her at the Express. She went and looked about but couldn't see him so she went and sat in the corner where they used to sit when they were in love. After a bit a man came and stood in front of her. He looked at her and said, 'You don't recognise me of course.' The voice was Malak's. It was the voice but not the man. 'You're not him,' she said. 'I don't know you.' He said he'd changed his face in Germany and later changed his name. He said his name was Munir now and he loved her. The girl was petrified. 'You're not him,' she said. 'And anyway I was afraid he might kill me, after the crime he'd committed.' She said she ran out of the café, scared the ghost would run after her. 'I don't know why they sent me this man who was pretending to be Malak. I'm certain Malak died in Tall el-Zaatar. He died and never called me once, died not loving me. How could someone who'd committed all those crimes love anyone?'"

What did today's Danny have in common with yesterday's?

It wasn't true that this Danny was the hero of an unwritten story, as Karim had thought in the past. Danny wasn't like heroes because heroes are frozen in our imaginations in the act of heroism. When they lose their balance and life preys on them they lose their magic and are transformed into mere shadows that break up in the light of ordinary life. The secret of Danny's allure lay in Sahar – a beautiful woman who worked so as to leave her husband free for political action. He'd disappear and she would wait for him, and when he returned she wouldn't ask where he'd been. With radiant face she'd lead him to the bathroom, remove his dirty underwear, and fill the bathtub with hot water covered with soapy, jasmine-scented foam. Then she'd leave him to go to the kitchen to fetch a glass of mint tea, sit on the edge of the tub, hold his wet hand, and sink with him into the silence of the steam that rose from the hot water.

This woman of waiting, who filled the life of Danny and his friends with joy, suddenly disappeared. No-one had any idea what had happened to her. She went on a trip to Italy to attend an architectural conference in Venice and that was the last anyone heard of her. One rainy night Danny had come to Karim's flat and said he was tired. He was sad and confused and couldn't hold his tongue. It seemed he'd smoked and eaten a lot of hashish before deciding he couldn't stay alone in the flat any longer. He said his wife's sister had taken his daughter to sleep at her place and he was feeling lonely. Then he told the story. He said Sahar had phoned him the day before. He said she'd disappeared three weeks earlier, when she'd been supposed to return after four days but hadn't and he'd had no means of contacting her. He'd told her sister about it two days ago. Her sister didn't seem worried or surprised by the news. She said she knew nothing about the matter and promised to come that day and take Suha. Half an hour after she left, Sahar phoned and said she was in Brussels, had found work there, and was never coming back to Beirut. She'd said strange things, that she hated Beirut, hated Lebanon, hated him, and wanted a divorce. She'd said she'd told her sister to get Suha's things ready because she'd decided to bring her daughter to live with her there in Brussels and she expected him not to object because he was busy with other things anyway, didn't know his daughter, and had no relationship with her. She'd said she'd give him free rein with their joint bank account once she'd withdrawn half.

Danny had talked like a parrot repeating things it doesn't understand. He'd spoken in a husky voice and the words had faltered in his mouth as though refusing to emerge. He'd said he was tired and wanted to sleep. Then his heart had begun beating violently and continuously. Karim had told him he ought to take him to the A.U.B. Hospital's emergency clinic because his heartbeat was racing "and I'm not a cardiologist. I don't know what to do. Come on, get up, and let's go to the hospital."

"There's no need," said Danny. "This always happens to me when I overdo it with the hashish."

Karim ordered him to lie on his back. He put three cushions under Danny's head, gave him a glass of cold water to drink, got a piece of ice from the refrigerator and ordered him to suck it. The heartbeat slowed but Danny didn't cease his raving.

"Better not talk now. We can talk later."

Danny never stopped talking. He was like someone speaking to himself. He went on for more than two hours while Karim sat next to him and tried unsuccessfully to break the accumulating sentences down into words. He heard the name Rana often repeated but what did Rana have to do with it? Rana was a member of the A.U.B. cell and was preparing to marry her boyfriend, with whom she'd been living for three years. Karim worked out that Danny had had an affair with Rana and that Sahar had seen them at the Mandarin Café on rue de Verdun when she'd thought he was fighting in the south. He said Sahar had come into the café where he was sitting holding hands with Rana. She'd been to the supermarket with her daughter, and they'd stopped by the café because Suha loved the *forêt noir*. "She saw me and I didn't see her. Suha ran to me and I didn't notice. It was all the effect of the hashish. I was on my way back from Baalbek. You know how the boys are there. It's cold, they light a charcoal brazier, sit round it, scatter hashish on the charcoal, and the smell rises – the sweetest smell and the best hashish and we'd get stoned without smoking. I left Baalbek stoned and instead of going home I made a date with Rana. I wanted to see her at her flat. She said it wouldn't work at home because her boyfriend might come at any moment and she suggested the Mandarin and I don't know why I agreed and we were screwed."

"So you love Rana?"

"God forbid! I love Sahar but Rana was, you know, a side dish."

"And she thinks you're a side dish?"

"Please, don't start getting philosophical! Marital infidelity is a necessity for the continuation of a marriage. That's how people are."

"So you've always betrayed Sahar?"

"What? You don't betray Hend?"

"Of course I don't betray her, what do you mean? I love her."

"If you don't betray her it means you don't love her."

"So Sahar knew you were betraying her?"

"I don't know. I think she knew but she turned a blind eye."

"Turned a blind eye?"

"Sahar is an intelligent woman. She knows that a man's imagination has no bounds, and imagination is the beginning of betrayal."

"Why didn't she turn a blind eye this time?"

"Because we were being defeated. Ever since the Syrian army came in and Kamal Jumblatt, the leader of the Lebanese Nationalist Movement, was killed, we'd been in defeat and were being dragged through the mud. And Sahar understood that maybe it was over, maybe she'd only loved me because I inspired thoughts of heroism. Maybe she loved the hero and the hero was being defeated, the hero was going to die. I didn't die, I became unemployed and unheroic. The revolution had failed and all that was left of it was the civil war and the civil war drags you through the mud, especially when it's in your home. When she saw me with Rana she couldn't take it anymore and I was like an imbecile, not seeing what was in front of me, with no idea what was going on till I found the girl hugging me and Sahar screaming at her so that she could leave and go home."

Karim didn't see Danny after that night. The man disappeared behind a veil of hashish smoke. Even when Khaled Nabulsi was killed and his wife came and sought refuge at Danny's flat, no-one could find him. He didn't answer the phone or open the door. This had put Karim in an awkward position and he'd felt like a traitor and a coward telling Khaled's wife he didn't know what she was supposed to do.

The woman disappeared behind her veil and Karim experienced his last moments of indecision in Beirut before deciding to go to France.

9

Later, when he returned to Lebanon, Hend had looked to Karim exactly as she always had. It was amazing how the woman hadn't changed, as though she were his Hend and age had added only more of the bloom of youth. He'd expected to see a woman with a body sagging from having given birth to three boys, one who exuded the smell of house and dust and never stopped clucking, like a hen. In the event, her brown skin, tanned and endowed with a new colour that seemed to clothe her in a second skin of beauty, gave her complexion the look of sun-ripened fruit and took him by surprise.

As soon as he'd cast off this girl whom he'd worn so long Karim had turned his back on Beirut. He hadn't lied to Danny: he had never betrayed her, not because he was uncommonly chaste or faithful, but because he couldn't. Her aroma, which was like that of shellfish, clung to all his five senses.

Once, they'd gone swimming in front of Rawsheh Rock in Beirut, Hend moving between the two formations, swimming on her back and using her arms as oars and he trying to catch up with her. He'd circled around her and dived beneath her while she surrendered herself to the sound of the sea and to its undulations. Dazzled by sun, water and salt she swam alone, heedless of his cries of love and water.

"That's enough. I'm tired," he said. "Let's go back."

She turned over and said he could go back if he wanted but she was going to swim to the cave.

It was her perpetual swimming rite. She would start by making a circuit of the two rocks that rise opposite the corniche at the lighthouse, then go to the large rock and swim on her back into the middle of the hole that time has created, forming from the lower part of the rock an arch that continues beneath the water. There she'd close her eyes and surrender to the spray from the waves that crashed off the rock covering her body with droplets of salt water in which burned threads of sunlight. Then she'd turn over and swim towards what the French called "the Pigeon Pool", where she'd enter the water's darkness and disappear. Karim had only once been into the cave. He'd swum at her side and they'd entered the vanishing light. He told her he needed air and could hardly breathe and heard her laugh. He pulled back and swam to the entrance of the cave to wait for her and when, after a quarter of an hour, she emerged he told her he'd been frightened for her because of the creatures of the sea.

"So why didn't you come back and save me?" she said laughing.

"I was afraid," he said.

"Afraid for me or for yourself?"

He'd wait for her at the entrance to the cave and then they'd return in one of those canoes that the Lebanese call a "fishbone" and go to the swimming pool at the nearby Sporting Club, where they'd drink orange juice.

Karim wouldn't speak much. He'd tell her about Danny and his Fedayeen comrades. It was the eve of the war but Hend had no interest in the subject. She thought politics was a way of killing time.

"You're like men playing cards. You know what they say when they play cards? They say, 'Come on. Let's kill some time!' You aren't going to kill just time, you'll probably end up killing yourselves and everyone around you too."

Karim hadn't surrendered in the face of this kind of talk. He believed time would change her mind and that this Hend, salted with sun and sea, would be his life's companion.

Shaking the water of Rawsheh Rock off herself and lying on a deck-chair at the Sporting Club, Hend said that three days before she'd had a terrifying dream which she hadn't wanted to speak of in case it came true, but then she'd changed her mind and decided to tell him about it because, that day, for the first time, she'd felt afraid of the darkness of the cave.

Hend said it had been a long dream. It had lasted all night, she hadn't forgotten any of it, and she was scared.

"Dreams are our repressed desires," said Karim. "Out with it, so we can see what your desires are."

Karim sat on the edge of the chair, lit an unfiltered Gauloise, took the first drag deep into his lungs, and waited for the story.

"What kind of a cigarette is that that smells so bad?" she asked.

He said the roasted black tobacco was less harmful and gave you a buzz. He didn't attribute it to Danny's influence, or mention that French tobacco had become fashionable among Lebanese leftists following the 1968 May Revolution in France.

"You and I were swimming beneath Rawsheh Rock and as usual I left you and went into the cave. It was dark. I swam. The water was very cold. Then I began to feel it was sticking to my body. I felt cold and was afraid. I tried to get out of the cave. I turned towards the entrance but instead of seeing light it just got darker. Usually when I turn around to go back I see the most beautiful view in the world. The sun looks as though it's sleeping on the water in the middle of the cave and the light is coming from under the surface. Come on, I thought, where's the entrance to the cave? I turned again and I couldn't work out the directions anymore. I kept turning around and around and screaming. I screamed but no-one heard my voice. It was as though my voice had disappeared. I knew no-one could save me."

"Where was I?" asked Karim.

"You'd disappeared," said Hend.

"I was alone and there was no-one with me and I screamed 'Father!' I don't know why it occurred to me to scream for someone I only know from pictures, and instead of my father coming to save me I saw him at home. He was sitting in the living room drinking a glass of whisky and my mother was coming and going to the kitchen because she was getting lunch. The doorbell rang. My mother told me, 'Get up, Hend, and open the door.' I ran towards the door to open it and found it was open and there was a tall man standing in the doorway holding a pistol. As soon as he saw me he shot me and I saw blood coming out of my shoulder but I didn't fall. I heard my mother screaming that her husband had killed her daughter, and hitting herself on the head, screaming that her daughter was dead. I stretched out my hands towards my father and said to him in a low voice, 'Help me, Father.' I looked out of the window and saw him stretched out on the ground, and the tall man who my mother said was her husband standing over him. I fell down . . . and was swimming in the sea and the sky was blue and clear and the sea was as smooth as oil. My father was swimming beside me and when I got to the rock I saw it was sinking. It was listing like a ship and instead of the big rock supporting itself on the small it knocked it over and the two of them sank together. I saw the rock sinking further and further under the water and started to cry. 'How are people going to know this is Beirut?' I said. 'If the rock's gone, so is Beirut, and me too, who's going to want to know me, now that I have no name?' And I felt myself sinking and screamed for my father and everything was dark and I was stuck inside the cave."

"And then what happened?"

"Then I woke up trembling. I went to the kitchen to drink some water. My mother was sitting on her own in the dark smoking a cigarette. I went up to her to kiss her and noticed her face was wet with tears. She was weeping soundless tears. I wanted to tell her that Rawsheh Rock had sunk but when I saw her in that state I didn't know what to do. I drank a glass of water and went back to bed."

Hend said that that day, for the first time in her life, she'd felt frightened of the sea and the cave. They were swimming at the beginning of April 1975; the Beirut spring sun had not yet taken the chill out of the sea air but Hend swam all year round saying she loved the shock of the cold water, it refreshed and revitalised the heart and stimulated the circulation. Karim didn't like the cold. He'd tried on innumerable occasions to put Hend off swimming out of season but it was no use.

He'd sat down in the chair and covered himself with the towel, seeking shelter from the cold air that infiltrated via his pores, and listened to the dream that Hend, stretched out on her back in her bikini with her eyes closed, had told.

"What do you think?" she asked.

"What do I know? Really, it's a strange dream. It doesn't make sense at all. All I know is that when you dream of the sea it means repressed sexual desire but your dream's very complicated."

"Like Meelya's dreams," she said. "Dear God, I'm afraid I'll end up like she did at the end!"

"Who's Meelya?" asked Karim.

"Her nephews were our neighbours and my mother told me strange stories about her. It's said her dreams used to come true and everyone was afraid of her."

"Then what?"

"Then how should I know?"

He said the best way to deal with dreams was to forget them and he was cold and wanted to get dressed.

When the war started he told Danny his girlfriend had prophesied it because she'd dreamed that Rawsheh Rock had sunk, and that that symbol of Beirut created by the French – which they'd put on all their postage stamps as an embodiment of Beirut under the Mandate – had to sink now that the old Lebanon had come to an end.

Danny just smiled the superior smile which was one of the hallmarks of his authority. He'd listen without interrupting, then pronounce in a single sentence his dismissal, for example, of the doctrines of Freud, which make man the slave of those dark irrational regions that they call the unconscious. It was only in France that Karim discovered that the French had nothing to do with Rawsheh. He'd been in Montpellier with Talal discussing the idea of Maroun Baghdadi's film when Hend's dream had flashed through his mind. He told Talal that the film ought to end with the vanishing of Rawsheh Rock and recounted to him the story of the symbol of the Mandate that had to disappear.

"What have the French got to do with it?" asked Talal.

"The French took the name they gave to the area from the rock. 'Rock' in French is *rocher*, from which we got the word Rawsheh and from then on we started saying 'Rawsheh Rock.'"

Talal didn't smile Danny's superior smile but he did explain to the Lebanese doctor that this was a common misunderstanding. "The French had nothing to do with it. 'Rawsheh' was originally the Syriac word *rawsh*, meaning 'head'. The rock was, according to our ancestors, who spoke Syriac, 'the head of Beirut', but in our ignorance we believed it was a

French invention." The French had called the area *la Grotte aux Pigeons*, referring to the cave close to the rock. The rock itself was one hundred per cent Syriac. Talal said his mother had told him the tale because she was an eccentric woman: "You know, she phones from Beirut, the shells falling around her like rain, and tells me about her linguistic discoveries. She told me the dictionary and the books of Anis Freiha were the best way to forget the war."

Talal took the story back to its beginning. Karim wasn't a friend of the young man. He would run into him at the bar, they'd drink a beer and they'd chat a little. Then Talal had invited him to meet Maroun Baghdadi and now he'd come along and, without realising, provided a different interpretation for Hend's dream!

When he'd first arrived in Beirut, and after the glass of arak at his brother's flat, Hend had contented herself with talking to him with, as it were, the tips of her lips. She'd asked after Bernadette, Nadine, and Lara and about life in France but shown no interest in hearing the answers, sitting at the table for only a few moments and spending the rest of her time coming and going between the kitchen and the dining room.

"Tell us about the girls. Did you bring pictures?" asked Salma.

Karim's attention was attracted to the thick black nylon stockings pulled over Salma's legs. The white that once had erupted at the edges of her black skirt was gone, its place taken by black spots that seemed to bespatter her calves and thighs. Karim hadn't been aware that Salma had reverted to wearing stockings of this kind after his father's death. Hend had told him that at the deathbed in the hospital her mother had cried out that the man had lost his sight and that afterwards she'd reverted to her old mourning dress.

"And what does Nasim think about Nasri?" he asked her.

"Nasim didn't say anything. When we got back to the flat, he was silent. He only spoke to me when he had to. He didn't even talk to the children. You've seen for yourself how he never says anything when we're sitting together."

Karim hadn't noticed his brother's taciturnity during his stay in Beirut. Quite the contrary, Nasim had talked a lot and in talking rearranged the whole story. In his version, everything was turned upside down. The older brother, who believed he'd preserved his purity both before and during the war, discovered that in his brother's version things were totally different and that he'd lost – amongst all his other losses – the ability to repair the holes that had opened up, all at one go, in his life.

That first night, after the welcome dinner, a rush of emotions had overwhelmed Karim as he became aware of the oppressive absence of his father. He'd discovered how powerless he was to fashion words of love for a man whom he'd believed he'd always hated for his overbearing ways. He had risen, wanting to go home.

"I'll drive you," Nasim had said.

"No, don't bother. Stay. We've drunk a lot of arak. I'd prefer to take a taxi."

Nasim got up, paying no attention.

"But you've drunk a lot."

"So what? I see better when I drink."

They got into the car in silence. Karim felt as though he was choking. The humidity, the heat, his inability to talk.

"How about a coffee on the corniche?" said Nasim.

"I miss the Beirut sea. In Montpellier the sea's all one colour, a kind of grey, and the beach is depressing, I don't know why. Every time I go to Palavas with my wife and the girls, I tell them about the corniche and Rawsheh Rock."

They'd stopped in front of Rawsheh Rock and were drinking espresso from one of the small vans serving coffee that were parked here and there along the corniche. The rock sparkled in the lights that refracted off the edges of the smooth waves breaking against it.

"This is Beirut," said Karim. "You know, I don't know what came over me in France. Every time I heard news of the shelling in Lebanon I'd be frightened that the rock would be hit and would sink. In fact I used to dream that the rock had sunk and feel that Beirut had become shapeless and all its houses and buildings were falling down."

"You dreamed about the rock sinking? Strange!"

"What's strange?"

"You know, it's like we were young again. Remember how Father would make us finish off each other's dreams? Now it's like you were telling me my own dreams."

"Your dreams!"

"Don't tell me you've come so we can go back to playing that game again! I thought you'd have grown up after being away so long. We're here to work. We've got a project that's better than a gold mine. In Lebanon today medicine is gold. But it looks like you don't appreciate the importance of the project and you've come to open doors onto memories that we'd closed once and for all."

Karim hadn't understood what memories his brother was talking about. He'd come back without giving his decision a moment's thought. He'd taken unpaid leave and arrived without thinking through the implications of his decision. He'd known Bernadette would never come to Beirut and he had no reason to destroy his little French family, which was his refuge from himself and his sense of loss. Despite this, and because he'd drunk a lot of arak while eating the kibbeh nayyeh, he'd slipped up and told a dream he hadn't seen.

"Strange," said Nasim, "I thought that was Hend's dream. Now you've got me confused and I don't know what to think anymore."

"Give me a cigarette!" said Karim.

"What? Seems as soon as you arrived you started smoking again. Didn't you tell us you'd stopped in France?"

Karim blew the cigarette smoke into the air and stood gazing at Rawsheh Rock, feeling pins and needles all over his body.

"You told me you dreamed Rawsheh Rock had sunk," said Nasim and burst into laughter.

Suddenly Karim began laughing too. Their laughter fluttered over the place. It was as though the brothers had gone back to being twins, tricking the world with their complementarity and finding themselves some room for independence from the overbearing presence of their father, who used to force himself between them on the excuse that he was the third side of their unbreakable triangle.

The triangle had come apart long ago. The duality, which the brothers had maintained despite the outbreak of the civil war and the fact that they were in two warring camps, had begun to come apart the moment

Karim decided to leave for France. It had disintegrated once and for all with the phone call during which Nasim had informed his brother of his marriage to Hend and Karim had choked on his cough and lost the ability to speak.

That Beirut night, in front of Rawsheh Rock, their duality was resurrected. They became two children once more, playing with words, tossing jokes at one another, making fun of everything.

"Tell me," said Nasim. "There's something I never understood. Father would hint at it and Suzanne drew the conclusion that it had happened. On your honour now, tell the truth. Did Brother Eugène really fuck you?"

"Of course not. Don't you remember what your father used to say about him and his sons being 'up a tiger's arse'?"

"What?"

"What's the matter with you? Have you forgotten everything? Whenever he drank he'd finish the session by saying, 'Thank God, I'm still up a tiger's arse.'"

"I don't remember but it doesn't matter. Tell me what a tiger's arse is first and then answer my question."

"Being up a tiger's arse means no-one can ride you. Who'd want to get that close to the tiger? That's my answer."

"O.K., so don't answer. Just tell me what it feels like when a man sleeps with you."

"You think I'm stupid? But I'll tell you all the same. It feels as though your heart has leapt from its place and something inside you is opening up the closed doors of your soul."

"So he stuck it in you. I knew, I swear, that that was your first betrayal of our relationship."

"You were an idiot and always will be. If you can believe that trite poetic stuff you can believe anything."

"You mean you're having me on?" said Nasim.

"As usual, *chérie*. Nothing's changed between us. I say, and you believe like a fool. That's how we were and how we always will be."

"You're the fool, *chérie*. I'm the one who played you and your father and made you think you were seeing stars at noon. I took you to the sea and brought you back thirsty, as they say. And Suzanne? Is it true you went to see her after I'd gone home and she threw you out saying, 'Go away, dear, and leave me alone, you, your father, and your brother. You think I'm running a charity?'"

"Me? It looks like you're the one that's drunk, not me."

"She told me. You know I'm not one to forget a favour. When the war started I went to the souk and got her out of there and put her up in a small flat in Ashrafieh and supported her till she died. She'd grown very old and her eyes, poor thing, seemed to have got smaller. The rheuminess had eaten away at them. She told me, 'You're the only real man in Lebanon because you're authentic' – and then she told me. Unbelievable! Who goes to his brother's girlfriend? Aren't you my brother? I swear I don't know."

"I didn't go to her," said Karim. "She must have said that because she was demented. Maybe she got us mixed up and she meant you when she said me."

"No way!" said Nasim. "Everyone got us mixed up except women. Women have a strong sense of smell. They never make a mistake."

"I can't be sure," said Karim.

"What do you mean?"

"Nothing, I'm just talking about the principle of the thing."

"If you mean something else forget it right now because there isn't anything."

Silence and night, and a sea stretching to infinity. Two rocks, one squatting over the sea and opening its heart to the water and the wind, the other like a piece of the first rock that the waves have separated and that stands there, waiting. And two men standing in silence.

Karim felt he'd fallen into the trap. His younger brother had prepared his revenge with care. He'd lured him with the hospital project knowing that Nasri's older son wouldn't be able to resist the temptation of returning to Lebanon. He'd lured him with the hospital so he could show him that inheriting everything from their father wasn't enough. He'd inherited from his brother too, and married a cultured woman who loved the sea, a woman whom in the past he couldn't have dreamed of approaching.

"You win," said Karim.

"Win what?" said Nasim.

"Everything, even though I didn't go to Suzanne and you must know I had nothing to do with it. But it looks as though it's what you say that's going to be taken as the truth. In fact it doesn't matter. What matters is what stays in our memory and your memory is stronger because you are stronger."

They parted in peace. Nasim took his brother to their father's flat, where he was going to live during his stay in Beirut, and went home.

When Nasim got home at two in the morning, Hend was asleep. He lay beside her in bed and felt the urge to have sex. He started to awaken her gently, kissing her here and there on her lips and closed eyes. Half asleep, she asked why he was so late and said she was tired. "Tomorrow, dear. It's very late now and I'm dog tired." Nasim kept on at her. He told her he couldn't stop halfway, he wanted her. "But, dear . . ." He silenced her with a long kiss on the lips, moved closer, and began to make his way in. Hend closed her eyes again and surrendered to the flood of her husband's desire. It reminded her of the days of their first love, when he'd always made love to her after they had eaten white grapes that gave off a smell of incense.

Hend couldn't resist and, despite the conflicting emotions caused by Karim's return, found herself swept away by that rush of love her husband was capable of giving, and which changed him in bed into another man. The night-time man seemed to be different from the daytime man and the man when he was present wasn't the same as the man when he was absent. By day she felt alienated from his mysterious secret world and during his nightly absences, from which he'd return exhausted, the smell of alcohol wafting from him, she hated him and felt the need to explode in his face and tell him that marrying him had been a mistake. And when she listened to him as he conducted the rituals of breakfast with his children she felt she was in the presence of Nasri, and that this man, who made no secret of his hatred and contempt for his father, was in fact his double.

That night, when he sat up in bed and lit his cigarette and coughed, she was overwhelmed by a sense of loss. Emerging from the furnace of love and sex she'd felt she was a stranger to herself and to her desire, which had escaped her control.

He told her he hadn't been able to talk to his brother. "I took him to the corniche to have a coffee and talk, and instead of talking about the hospital project and how he wanted to run it and whether he was prepared to leave France and come and live in Lebanon or if he wanted something in between, like six months there and six months here, the idiot started telling me his dreams. I don't know what's happened to him. Things seem to be mixed up in his head. Maybe he thinks I know how to interpret dreams. And we couldn't talk, and in the end I had to explain his dream to him."

"And what was your explanation?" asked Hend.

"Why? Did he tell you the dream? Or maybe you dreamed the same dream. God, what a bind I've got myself into!"

"What are you talking about?" asked Hend.

"And you pretend you don't know either!"

"For God's sake, stop talking in riddles, or you'll spoil everything. If you don't want to talk sensibly let's go to sleep."

Since their first night, when they were at the chalet, Nasim had been smitten with astonishment when Hend's eyes shone after making love, and even though he'd insisted on not touching his girlfriend's virginity, the kisses on their own had been enough to turn her eyes into mirrors with shining depths.

He looked into her eyes and said, "For my sake, get up and look at your eyes in the mirror so you can see how they shine. God, it's beautiful!"

"It's alright, dear. Tomorrow the two of you can meet and talk. Let's sleep now."

"Don't you want to know the dream?" he asked her.

"You already told me I know it."

"So you do know it?"

"Please, get these ideas out of your head and let's sleep."

She covered herself with the blanket and asked her husband to turn off the light in the bedroom but he sat up straight, lit another cigarette, and told her that his brother had told him her dream about Rawsheh Rock sinking and claimed it as his own.

"Your brother's crazy," she said and turned off the light.

"Don't you want to know how I answered him?"

"I want to sleep."

She heard her husband breathing deeply at her side and saw herself in the wakeful darkness. As she went over again in her memory the story of her disappointment with Karim she found herself unable to sleep. Why had he run away like that? Why had he left her feeling undesired? Had he left after the Khaled Nabulsi affair, as he'd said, or after he was asked, supposedly, to write a book about the death of Jamal? On the eve of his departure, sitting in Uncle Sam's, she'd told him she didn't believe him and that she'd never have gone with him anyway, not because of her mother but because for a while now she'd begun to smell another woman on him.

"That's not true," he'd said.

"True or not, what matters is that that's how I feel."

He'd asked the waiter for the bill and left.

Karim had left because he'd had to leave: after Khaled's death, the Jamal incident, and Danny's terrible breakdown, the man had been incapable of regaining control of his life. His life had seemed like a rubble of events and memories that it was beyond him by then to reorganise.

"Life is context," he'd said to Bernadette as he tried to convince her of the merits of the project in Beirut.

His French wife had looked at him with her blue eyes and said she didn't know what he meant.

What context did Karim have in mind? Hadn't he told her in the first days after they met that he wanted to begin again from scratch, that he'd left behind his life among the bombs that had made gaps in his soul and his memory precisely so that he could begin a new one? He'd told her he would never look back because what lay behind was a darkness where the ghosts of the dead held sway. Even the living whom he'd left behind in Beirut now seemed like ghosts. He'd told her he was running from the blackness to the blue of her radiant eyes, that he had become a new man.

When drinking French wine and carried into his memories on the clouds of inebriation, all he'd talk about was Sinalcol. Sinalcol, whom

Karim had never once met and whose real name he didn't even know, was the story behind which Karim had hidden.

"Why do you talk to me about no-one but Sinalcol?" she asked him.

"Because he's my spiritual twin and my Lebanese mirror," he said. "Sinalcol's is the only story that's stayed with me from there, maybe because it isn't like other stories. Usually we tell stories we know but with him I know nothing. All I know is a few rumours that no-one can confirm and yet I feel him here, before the glass of wine and before your blue eyes."

When Karim recalled his obsession with Sinalcol in Montpellier and compared it with his aversion and indifference to him here in Beirut, he couldn't make sense of what had happened. Perhaps it was because his extreme drunkenness in the bar the day he met Bernadette for the first time had made him claim his name was Sinalcol and the name had stuck to him without his meaning it to.

In Beirut he hadn't thought of Sinalcol until Bernadette had mentioned him. He was talking to her on the phone and telling her about the hospital project and his proposal that he split his time in two – half in Beirut and the other half in Montpellier –which would allow him to take a break from his exhausting job in France and devote himself to his hobby of reading novels, when she asked him for news of Sinalcol.

"Have you found out anything about Sinalcol?" she asked.

"No, I haven't been to Tripoli yet."

"But you told me the first thing you were going to do was visit Tripoli."

"Don't worry, I'm not coming back to France without a photo of Sinalcol, but I'm really busy now."

Karim hadn't been telling the truth. He was planning to go to Tripoli, but to meet Radwan. Even Khaled Nabulsi, whose grave he was never to find, he'd tried to forget about, despite the fact that throughout his Beirut stay he was gripped by a feeling of responsibility towards Khaled's wife, Hayat, his aloofness and hesitance towards whom when she'd visited him at his home to ask for help after Khaled's assassination he had never been able to justify to himself. He hadn't known how to get rid of her. The fear had traced itself on his jaw, which had started to tremble, and the woman had understood and left without waiting for an answer.

The other woman, the one whom Hend had smelled on him, was none other than Jamal, though she wasn't. Or she was. He didn't know and didn't discover why until he read her diaries.

After the killing of Jamal on 11 March, 1978, a poster had appeared showing her with a scarf around her neck, crouching with a Kalashnikov. She was surrounded by photos of the other Deir Yassin Group martyrs. Underneath it said "Leader of Operation Kamal Adwan". He'd understood then why the girl had looked at him in surprise when he'd met her at the Café Jandoul.

Jamal hadn't asked him "What do you want with me?" She'd let him flirt with her while apparently not listening to what he was saying. In her eyes he'd seen an abyss of white emptiness. When he recalled her eyes all he could see was a white vastness, as though she didn't see him, or saw nothing, as though she was in some other world.

He'd met her at a military training camp in Baissour in 1976. Danny had taken him there after telling him that the great battle was about to begin and every member of the organisation had to take intensive training courses: everyone was expecting an incursion by the Syrian army to prevent the Lebanese Left and the Palestinian resistance from deciding the struggle for power in Lebanon.

Karim hadn't understood what all that meant or how it would be possible to stop the Syrian army, which had occupied the heights of Sannine and decided the battle before it began. But he went, and there he met the martyrs. Later, dozens of the young people on the training course were killed at the Battle of Bhamdoun but Karim didn't go to Bhamdoun with the others. They attached him to the Red Crescent station at Baissour, as though he were a doctor, which was how he escaped death. Jamal had been to Bhamdoun and not died. She disappeared from his life, and when he asked about her Danny told him she'd left the Student Brigade when the brigade leader had told her to get out of the camp because she was the only girl among dozens of male fighters. Danny said Jamal had joined one of the groups attached to the Western Sector, meaning the Occupied Lands sector, which was under the command of Khalil el-Wazir – Abu Jihad – and he knew nothing more about her.

Two years later, in early March 1978, Karim met her by chance at the clinic in Burj el-Barajneh camp and invited her to have coffee at the Modeca Café on Hamra Street. She agreed but asked if they could change the place: she said she preferred the Café Jandoul on the corniche at Mazraa because it was close to her parents' home.

At Baissour Jamal had been a different girl, brown-skinned with large honey-coloured eyes, a delicate nose, full lips, short black hair, and a scarf tied around her neck. During the evenings at Baissour, where he spent two weeks, Karim would make a point of sitting next to her and talking to her. He had no idea where he'd found the words after the boring lectures on the People's War, the theories of General Giap – hero of Dien Bien Phu – and the thoughts of Mao Tse Tung on "the principal contradiction and the secondary contradictions". When the political discussions finished he'd find himself sitting next to her, talking about everything and nothing. Nothing that was said then had stuck on memory's tape, but the curve of the girl's shoulders, her dissatisfaction with everything, and her insistence on talking constantly about the martyrs had stirred in his soul waves of desire that did not dare show themselves. He contented himself with short walks with her in the forest, where their talk began to take on the form of love. She told him stories about her father, who had fled on foot from Jaffa to Lebanon under the bombardment to which the city had been subjected.

Karim left the training camp and those who died at Bhamdoun died. The Palestinian girl's shining eyes, however, continued to keep him company, though he had no idea what to do with the mysterious emotion he felt.

At the Café Jandoul he told her he loved her.

Jamal's look, however, remained filled with white spaces. She sipped a little from her coffee cup and asked him if he was ready to die for the woman he loved.

"If I love her I have to live for her sake."

She smiled, lit a cigarette, and blew the smoke into the air before asking him again.

"That's not what I meant. I was asking you if you'd be ready to die with her."

"I don't understand," he said.

The girl seemed to hesitate, as though she wanted to say something, but she didn't say it.

"It doesn't matter," she said.

"But I feel a strange attachment to you," he said.

"You'll forget soon enough," she said.

"Why should I have to forget when we haven't yet begun?" he said.

"You know, Doctor, I think all intellectuals are cowards. A large intelligence turns one into a coward. I listened to your comments during the course on what you called the naïveté of the thoughts of Mao Tse Tung and especially his theory of paradox and you may be right, but without naïveté we wouldn't be able to fight. Without a simple clear idea that can take over your heart, like a religious idea, you can't do battle."

"But we're secularists and Marxists and have to liberate ourselves from religion."

"True, but there's no other solution," she said.

"If we turn into a religion we'll lose everything," he said.

"You know you're more intelligent than I am and are going to win the argument but that's not the point. The point has something to do with cowardice and courage and not being afraid of death."

"Is there anyone who isn't afraid of death?"

"Me," she said, and prepared to get up. He asked her if he'd see her again and she said, "That would be nice." He said they could make "That would be nice" into a reality now. "I could see you in two days. Let's go out and have dinner together."

"That would be nice," she said and left.

Karim only understood the meaning of her hints two days later, when pictures of Jamal filled the front pages of the Beirut newspapers. She was lying on the ground on the coast road between Haifa and Tel Aviv. An Israeli officer was crouched over her bullet-riddled body, as though searching the corpse.

Had she wanted him to go with her to their death? Had she meant by her hints at the Café Jandoul to invite him to join her group, which had made its way by stealth in rubber boats to the beach at Haifa and hijacked two Israeli buses before clashing with the Israeli army and dying?

Was suicide the other name of love? Or was it that Jamal, on the eve of her decision to lead a suicide operation inside Israel, was unable to love? What it came down to was that her heart had needed words, for at the moment of death, just as the lips feel a thirst for water, the heart thirsts for words.

Jamal Salim Jazayri was born on 12 January, 1958, in Beirut. She was the eldest daughter of a Palestinian family from Jaffa. Her father, Salim Jamal Jazayri, had left Jaffa on foot the day the city fell, at which time he was twenty. His entire family had already left the city in boats but the young man, who had fought in the ranks of the Jihad Muqaddas Brigades, had refused to go with them and fought on in the city until the end. The city's fall and the invasion of its quarters by men from the Haganah forced him to bury his rifle in the garden of the house and flee on foot to Lebanon. In Lebanon he never met up with the other members of his family, whom the winds of fate had tossed to Damascus, where they took up residence in Yarmouk camp. He made it to Beirut, where he refused to live in one of the camps set up for Palestinian refugees. Instead, he rented a room in the Mazraa district and worked as a mechanic in the garage of Hajj Feisal Mughrabi before becoming the owner of his own garage and turning himself into the best car-repair mechanic on the Mazraa corniche. In 1957 he married Dalal el-Batal, a Palestinian from the village of Tiret Haifa, eighteen years of age, with whom he had four children, Jamal being the oldest; and though he had three boys – Salim, Amin, and Nasir – he continued to be known for the rest of his life as Abu Jamal.

At the Baissour camp Jamal had told Karim her family's story, and also how her father had encouraged her to take part in training courses organised specially for young girls. He hadn't objected when she decided to join the Fedayeen after she got her secondary school certificate. She said she preferred the university of the revolution to a regular university. She couldn't understand why all young Palestinian men and women didn't join the Fedayeen: she wanted to be a model of the Palestinian woman in the resistance, just as Djamila Bouhired had become a symbol of the Algerian.

When Karim read the details of that operation led by a woman and saw Jamal's corpse on the ground being messed around with by an Israeli officer, he was stupefied. She'd become a symbol, as she'd wanted. There she was, the girl from the Baissour camp, at whose presence alongside the men in another camp some of the youths there had grumbled, proving to them all that she was the bravest, the most beautiful, and the most capable of sacrifice.

A girl of twenty, she'd led ten Fedayeen, including two Lebanese and two Yemenis, and taken them by night in two rubber boats to the beach at Haifa. There they hijacked a bus carrying fifteen passengers and two hours later they hijacked another. Then they set off for Jaffa, firing into the air to clear the road.

The first bus was taken over at 2.30 p.m. on Sunday, 11 March, and at 4.40 p.m. the Fedayeen moved with their hostages, who at this point numbered more than sixty, to a new bus. At 5.30 p.m. the bus found its way blocked by a barrier set up at the used car market in Herzliya, close to the County Club.

Helicopters and tracked vehicles barred the way and the battle began. The bus was set on fire. The Fedayeen jumped down onto the road and engaged with the Israeli forces. Eight died, two were taken captive, and thirty Israelis were killed.

The moment he heard of her death, Karim felt he'd lost the woman he loved. It was as though Jamal had been hiding beneath Hend's skin; as though the two young women were one, or had become so.

"Why did they send her to her death?"

When Danny came to him with the strange proposal, he'd felt panic.

"Why me?"

"Brother Abu Jihad wants to meet you. He read your article on the history of Shaqif Castle in the magazine *Occupied Palestine* and he wants you to write a pamphlet on Jamal."

"Me?"

"Yes you," said Danny.

"But how did he know I wrote the article when I published it under a pseudonym? I don't want anyone to know I wrote for *Occupied Palestine*.

You know how my family's placed, living in East Beirut. I don't want them coming to any harm because of me."

"Abu Jihad isn't just anyone. He's the real leader of the revolution and he knows everything, including that your brother Nasim works with the Phalanges."

"What's my brother got to do with anything? I beg you, don't mention that to anyone!"

"The important thing, my friend, is that Abu Jihad was much taken with your storytelling skills and asked which of the boys who knew the Martyr Jamal wrote well, and he chose you. He said your article on the crusaders was excellent because it was made up of stories and he wants you to go and see him at ten o'clock tomorrow night at Centre 38 so he can talk to you about it."

"Where's this Centre 38?"

"I'll go with you," said Danny. "Do you have any idea what it means that Brother Abu Jihad chose you to write about Jamal? Do you know what she meant to him? He's the one who chose her *nom de guerre* 'Jihad', because she was like one of his children to him."

"If he loved her so much why did he send her off to commit suicide? Anyway, I'm not a writer. For me writing's a hobby; I prefer to read. I wrote the article about the history of Shaqif Castle to say that while it's true the Franks occupied our country for two hundred years, in the end they went away and all they left behind was castles and shankaleesh and that's the way it's going to be with the Zionists in Palestine."

"That's what Abu Jihad liked about it. He said your article was 'an expression of historical optimism: no matter how long the Jews stay and impose their rule, in the end they are destined to abandon the country to its inhabitants.'"

"I didn't say the Jews, I said the Zionists and that's the heart of the matter. We're for a secular democratic state in Palestine and we mustn't use the word 'Jews' to describe the Israeli occupiers. If Abu Jihad said Jews, I don't want to work with him."

Danny explained that all members of the generation that lived through the Palestinian catastrophe in 1948 used the word "Jews" for the Israelis, for the simple reason that the Israelis, before and after the founding of their state, insisted on calling themselves by that name. Saying "the Jews' army" in 1948 didn't carry any intrinsically racist connotation. It was just a name that the peasants gave to the members of the Haganah forces.

"But we do distinguish between Jews and Zionists," said Karim.

"Absolutely," answered Danny, "and Brother Abu Jihad does so too but when you're dealing with people of that generation there's no call to be stubborn over words. We'll meet tomorrow at nine at Café Jandoul and I'll go with you to Centre 38."

"I like being stubborn over words because I've been split in two. Here in Lebanon, where we're fighting a civil war against the fascists, all I hear you talking about is 'the Christians'. I've turned a deaf ear a hundred times but I've had enough. I don't want to go on being a fool because that way the sects will swallow us up, the Left will die, the Palestinian cause will become a religious cause, and we'll lose everything. Tomorrow, if Abu Jihad says 'the Jews', I'm going to turn around and leave."

They met at nine on the evening of the following day at Café Jandoul. Danny had chosen the café because it was close to Burj Abu Haydar, where Abu Jihad had one of his clandestine offices, known as "Centre 38". Karim took it differently, though. He believed the choice was a secret message addressed to him by Jamal. It was there that they'd met for the last time and there that he'd discovered the beauty of her short black hair, a single small lock of which hung down over her right eye, and there that she'd admitted – by inviting him to die with her – that she loved him.

Danny came in all his elegance, an elegance over which this professional revolutionary – for whom it was a matter of pride that his wife was the most beautiful woman in Beirut – took as much care as a cockerel. He would wrap a long scarf around his neck and choose shirts ranging from sky blue to indigo, which had to be ironed to perfection. His shoes shone like his hair, which was fairish. The image would have been impeccable were it not for the smile, which revealed small teeth stained black by the French cigarettes he smoked. Danny ordered a chocolate *sablé* and a glass of Rémy Martin. The waiter turned to Karim, who ordered the same but Danny told the waiter, "Two *sablés*, one cognac, and a tea."

"You don't like cognac anymore?" asked Karim.

Danny smiled and said in faux-classical Arabic, "Nay, Brother! The tea's for thee, not me," explaining that it would be inappropriate for him to go to a meeting with Abu Jihad with the smell of alcohol on his breath.

"Why? It's forbidden to drink alcohol?"

Danny shook his head. "You're totally unworldly, Brother Karim. It's about what Chairman Mao taught us: respect the masses and their traditions."

"I swear I don't understand you people. What? Is Abu Jihad the masses?"

"Brother Abu Jihad doesn't drink and doesn't like those who do, end of story. If you want to be part of the struggle you have to know where it is you're living. Come on, drink up your tea and stop pestering me. We mustn't be late."

Karim swallowed the hot tea while he watched Danny sniff the cognac, take the glass in the palm of his hand to warm it, and then sip the liquid drop by drop as carefully as if he were distilling each one in his mouth.

Did Karim's problem lie in the fact that, contrary to what he now claimed, he hadn't spoken his mind? Or was it that he was so dazzled by the Fedayeen that his criticisms evaporated when he found himself face to face with their heroism? He'd told Abu Jihad shamefacedly that he didn't support suicide operations – he didn't say that exactly but he did say "It's a sin to send young people to their death that way! A sin, Brother Abu Jihad!"

"Where's the sin?" asked the leader as he gazed at the map for the Martyr Kamal Adwan operation that lay on his desk.

Instead of explaining his position or responding, Karim found himself gasping with admiration as he looked at the map and saw the points at which the Fedayeen had stopped before arriving at their death.

Danny had taken him to a building in Burj Abu Haydar. A guard carrying a revolver asked them what they wanted. "Deir Yassin," responded Danny. It seems that was the password, for the moment he heard it the guard spoke into a walkie-talkie. A few minutes later a youth wearing khaki appeared, asked which of them was Karim, and gestured to him to follow.

"I'll be at home if you need anything," said Danny.

Karim entered the building with the youth, whose Tokarev pistol was visible at his waist, and they descended endless steps. Karim was silently counting the steps and when he got to sixty he saw in front of him a door, which opened, dazzling him with light.

The youth had left him in front of the door and begun to climb back up the stairs. Karim hesitated a little, then heard a voice calling to him to enter. This was the only time he met Abu Jihad. The leader was wearing a dark grey shirt and sitting behind his desk.

"Welcome, Brother Karim! What would you like to drink?"

Abu Jihad poured two glasses of sage tea from a thermos in front of him, offered a glass to Karim, drank from his own, and said he was pleased to meet him.

Abu Jihad said he'd chosen him for three reasons. The first was that he'd known the martyr and it had come to his knowledge that an innocent friendship had developed between the two of them at the Baissour camp two years before. The second reason was that he'd read his article on Shaqif Castle and been impressed by his ability to recount and summarise history and put it at the service of the cause; his attention had been caught particularly by Karim's citing of a story by an Israeli author called Yusha about a Palestinian with a severed tongue and his ruined village.

"Yehoshua," said Karim.

"Right, Yehoshua. You read Hebrew?"

"No, I read it in English."

"You're from the Shammas family of the Galilee – Fasouta, I think."

"I'm not Palestinian," said Karim, "I'm from Beirut."

"Anyway, we're all one people."

"Thank you," said Karim.

"Where were we? The third reason is that I don't want professional writers. I want what's written about Jamal to be full of life, which is why it has to be a writer like you, meaning a writer who isn't a writer."

Abu Jihad started explaining to Karim the map in front of him and how the young people had infiltrated using a commercial ship. Then, when they reached a point opposite Haifa beach they'd thrown their rubber boats into the sea and themselves into the midst of the waves to get to them. Two of the youths had become martyrs by drowning, and had it not been for the intensive training they would all have drowned before getting to the boats. Then he spoke of the two buses and how the Israeli army was responsible for the massacre that took place. "The orders to Jamal and the boys were not to kill any Israeli hostages. They were to get to Jaffa and negotiate there the release of a hundred Fedayeen captives and their safe exit from occupied territory. But the Israeli army closed the road at Herzliya, bombed the bus from helicopters and the massacre happened."

"But I know from Jamal, Brother Abu Jihad, that the chances of not dying were zero."

"Not true. We prepare the young people psychologically for martyrdom but that doesn't mean that the chances of returning safely are zero. That's not true."

Karim asked what it meant to say that "the chances weren't zero". Abu Jihad smiled bitterly and said, "They're like my own children and in any case the road we've chosen can lead only to martyrdom. I'm certain that the moment when I shall meet them again is near. It will be the happiest of my life."

Abu Jihad explained to Karim that he expected a short text from him – enough to fill a five-page pamphlet – that would tell the story of Jamal and turn her into a symbol of Palestinian womanhood.

"But to write, I have to have all the facts," said Karim.

Abu Jihad opened his desk drawer and took from it a spiral-bound book that had been placed in a closed brown envelope. "I made you a copy of the diaries kept by the martyr. I'm sure they'll be a very useful source. There are only two copies of these diaries. The original is with me and the photocopy with you. Absolutely no-one must see this text. Take your time and write at your leisure and if you have questions phone Brother Nabil directly. He's the one who's going to take you home. I'm ready to answer all your questions anytime you call. It's a big responsibility that the revolution is placing in your hands. Please don't spend a lot of time on some of the personal issues, they're not useful, but you have to know about them so you can write."

Karim took the brown envelope with trembling hands and, seeing the leader stand, stood up too. Abu Jihad put out his hand and shook Karim's, and Karim heard the voice of Brother Nabil, who had suddenly appeared in the room. They went out into the darkness of the stairs and climbed in silence. He got into a small Volkswagen next to Nabil. Nabil drove the car carefully through the empty streets and didn't ask where he was supposed to be taking him. The car stopped in front of Karim's building on Abd el-Aziz Street. Nabil gave him his number and said he'd be waiting for him to phone. Karim opened the door of the car and made to get out but Nabil's hand reached out for his knee and stopped him.

"Forget where you met Brother Abu Jihad. No-one must know where 'Centre 38' is."

Karim nodded and quickly got out of the car. Because there was an outage he climbed the steps to the third floor where he lived, lit the paraffin lantern, and sat down on the only sofa in his room, where Jamal's words started marching towards his eyes. He felt as though he was choking; he felt thirsty and the words danced over the shards of light from the lantern, which, seen through his tears, appeared upside down.

Why hadn't he dared tell Abu Jihad that he would never write the pamphlet? Was it cowardice, admiration for the man, or a mixture of the two?

He wanted to tell him that suicide operations were a sin, they did no good, and that he was against them because the killing of civilians wasn't a revolutionary act. At the same time, though, he admired and was enchanted by this girl who had fashioned heroism through her death. Things were mixed up in his mind because he wasn't against the heroic operation that Jamal had led: he'd wanted it to happen and to succeed and in so doing to shake Israeli society to its roots and make it feel the significance of the catastrophe that had befallen the Palestinians and of their expulsion from their homeland. But he'd also wanted Jamal to emerge alive. The problem of the revolution is that the men and women who die for it and are transformed into posters and photos and they don't see their own posters. They die imagining the poster. Truth becomes an illusion in their lifetimes, and their lives vanish into the darkness of death.

He lost himself amongst Jamal's words. He felt they'd become traps into which he'd fallen and from which he would never escape. Why had Abu Jihad chosen him for this impossible task? Did the man know of his silent love for the martyr and had he chosen him to make him pay the price of his cowardice? Jamal would never have been able to invite him to die with her without first consulting her commander. Maybe they thought they needed a doctor, but a doctor can't treat suicide if he commits suicide along with the rest. What a bind! How was he to write of his disappointment? How was he to write after reading what Jamal had written about him? Was it true that he used to weep at Baissour, and if not, why had she pictured him so? Had she wanted to castrate him to justify to herself her failure to respond to him? But she had responded. True, she'd been reserved at the camp, but at the Café Jandoul she'd been different – distant and close, her eyes wandering as though she wanted to say and not say. And then there was the meeting at the clinic in Burj el-Barajneh, which had happened by chance. Karim was certain it hadn't been a coincidence at all, and that Jamal had dropped by the clinic deliberately so that she could run into him because she'd wanted to convey to him a precise message. That was why she'd agreed to his invitation to coffee at Café Jandoul, though there she'd hesitated and hadn't said what she'd meant to.

Karim spent the whole night up, reading and rereading. He didn't tell Danny what had happened at his meeting with Abu Jihad and Danny didn't ask. Karim lived with Jamal's diaries for three days. He was stunned, reading words that were next to one another without arriving at their meaning, the meaning fleeing the text before it could enter Karim's consciousness. He read and reread and discovered he'd never be able to write anything. How could he rewrite a text that had been taken apart by death and then reassembled? How was he to interpret a voice coming to him from the other world? What could the dead say to the living? Jamal had written poetry. He read the poetry and reread it. He would see the poem, or something like the poem, disintegrate and then reassemble itself, its rhythms dissolving in his eyes. He read the poem ten times. He read it in a low voice and in a loud voice. He read it with his eyes closed and he read it with his eyes open.

When he read the news of Abu Jihad's assassination in Tunis Jamal had awoken once more in his memory.

He'd run into Talal at the café in Place de la Comédie. The Lebanese student was carrying *al-Safir* and started reading an article describing Abu Jihad's funeral at Yarmouk camp in Damascus. All he could remember of the description was the scene of the bier flying over upraised hands. "The whole camp came out and all the villages of Galilee congregated to bid farewell to the leader of the intifada of the 'children of the stones' in Palestine. And then the bier flew. The bier hovered over the throng and moved over the tips of the fingers of the hands raised to bear it. So thick were the crowds that it was beyond the power of those carrying the bier to move forward. They were stuck fast but the bier knew how to complete its journey to the grave. Wrapped in the Palestinian flag, it flew over the fingertips, the hands of all those gathered to see him off rising to receive it. The bier appeared to be flying, the raised hands seemingly making for it a pathway in the air."

Talal put the paper aside and asked Karim what he thought of the beautiful description and at the same instant Karim saw himself sitting in front of Abu Jihad, who was telling him he wanted him to draw a map of hope over the map of death that was open on his desk. At that same instant Jamal's words also returned to ring in his ears. Only a few lines of her poem had stayed in his memory but there, in the Café Comédie, he could her voice as clearly as though time had evaporated, as though he was with her on the Mazraa corniche and they were sipping coffee at the Café Jandoul. With head bowed and a lock of her hair covering her right eye she'd gazed ahead and recited.

> I shall walk and walk
> And read out the communiqué of the stone
> And read out the communiqué of the tree
> And embrace my love
> And build for my heart
> Houses of sadness and of memories
> And I shall sit alone
> With death alone

And my voice there
Like my voice here
Shall be a call to my land
That traces the face of the rain.

"That's Romantic poetry," said Karim.

"I'm not interested in the terms. Soon you'll see that I've written the most beautiful poem of all."

"What?"

"I'm not talking about this poem because poetry must take the poet by surprise before it can take the readers by surprise. I'm talking about a poem written in a different way. Tomorrow you'll read it and think of me and say, 'Thus spoke Jamal.'"

Memory tossed him this way and that, her voice wrapped itself around him, and he regretted not having written the pamphlet he'd been commissioned to write. He'd read the text dozens of times, read the details of the suicide operation, and looked at all the available pictures. Brother Nabil had even got hold of a photograph for him of a place in Israel they call the Cemetery of the Numbers, where the Fedayeen are buried by number and not name. Nabil said that he didn't know Jamal's number at the cemetery but it wasn't important; the important thing was to draw the lesson, which was that even their dead had become numbers, and that he might want to focus on this point to make a comparison between the numbers tattooed on the arms of Jews in the Nazi death camps and the numbers given to dead Fedayeen.

The idea didn't appeal to Karim. He told Nabil such comparisons weren't useful: the Palestinians were victims in their own right and didn't need to be compared to other victims to prove the reality of their tragedy.

It had all come to nothing. The text hadn't been written, Nabil had been killed in an explosion in the Fakhani district, and the connection to Abu Jihad had been lost.

The strange thing was that no-one ever asked him for Jamal's text. The likeliest explanation was that her story, like other stories, had been forgotten. The martyrs were a surging throng, the newly dead obliterating the dead who had gone before. Thus was Jamal's story lost, and all that remained of it was the image of heroism represented by her body lying on the road at Herzliya.

Karim remembered that the one precious thing he'd taken with him to Montpellier was Jamal's text. On the eve of his departure, when he'd thrown all his papers into the wastepaper basket, he'd found himself incapable of throwing Jamal onto the rubbish dump of his memories.

He'd left Talal going on about the plot of the first-ever film shot in Lebanon about muscles and body-building and set off home at a run. He'd gone into his bedroom and opened the drawer in the bedside table where he'd put the brown envelope, but failed to find it. He opened the doors of the wardrobe and had begun going through it when Bernadette came into the room.

"What are you doing?" she asked.

"It's O.K. I'm looking for something I brought with me from Lebanon."

She said nothing got lost in her house and that she could look for it but was busy at the moment with Lara. She said they'd summoned her to the school, where the teacher had told her Lara had wet herself, which wasn't normal for a girl of seven, and that the psychotherapist at the school would have to see her because these sorts of things pointed to a disturbance in her relationship with her parents. She'd been obliged to take the girl back home to change her clothes, and when she'd returned her to the school she'd met the psychotherapist, Monsieur Charles, who had deduced from his interview with the girl that she was suffering from a disturbance in her relations with her father, and said he'd like to meet the father.

"Monsieur Charles has given you an appointment for a week from now and says you have to go."

"Fuck him."

She asked him not to swear and said the only Arabic she'd learned was the swear words, as though they were all the language had, and that it was his duty, instead of getting upset, to think about how he could improve his relationship with his children because the girls hardly ever saw him. Even when he took them to the public gardens or the Place de la Comédie he didn't talk to or show any interest in them.

"How silly can you get? When I was seven I shat myself at school. Father didn't make a fuss. He just told me to forget about it and I did. Maybe the girl was scared of the teacher because she didn't know how to write some sentence – no more no less. And now they're trying to tell me the girl's messed up psychologically. Nonsense! You want to tell me that when I shat myself at school I had a psychological problem?"

"Definitely," answered Bernadette.

"Me?"

"Yes you."

"No, *madame*. The messed up one with psychological problems is you not me."

She said she couldn't talk to him anymore because he lost his temper so quickly and refused to face up to problems, large or small, and that instead of thinking about how he could take care of his daughter – which he ought to, given he was the reason for the problem – he just shrugged the charge off and pinned it on her.

She asked him, the shaky calm of her voice concealing her anger, to stop behaving that way. If he believed she was responsible for the girl's psychological disturbances, she was ready to listen to him.

"I don't think there's anything wrong with the girl and you should stop talking about 'disturbances'. If there's anyone creating tensions in this house it's you."

Bernadette had left the room in a fury but returned a few minutes later with a brown envelope in her hand. She said she'd hidden it because she'd found it discarded among his socks. "I was sure you'd look for it one day so I hid it in the drawer where I keep the deeds to the flat. Here you are, and please stop making a mess of the wardrobe."

He apologised to her, said he hadn't meant anything, and that it was "just the way the words came out". He was on edge and would pay more attention to the girls, but right now he had to read that file.

He took the envelope from her and sat at the dining table. His hands trembled as he saw the letters leap out of the darkness of death and heard the voice of Abu Jihad saying he wanted to turn Jamal into a symbol of the Palestinian woman.

He emptied out the envelope and found three photocopied files taken from the diary in which Jamal had written her text. The date was printed at the top of the pages. Jamal had started writing on Tuesday, 26 December, and finished on Monday, 18 September. On the last page she had written a single sentence in big letters that filled the entire space: "The Revolution will be true to my blood. Your Sister Jamal Salim Jazayri (Jihad), 2-9-1978" – which meant that the dates at the tops of the pages bore no relation to the real dates. The diary had been manufactured to fit writing in French or English, in other words from left to right, but Jamal had used it to write in Arabic and had written from right to left, so the dates at the top of the pages went backward instead of going forward and had lost their meaning. That didn't matter, Karim thought. He read the diaries from beginning to end and discovered that the parts of Jamal's poem which had stuck in his memory were not in fact the poem, because his memory had added to and subtracted from it. That's what memory does. Jamal too had been betrayed by her memory, and the first lines of her only poem weren't in fact by her but part of a poem entitled "The Land" by Mu'in Bseiso that he'd recited at U.N.E.S.C.O. Hall in Beirut on Land Day in 1974. Her memory, however, had betrayed her and rewritten it.

Now that it was clear that Jamal had been Karim's biggest delusion, why did he still want to read? In Beirut, when he got to that part, he'd closed his eyes. He hadn't thrown the exercise books aside or risen from the only couch in the small flat and stopped reading, but had closed his eyes and fallen into a doze. What would he do now? Would he close them again and doze? Or would he read and focus on the deception?

Jamal had written about everything. She'd put her finger on all the different manifestations of corruption in the Revolution and their underlying causes, and yet she'd gone to her death despite this, for the sake of a revolution in whose children she no longer believed. That was the paradox of her death and the magic of her heroism. She wasn't so naïve as to believe but she was such a believer that she ignored what she'd seen. That day, in the distant French city, Karim could speak of naïveté and belief, but in Beirut, when revolutionary words had had the power to ignite within him the volcano of possibility, he hadn't realised his naïveté. Even the fear that had controlled him and paralysed his every movement had become a conscious feeling only after he left Beirut. He'd spoken, during his last days in Beirut, of his disgust with the war and the transformation of politics into an endlessly repeated exercise in futility. But it was only there, in "the land of the French", as his father used to call France, that he'd acknowledged that the whole thing had had nothing to do with his political convictions but was, rather, an embodiment of that incapacitating feeling whose name is fear.

He'd been incapable of explaining to Hend that his desire for her hadn't evaporated because of some other woman – even though at the time he had himself been convinced that Jamal was that other woman – but had done so out of fear. One who is afraid neither eats nor wants to. One who is afraid simply fears.

Jamal was, but also wasn't, the "other woman". He'd run into her more than once at Fatah's Western Sector office in Fakhani but those had all been brief encounters. They had drunk tea several times at the Café Shumoua but being in a café so crowded with Fedayeen had made of their time together a mere shadow of the relationship he'd built up with her at the camp at Baissour, and whenever he asked her for a real date she'd say she'd call him.

Why had she resolved to see him a few days before her death, accepted his invitation, and specified the place? She hadn't refused to go to Café Modeca on Hamra Street only to impose on him some sad and insipid meeting at Café Shumoua. Instead, she'd specified the Jandoul. Had she been hesitating, or was she, in her own fashion, saying goodbye to the world? He remembered she hadn't asked him to stop when he'd spoken poetically of the beauty of her eyes. When he'd stretched out his hand towards her she'd stretched out her own small shy hand, and when she'd bent her head to listen to his words of love she'd radiated shyness and desire. Why then had she spoken of him as she had in her diaries?

He'd returned to the diaries because when listening to Talal reading about Abu Jihad's funeral procession in Damascus the mix of passion and sorrow he thought he'd left behind in Beirut had filled him once more. He'd felt the same paroxysm he had the day he heard the news of Jamal's operation and her tragic death in Herzliya.

He reread the spiral-bound books line by line, read Jamal's criticism of the corruption and of her belief that women, if they were to win their right to equality, must fight exactly like men. He read her concerns about the company commander who had ordered her to leave the Baissour camp because she was the only young woman in an eighty-strong group of men. He saw her admiration for the leaders Majid, Abu Azzam, and Saad Jradat, and paused at her description of the harsh training in the use of rubber boats – the means used by the group to reach the beach at Haifa.

"Picture to yourselves how I used to sleep! I used to sleep together with four young men and not feel shy, because each rubber boat carried only five. Even so, we all worked together as one and took all our decisions together, united by our determination, our will, and our devotion. We sang and trained and waited for the moment when the operation would be launched."

She'd gone through a lot and had had to put up with the ship, which had no proper latrine. "You may not believe it but during the four days that we spent on the ship I never relieved myself, but waited until we'd reached the beach. At sea I endured sickness, hardship, and exhaustion but I would raise the boys' morale, sitting with them, singing with them, and making food and tea for them."

Jamal had gone through a lot to arrive at the moment of her radiant appearance on the poster. Karim read as though listening to her speak. He heard the sound of her voice through the written words and understood why he hadn't been the one she spoke of. He hadn't lived with her the moments of tension, fear, and endurance during the training on rubber boats. So what had happened to him when he read the section about the youth whom Jamal had loved? Why had he been afflicted with sorrow and a sense of loss as he read her description of him and her account of her relationship with him in the diaries? It was because he'd thought at first that he was the man to whom she alluded and had felt his heart burn, but then discovered it had nothing to do with him for she was speaking of another. He felt his soul disintegrate and his body evaporate and was struck by the sorrow of one who feels he has been deceived.

"During the time we were in the camp I treated one of the brothers differently because this brother was in need of someone to stand beside him and help him and feel with him. He'd consult me about everything he did and if I didn't respond and talk to him and laugh with him and sit next to him, he'd get upset – he was always crying. If I pointed out to him some mistake he'd made, he'd feel shaken, take it personally, sit on his own, and not eat, drink, or sleep. His crying cut me to the quick and I'd tell myself he was crying because of me . . . and then the camp commander would shout at me for going with him and being late and I'd have to lie so that the brother in question wouldn't get upset."

"Why does she write about me like that? I'm not like that!" Karim had shouted, flinging the book from his hand.

That was how he remembered himself in his flat in Beirut: alone and reading and shaking with sorrow and anger. But he hadn't cried. He remembered he'd cried *once* during the night at Baissour – he'd been walking with Jamal when she asked him about George. And he hadn't cried because Jamal had reprimanded him over some mistake he'd made, he'd cried because George had been his friend. George, a Palestinian student at the American University of Beirut, had died. He'd returned on a stretcher, crowned with the white snow of Sannine, and when his mother had asked that a cross be set up over the grave of her only son, who had been buried in the Islamically themed Palestine Martyrs cemetery, everyone was struck dumb. Marwan, who ten years later would be assassinated in Cyprus, had declared, however, that the cross would be there. He brought a large black cross with the name of the martyr on it and planted it over the grave. The wooden cross was a metre and a half tall and didn't look at all like the cross that had been inscribed, in a place where it couldn't be seen, on the tiling of the tomb of Kamal Nasir.

The A.U.B. student group had received an order from Danny to protect the cemetery and ten of the boys, Karim among them, had gone there, fully armed, to provide a guard for the ceremony. Danny had arrived glowering and said that the priest of the Orthodox Church of

Our Lady had refused to come to the cemetery; he'd fled, so Danny had been forced to bring in a Palestinian Protestant minister who'd come to attend the funeral prayers at the church. The moment the bier appeared, though, the armed members of the protection detail fell to pieces at the sight of their comrade lying on a wooden plank and wept. The stern orders that Danny had given them to form a cordon around the cemetery lost all meaning.

No-one had provided protection for the funeral. George had no need of it, for those days were different from these, as he would later tell Khaled, who used to talk to him about Islam and the necessity of joining the fundamentalist tendency as it was the future, now that the defeat and collapse of the Left had become an established fact. The day Khaled said that, Karim had asked him, "What shall we do then with George and the cross we put up at his mother's request in the middle of an Islamic cemetery?" and Khaled had hung his head and found nothing to say.

If Karim had spoken while reading Jamal's memoirs he would have said he'd never cried and that Jamal had disfigured his image. The lover commits suicide only if the beloved dies; perhaps that was why Jamal had talked of their dying together.

He'd gone on reading, only to discover that he wasn't the hero of the story. Jamal spoke of another youth, giving his initials as "N.A.". Karim couldn't remember if he'd noticed those letters when he'd read the text the first time, in Beirut. "N.A." had trained with the suicide group, injured his foot, and gone to hospital three weeks before the operation, and was thus rendered unfit to go through with the mission. He'd visited her at home, limping, and begged her not to go to her death. When she refused he'd threatened to tell her mother the facts of the suicide operation but had been too much of a coward to do so.

Now, in France, these lines jumped out and struck him in the eye. Had the story of his love for Jamal been nothing but an illusion? Had he invented the tale of Jamal to make it easier for him to abandon Hend? And why had he abandoned Hend?

True, she'd said she couldn't leave her mother. He could have gone abroad to finish his studies, then returned and married her, but he'd decided not to return and to run away from Salma and his father, and from Danny's descent into the abyss following the death of Khaled and the phantom of death that Khaled had seen in the eyes of the Syrian general. He had, therefore, cooked up for himself a fictitious love story.

Jamal was alone in the Cemetery of the Numbers there, somewhere in Galilee, and he was sitting in his flat in Montpellier chewing the cud of his memories.

He'd come to France to erase his memories and manufacture new ones, in a new country and with a new woman who had nothing to do with his past.

He remembered saying "I've found her" when he awoke the next morning with Bernadette beside him in bed and he discovered she was a nurse. A white-skinned woman, her skin so clear that it allowed a whiteness that dwelt deeper down to show through – as though the whiteness weren't a colour but an incandescence that shone out from the depths and rose through her body, colouring it, before continuing in an infinite outpouring.

During one of his drinking bouts, while listening to the songs of Edith Piaf, a line of pre-Islamic poetry had come to him. He'd tried to ignore it and travel with the voice of the French singer but could not. He'd declaimed the verse, then sung it in a low voice, the way his teacher – the one whom the students called "the Lord of Literature" – had done in the baccalaureate class, and finally the poetry had exploded on his tongue and he'd felt the voice of Muallem Butrus Bustani emerging from his throat, quivering with the rhythm.

Bernadette turned down the volume of the tape recorder and asked him what he was saying. Instead of answering her he repeated the line again, and again the voice of the Lord of Literature emerged from his throat.

He tried to translate the line for her but couldn't. He said it was attributed to a pre-Islamic poet who'd lived in the Arab desert, and sung the praises of the beauty of a white-skinned woman by saying that her whiteness was a skin to her skin.

She asked him where the Arab poet had seen a white-skinned woman.

He explained to her that white skin was widespread in the Arabian Peninsula.

"But you told me the opposite," she said.

He tried to say that what he was interested in at that moment was *her* whiteness and *her* beauty.

When Karim had woken up after his night of drunkenness and found Bernadette in his bed, he'd been struck by "the shock of beauty", as he would later refer to the instant at which he'd become immersed in her eyes. She recounted to him how she'd come across him beneath the breasts of that whore, and how they'd walked aimlessly through the streets of Montpellier; when she'd told him she was tired and had to go home he'd put his arm around her neck and refused to let go.

"Then I discovered you were drunk and I couldn't leave you alone, so I decided to walk you to your flat, and there you tricked me and took me to bed, and in the morning you asked me my name and what I did and when I said I was a nurse you said you loved me, and I couldn't help laughing."

"Me?"

She said his cough was nervous. "I'm sure you don't cough or yawn at the hospital but the moment you reach the flat and have to talk to me or to the girls you start coughing. I don't know you anymore and I don't know what made me agree to resign from the hospital so I could stay at home and devote myself to looking after the children; I've wasted my life. The girls are at school and you're at work and I'm waiting. You turned me into an Oriental woman and now you want to leave me and go to Beirut? We're not going to ruin our lives to go with you just because we're supposed to put up with the sudden whims of the Arab beast sleeping in your depths. You hid the beast from me and from yourself but today it's woken up to take revenge on me and on you and on all of us."

He didn't tell her that a person cannot live without his mirrors. He'd exchanged Nasim, Hend, Jamal, Danny, and Malak for French mirrors but had come to feel he could no longer see himself in his new environment, as though Karim had evaporated and no longer had an image. All he wanted to do was recover his image before deciding what he should do with the years that remained to him.

*

Karim was close to forty when he decided to agree to his brother's proposal. He'd told Nasim on the phone that he wasn't promising anything: "Let me see and then I'll decide." The strange thing was that the conversation between the two brothers had sounded as though it was taking place between two businessmen, without emotion or yearning or jokes – just dry words devoid of feeling, as though the twins were using words to cover words.

The only emotional words spoken were uttered by Nasim.

"Come now and we'll see. We'll soon be forty and life is passing without our noticing."

The idea of life passing struck him with terror. The image occurred to him of Nasri gripping his glass of wine with trembling hand, bringing it close to his lips, and saying that life was like a dream; then his eyes would fill with tears before he burst out laughing.

"It's a lie. Life's a lie and the only certain truth is that we're all going to die."

"What are you saying, Father? You're still a young man," Nasim would say.

Now Karim was discovering that the only truth was one's later years. At forty a person discovers that what's passed hasn't passed; it's more as though it's slipped through one's fingers, with what lies behind having become greater than what lies ahead.

The Lord of Literature was an eccentric teacher. Age had inscribed its wrinkles on his face, his eyes had grown smaller and his nose larger, and he'd become thin as a piece of string. He would shake with ecstasy as he recited the lines of al-Mutanabbi in which the poet mourns the passing of the years:

And how shall I take pleasure now in the evenings and the forenoons
When that breeze that used to blow is nowhere to be found?
There I recalled a union as tho' 'twere one that ne'er had happened,
A life as though traversed in a single bound.

Karim felt that life had carried him off and stripped him of everything, leaving him a stranger in a strange land. Only those who'd died had been able to cheat the game by refusing to drink the cup of the slow slide into the abyss of the years.

He'd read Jamal's texts and understood. The young brown-skinned Palestinian woman had never loved him and had probably been quite unaware that he'd harboured the emotion that now, sitting in the dining room of his flat in France, he claimed to feel. Maybe she'd wanted to meet him to escape the fearful look in the eyes of her true beloved, who'd found a way to elude death at the last moment. Jamal had taken a firm grip on the only two moments at which a person can challenge life and vanquish time – those of love and death. Her first lover had wanted to strip her of death as the price of love but she'd refused. Karim on the other hand had been just a little story by means of which to prove to herself that she could hold both embers in her hands at once.

The sound of the waves at the Sporting Club swimming pool restaurant grew louder and Danny was drinking arak like there was no tomorrow. He looked strange, as though he weren't the old Danny but a replica. It occurred to Karim that this Danny who kept telling him the same stories like an older man looked so much like Danny he could have been his twin but wasn't in fact him. There was a relationship of resemblance, mingling, and contrast which resembled that between himself and his twin.

When they'd met after all those years, Karim had felt as though the roof of the sky had come closer and that the sea, instead of being an extension of the city, had come to resemble a valley threatening to swallow it. Memory had taken him back to a friend of Danny's who'd called himself Camille. This Camille was an odd man. He'd come from his distant village in the Beqaa to be a "revolutionary writer", as he styled himself. He spent most of his time in his small room in the Watwat district drinking vodka, eating meat, and writing. No-one had read any of the novels he claimed to have written. He maintained that he refused to publish because he was writing for a time which had yet to arrive. He used to visit the military positions in Danny's company, his little pointed beard giving off a smell of alcohol.

He asked him about Camille and Danny smiled, his eyes clouding over vacantly. He took a sip from his glass of arak. "We're all criminals," he said.

"No, that's not true. Me for instance – I never killed anyone," said Karim.

"You never killed anyone because you're a coward. Your cowardice stopped you from killing but you're still a criminal."

"I . . . I wanted to . . ."

"You wanted to kill but you couldn't. I could, but what difference does it make? Even Khaled was part of the same story, the one whose heroes aren't heroes. You're going to reproach me because when Khaled was killed I vanished and when his wife came to visit me at home and knocked on the door I didn't open it?"

"She told me. She came to my place and asked me about you."

"And what did you do? You gathered up your things and took off for France and now you've come to see me so you can ask me why I betrayed Khaled? You're a traitor too, my dear."

"So what? I was afraid."

"And I too could say I was afraid but I'd be lying to you the way you're lying to me. The truth is I was tired and lonely and sad. When my wife left I felt I was finished. I knew she wanted to run away and not come back. I told her to do that because it would put an end to the story, but when she did it I went crazy, as though I'd forgotten what I'd known. Failure is when someone forgets the things he knows and ends up as though he knows nothing. Then it's as if he was dead. I really did feel as though I was dead. You want me to have opened the door and saved the woman from death? Why didn't you open your door?"

"I did but I told her I couldn't hide her at my place as it wasn't safe."

"Meaning you lied to her and left her to die."

"You're telling me she died?"

"They killed her and her daughter. They went by their house and cut their throats with knives. They cut the mother's throat and they cut the daughter's throat and they wiped their blood-covered hands on the walls."

"They cut their throats?"

"You're telling me you didn't know?"

"I'd left the country."

"No – they cut their throats before you left."

"And what about Sinalcol? Did they kill him or is he still alive?"

Karim's voice, as he asked about Sinalcol, sounded like that of a comedian in an empty theatre. He'd listened to how the woman and her daughter had ended up with their throats slit. It was the completion of vengeance, a way of making Khaled pay the full price. But instead of feeling ashamed and staying silent all he could think to do was ask about a ghost of whose existence nobody was even sure.

Danny looked at him with half-closed eyes and said he had to go. He asked for the bill, paid, refusing Karim's attempt to do so, put his weight on his stick, and limped off without looking back.

10

Hend couldn't put life with her husband into any sort of context. The man who'd taken possession of her heart while she'd been momentarily distracted was so full of inconsistencies she'd come to feel she wasn't living with just one man. Rather, the man called Nasim Shammas who had given up dealing in drugs and gone into timber and petrol imports was many men in one.

He'd be tender when the boys needed tenderness, amorous when he felt the need for love, when drunk lewd and foul-mouthed with her in bed, sweet when sleeping next to her like a child, frantic when he failed to find her at his side, hilarious when facing difficulties – a mass of inconsistencies gathered together in one man. She didn't know whether he loved her or whether marrying her was simply his way of taking revenge on fate, an attempt to prove he deserved better than his brother because he was braver and more truthful with himself and with others.

Nasim was incapable of hiding his feelings. Things traced themselves on his face as though it was a blank page waiting to be inscribed with the truth. It followed that he couldn't lie to or hide anything from his wife or invent excuses with which to cover for himself, as most people do.

"Don't lie, I can read everything in your face," Hend had told him after she'd stayed up for him one night till three in the morning. It was raining and there was shelling. She'd felt in her heart that there was bad news and she believed her heart because it never lied to her. She'd had an intuition that her husband had been killed and his body thrown under a bridge, as was the custom in those days, so she'd sat vacantly in the living room. The idea of her husband's death had struck her hard but she hadn't wept. Even sorrow had evaporated before her feeling of emptiness.

When he returned she was surprised he wasn't dead. She looked at him sideways with her closed eyes and said nothing.

"I'm sorry, love, you must have been worried but you know the phone isn't working."

. . .

"Come on, let's go to bed."

. . .

She got up sluggishly and said she'd been surprised by his return. She'd been sure he was dead and was shocked at not being glad to see him. She said all she'd wanted while waiting was that he'd come back, "and then I gave in to the idea of death. I was sure you'd died and it's odd but I relaxed. Instead of getting upset, I got sleepy. Death makes one sleepy."

She watched his face while he got undressed and said she didn't want him to talk because she knew everything and was amazed that he'd risk his life in the dead of the Beirut night with all its dangers for the sake of a woman of that sort.

"I told you, I had work and I want to go to sleep. Please, I don't have the energy left to file a police report with you."

She said she wanted to remind him she could read everything in his face, didn't need to listen to his lies and knew everything because her life with him had taught her how to smell other women. "You know something? You've made me forget what a man smells like. Whenever you come near me I smell women and right now I smell women and women are written all over your face. You know the worst thing about you now? The worst thing is that because of you I can't go to sleep. Your supposed death made me sleepy and your infidelities have woken me up again. Keep away from me. I don't want to hear."

How was he to explain to her that he hadn't been unfaithful to her, had never been unfaithful to her in his life, and that all this had nothing to do with him? It was as though the person who went out with women wasn't him but another man. He'd wanted to say this, but he knew that words turned into wounds for this woman whom he loved.

He hadn't told her that since marrying her he hadn't been out with another woman. All the women he'd been out with were whores and a whore, though a woman, isn't like other women: she has the shape of a woman but she doesn't remain on the body or leave her traces on the soul.

Nasim knew this wasn't true but "war makes wrong right", as Nasri used to say. Nasim's double disappointment had been with Suzanne, whom he'd never abandoned even though she'd abandoned him as a result of his father's stupidity and fear for his son – despite which he still dared to maintain that whores didn't remain on the body or leave their fingerprints on the soul. Nasim hadn't put his relationship with Suzanne in the same category as his relationships with prostitutes; she'd been a different story. He'd gone to her in the midst of the shelling to pluck her from the souk after it turned into a battleground and the Phalangist militia started raping women preliminary to issuing them with a warning that they had to get out.

Nasim had been sitting with several youths from the S.K.S., the Phalangist police, in the barracks in the Three Moons School in Ashrafieh, drinking arak with them, smoking hashish, and counting the shells when he'd had a vision of Suzanne. The boys were talking big and saying Boss Dib had begun to put his threat into operation. Ronny, who was nineteen, spoke about how the day before he'd been at the Ashrafieh roundabout and the scene had been like something from a horror film, and Boss Dib had put an end to it. He'd pulled the boys out by sheer force because it was a revolting sight and told the women they had to leave the place by 6 p.m. that day. "And he said, 'Tomorrow at six p.m. I'm going to shell before launching a new attack and anyone who's here and doesn't die in the shelling will be killed by the boys. My orders are clear. Got it?'"

"Where are they supposed to go, boy?" asked Nasim. "They don't have families."

"Who gives a damn whether they go or not? The Bash has ordered the prostitutes' market closed and Boss Dib thinks this is the best way – shelling and then attacking. I really wanted to go with the boys today but the boss said no. I don't know what happened to me yesterday. After we'd done stuff to the women I started throwing up and turned as yellow as saffron."

"Were you afraid?" asked Nasim.

"Don't be dumb! What was there to be afraid of? A few poor women.

They made out they were too proud to take our boys, so we were forced to rape them. Whoever heard of a prostitute being raped?!"

At that instant a vision of Suzanne appeared before his eyes. He saw her lying in the middle of the street moaning, the blood spurting from every part of her. Nasim stood, picked up his rifle, and set off towards his car.

"Where are you going in all this shelling?" Ronny asked, running after Nasim and trying to stop him before he could get to the car.

"I'm going to the souk. There's a woman I have to get out of there."

Nasim rushed to his car and drove like a madman, the shells flashing in Beirut's empty sky.

He reached the souk, parked his car near the shawarma restaurant, which was almost demolished, took his Kalashnikov in his right hand, and rushed up the stairs to the third floor. The shelling was all around and the door stood open. He went in calling her name, heard a low moan coming from the direction of the kitchen, drew closer, and saw her. Suzanne was sitting on the floor with her hands over her ears. He went up to her through the whining of the shells as they traversed the incipient darkness, held out his hand to her, and asked her to get up.

Instead of turning towards the source of the voice, Suzanne hunched over herself in the corner of the kitchen and moaned louder.

"Get up and come with me," said Nasim in a low voice.

"Get away from me. I can't take any more. Please, I don't have anywhere to go. Kill me but don't come any closer. It's wrong. It's so wrong. Don't you have mothers? Why are you doing this to us?" – and she screamed in a mighty voice, "O Jesus! Come and see what the sons of whores are doing to the Magdalens!"

"Stand up, Mother. It's Nasim."

"Who?" she said in a hoarse voice.

"Nasim."

"Nasim who?"

"Nasim the son of Nasri the pharmacist. Get up for me so we can get out of here!"

Suzanne took her head in her hands and began to cry. Her whole body shook with sobs that emerged from her chest and through her hands.

He grasped her by the arms to make her stand up and she cringed where she crouched. He bent over, pulled back, squatted at her side, and explained that he'd come to rescue her, that she had to go with him before the shelling stopped and the militia invaded the place. He said he'd take her to his house and shelter her the way she'd sheltered him when he was young. "Don't be afraid. I'm with you. Get up and let's get out."

The woman pulled her head back and looked at the young man sitting next to her. "You're Nasim, that's for sure. What do you want with me, boy? Go back to your family."

Nasim sat down on the floor, took Suzanne in his arms, clasped her to his chest, and said in a whisper that she had to go with him and that if she refused he would stay and die with her.

The woman got up, went into her bedroom, and began gathering her things. "Leave everything where it is, there's no time. Can't you hear the shelling? They're coming now. Let's get out of here."

She stopped, hesitated, went to her bed, took a small icon of the Virgin Mary from beneath her pillow, placed it in her bosom, and left, leaning on Nasim.

Thus did Nasim win back the woman who had thrown him out. He took her to the small flat in which he'd lived before marrying Hend and after leaving his father's, and Suzanne lived with him there for about a week. Then he found a flat in the Badawi district whose Muslim owners had been chased out and she lived in it for ten years until she died. During this period Nasim visited her once a week, at 5 p.m. every Friday, and every Sunday morning he sent her a platter of kenafeh-with-cheese.

He told Ronny that what had happened at the souk wouldn't do – "What fault is it of the women's?" – but his words fell on deaf ears, so he went deaf himself. Michel Hajji advised him not to get caught up in such things: "It's a bigger issue than just that. We're defending the Christian presence in the East and a few excesses here or there mustn't put us off."

Nasim understood that he would have to turn a blind eye and that the true fighter is one who closes his eyes and throws himself into the war and asks no questions, letting things take him where they will. This was why he asked Suzanne to stop telling him the same story every time he visited her, saying she had to forget and should spend the days that were left to her remembering the beautiful things she'd lived through rather than repeating to him the story of Faten the Egyptian.

Suzanne refused to forget. She told him that a vision of Faten, her belly slit, came to her every night. "Why? Can you tell me why your people did that to the women? Why did they take the Egyptian and the Turkish girls and the ones from Aleppo and kill them that way?"

What did happen at the souk on 14 January, 1976?

The stories had vanished along with their heroes, all of whom had died, as Nasim had said to Ahmad Dakiz, who was telling him about the plans to demolish the old parts of Beirut and build a new Beirut in its place, claiming that "Beirut is going to be like Paris or even lovelier".

"But the war isn't over yet," said Nasim.

"And it mustn't end now," said the engineer. "War is the best architect. It demolishes so that we can clear and rebuild."

The souk, or Mutanabbi Street, with its Ottoman arcades and illuminated neon signs adorning the balconies and announcing the names of the prostitutes, was still standing, a witness to the massacre, the memory of which would be erased only ten years later when Suzanne died.

Was Suzanne's account true?

Was it true that the boys had separated the prostitutes according to ethnicity after raping them horribly, and had then killed the Egyptians, the Turks, and the ones from Aleppo, ordered the Lebanese Muslims to leave immediately, and given the Christians a stay of execution until the evening of the following day?

Nasim asked Ronny what had happened but the boy's memory was so messed up he couldn't sort out the events. He recounted only bits and pieces, full of inconsistencies, laughing hysterically as he did so.

Why did Nasim wait all those years to find out from his brother why Suzanne had thrown him out when he went back to her that Sunday morning as agreed?

Why hadn't he asked her, and broken the wall of silence that had risen between them over those ten years?

Nasim had felt remorse that day. He'd poured insults on his brother and threatened to kill him, but he'd hated himself, and his inability to speak, even more.

Suzanne said almost nothing during his weekly visits to her. All she could think to do was call blessings down upon him. When he spoke of his memories with her, silence enveloped her; and when he asked what was wrong with her she said she was cold. Suzanne always felt cold and Nasim failed to understand why. Like an idiot, he believed she felt cold even at the height of summer because she was a whore and a whore couldn't sleep alone without a man in her bed. Nasim didn't understand that true cold, which penetrates bones, results from an inability to speak. He felt the need to visit her grave and stand in front of it and say he hadn't been unfaithful to her, that he hadn't broken his undertaking to her, that the one who'd been unfaithful to her and to him was his other half. He'd told his brother what had happened because it was like telling himself: he'd never expected his twin to betray him by telling the story to his father. Nasim could see Suzanne, humiliated beneath Nasri's pitiless gaze, his viciousness, his lack of compassion. Now he understood why Suzanne hadn't been able to forgive him. When he'd brought her to his flat he'd felt gallant and heroic; he'd risked his life and forgiven. He'd never once asked her why she'd thrown him out because he hadn't wanted to embarrass or demean her or look as though he was now doing her a favour. He tried to talk to her and behave as a friend who was like one of her children. But she wrapped herself in silence and he respected her sorrow and her loneliness.

Nasim hadn't gone to the grave and covered Suzanne with words. He knew well that people cover themselves with words for warmth but he didn't know where to find Suzanne's grave. The woman had been buried in the common graveyard because she was not of a family that owned a grave plot, so he had no way now of finding her. Suzanne would stay cold forever and Nasim would never be able to find the words.

He tried to tell Hend that he wanted to speak, but the words tripped over each over in his mouth, for words, like seeds, need ground to receive them and Hend's ears weren't ready to listen. Or, at least, the fault wasn't Hend's, for Nasim hadn't dared speak because he didn't know how to, or what to say. Should he repeat what his father had said, to the effect that wrong had become right because of the war? But that wasn't true. His father had said that the Lebanese had made a Wailing Wall out of the war

to justify men's villainy, their cowardice, and their inability to understand the tangled inner jungle in which dwelt their minds and souls,
and this rendered them them incapable of understanding their actions.
"Tomorrow," he'd say, "when the war ends, what shall we say? Shall we
yearn for it because it filled the emptiness of our lives with another emptiness? Or shall we chew the cud of our memories till the end of our days?"

"I swear to God, I thought of killing you! You made me feel like shit
and made the one noble deed I'd done in my life seem pathetic. You
know what Suzanne did when she saw me in her place, when I went to
get her in the middle of the shelling? She covered her face with her hands
and said to me, 'Not you. I don't want to.' I thought she was embarrassed
to see me but later I realised she despised me and did so till the day she
died, and all because of you. You can't imagine the thoughts that came to
me: I felt I could kill you. Damn the Devil and all his works, you're a traitor, my brother, my dear friend, and I forgive you. Let's take a look at
what we can do with the hospital."

Sitting alone with his brother while they waited for Ahmad Dakiz to
arrive bearing the plans for the building, Nasim had spoken of the hospital. Hend wasn't at that particular meeting: she was sitting in the dining
room helping the children with their homework. She'd told Nasim that
she despised the architect, whose sole interest was in making money and
who was working for a property company while preparing to emigrate to
Canada. He spoke of the beauty of the old city in Montreal while con-
tributing to the demolition of old Beirut! She didn't like his wife either,
because she never for an instant stopped playing the seductress, as
though she couldn't forget she was female, as though her centre of grav-
ity was located between her thighs – "and you, my dear, like that type of
woman. I regret I can't be of service to you, or be a friend to your friends."

The question about the war was meaningless. The real question was,
how could Nasim tell what couldn't be told?

What should he say to Hend? How should he explain to her that he
didn't know what was happening to him, that, without knowing why or
how, he'd gone back to the life of the night, of which he'd been cleansed
by the love she'd brought him, and that this had nothing to do with his
love for her?

How could he explain to her what he couldn't explain to himself?

How could he tell the story of the difference between the truth and its opposite? How could he say that though he didn't know much he did know that his life at home with her and the boys was the reality and the other things were like the shadows of things, that the person whose behaviour she found so upsetting wasn't him but his shadow, and that he trod his shadow underfoot each day and felt no pain?

"That's what you have to feel. As though what's being stamped on is my shadow, not me. I stamp on my shadow so you can see me."

Hend couldn't get to the bottom of the mystery of her husband, especially after his father died. His life had been turned upside down. He'd decided to enlist his brother's help in turning the page of the past once and for all and start anew from the point where everything had come to a stop.

He hadn't invited his brother to Beirut to wreak vengeance on him or show him that it was he, the failed twin, who'd done well in the end. It was Hend – who changed utterly from the moment she heard of the hospital project – who had imposed this idea, which left its mark everywhere on his brother's journey of return. She hadn't been able to stamp her foot and say no, as she had when he tried to get her a Sri Lankan maid. This time he was ready with his excuses. He told her the past was over and done with, that he'd become disgusted with himself once he'd repented and turned to the Lord, that his business was going to change. From that day on there'd be no more smuggling, no more parallel life. "We'll build the hospital. I'll take care of management and Karim will oversee the medical side, and the war will be over." He told her God had accepted his repentance but she hadn't, and that she was being unfair; he had shown her he could change.

Nasim had wanted to tell his brother that he felt as though his eyes had been opened after his father died, and he had seen what before he could not. Strange, one's relationship to life! He ought to have seen Nasri before he died, but the closing of the father's eyes seemed to have been a condition for the opening of the son's. He'd wanted to tell his brother he understood now why the ancients had worshipped their ancestors: it was because they, like us, felt guilty and failed to understand that a person's relationship to life starts at the moment when death draws close, when he runs head on into the possibility of absence. This is why the relationship between the living and the dead rests on a deep sense of regret.

Nasim understood this because, at the moment his father died, he'd felt death draw close to him too. He'd realised he'd lost the chance of an encounter with the man his bond with whom had been severed the day he'd fled from home to Suzanne, to be restored only when Salma screamed that Nasri had lost his eyesight. Why hadn't Nasri told his son about his eyes? Had he been afraid of being treated with contempt? Or had he been wary of seeing a gloating look in his son's? The result was that his blindness had remained a secret he shared only with the dark.

"Things are their smell," Nasri used to say, "and when the smell goes everything's gone."

Karim had returned to a city that had lost its smell. Even the flat no longer smelled of itself. Nasim had painted the walls, changed the curtains, and bought new furniture to replace the old, which had worn out. He'd put a large oblong mirror in the bedroom to replace the convex mirror that Nasri had stood in front of every morning before leaving the flat, enjoying his rounded image. "Why did you change all the furniture?" asked Karim, who was convinced his brother had used the family home to meet women.

"I changed it because it was worn out and so I wouldn't have to hear Father's voice ringing in my ears as he stamped over the carpet, spat on it, and said, 'This damned carpet's going to last longer than me. Screw life!' I changed everything so that the things wouldn't outlive the man."

"But that's wrong," said Karim and he asked where his brother had put the Persian carpet Nasri had inherited from his grandmother.

"Remember what Abu Sultan did?" said Nasim. "I did the same. Everything went to the rubbish tip, so that I wouldn't see anything that reminded me of death."

"I just hope you found the money in the pillow too!"

Nasim smiled and told his brother he'd never understood Nasri, and how the approach to death's threshold had changed him. "After he died, I found out things and felt sorry, but what's the use of feeling sorry?

Salma's the one to thank for everything. She's the one who made me open my eyes but what's done is done."

Hend too had wasted the opportunity to discover what had happened to her husband and how his life had changed. At first she couldn't believe him. Then, when Karim came back to Beirut, she felt a sense of loss. The past came back to her with all its bitter memories but a strange feeling took possession of her: what she'd thought was hatred for that "monkey of a doctor", as his brother used to call him, and contempt for that cowardice of his that had driven him to run away, had turned into a crushing sense of loss and an awareness of the need to recover her dignity.

When grief consumed her daughter upon Karim's departure for France, Salma had told her that the feeling, which seemed so natural, was simply an illusion. "I know, my girl. Just ask me! A woman can't accept that she's not desired or loved. All she has to do to get men is to make her desire obvious. That's why when she's rejected she can't take it in and is willing to do anything to recover her status. But it's an illusion, my girl. It's over, forget about him. He's a dog and the son of a dog. It's over!"

"But I love him! I'm not talking about desire, I'm talking about love!"

"Sod love. Men don't know what love means. It's over."

"And my father, who was ready to die for love for your sake?"

"You father was different. God rest his soul, he put me through hell."

"Put you through hell?"

"He put me through hell because he died. I left everything for him and for love and ended up with the dead. Don't bother me with talk of love! Go see what you can get out of life! You're a pretty girl and educated and a hundred men will want you."

At the time Hend was convinced. She'd ripped Karim out of her heart and said, "It's over!" But the moment she saw him on the night of his return to Beirut, when her husband brought him to their home, the feeling had returned that a deep valley was being gouged out in her chest, and she'd found she couldn't breathe. She saw how Karim had preserved his slender figure, as though he were still twenty, while her husband's belly sagged over his belt, and his face, on which black spots caused by overindulgence in alcohol had begun to appear, had gone flabby.

No-one believed him but Nasim believed himself. He'd taken his decision calmly, had phoned his brother, and had put to him the idea of building a hospital. He'd decided it would be called Shefa Hospital after his father's pharmacy and would have attached to it the largest pharmacy in the Middle East. He'd started to reduce his trading activities, put an end to the import of timber and iron, and kept only the trade in petrol, which he would bring to a close with a huge import operation using the Cypriot tanker *Acropol.*

He had withdrawn quietly and without fuss, having decided to maintain his relationship with the Phalangist militias in order to guarantee protection for the hospital. This was despite his conviction that the days of the militias were over and that the Christian militia was on the verge of collapse following the failure of Israel's 1982 invasion of Lebanon. He reckoned that the war would end soon, as Nasri had predicted, with a fatal blow to all those who had put their money on the alliance with Israel.

He was at home. Nasri was taking his afternoon nap, and Nasim was talking with his friends from the Phalangist B.G. Squad. Said was in a state of excitement over the trip he was going to make with a select group of his comrades to receive training in Israel – the same Said who would be afflicted with hemiplegia after being wounded at Bhamdoun in 1984 in what would be known as the Mountain War which broke out between the Christians and the Druze following the Israeli withdrawal from southern Mount Lebanon. This would result in the total defeat of the Christian militias and the destruction of about eighty villages and the expulsion of their inhabitants. Said talked about the preparations and told Nasim he hoped he too would be lucky enough to make a similar trip someday.

"Real training, by God! Tzahal is amazing, it may be the best training in the world!"

"What does 'Tzahal' mean?" asked Nasim.

"It's Hebrew. It means 'defence force'."

"You know Hebrew?"

"No. The training there will all be in Arabic, but one has to learn Hebrew, it's the language of the future," said Said, launching into a lengthy paean in praise of the Jews. "A minority like us, but they knew how to walk all over the Arabs and bust their heads."

At that moment Nasri appeared in the living room. He was shivering in grey pyjamas that hung loosely on his thin body.

"Do you need anything, Father?" Nasim asked.

"How do you do, sir?" enquired Said.

"Fine, but it seems to me I heard something about you boys going to train in Israel? Be careful, fellows! It's silly tricks like that which will end up sending us all to hell."

"The boys are just gabbing," said Nasim. "Go finish your nap. If you don't have your siesta you'll get a headache."

Nasim told his comrades that ever since reaching forty his father had routinely taken an hour's siesta, sleep in the afternoon being the best way to rest the brain via descent of blood to the stomach. "Tell them about your siesta, Father, before you go back to sleep."

"A siesta is a necessity for the preservation of the health of both body and soul. As the proverb has it, 'Eat lunch and stretch out. Eat dinner and go out.' But Israel? No way! Be careful!" said Nasri.

At this point Said, whose smile had never left his face as he watched the elderly man in pyjamas saying strange things dredged up from the world of the ghosts of the past, wiped it off, knit his brows, and told the man he'd do better not to interfere in things that didn't concern him. "We're discussing very important matters, old fellow, that have to do with the destiny of the Christians throughout the East and not just Lebanon. You'd do better not to worry your head over them."

"I told the bastards," said Nasri, pointing to his son Nasim. "One calls himself a communist and wants to save the Palestinians and the other calls himself a Fascist. They've become like Cain and Abel, brother is going to kill brother and then die. But that's not the important thing. The important thing is that I explained to them we're a minority in the East and minorities have to mind their p's and q's and not behave like arseholes with the majority, because in future they'll have to pay the price on their own and the price will be very high."

"What kind of a *zimmi* mentality is that? We aren't *zimmis* anymore and we won't put up with being treated that way." Said turned to Nasim and said, "It seems your father's still living in Ottoman times. The Ottomans have gone, old man, they're over and done with."

"Gone, yes," said Nasri, "but it's not clear they're over and done with. What goes comes back and what sleeps awakes. Where do you think you're living? We're a minority in this East and we have to maintain our existence in a rational fashion. Watch out for Israel! Allying ourselves with the enemy of the Arabs will mean the end of us, forever. Be careful!"

"Stop talking that shit, Father! You're making me look a fool in front of my friends. Us a minority!? The Ottomans coming back!? That's drivel, Nasri. Did you hear what Bashir Gemayel said: 'We're the devils of the East, and its saints!'?"

"Devils, maybe, saints would be better, but devils and saints together doesn't work. You're crazy. Your leader will be the ruin of us all."

"O.K., so take the Jews – a minority like us, and look at all the stuff they've pulled off and how they've won victories over all the Arabs."

"A minority, true, and they've won victories, true as well. But no-one can be victorious all the time. Fortune is a wheel, which is why they have to learn to be polite and get off the Palestinians' backs. Wasn't it enough for them to steal their country? Explain to me why they still occupy the West Bank and Gaza."

"The Palestinians are the enemies of Lebanon!" screamed Said. "You're defending the enemies of the Christians!"

"Enemies of Lebanon? It's not so clear, but let us suppose hypothetically you're right on that point. You still shouldn't go where you're going. It means ruin."

"The Jews are a minority and they've won and it follows naturally that they should make alliances with other minorities," said Nasim. "Please, Father, go and sleep! What are my friends going to say about you?"

The grey ghost turned his back and returned to his room, muttering incomprehensibly. That evening he told his son they were crazy and that the destiny of the Jews of Israel would be no better than that of the Christians of Lebanon. "Soon, after I'm dead, you'll think of me and say, 'Nasri was right.' The Israelis' problem is that they're drunk on their military power. They'll discover soon enough that power doesn't last. If they want to stay in the East, they're going to have to behave better. There's a thought for you and a nice one too – that you've got to behave better, which means being humble and knowing who you are and where you live."

Unlike many of his comrades, Nasim didn't go to the training camp set up by the Israeli army on the lands of the Palestinian village of Saffouriyyeh, whose inhabitants had been chased out in 1948 and which had been converted into a settlement under the name of Tzippori. During the Hundred Days War he was hit in the foot by a piece of shrapnel, which kept him limping for about three months and prevented him going on the main course, in which three hundred Phalangist fighters participated. At the same time the death of Michel Hajji and the sight of his corpse, rigid in the morgue at the Greek Orthodox hospital, made him distance himself from the fighting and follow his own course in life, far from the trenches.

Was Nasri right?

Nasim had wanted to tell his twin that these truths, which Nasri had uttered before anyone else, in no way meant that Karim had been correct in the political choices he'd made and that had led him to exile. "We're wrong and you're wrong, which is why we both got shafted. The Palestinians and the Leftists you belonged to lost and the Phalanges and the forces I belonged to were defeated, and Syria came and swept the board."

"The Syrian regime, not Syria," said Karim. "They swept the board with the brush you gave them, but what do I know? Maybe it was all wrong from beginning to end. God have mercy on those who lost their lives."

Karim hadn't come to East Beirut in a mood of penitence or regret. He didn't believe the history of the war could be summed up in the expression "It was all wrong from beginning to end"; it might apply to him personally – because, despite not being a member of the Communist Party, as his father had believed, he hadn't been able to take the consequences of the defeat of the Lebanese left after the Syrian army entered Lebanon – but it didn't apply to the war. He'd wanted to tell his brother that the Lebanese had to acknowledge their mistakes in the war.

Everyone had made mistakes, but there was a difference between a mistake and a sin. Likewise there was a difference between those who had fought for a secular republic and those who had fought in defence of the sectarian system. What could he say though, now that he'd lost the power of speech? Khaled Nabulsi had turned him into something not unlike a mute; since the day of the man's killing he'd felt he no longer had the right to speak of anything. Anyone who'd been afraid to provide refuge to a widow and her daughter upon the assassination of the woman's husband and who later found out that both the woman and her daughter had had their throats slit would do better to keep his mouth shut.

Why then had Karim returned to Beirut?

He hadn't returned to revoke his history and erase it, nor had he returned to resume where he'd left off. Bernadette was right: the man had returned because, as they say in detective novels, a criminal always returns to the scene of his crime.

When Hend told him how his father had died he was afflicted by a headache that stayed with him throughout his remaining days in Beirut and that later he'd refer to as "the criminal's headache". He thought that, of all directors, only Maroun Baghdadi could make a film with that title: it would tell how the criminal returns to the scene of his crime because he has a killing headache that starts at the eyes and spreads till it comes to settle in the centre of the brain. Karim, though, had had nothing to do with his father's murder. He'd wanted to tell his brother that it was he, Nasim, who was responsible: had it not been for Nasim's hatred of his father the crime would never have taken place. But then he remembered no-one had suggested that Nasri's death was a crime. The film he might propose to Maroun Baghdadi would have to be about another crime, one called "The Killing of Hayat and Her Daughter Following the Assassination of Khaled Nabulsi". At this point the headache would acquire its moral correlative and Karim would find himself facing a court of justice.

Karim hadn't returned to look for justice. The issue of justice had assailed him only once he was in Beirut, where it took the form of a throbbing pain in his head, and all because of Hend and her ambiguous tale of his father's end.

He decided to check the details of the story with Salma, but where was he to find the courage to confront a woman who'd told him that the war would never end?

On his first night in Beirut, while eating the kibbeh nayyeh that Salma had prepared, the black-clad woman had looked closely at him and asked about his situation in France and his wife and daughters. Before he could answer she said everyone received their apportioned lot in life, "and more has fallen to our lot, praise God, than we deserve. *Hate nothing – it may be better for you.*"

Nasim looked at her with furious eyes to make her shut up.

"I'm talking about the war, son. Who would have thought the war would go on so long? It's amazing – we'll be finished before the war is, as though it came out of our insides. Plus, who would have thought that a person could live through war and have children and make money. Praise God! *Hate nothing – it may be better for you!*"

With these words Salma put paid, on the first night of his return, to any possibility of discussion.

When Salma had heard the news of Karim's return she was terrified. She told her daughter it was her duty to convince her husband that the hospital project was a mistake from the outset. "It's all wrong from beginning to end, my girl. Thank God your husband has repented and become domesticated and god-fearing. But it still won't work out right. It's bound to lead to ruin. The project has to stop or your life and your family's will be destroyed."

Salma was convinced that the idea of opening a branch for treating drug addicts had been the doctor's. She saw in the project as a whole an attempt by Karim to exploit his brother's turning over a new leaf: he thought he could return to Beirut and luxuriate in the wealth his brother had collected through the sweat of his brow and get a free ride.

"I'm sure that monkey of a doctor came up with the idea so he could get a free ride out of his brother the way he's done all his life. Anyway what's it all about? Tell your husband that that's not how you turn over a new leaf. First they sell poisons and drugs to make money and then they treat the addicts, and that way they make even more money. His brother must have exploited his desire to repent and sweet talked him with some story about treating addicts. What does that monkey, who makes out he's such a saint and so humane, know about treating addicts? He's a doctor for syphilis and skin and venereal diseases! What's he got to do with all that?"

He'd gone to Salma because he knew she was the only person who understood the story from every angle. But what does it mean for us to know exactly what happened, how Nasri died or was killed? Nasri had died before he died. He'd died the day the civil war started, when he turned into a ghost lost in the foggy maze of his memory. Suddenly his world had collapsed and he hadn't been able to salvage anything from it. He hadn't been able to understand where his sons and their comrades got their passion for war and destruction. Nasri belonged to another world. His memory didn't go back before the Second World War, when people in Beirut heard of the woes of war but paid none of its costs. Even the Palestine Catastrophe of 1948 had seemed to him more like a movie; he'd been convinced that the early Hebrew state would be no more than a place of refuge for the Jewish minorities and that it was destined to blend into the region. War never crossed his mind. He believed it was the duty of the inhabitants of this country of theirs to take everything in their stride. True, he remembered some of his father's stories about the terrible famine that had struck Lebanon and wiped out a third of its population during the First World War. However, he'd never troubled himself to think about the destiny of this small nation which had been put together from the rubble of an empire – the Ottoman Empire – which had collapsed, and of a kingdom – the Arab Kingdom founded by Feisal I in Damascus – which had been intended to gather together all the parts of "the Land of Shem", namely Syria, Lebanon, and Palestine, but which had existed only as a mirage. He was certain what had happened and would happen were no concern of the Lebanese, that life was more powerful than politics and conflict. He'd ended up, though, a stranger in a land he didn't know, as though the sleeping devils of war had suddenly awoken, emerging from he knew not where, and carried off his sons and most of that accursed generation; as though the calm that Lebanon had known for a hundred years, since the end of its first civil war in the nine-teenth century, had been just a break or a truce.

If Nasri had spoken he would have said that his blindness was a part of his decision to not see, for when you don't understand you don't see even when you do, and Nasri didn't understand. He was sure his sons were in the wrong but didn't know what the right was. He'd become like Jeha in the story he used to tell his sons when they were little, to prove to them there was no justice in this world. He'd shout and argue; then, when asked for his opinion and how to save Lebanon from its wars, he'd fall silent because he didn't have the answers.

This is not an accurate picture of Nasri after the outbreak of the war. Nasim's memory had refashioned the image starting from the end, as memory usually does when it reduces persons and events to a summary and fossilises them within a closed moment. The problem with memory is that it cannot stand inconsistencies, so it draws an immutable picture of things. Thus, in Nasim's memory, the image of Nasri was transformed after his tragic death from that of a monster into that of a saint. However, it wasn't true that Nasri died the instant war broke out, or that his appe-tite for life had suddenly disappeared and he'd lost his way in the milky whiteness that traced itself over his eyes.

Nasim had decided he would remember of his father only the final image of him that Salma had drawn as he lay on his deathbed, as though a new man had been born in his memory after the death of the old. Who can say if Salma was telling the truth? Or, supposing Salma reported accurately what Nasri had told her, what reason is there to believe a man who had lied to everyone throughout his life?

Karim wasn't convinced by the idealised image his brother drew of his father. At first he'd objected to the name of the hospital, not wanting it to inherit the name and lore of the pharmacy, but he'd resigned himself because he saw in it a sign of his brother's atonement for his sins. He did, however, refuse absolutely to allow the laboratory attached to the hos-pital to be named the Nasri Shammas Laboratory. "That I will not agree to. We're starting from scratch, not inheriting a hospital. Not to mention that you know very well, my dear brother, what Father did to people and the uses to which he put his concoctions."

Nasim looked at his brother uncomprehendingly, as though he'd traded in his old memory for a new one, as though it hadn't been Nasim who'd uncovered his father's scandalous doings when he revealed the secret of the cupboard in one of whose drawers Nasri had put pictures of the women who were his victims.

Nasri hadn't died with the outbreak of the war as Nasim had tried to imply to his brother. The man had died by degrees, as everyone does. He had at its outset treated the war as a silly game in which he could see a repetition of the Lebanese megalomania which turned the disasters of the country's modern history into a kind of joke. He supported his argument with two names – Said Aql and Charles Malek. The first was a well-known poet who had learned nothing from al-Mutanabbi but self-conceit, which had led him in the end to call for the adoption of the Latin alphabet in place of the Arabic and to a *folie de grandeur* which made him believe that Lebanon was the greatest country in the world. He had also made the embarrassingly racist statement that "it is the duty of every Lebanese to kill a Palestinian". The second was an Americanised philosopher who ended up prostrating himself before Camille Chamoun and pleading with him not to leave the Lebanese Front (an alliance that brought together the right-wing Christian sectarian parties during the war). He also proclaimed that Bashir Gemayel had created the first Christian army in the East! This happened after the Phalangist militias annihilated Chamoun's in a bloody massacre at the Safra Marina, leaving a swimming pool full of corpses floating in water and blood, and the Lebanese Forces as the sole army of the Christian Right.

"One preening his moustache and the other on his knees – that's your war!" Nasri screamed in Nasim's face.

"What? You think your clever son Karim's Palestinians are better than us?"

"God damn the hour!"

"What hour?" asked Nasim.

"The hour I fathered you. No-one else has had it like me. Is this some kind of bad joke? The war's come right inside my house."

Despite his harsh words against his sons, Nasri didn't take the war seriously. He thought it was just a little game that would end in a few months. But as time passed and the war became a way of life, he began to feel his world was dying and that he'd lost both his place and his status. The twins had separated forever and his pharmacy was now desolate. In the war, amidst the downpour of shells, Nasri discovered how the city had aged. Beirut, which to him had been a symbol of youthfulness and renewal, shrank into itself. Its skin cracked and it ended up resembling a blind old woman wrapped up and bent over as she walked, her back humped and her head buried in her chest. Beirut had come to look like an old woman called Catherine, distantly related to his mother, of whom he could remember only her hunched back, her long toenails that she couldn't clip, and her black clothes. The image of this aged woman rose up unexpectedly from some hidden corner of his memory. Nasri couldn't remember where he'd seen her, for she'd died when he was six, and her image, like most images of the first stages of childhood, had formed only through what his mother had said about her. And his mother had spoken of her only every 20 September, on which day she would hold an annual memorial service for the dead in her family and include Catherine in the list.

This image of an aged hunchbacked woman began to replace that of Beirut as Nasri started to notice the ageing of the city and smell its decay, which was like that of the bodies of the old.

Nasri sank towards his end without realising it. He mocked a city that could behave like an old woman. Once, he told Karim – who was reciting verses by Khalil Hawi in which the poet calls Beirut a whore in order to justify its necessary destruction – that he didn't like that kind of literature, which converted entities into metonymies: the metonymy is the ugliest form of simile and to speak of the city as "a woman" or "a whore" was to create bad literature because literature shouldn't imitate reality: reality should imitate literature, not the other way round.

He only learned that the poet Khalil Hawi had committed suicide during the Israeli incursion into the city in 1982 when Karim phoned him from Montpellier and told him in a sad voice that Khalil Hawi had killed himself with a shot to the head from a hunting rifle in protest at the Israeli occupation.

Nasri was on the verge of laughter as he told his son, "How stupid! Wouldn't it have been better if he'd shot at the Israelis instead of himself?" But his tears poured out and he started sobbing. Karim had rung off in his father's face and didn't hear him weep. At that instant Nasri had seen a vision of Catherine in front of him, but she'd turned into a man who looked like him. He'd brought the woman back from his memories to make her a metonymy for Beirut, and so hide his old age from his own eyes. He'd come to understand why writers and poets resorted to metonymy: metonymy is the world's senectitude which resembles childhood only in its inability to distinguish among feelings, which it jams together, so that laughter becomes a synonym for weeping.

Catherine had turned into a man and the man was bending over the remains of the herbs that had rotted in a nearly deserted pharmacy located in a city consumed by rust.

"I am Catherine," Nasri said to his reflection in the mirror. He was standing in front of a huge looking glass that he'd placed in the back room of his shop, where he would transform herbs into remedies and have sex with women whom he'd intoxicated with love of life via the herbal mixtures distilled in his small alembic. There, in front of the mirror reflecting the image of his secret room, Nasri stood alone and saw the image of the hunchbacked woman on whose thick skin rings like those on tree trunks had erupted. She had dressed herself in him and taken him off to taste the bitterness he felt each time he imitated one of his father's movements, or performed some involuntary action that reminded him that he was now an old man.

Against his own will, Nasri began to see himself as his father and began to hate himself. He had never loved his father and had loathed his smell, which was of a kind of old-fashioned jasmine in which the foetid scent of the flower mixed with that of cheap cologne.

Catherine came and the smell of musk, which Nasri used to perfume himself, was overlaid by the smell of foetid jasmine. It was like the smell of urine, and Nasri's battle with his father's smell, which had taken root in him, began. It was an unwinnable battle in which no soap or perfume availed.

The first battle Nasri lost was to smell and thereafter one defeat followed another, reaching a final climax with his collapse in front of Salma, who believed him only after he was dead.

That day he'd stood in surrender before the mirror. He'd lost all his desires at one go. He'd lost all appetite for food, for women, for wine. He'd lost his desire to play backgammon. He felt the city was mendacious and deceptive: it insinuated to him its own death so that it could kill him and take him to the end.

He wished he could bring his two sons together just once more around the breakfast table to tell them he didn't want to die but was going to despite himself. He didn't want them to promise him anything because he knew now that they would in the end become one man, as he'd hoped they would, though all that man would find before him to cloak himself in would be the image of an aged father. After that day he wouldn't want to see them again, so that their image would deteriorate no further and they wouldn't end up, as he had now, hating it and despising human nature.

"The man's thoughts were very confused," said Salma. "He came to see me a number of times but would stay for only a few minutes. I don't know what happened to him during the last months. When he told me he couldn't see anymore he said it was a psychological thing."

"I've stopped seeing because I hate myself. The whiteness has descended to save me from my own image. It's so horrible. In the mirror I see the image of my father and hate myself. You know, the idea of the killing of the father is silly. If you kill him you're killing yourself, and if you don't kill him you're committing suicide. I tried to explain the idea to Nasim but he can't take in anything new and he decided that I meant to kill him when I did the operation on his thigh after he got hurt. And the other one, the smart one, isn't here. I'm sure he's become French and made up his mind to forget us. And I hate people now. I see myself in their eyes, as though their eyes were mirrors. I spit on life!"

Salma said that on his last visit to her, a week before his death, he'd complained that the image of his father was pursuing him. He said a person's life wasn't worth an onion skin and that the end was like the beginning because one was compelled to imitate someone else in order to exist. She said she could think of nothing to say and had tried to cheer him up. She told him she was going to make him a glass of lemonade the way he liked it, meaning by chopping the unpeeled lemon finely with sugar, then adding water, orange blossom water, and rose water to it. "I left him sitting in the living room and when I came back with the lemonade he'd gone and that was the last time."

Nasim asked what she'd done with the lemonade and she didn't answer.

A smile more like a grimace traced itself on his face as he gripped the glass of chilled lemonade his mother-in-law had brought him from the kitchen and drank it at one go.

"Just like the departed," said Salma. "Your father, God rest his soul, was like you, he loved lemonade. Sometimes he'd put qarqashalli biscuit into it and take out the bits with a spoon and eat them. God rest your soul, Nasri, you died hard done by."

When Karim told Ahmad Dakiz that he longed to visit Tripoli so that he could stop at Batroun on the way and stand in the Hilmi Café and drink the finely chopped Batroun lemonade whose flavour he craved so much, his brother looked at him in surprise and said, "You like lemonade too?" But Ahmad Dakiz picked on his words as a cue to say, "Who doesn't like Batroun lemonade? Surely you must know the two verses that speak of lemonade and its relation to love?"

"Please, Ahmad, we don't want to hear that," said his wife Muna.

"Let's hear them," said Nasim.

"The madam will get upset," said Ahmad. "Whatever you say, my dear. I won't, but if you ever want to go to the Fragrant City, and you should, you can forget about Batroun. Go to Ash'ash in the port. It's a small café opposite the Dakiz mosque where they make lemonade ice cream. It's to die for. You get the authentic taste of sailors!"

Nasim smiled as he told his brother that the people of Tripoli refer to bitter lemons as "sailors" and have a strange way of talking.

"If you want to hear a really strange way of talking you should pay a visit to Ahmad's father," said Muna. "Tell them about your father, Ahmad."

"I'd like to visit your father," said Karim. "It's been ages since I went to the Fragrant City."

"I'll come with you," said Nasim.

"Many thanks, dear brother, but I'd rather go on my own."

Ahmad wrote his father's telephone number on a small piece of paper and gave it to Karim.

"But God help you if you get in touch with him! He'll talk till kingdom come. Those old codgers don't know how to stop talking once they get going."

Later, in bed, Muna would recite the two lines of verse about lemonade to the doctor, rocking with laughter at the childishness of men:

He who stops off at Batroun
And doesn't taste the lemonade he fancies
Is like someone who sits a girl down beside him
And doesn't get a hand in her panties.

Muna laughed, then said, "Ahmad thought he was giving me what I wanted but I was exhausted. He'd take me on trips to Tripoli, up to the Castle of Saint-Gilles, and give me a tour of the city's markets, thinking that would make me fall in love with him. I did fall in love with him, I can't deny it, and then I got sick of all the talk about love and told Ahmad, 'Come on, let's get married,' and we did, and now we're off to Canada."

She told him men were like that. They know but they behave as though they don't because they can't face the truth. She laughed as she told Karim she was sure he was no different from other men in such matters, and that it was all attributable to a cowardice that could only be explained by men's fear of women and of the secrets they believe they harbour.

Had Nasim been afraid of Hend and her secrets?

She'd told him she didn't know him. "After six years of marriage I've discovered I don't know you."

He told her she was mistaken and that she didn't want to believe that he'd turned over a new leaf.

Hend would never forget the night of 22 December, 1988. Nasim had come home early carrying a large bag and a bottle of champagne.

"What's that you've brought?" Hend asked.

"A present and champagne," he said.

He said he'd got a present for himself, for his birthday.

"I'm sorry, dear, I completely forgot it's your birthday today."

Hend always forgot her husband's birthday and always apologised a few days later, when Nasim would say he didn't like celebrating his birthday. That year he'd departed from custom and decided to celebrate his birthday in a special way.

"O.K., so let's see the present," she said.

"Not now," he answered. "When the boys have gone to sleep we'll open the champagne and you'll see what a nice present I got."

Nasim opened the bottle of champagne and turned on the tape recorder with George Wassouf singing "Forget You?" by Umm Kulthoum.

Hend stood up and turned down the tape recorder while they were drinking.

"Why did you turn it down?" Nasim asked.

"So I can talk to you," she said.

"Tonight there's no need to talk in words. Tonight we're going to talk another language." He bounded into the bedroom and returned carrying the gift.

He opened the bag, took out an oblong cardboard box wrapped in shiny red paper, and presented it to his wife.

"It's your birthday today. The present's supposed to be for you, not me," said Hend as she took the gift from her husband.

"Open it!" he said.

"The present's for me?"

"For you and for me. Just open it and see the lovely surprise. It's something you never would have thought of."

And a surprise it was!

When Hend took the Oriental dancer's costume from the box she was speechless. She took the costume, threw it on the couch, hung her head, and said nothing.

Nasim stood up and went over to her. "It's for you, my love. Today's my birthday and I want you to dance."

"Me?" she said in a husky voice and burst into tears.

She wept from the depths. Everything in her wept. She shook, rocked right and left like a mother that has lost her child, and moaned, though all that emerged from between her lips was a croak.

"Why are you behaving this way, Hend?" he asked. "All women dance for their husbands. What sin have I committed? I just want us to be happy."

Hend pulled herself together, picked up the dancer's costume, and threw it in his face. "Get out of here, you and your fucking prostitutes! You want to turn me into a prostitute like them?"

It was the only time in her entire life that Hend had used bad language: never before had this shy brown-skinned woman used a vulgar expression; now she found herself with no choice and the abuse poured out of her. "God forgive me!" she said and went to the bedroom, closing the door behind her.

The night of his birthday Nasim slept on the couch in the living room. He turned off the tape recorder, emptied the bottle of champagne into his guts, and went to sleep.

Nasim had committed no mistake requiring an apology but the following evening he had to apologise all the same. He said he was sorry but Hend refused to forgive him. Later, when he announced his final turning over of a new leaf, she told him she forgave him everything except that one stupidity.

"I just want to know, what did you think I was?"

"Honestly, love, I meant no harm. All my friends' women have dance costumes and dance for their men. I thought, why not, maybe our sex life will improve, but 'instead of setting the leg I broke it'. I apologise a second time."

He'd wanted to tell her that it was Ahmad Dakiz who had given him the idea but he didn't so as not to complicate matters further, especially as Hend despised Muna and believed the woman could think of nothing but how to show off her sensuality, as though her whole body were one large multi-purpose sex organ. Ahmad had told Nasim that the only way to overcome the tedium of married sex life was with games; he found Oriental dancing at home to be the best stimulus. Nasim was attracted to the idea but failed to interpret it correctly: Dakiz had been talking about stimuli for him, not for his wife. Nasim, on the other hand, suffered from frigidity in his wife, which was not about to be cured by making her dance.

"Is that how your friends are? They treat their women as though they were prostitutes?"

"Oriental dancing is a refined art, not something for prostitutes," he said. "Do you know how belly dancing began? It began in Egypt in the days of the pharaohs and took place in temples as a rite of worship. The dancer used to arch her back to present her navel as a gift to the gods."

"You're trying to tell me that when you brought the dance costume and made me drink champagne you wanted me to pray? What do you take me for? An idiot?"

Hend didn't like her husband's turning over a new leaf, which had grown into an obsession with religion, because she had no interest whatsoever in religion. She had never posed herself philosophical questions regarding the existence of God and didn't think the issue concerned her. She'd grudgingly agreed to let her children be baptised in church "because it can't be any other way", as Nasri had said, but she kept religious rites and traditions out of her house. Likewise, the boys were totally shielded from such things as she'd put them into the Lycée Français, a secular school.

Nasim was bowled over by his father's death. He stopped spending his evenings outside the flat and took to attending mass every Sunday. Then he began taking the boys to church with him and discovered that a lay organisation existed to offer religion classes to children after mass. He enrolled the boys in Sunday school and things got to the point of his volunteering to teach in it himself. He started reading religious books and invited his wife to go to church with him and the boys. She refused and said that his religious mania was part of a general despair resulting from the long civil war.

She couldn't explain how she'd agreed to go with him to one of those evening meetings called "vigils", where a group of men and women had met around a monk who looked as though he lived in a cave in the wilderness and whose flowing black robes spread out around him making him seem bodiless, or as though his body were made of some ethereal matter. His eyes were large but vacant and dead, in a face consumed by a long untrimmed beard. This monk had returned from Mount Athos in Greece, where he'd spent twenty years, to found a monastery in a distant village in Akkar. Hend had no idea what had brought him to Beirut or why this particular group of people gathered around him. She thought she'd hear about his experiences of "the mountain of the monks" in Greece, but the monk, whom they addressed as Father Fadi, disappointed her and uttered not a word. The vigil, when it began, consisted of the recitation by candlelight of endless prayers and hymns, in an atmosphere reminiscent of the summoning of spirits. The participants in the celebration appeared to be almost unconscious; from time to time the lady of the house would appear carrying a brass brazier from which incense poured and give it to the monk, who would wave it right and left over the heads of the seated. Hend felt dizzy and drowsy and her eyelids began to droop, while the eyes of the monk, in contrast, would flash and gaze into hers before the light in them died out once more. She stayed about three hours, resisting sleep and fighting off the monk's eyes, and at around one in the morning, when he raised his hand to announce a short break and cups of sage tea circulated, she turned to her husband and said they had to go home.

On that night, redolent of the scent of incense and the flavour of sage, Hend had a strange dream that came from she knew not where. She saw herself dressed in an Oriental dancer's costume, surrounded by a circle of people praying. She was dancing like a professional, shaking her buttocks, going down on her knees, arching her belly, and then letting her head fall back and raising her navel towards the greedily waiting eyes of the monk.

11

She said her name was Ghazala.

She said she was from a village called Shuhba in Jabal el-Arab, or Jabal el-Durouz, in Syria.

She said she was the mother of two small children and didn't do houses but had said yes for Khawaja Nasim's sake. "Nasim and Matrouk are like brothers. Matrouk hasn't worked with anyone else in Lebanon. To tell you the truth, Doctor, if it hadn't been for your brother, we wouldn't have stayed a moment in Beirut. Who can live in this city? When I married Matrouk all I wanted to do was go to Beirut and when I got to Beirut I wanted to go back to the village. I was so scared and – how can I put it? – it's like the night we arrived the whole place was lit up with the shelling and I was trembling and all I wanted to do was hide."

She said she'd agreed to work for Madam Hend "to help her – I'm not a maid, Doctor, and Matrouk doesn't allow me to work as a maid in people's houses but Madam Hend's different. I couldn't disappoint Khawaja Nasim. I was with her for several months. What a woman! A gem! When she saw me at work cleaning the flat she'd jump up and help me and work with me, like we were friends. Then she told me I wouldn't be coming to do work anymore but that I was to visit her once a week. Every time I go to her she sits with me and won't let me do a thing. We drink coffee and talk and she starts asking me about the village. She likes me to tell her stories and the one she likes best is the one about my grandmother. She keeps asking me to tell her the same story and then gives me presents for the children and she never gives me used things. Now that's what I call a lady! She's got a heart of gold and I feel like she's my friend and a sister to me."

She said she'd agreed to her husband's request that she work at the doctor's flat because he was Khawaja Nasim's partner in the hospital project and she considered her work a service to a friend. "Don't get me wrong, Doctor. All I want is for the hospital to go well and then we'll all get a break. Matrouk can stop working as a labourer and a driver and take over the supervision of cleaning operations at the hospital and that way we'll all get a break."

Karim asked her what she wanted most and she said she wanted to buy a flat in Beirut "and be a lady like the other ladies, like having a Sri Lankan maid and taking a break."

"A maid!"

"That's my dream. I know it's not an easy dream to come true but that's what I think about. I see myself as a proper lady."

He told her Hend had refused to have a Sri Lankan maid.

"I know. She told me the story. Hend's a gem. I told you she's different from other women. She won't ever agree to have a maid because that's her opinion and I love her and I love her opinion but you asked me about my hopes and dreams and I gave you a frank answer."

Their first meeting was strange. At 7 a.m. Karim heard the sound of the doorbell, seemingly coming from somewhere far away. Then he heard the key turn in the lock and the door open. He leapt out of bed, rushed to the door, and found a woman standing on the doorstep. She was bending forward a little as though about to come in but not coming in. She was holding the key in her right hand and smiling.

"I'm Ghazala," she said.

"Who?"

"Khawaja Nasim gave me the key and told me you might not be home. I thought I'd come early, sorry to disturb. I thought that way I'd finish my work and get home before the children come back from school."

"Who are you?" asked Karim, rubbing the sleep from his eyes.

"You go back to bed. You look tired and I won't get to your room for a couple of hours."

Karim focused, sleep now banished, and asked her who she was and what had brought her there so early.

She said she was Ghazala and Khawaja Nasim had sent her to clean the flat. He'd given her the key and asked her to leave it with the doctor if she found him at home, or if not he would get the key the next day from her husband Matrouk.

She held the key out to the doctor, who took it from her hand.

"Would you like coffee?" she asked.

"No, that won't be necessary, I'll make the coffee. But Nasim didn't say anything to me."

"The khawaja's like that," she said. "He's always making surprises for people he likes."

Karim went into the kitchen to make his morning Turkish coffee and Ghazala caught up with him and started cleaning up the sink, in which dirty dishes were piled high.

"How do you like your coffee?" Karim asked her.

"What an idea, Doctor!" she said, and went over to the stove to make the coffee. Her brown arm bumped his. She pulled her arm away quickly and looked at him with eyes that she lowered in a coquettish display of false modesty, making Karim feel he was watching a third-rate Egyptian movie. He withdrew from the kitchen to his room and heard Ghazala's voice asking him how he liked his coffee.

There was a sort of seductiveness in her voice, but it was that of a black-and-white melodrama where the maid seduces the hero, or the hero exploits his position and authority to drag the maid to his bed.

He said he liked it Ottoman-style and she asked him what "Ottoman-style" meant, so he answered, "It means medium sweet with just a little extra sugar." He thought the melodrama was like the coffee that the Lebanese attribute to the Ottomans: there was something in it of the coquetry of the sugar which permeated the gravitas of the coffee, leaving nothing at the bottom of the cup but the residue, which resembled the tears that girls wept over "Ustaz Wahid" as played by the Egyptianised Syrian singer Farid el-Atrash. Karim had never dared proclaim his love of Farid el-Atrash and his passion for his song "Torment", which went so well with his husky voice. The feelings of torment emerged broken from the singer's throat, leaving love as a question mark suspended in the space of the *hujazkar* mode with its repetitive rhythms and Kurdish melancholy. The embarrassment he felt at his affection for the songs of Farid el-Atrash was equalled only by that which he felt at his passion for melodramatic movies, such as that in which Ustaz Wahid weeps over a lost love in "Letter from a Woman Unknown". In his youth and during the days of leftist tumult he hadn't dared reveal this side of his personality to anyone; the fashion was for Sheikh Imam and his revolutionary songs, and Karim loved those songs and learned them by heart, especially "Guevara Is Dead". But nothing could reach into his innermost soul like the husky voice of Farid el-Atrash with its mixture of repressed desire and pain.

What had happened with Ghazala? How had things developed? Why had he felt as though his heart was being almost ripped from its place every time he heard the two successive rings of the bell that announced her arrival? And how did it come about that he'd sit in his room waiting for her to finish cleaning the flat so that she could come to him and lead him to the bathtub, where her hands would be waiting for him?

Everything had started when his arm bumped hers. He'd gone to his room as she'd told him to, sat on his bed reading a paper, lit a cigarette, and closed his eyes. Suddenly the smell of coffee erupted and spread like pins and needles through his joints. Ghazala came in, her hair up, and the smell was everywhere; and the two ebony hands reached out holding a tray bearing a coffee pot and a cup from which wafted the fragrance of orange-blossom water.

Karim was intoxicated by the aroma and asked about it. She said she'd put a little orange-blossom water in before boiling the water: "There's nothing better than the smell of orange-blossom spirit." She said she'd only found out about orange-blossom water here in Beirut. "In the village we didn't have orange blossom or anything of that sort. We plant olives, wheat, and barley. If you could only see the black soil of the Houran plain, Doctor! It breaks your heart. The land is cracked with thirst, its skin is broken, and no-one can do a thing."

She asked him why the Lebanese called orange-blossom spirit "orange-blossom water". "It's a spirit, Doctor. When you get a whiff of it you feel your spirit expand."

"Where are you off to?" he asked her. "Sit down and drink a cup of coffee with me."

"My coffee's in the kitchen," she said, "and I don't like sugar in coffee. The sugar destroys the dignity of the coffee and I don't know why you people in Lebanon drink your coffee like that, as though you were afraid of the taste and smell of the coffee itself."

He decided to pick up his cup of coffee and go after her into the kitchen. He noticed the heels of her cracked naked feet and felt the flames of desire but stayed where he was and couldn't summon up the courage to do anything about it – throw her to the kitchen floor and take her like that without preliminaries or talk, raise her legs and enter her. The doctor's right hand shook and the thought of rape flashed through his mind.

Sitting there in Beirut, Karim suddenly was intoxicated by the thought of rape, which blended with the spirit of the orange-blossom water and the flavour of roasted coffee. He thought Ghazala was right and he should drink Turkish coffee without sugar. She'd told him that the coffee spread on the tongue and coated it with taste, and that sugar spoiled its flavour.

Everything had started when she'd left his room barefoot after putting the coffee pot on the bedside table and he'd noticed her cracked heels. He'd felt the desire to grab them, pull her down to the floor and throw himself on top of her. He pictured the scene as vividly as if it were happening in front of him and discovered that every cell of his body wanted the woman. But he didn't dare. Once again Karim discovered that his nobility, or what he claimed as nobility, was just a cover for his fear.

He sat down on his bed, drank a little of the coffee, and a tingling ran through his body; he thought many times about getting up off the bed but didn't.

He found himself in the kitchen. He didn't know how he had risen from the bed, or where he'd found the courage to stand in front of Ghazala and tell her he'd decided to try her bitter coffee.

He drank the coffee standing in the kitchen while Ghazala came and went, looking at him out of the corner of her eye and behaving as though she didn't see him. He felt the bitter taste invade his tongue, grew intoxicated on the coffee's smell and burning taste, and decided that from then on he'd drink only sugarless coffee.

The rape episode had ended with a cup of coffee. He'd stood there waiting for Ghazala to look at him and only awoken from this state of expectancy when he heard her asking him to leave the kitchen as she wanted to wash it down.

This first encounter bore no relation to what would take place later. The short stormy relationship that ended two months after it began, only to take on a bizarre aspect thereafter, had left the Frenchified doctor with the taste of confusion on his tongue.

Karim might say that Ghazala was a symbol of the confusions of Beirut and thus absolve himself – after the moments of terror he lived through as he drank arak and chewed grilled chicken – of the naïveté of the look that had described itself on his features when Matrouk told him the story. When we resort to turning things into symbols it liberates us from responsibility and makes of human experience an arena of random happenings, so that life becomes no more than a story.

Karim had come to Beirut to repair his mirror and redraw his image, only to find himself in a reality susceptible to neither symbol nor explanation. Civil war is superior to all other kinds of war in that it resists explanation. It is total stasis, naked exposure to word and caprice. Ideas can last only if they are put in a vessel that imposes form on them, adding to and subtracting from them, but a civil war has no vessel. It is an assemblage of broken mirrors that run parallel to one another, making of the fragments images that reproduce each other but refuse to form a coherent whole.

The difference between Karim and his twin was that when the doctor had found himself incapable of imposing form on things he'd fled to France, where he'd set about erasing his memory. All that had been left of the days of war was the vague image of a ghost which his memory, awakened by extreme drunkenness, had decided to preserve, making of it a vessel for the first stirrings of his love for the Frenchwoman.

His brother Nasim on the other hand had set about adding, not subtracting, for he wasn't content with his own personal memory. Rather, he had mixed his brother's into it by taking possession of Hend, who had experienced something resembling a nervous breakdown following Meena's arrest and expulsion from Lebanon.

Ghazala and Sinalcol overlapped in Karim's memory even though the woman took up residence there only briefly before withdrawing and turning into an elusive shadow, while the man was never fully present.

He was a ghost woven out of people's words, a shadowy thug whose presence could be detected through the submission of others to his commands because of their fear that his explosive charges would blow away the doors of their shops, spilling their guts onto the street. This ghost had turned into a real person whose identity Karim was able to assume, and of whom he told tales that mixed truth and fiction, piquing both the curiosity and astonishment of his French wife.

Karim never dared tell the Ghazala story to anyone, and it would have remained wrapped in oblivion if Ghazala hadn't come to see him three days before his departure from Beirut, wreathed in smiles, to say that Matrouk had made up with her following Khawaja Nasim's intervention.

"As you know, Doctor, I could never say no to Khawaja Nasim."

At that moment Karim had understood that his brother had decided to announce, in the midst of the collapse, that he could still keep score, and that Nasim had known what was going on all along – and had managed, perhaps, to possess this woman's body too.

The Ghazala who returned to tidy the flat and help Karim gather his things for his final departure was not, however, the same woman. The brown-skinned woman of medium height with the well-turned calves and full thighs pulled back at the moment of orgasm, her naked feet cracked with pleasure and water, the Ghazala of the long black hair whose regularly spaced waves cast shadows on the pear-shaped, slightly pendulous breasts that perked up at the ends as they rose towards rosy nipples, the Ghazala of the large mouth and bee-stung lips, black eyes, and long neck – this was not the Ghazala who returned when the maid came back to help him gather up what he wanted from the flat.

The woman who came back was different in every way. She had cut her hair and wore a wide dress that erased the contours of her body. Her eyes were without fire and there was a slight stoop to her shoulders.

She said she had to apologise to him for getting him mixed up in something that had nothing to do with him. She said she felt it was her duty to tell him the truth and he answered that he didn't want to know. But he drank her bitter coffee and listened to her story, feeling the knives cutting up his heart.

"You don't have any right to be angry with me, Doctor," she said. "You were with Madam Muna too."

"Don't you dare say a word about Muna!"

Nasim had told him he could take what he wanted from the flat: he'd decided to sell it along with the unfinished hospital building and the pharmacy and the plot of land in the village of Brummana where Nasri had dreamed of building a three-storey summer house for his two children and theirs. He'd asked him to sign a general power of attorney that would allow him to make the sale so that he could pay off a part of his debts. Karim had signed without discussion. He'd agreed because there was nothing else he could do. He'd left his city stripped of everything, realising as he signed that he would never be able to go back.

Ghazala had appeared from he knew not where.

On the first day of his encounter with her, the seduction had revolved around coffee and naked feet. Karim hadn't raped the beautiful maid who had come to his flat, bringing with her an aura of seduction. The idea of rape had lingered in his mind and become a source of drowsy fantasies that filled that night and the four other nights he spent waiting for her.

He'd left the flat for a meeting with the agent of a medical instruments company, then returned at five in the evening to find everything in his flat shining – but no Ghazala. His meeting had been with Ayoub Tayan, a distant relative of his mother's whom he hadn't seen for thirty-five years; in any case the man and the child had nothing in common. He said he was the agent for a medical equipment company and had re-equipped the Greek Orthodox hospital, and that he attended mass every Sunday morning because he was a lay leader at the Church of Mar Niqoula. Karim failed to grasp the connection between work and church services and he had a strange feeling about this short fat fifty-year-old, the contours of whose face were consumed by flesh and the hair of whose eyebrows covered his small eyes so thickly you couldn't see them. Then he learned from his brother that "the Yoyo", as the man's mother, Tante Rose, had called him, was a member of the B.G. Squad, the special strike force set up by the Phalangists during the war and the instrument with which they had forced Beirut's Ashrafieh district into submission.

"The Bash brought the world to its knees with the B.G. Squad," said Nasim.

"Who's the Bash?" asked Karim.

"The Bash was Sheikh Bashir, God rest his soul. After all this time you still don't know who the Bash was!"

"And what's the Yoyo got to do with it?"

"He was one of the Bash's right-hand men, but it was his mother's fault. His mother went to the metropolitan and said to him, 'Help me, my lord. Your son is going to be lost to us. Bashir is about to send him to his death, along with all the other young boys.'"

Everyone had their doubts about the Yoyo's parentage. Ayoub was the only son of Qustantin Tayan, who died in mysterious circumstances at the start of the war. It's said he was sitting in his living room when he was struck by a stray bullet in the upper thigh. The bullet struck an artery, causing him to bleed to death within minutes, and it is thought that he died before the ambulance men could get him to the hospital.

At the time, many accused the metropolitan of having killed his rival, but nothing is sure, for dying in war is like living in it – the product of mere chance. There was however a consensus that the Yoyo looked too much like the metropolitan, and that if you were to hear his voice without seeing him you'd think you were listening to His Reverence Samu'il.

Nasim made a lot of his opinion that the Yoyo was the son of the metropolitan and asked his brother whether he'd met His Reverence Samu'il in Paris.

After the meeting with the Yoyo, in which Nasim had also participated, was over, Nasim insisted on taking his brother to the Chez Sami restaurant in Maameltein. Despite the doctor's refusal and insistence on returning to the flat, he found himself in his brother's car, heading for the restaurant. Thus the possibility of Karim finding Ghazala at home, which was something he'd promised himself, was lost.

Karim wasn't interested in hearing the story of the metropolitan's affair with Tante Rose, or how the Yoyo's relationship to the Bash had continued after Bashir informed him that he had to move from military to economic activities – which resulted in his becoming the biggest commission agent at the Port of Beirut's Dock Five. The Yoyo was no different from many other contractors who had clambered over corpses to garner vast wealth, creating in the process a class of war profiteers. The story about Metropolitan Samu'il bequeathing the Yoyo extensive lands in the hinterland of Jbeil was equally meaningless. Even the tales about the disintegration and crumbling of the metropolitan's bones during his final days, to the point that his body shrank and turned into a ball, and how Tante Rose abandoned him and refused to visit him in hospital because she couldn't stand to see him in that state – all these were just banal everyday stories such as one might find in the television soap operas of those days. What did interest Karim was the man's nervous collapse when he found out that the Frenchwoman whom he loved was being unfaithful to him.

Nasim said that all the man's friends had come together to help him regain his psychological balance, and that confiding to him the task of equipping the hospital was part of the treatment.

Once, when his words, being larded with something of the desire that gives them their taste, were still able to reach her, Karim had told Bernadette that what he feared most was his feeling that Beirut had become merely a mirror. He'd told her of the torment of the mirrors – that when he could no longer distinguish between his image and the mirror, he'd decided to flee. "A mirror, my dear, feels pain, because it exchanges itself for what it reflects, so that it forgets who it is. Then, when it tries to recover itself, it discovers it is no longer capable of distinguishing between its own identity and that of others and is forced to forget itself and melt into those reflected images."

Bernadette had knitted her brows, as she usually did when facing something difficult to understand, and said she understood. A moment later, though, she burst out laughing and said she hadn't understood a word. She told him the nicest thing about her relationship with him was that she had never once understood what he meant, and that that was what attracted her to him: "A mysterious love brought about by your mysterious words."

She laughed and he laughed and he stopped trying to explain because he was unable to put his feelings about mirrors into clear speech.

Why was his mysteriousness no longer capable of bringing out the shadows of love in his wife's eyes? Worse, his inability to express himself, which Bernadette called mysteriousness, had begun at some point to change into a reason for her to turn on him and criticise his behaviour.

When Karim got back to the flat and entered it in the dark of the power outage, he didn't find Ghazala. He'd lost Ghazala in the restaurant listening to a trivial story about a trivial man who had made up a trivial love story for his trivial brother to tell him. He had wasted his day in an excellent restaurant that would have served better as a place for lovers' trysts than for making fun of a love story, however stupid.

Ultimately, the Yoyo proved his story wasn't stupid by finding a tragic ending for it appropriate to a lover's tale. Karim though, at the very time he believed he was living a story of physical passion with Ghazala, found himself descending into the depths of melodrama.

The Yoyo committed suicide. He put an end to his feeling of humiliation at the mockery of others by shooting himself in the side of the head.

Not so Karim.

Karim had thought that Ghazala could fill the empty spaces of Beirut with a love that wasn't like love because it was stripped of all feelings – love without talk of love, desire without the soul being consumed in flames.

Ghazala was pure sex without pointless extras. With her the Frenchified doctor threw himself into a sea of those traditional delights according to which the woman is pawn to the will of the man. The man plays the role of the undisputed master, amuses himself with the woman, and takes her wet with the water of desire. Then, upon rising from the bed of pleasure, he washes her off his body as though she had never been and goes back to life.

Karim's problem was that, in spite of his attempts to convince himself otherwise, he'd found nothing in Beirut to keep him busy. He came and found that the plans for the hospital building had been made. He'd met with Ayoub so that they could study together equipment purchasing options, but Nasim had decided that the equipment and doctors' contracts would have to wait a while because he was expecting a large sum of money to arrive. At the same time, Ayoub's suicide came as an early indication that the project was faltering. Karim's job was reduced to waiting and going to the construction site, where he would listen to the building contractor's explanation of the progress of the preparations for the start of the work. When he got back to the flat he'd sit at the table in the office and draw up plans that he knew in his heart would never materialise, despite which he decided to continue the game.

"What does it matter to you? From the moment of your arrival in Beirut the hospital director's salary has been deposited in the bank in your name. We agreed on five thousand dollars and the money's there. Think of it as a holiday, brother, take things easy, and the moment the money arrives we'll start on the construction."

Nasim had been clear from the start. He'd told his brother that he would underwrite all the costs and the hospital would be a joint-stock company with Nasim holding 51 per cent of the shares and Karim 30 per cent, the rest to be distributed among the doctors they employed.

"All of them will pay for the shares they buy except you. You won't pay because this will be in place of your share of what our father left. He didn't leave us anything worth mentioning but it doesn't matter; and your salary as a director has nothing to do with what you earn as a doctor. In other words, old boy, the door to a fortune has been opened. The biggest fortune anyone can make in Lebanon is from medicine. Medicine in Lebanon is an oil well. People will pay whatever we ask so long as we maintain an impeccable reputation. And your reputation, which has preceded you to Beirut, is that in France you're a famous dermatologist. Soon, before we start work, we'll set up a telephone interview for you about your work in France and from then on your path will be strewn with gold. Money, my brother, is word of mouth. Get some good word of mouth going about yourself and just see how the money flows in."

It wasn't true that Karim had believed in the potential riches of which his brother had spoken. That wasn't what he'd come in search of, and had he wanted money he would have gone to the Gulf, where inexhaustible wealth awaits those who wish for it.

He'd never told his brother the story of Sheikha Murjana, the wife of one of the Gulf sheikhs, who'd come to him at the clinic in Montpellier after a series of cosmetic operations all over her body and asked him to treat her skin, which was thick and given to sweating. He'd prescribed some ointments and told her – when, glorying in the achievements of French cosmetic medicine, she'd shown him an old photo of herself – that he couldn't recognise her, she'd changed so much. She laughed, revealing two rows of sparkling white teeth, and said she'd been reborn but wanted him to solve her sweat problem. She used vulgar expressions and laughed loudly, as though she'd left modesty behind in her hot country and become another woman at the hands of some French doctor who had managed to redesign her face, making her nose smaller, lips fuller, forehead higher, and cheekbones more pronounced.

The vulgar expressions this fortyish woman used made Karim feel she was wearing a mask. He asked if she covered her hair in her country. She said she covered her face and neck as well, with a thick black cloth that hung down from below her eyes.

The Lebanese doctor cleared his throat as he searched for words to express himself but the woman pre-empted him, saying she had had the cosmetic surgery for her own sake, not to please a particular man or for any other reason. She said it was through such operations that she'd regained her self-confidence, her need to appear attractive to herself.

She said a woman not attractive to herself would never be able to attract a man, and that the essence of the game was a dialogue within the ego.

"But after all that surgery there shouldn't be any need for you to cover your face since the face we see today isn't your face and you aren't you."

"And who told you, doctor, that everyone isn't like that? With or without cosmetic surgery, with or without a veil, we all cover and change."

Sheikha Murjana had studied psychology at the American University in Beirut. "I used to take my veil and mantle off at the door of the plane the moment I arrived in Beirut. I'd wear jeans, put my long black hair up, and recover my body by surrendering it to the looks of the passers-by. But I had to go back to my home country to get married to my paternal cousin, and I married and had a boy and two girls. That's how the world goes round."

She said she didn't understand Lebanese women anymore. "We used to escape from our veils to their unveiledness. What's happened to your women? Half the women of Lebanon wear veils and the other half go about half naked. Why?"

Karim couldn't come up with an answer. Should he tell her that Lebanon too was a mirror? And what would such casuistry mean to a woman who came with specific questions and expected clear answers?

He gave her medicine for the sweating, prescribed her a diet, and promised her everything would be fine. As to what she thought was "thickness of the skin", it was, he told her, a simple illusion as there was no such thing as thick skin and thin skin. Her dark complexion made her think that; but it needed to be borne in mind that dark skin was preferable to white as it absorbed heat better.

He massaged her wrist as he told her that her skin was smooth and attractive and only needed some creams to shine and radiate.

To this point there was no mention of a story that was still to unfold. This started four months after this encounter, when Karim Shammas received a phone call from Sheikha Murjana thanking him for his medicines and his advice and saying that she was now completely cured of the sweat that used to soak her body from head to toe whenever Sheikh Zeidan came near her. She said she'd discussed matters with Sheikh Zeidan and invited Karim to the Gulf to work there; she mentioned fantastic figures such as he'd never dreamed of.

Karim had gone only once, to treat a group of the Sheikha's friends. He discovered there that the number of foreign workers in the country was far greater than its inhabitants, who were referred to as "citizens", and all of whom, women and men, wore traditional dress to distinguish them from the workers, who were referred to as "newcomers".

When Sheikh Zeidan broached the topic of his staying on to work in the small emirate, Karim felt at a loss as to how to turn down such a generous offer, so he used his French wife and daughters as an excuse. At his only meeting with Sheikh Zeidan, Karim listened to the strangest analysis he had ever heard of the relationship between the two blessings – Islam and oil – for which the Arabian Peninsula provided a stage. The sheikh recounted that Islam had forced people out of the Arabian Peninsula: Islam was a gateway to conquest, extension, and expansion, so people had left this hot naked uninhabitable desert land and settled in the various countries and great settlements of the world, where they lived in the luxury of cities traversed by rivers. Had it not been for the duty of pilgrimage to Mecca, the country would have been emptied of its inhabitants, or of the best of them at any rate. The Arabian Peninsula then had to wait for its new dawn, which began with the discovery of oil. "With oil came air conditioners and instead of people emigrating this became a land for immigrants looking for a crust of bread. Islam gave us glory and forced us out of this land; oil brought us back to it and made us lords of the world once more. The rebirth that began here will radiate to the entire world. It is the product of this encounter, which is a manifestation of the divine wisdom."

"But you don't allow people to become citizens of your country."

"And we must not, or we shall disintegrate and all trace of us will be lost," answered the sheikh as he invited the miracle-working doctor to reside in his small emirate.

He said his wife had become ethereal with beauty through use of the magical medicine the doctor had given her and he didn't know how to thank him; that he didn't want to seem ungrateful but hoped the doctor would convert to Islam and take up residence there, "thus making God's favours to us complete".

The magical relationship between oil and Islam had never before occurred to Karim. Poor Khaled Nabulsi! He'd joined a fundamentalist Islam that had no oil so as to complete the revolution, and his body had been ripped to pieces – after which the revolution had continued on its course without him and his like! The revolutions of the day were in need of oil wells. Money oils everything and is "the adornment of this present life", as it says in the Koran. For his part, Karim had no idea how to respond to the sheikh's offer. The man was kind and didn't insist, telling the doctor that he was one of the People of the Book "and the People of the Book are under our protection". He said he'd only wanted to honour him with the best possible offer; however, there was "no compulsion in religion".

Nasim thought medicine was Lebanon's oil and that through the hospital that he'd decided to build he would be able finally to put his relationship to the war behind him and start a new life as a respectable businessman. In no way then would he resemble the thug who'd risked his life for every penny he harvested from the fruits of war.

But the hospital needed a certain deal to go through before it could be completed. And when Karim tried to enquire about the nature of that deal his brother said it was nothing to do with him; his job now was to wait, draw up the plans, and supervise the preparations.

The wait was long. Six months of nothing, of wasted time, of abortive affairs that left only a bitter taste on his tongue.

When Ghazala appeared, in all her glory, Karim's body was filled with tremors of desire such as he had never realised lay concealed in the darkness of his soul. He started with the lust to rape and ended a total captive to this terrifyingly beautiful woman; he told her her beauty was "terrifying" because he could find no more suitable word to describe it.

She came the first time on a Tuesday morning and said she would come twice a week, in accordance with the instructions she had received from Khawaja Nasim. She didn't specify which days, and Karim had to wait since he didn't dare to ask.

She came on Thursday, but not early, as he'd expected. It was about 11.30 a.m. and Karim had grown fed up with waiting. He'd agreed to have lunch with Ahmad Dakiz so that they could discuss things to do with the building.

She came, resplendent, her dark face shining above her long neck, her black hair tied behind in a ponytail, wearing a dress that reached just below her knees. She rang the bell and waited, and when she saw Karim she smiled and said she'd meant to come early but was late because she'd had to visit a sick friend.

She entered and a musky perfume erupted from her rustling dress. She left him holding the door and went into the kitchen.

He didn't know what to do. Should he go after her or go to the living room, open a book, and pretend to read? He went to the living room and phoned Ahmad Dakiz to apologise for not being able to accept his invitation to lunch, saying he was involved in an emergency. He sensed she was listening to the call but didn't care. He sat on the couch, opened the first book he found in front of him, and pretended to read.

The smell of coffee wafted in. Ghazala brought the coffee tray and poured two cups. He took his cup with trembling hand, drank a drop, and felt the catch of the bitter coffee as it spread over his tongue and through his mouth. She took her cup and bent forward, as though about to set off for the kitchen.

"Sit down and drink your coffee with me."

He shifted to make room for her next to him on the couch but she knelt, sat cross-legged on the floor, took a sip from her cup, and made a motion with her fingers, as though she were holding a cigarette.

Karim took a cigarette, placed it between his lips, lit it, and gave it to her.

Then he took a second cigarette to light for himself.

"No, you don't have to light another. I don't usually smoke but I just happened to think of a cigarette now, I don't know why."

They smoked the same cigarette in silence. She put her hand on the couch to get up and he took hold of it. Instead of helping her rise he fell to the floor and found himself rolling over her body.

When Karim thought back to how things started he'd tell himself she'd pulled him down and he'd found himself lying on the floor without having decided to before the fact.

But the point isn't who started it: the beginning had been already sketched out to the rhythm of the smell of musk that wafted from the edges of the wine-coloured dress that covered her body.

The story began on the living-room floor, on the red carpet put there in place of the Persian rug Nasri had so angrily stamped on, swearing the damned thing would outlast him by many years.

On that pale red carpet Karim Shammas discovered he was still a primary school pupil when it came to the art of love. There he learned to sip the woman drop by drop and melt before her. With his eyes and all his senses he saw how the dew covered Ghazala's body and how she entered his insides as he entered her and how desire renewed itself at the moment of its ending.

Ghazala's nakedness glittered on the floor, and instead of him taking and entering her, she took him. When they took off their clothes, he asked that they move to the bed. She said no with raised eyebrows and pulled him to her. He tried to lift her legs so that he could enter and she pushed him away, then with a motion of her finger ordered him to lie on his back and close his eyes. The man closed them in surrender as a sensual thrill spread to every part of his body. She swept his whole body with her long hair, kissed him, kneaded him, panted above him, inundated him with the water that sprang from her, whispered and sang, and, when she let him enter, he was released inside her like a slow musical refrain.

She was hot and tender, aflame and glowing, knowing when and how and what. The smoothness of her skin enveloped him and the strength of her desire melted into a diaphanous film of sorrow that covered her eyes. Her soft moaning entered his pores and her groans of pleasure mingled with the evaporation of his will.

Karim was incapable of describing the feelings that possessed him on the living-room floor, or what exactly happened or how. On reaching one peak of pleasure he would find another waiting, but he didn't have to climb the peak in order to arrive, for it spread from the ends of the hair on his head to his fingertips.

Karim found himself in the bathroom. Ghazala filled the tub with hot water, slipped into the water, and held out her hands; he slid towards her and found himself immersed in water and soap.

In the bathtub he closed his eyes and began learning to read the woman lying before him with his fingertips. He caressed the smooth skin that made of her chest a mirror covered with the warm exhalation that arose from her pear-shaped breasts, which hung down in a slight curve before being lifted once more by the eruption of pomegranate blossom. He discovered the neck and shoulders, then descended to the buttocks and caressed what lay between her thighs, which gleamed with soap, and when he reached the cracked heels he caught fire again. He tried to slip inside her but Ghazala stood up, turned on the shower, and began roaring with laughter.

Karim, enchanted by what he believed was a rare moment of genuine encounter between two bodies, still had his eyes closed, and Ghazala's guffaws as she swayed naked beneath the shower took him by surprise. He held out his hand, calling her to him again, and heard her tell him to get out of the tub as she was hungry.

"What do you fancy eating?" she asked.

He told her he wasn't hungry and wanted to stay where he was.

She jumped out of the tub, dried herself, and ran into the living room where she put on her clothes, and he heard her summon him to table.

Karim fidgeted in the tepid water and began piecing together the different parts of him that had been dissipated so he could stand. He felt a sting of cold, then leapt out of the tub, dried himself, got dressed in a hurry, lit a cigarette, and sat in the living room waiting for her.

He heard the sound of plates being put on the small Formica table in the kitchen and smelled the smell of fried eggs, mixed with garlic and sumac.

"Come and get it, Doctor."

Suddenly he felt hungry. He went into the kitchen and found Ghazala seated in front of the frying pan, and on the table a bowl of tomato salad and a loaf of bread.

"There's nothing in the house, Doctor. It's good I brought a few eggs and some tomatoes with me."

She talked about the types of food she made well, laughed as she picked up small mouthfuls of bread which she filled with egg, then dipped in a garlic and sumac broth, and swallowed with gusto.

Karim needed silence. He wanted to enjoy the aroma of garlic and sumac, but Ghazala's inner self seemed to have opened up entirely.

She ate and laughed and talked. She told him about her husband Matrouk who loved lentil soup after sex, and said she knew that whenever he asked her to make it she had to get ready and wash herself with musk.

She said "musk" and then fell silent, as though she felt she'd made a mistake she couldn't retract.

"So you'll be making soup tonight," he said.

She didn't answer and ate in silence, then got up, while the doctor looked out of the window.

When Karim went into his room and lay on his bed, and the drowsiness began hovering around his eyes, it occurred to him that the siesta was the best thing ever invented. In France, where it didn't exist and the working day lasted till evening – as though food at lunchtime were not the dividing line between two distinct parts of the day – he despised the siestas of the Lebanese. He thought of them as laziness, remembering how his father would close the shop at noon, eat lunch, and sleep for an hour on the couch in the room at the back so that he could begin life over again. Here though, after two weeks of living in Beirut, he'd realised there was no doing without the siesta. The smell of the city was different after lunch, its sounds died away, and drowsiness spread to all its nooks and crannies.

Karim began his siesta feeling a bitterness that he would later discover to be unjustified. Instead of dying away with the ghosts of sleepiness, his bitterness started to increase. He felt the woman was a devil: instead of his tricking her or exercising power over her, as was supposed to happen in an affair between a man and his maid, she'd taken charge of everything, aroused desire, and then deftly and mockingly withdrawn. The magic had melted in the frying pan with the eggs, and the desire had uncovered the musk with which the woman washed herself for her husband's sake, not his.

There was no jealousy – not only because Karim knew that jealousy of a mistress's husband incurs laughter and has no place in the expression of love, but because he'd decided at that instant, as sleep benumbed his limbs, that his relationship with this woman must never be more than purely physical. True, the role of rapist that he'd decided to assume had come to an end on the living-room carpet and evaporated entirely in the bathtub, but he was capable of imagining another relationship similar to rape without actually being rape, a relationship of body on body that ended immediately orgasm was reached and was erased the instant the desire to make love had been satisfied.

Karim nodded off, or it seems he did so, without realising, because when he opened his eyes all he could see was darkness. It seemed he'd slept many hours without feeling the tingling of sleep that accompanies dreams. He got out of bed. The flat was swimming in darkness. He turned on the light and went into the kitchen.

On the kitchen table he found a pot of cold coffee covered with a small plate and placed on a tray with, next to it, a folded piece of paper. He poured the coffee into a cup, drank a little, discovering that it had been flavoured with orange-blossom water, opened the folded sheet, and read a single word written in an oddly childish hand. He read "Thanks" and smiled, feeling his manhood restored to him.

This sexual rite would be repeated twice a week, with the addition of a cooked meal that Ghazala would prepare to make the session "cosy", as she put it. Over the table she told him many stories of her village, her childhood, her grandmother, her husband Matrouk, and her love for and fear of Beirut. She filled the place with random talk that blended with the taste of the arak that Karim drank at the table on his own because Ghazala said she was afraid of what might come over her if she drank arak. She'd drunk it a few times, and each time had felt another woman come awake inside her. It had made her afraid and she'd decided never to drink. When Karim insisted she drink a little from his glass, she took it and sucked at the white liquid. Her eyes glazed, as though she could get drunk on a single drop.

Two months of heedless pleasure uninterrupted by a single moment of unpleasantness. From the second week, Karim would put what he called "the weekly gift" on a plate in the kitchen and she'd take it without saying anything. She'd take it as though she weren't taking it, in exactly the same way as, in bed, she took as though she were giving. Karim felt no regret about the gift: it was her due as maid and mistress. Her sudden disappearance, however, caused him anxiety. Suddenly she'd disappeared and she didn't phone. Karim waited a week before asking his brother about her and the answer only made things more mysterious: "Forget Ghazala. Tomorrow I'll send you a better maid. Don't worry about it."

"Why? What happened?" asked Karim.

"What happened happened," answered his brother. "Why would you want to get involved? Tomorrow I'll send you another woman to clean the flat."

At first Karim was afraid Ghazala had discovered he was having an affair with Muna. She must have known. She must surely have made herself a copy of the key: this woman who was such a strange combination of cunning and naïveté knew her own interests very well.

*

The affair with Muna came about by coincidence and was innocent compared to the one with Ghazala. The love he practised with Muna was full of concealment and shyness. The woman, who had come to him to have her skin treated, said nothing in bed. He would feel her interior quiverings, though not even a sigh escaped her, as though her thin body was the opposite of Ghazala's in every way.

Why then had he initiated an affair with this woman in the midst of the waves of desire that wooed him? Was it because he wanted to extinguish his desire for Ghazala's body, that storehouse of inexhaustible convolutions of lust, in that of another woman who seemed soaked in drowsiness and governed by shyness?

Karim didn't know the answer, or at least he did but didn't dare confess that he was being an out and out bastard. That was what Sawsan had told his brother when he gave her a respectable old age and saved her from abuse and death. For him to say he was a bastard, though, was meaningless. He hadn't come to Beirut for the sake of Ghazala or Muna, he'd come for the sake of another woman. He'd discovered, however, the moment he entered his brother's flat, that that woman no longer existed because the man she'd loved many years before had disappeared.

"The issue, my dear," he'd said to Hend, "is that exile forces us to recompose ourselves; one has to reinvent oneself each day or lose oneself. But someone who remains in his own country and among his family doesn't have to do anything. He stays who he is without effort and without having to try to fabricate himself."

Hend smiled wryly and said exile had made him forget how people lived in Lebanon. "You've really got things the wrong way round. Beirut may be the only place in the world where a person has to reinvent himself every day."

She spoke of Beirut as a city that was sliding. She said Beirut had decided to die ages ago but its inhabitants refused to acknowledge the fact; each time the city died its population raised it from the dead against its will. The hardest thing wasn't dying but coming back from the dead, because then one was obliged to reinvent oneself once more. That, she said, was why she didn't like the story of Lazarus in the Bible. "Your brother doesn't understand why I don't like to take the children to church on Palm Sunday."

"Who doesn't like Palm Sunday?" said Karim.

"I don't," answered Hend.

"What about the candles and the olive branches and the palm leaves? You must be joking. The way I see it, those kinds of celebrations are the only nice thing about religion."

She said she hated Palm Sunday because instead of singing hymns to Christ the King who had entered Jerusalem on the foal of an ass, there to be crucified, they sang hymns to the resurrection of Lazarus. Had anyone asked Lazarus his opinion? The poor man hadn't uttered a word after his rebirth. Only Khalil Hawi had understood and written his poem "Lazarus '62", in which the protagonist calls on the gravedigger to deepen his grave because he doesn't want resurrection.

"Have you read the poem?"

"*Deepen the hole, gravedigger! Deepen it till it has no bottom!*" intoned Karim.

"My, my! You like poetry now? When we were together you used to say poetry and Umm Kulthoum were the reason for the Arabs' defeat."

"And now I like Umm Kulthoum too but that's not the point. The point is I don't like symbols. Khalil Hawi did to Lazarus what the Bible did: he turned him from a person into a symbol. No doubt the poet was right, the man wanted to go back into his grave, but his reasons had nothing to do with the poet's. He wanted to go back into the grave because he was afraid of life and the poet wanted to turn him into a symbol for the failure of Arab nationalism and the failure of the project of rebirth. I hate symbols in literature, politics, and life because in the end the symbolist poet or writer is obliged to die symbolically, meaning he never savours the flavour of death. That's what happened to Ghassan Kanafani and that's what Khalil Hawi did when he committed suicide," said Karim.

Hend nodded but didn't reply. She felt that this man who had come back from faraway France no longer meant anything to her. He'd become a mere form emptied of its content, a body without a soul.

Nasri had spoken to her once about the soul. Hend had been impatient with the spiritual transformation that had overtaken her husband, with how he had so suddenly donned the garb of faith and taken to insisting on going to church to attend mass on Sundays. He never forced her to go with him. He said he respected her opinion on religion, but had discovered faith and would be taking the boys to church every Sunday. Hend made no comment. Religious mania had seized the Lebanese during the civil war and there was no reason her husband should be immune. Devotion to religion was better than working for a Fascist party or taking or dealing in drugs. She told him he was free but had to leave the boys their freedom of choice and he shouldn't put any pressure on them. He said children had to follow the religion of their fathers and that her view that he'd given up one opium in favour of another was naïve and not of their age, which was religious at all levels.

Nasri had come on a Sunday morning bearing manaqish with thyme and found Hend alone in the flat. When he asked her where Nasim and the boys were a wry smile traced itself on her lips.

"No, my dear," said Nasri, "you mustn't make fun of your husband because he's rediscovered his relationship with his Lord."

"If that's what you think why don't you go to church too?" she asked.

"Sit down and I'll tell you," said Nasri.

What he said scared Hend. At first his words seemed pitiable but soon fear filled her eyes and the mockery in them died. The ageing man spoke from the depths of his soul. His voice sounded rough and warm and tinged with sorrow.

He said he'd lived his whole life without faith in anything. "I had faith neither in religion nor in the beliefs of the secularists. The only thing I had faith in was life. I believe in life in spite of everything because life is magnanimous. Even when it takes, it takes so it can give. All my life I was certain my body was my soul and that I was an indivisible unity. Religion, my dear, rests on the division of the human self into two parts, body and soul, and some say it's three parts, meaning body, spirit, and soul. All my life I could never understand the meaning of the spirit as something that is attached to the body and is extinguished with it but I've come to realise the meaning of the soul remaining alive after we die. I thought it was an illusion – how could the life of a beautiful woman continue without her body, and what could that mean? These were myths, or so I thought, and I believed, and still do, that death is the end of everything. We go back to where we came from, and we came from nowhere. All the same . . .

"That 'all the same' did for me because it says everything while saying nothing. What matters, my daughter, is that I began to discover my mistake. I discovered it gradually as I aged. People liken old age to childhood but that's wrong. Absolutely not. In childhood your body and soul grow up together. In old age the body ages while the soul stays the same. I swear the only way I know I'm an old man is from the eyes of others or the pains in this inconsequential body. Am I as inconsequential as my body? It's not possible. I can't believe this is my body. It disgusts me now. But my soul is still as it was. That's why I've begun to be convinced that a person is two, a body and a soul, which means that in all probability the soul has a life independent of the body."

"Why don't you do the same as your son and go to church?"

"That's another subject. Belief in the existence of the soul and the issue of the existence of God have nothing to do with one another. Even if God exists I can't bring myself to make peace with Him. I couldn't accept such a thing for myself and He wouldn't accept it either. No, it's out of the question. But what I was trying to do was to ask you to be patient with Nasim. He may be right and we may be wrong."

Hend told Karim that from the first time she'd seen him again at her house she'd called him Lazarus. "I began calling you Lazarus to myself and began seeing you as one who'd risen from the grave and didn't know anything, like a sleepwalker: he walks and talks like a sleepwalker and he doesn't understand anyone and no-one understands him. Why did you come back? Wouldn't it have been better if you'd remained dead to us? We'd have been able to tell our memories of you, sweet and sour. Now everything about you is sour."

She said she hated him and hated herself and hated her emotions. "It's as though I've been sentenced to life with this family. Plus you've reopened the story of Nasri's death, which we'd all decided to forget. You came back and brought all the horrible memories back with you. From the first day, my mother said you hadn't come to set up a hospital, you'd come to open graves, and I didn't believe her. But then I discovered she was right and I shouldn't have let my husband go ahead with the hospital project."

"Your mother must know because of her extensive experience of life."

"My mother's the most honourable woman in the world. Watch out you don't start being offensive and making insinuations about Salma!"

"I'm not talking about honour," he said.

"What are you talking about?" she asked.

"I'm talking about talking, but it doesn't matter. You may be right, you probably are, but I'm here and I don't know what I'm supposed to do."

Ghazala disappeared. She melted away as though she'd never been, and when he badgered his brother for the reason he got a mysterious answer about a major problem between Ghazala and her husband. When he sought greater clarity his brother said he only knew what Matrouk had told him. Nasim said Matrouk had told him he'd been on the point of killing her but hadn't done so out of pity for the children.

"Why did he want to kill her?"

"Really I don't know," answered Nasim. "Anyway, why are you so interested? I hope you haven't fallen in love with the maid too."

"God forbid! What a thing to say! I just wanted to know."

Karim didn't know what his brother meant by "too". Had Nasim had an affair with her as well, or did he mean the deceived husband?

"Why didn't he kill her?" asked Karim.

Nasim didn't hear, or perhaps ignored, the question. He told him he'd be sending him a Sri Lankan maid. She'd come to him once a week and "that way your problem will be solved".

Three days later he got an unexpected phone call from Matrouk, Ghazala's husband. The man's voice was hoarse and hesitant. He introduced himself as "Ghazala's husband – you don't know me, Doctor, but I'd like to come and see you tomorrow and have a cup of coffee." The man said he'd come at 1 p.m., during the lunch break at the hospital site, and though he didn't want to take a lot of the doctor's time it couldn't wait.

Karim did not sleep well that night. He felt he was in a trap and facing possible disaster all on his own. Why should the husband want to meet him? Had she told him? Had something made him suspicious? Also, he didn't know what to say. Should he admit the truth or deny it? And what if she'd confessed? Wouldn't his denial just be a confirmation of his bad faith?

Before going to bed he found himself phoning his wife. He didn't know what impelled him. Was it loneliness or was he looking for a refuge now that he felt everything was closing in on him, as though he were in a darkened cell? He asked about the girls and said he missed them and heard Bernadette's voice asking him tenderly to "come back to Montpellier because we've missed you and Nadine and Lara ask about you every day". Why didn't he come back, she asked, and what had he been thinking of to endanger his job and his position at the hospital in Montpellier? He said he'd be back soon but couldn't abandon the project right then. He heard her kiss on the phone as she told him, before hanging up, that they'd be waiting for him.

He slept intermittently. In fact he didn't sleep properly until dawn, so didn't open his eyes until ten-thirty in the morning. He phoned the architect to reassure himself that the work was progressing but couldn't get hold of him. He dressed and walked the streets aimlessly. He walked to kill time. He didn't like just waiting about.

He reached Sassine Square, took a seat at the pavement café, ordered a cup of coffee without sugar, swallowed down the bitter catch in the throat *à la* Ghazala, and contemplated the memorial to Bashir Gemayel and his comrades killed in Ashrafieh on the Feast of the Cross in 1982. The Phalangist militia leader was portrayed as a young man bursting with vitality, which was etched on his face in lines of shadow. He thought about the absurdity of the moment that had brought him – a former fighter in the leftist Palestinian Joint Forces – to sit opposite the image of the man who had once been the embodiment of the merciless enemy. He smiled when it occurred to him that only the dead can embody the vitality of life, for had Bashir lived to be sixty and died of an illness he would probably have committed additional horrors that no intercession could have erased.

He smoked three cigarettes, then began to feel hungry. His watch showed twelve-thirty. He thought he'd better go home because the hour of his appointment with Matrouk was near. He decided to buy a grilled chicken sandwich from Abu Esam's, next to his building. He walked in the direction of Sofiel, reached the Tabaris roundabout, turned right, entered Haramiyyeh Lane, and started the descent towards Gemmeizeh.

Thick dust in the air? Where had it come from? Borne on hot winds the dust formed a cover over the city, but Karim felt a shiver of cold. Since receiving that phone call from Matrouk he hadn't known whether he was cold or hot. Everything had got mixed up with everything else. He felt he was about to fall down in a faint; he leant against the wall, rubbed his eyes, and continued on his way like a blind man.

He reached Abu Esam's place, saw grilled chickens, fire surrounding them on all sides, turning on spits in front of the shop, and, instead of asking for a sandwich, as he'd decided to do at the café, ordered a whole chicken. He could smell the arak Abu Esam was drinking to go with his salted chickpeas and decided he'd drink a glass of arak with the chicken. He took the grilled chicken, which Abu Esam had wrapped in a flat loaf of white bread before putting the whole into a plastic bag alongside two small tubs of finely mashed garlic in olive oil. The smell of the garlic wafted everywhere and the man began salivating as he took the bag in his hand and set off for the flat.

He reached the entrance to the building, remembered his refrigerator was empty, and instead of climbing the stairs to the second floor, where he lived, walked about fifty metres to Emile the greengrocer's. He bought a kilo of large mountain-grown tomatoes and a kilo of cucumbers. He looked at his watch. It was one. He hurried back to the building, took the stairs at a run, and on reaching his door gave a start, as though he'd received an electric shock. A man was standing there, waiting for him. He retreated a little, apologising for being late; this tall brown-skinned man had to be her husband. He opened the door to the flat and asked him to go ahead, but the man hesitated and said, "That won't do – after you, Doctor." They entered more or less abreast, their shoulders bumping as they entered. The man pulled back and Karim turned slightly. "Sorry, sorry," the man said, smiling. His white teeth showed. Karim patted him on the shoulder and asked how he was, and how Ghazala was.

The man went into the living room while Karim went to the kitchen, washed the tomatoes and cucumbers, prepared two glasses of arak, took the chicken out of the bag, and put two plates, two knives, and two forks on the Formica table. Then he went to invite the visitor to eat lunch.

"You shouldn't have gone to all this trouble, Doctor. There's no need for lunch. I just need a couple of words with you."

"It's no trouble, you're most welcome," said Karim. "I was passing Abu Esam's, fancied a chicken, and thought we could have lunch and drink a glass of arak together."

The man thanked him, then breathed the smell in deeply, relaxing his thick lower lip and closing his small eyes, which looked as though they'd been gouged into his face. He said garlic called for arak: "I only have to smell garlic to think of arak." He said he'd learned a lot about garlic from Madam Salma, Khawaja Nasim's mother-in-law, and was always seeing her sitting in her daughter's flat peeling garlic and eating the cloves because garlic was good for blood pressure. "She eats raw garlic, with nothing else, and she told me about its health benefits. Madam Salma says that a clove of garlic in the morning opens the heart just like the sun opens the day, even with fried eggs. There's nothing better than fried eggs with garlic. That's how we eat eggs in the Jabal. We fry them with garlic and that's it. I don't know where Ghazala learned to do them with sumac, I like just garlic. It reminds me of the way my mother used to smell."

When Matrouk started talking about eggs and sumac, Karim felt the fellow had come to the point and put him in the dock from the outset. Matrouk drank a little from the glass of arak in front of him. He picked up the grilled chicken and started breaking it apart with his hands. He looked at the doctor and said he was sorry but he could only eat using his hands. "Ghazala always laughs at me. She says I was born a peasant and I'll die a peasant, but I can't taste the food properly unless I eat with my hands." He took a chicken thigh and put it on the doctor's plate.

"I prefer the breast," said Karim.

"'Breast for the bereft', as they say," answered Matrouk.

"The breast's healthier because it doesn't have fat."

"Whatever you say, Doctor," said Matrouk. He took away the thigh and put a piece of breast in its place, saying food without fat had no taste.

They drank and ate in silence. Suddenly, Matrouk stood up, tugged at something at his waist with an irritated expression, pulled out a revolver, laid it on the table, and went on eating.

The doctor choked and found himself unable to swallow a morsel of food that had lodged in his throat. He picked up his glass of arak with a trembling hand and took a large gulp, feeling the blood drain from his face.

Matrouk's expression changed when he placed the revolver on the table next to the chicken breast, which the doctor hadn't yet eaten. The anger that had creased his brow dissolved; it sagged down into his facial features, which lengthened with sadness. He stopped eating and looked at the doctor with eyes so dimmed with grief that he failed to notice the panic that had transformed his host into a wet rag.

There was silence, through which they could hear each other breathing, and then Matrouk suddenly broke the silence, cleared his throat, drank a sip of water, and told the doctor that he'd come to consult him about Ghazala. And he started to talk.

He said that at first he'd decided to kill her. "I found out she was being unfaithful to me with another man and when a woman's unfaithful to her husband, only blood will wash out the stain."

Matrouk lit a cigarette and said later he'd changed his mind. "How can I kill her? She's the mother of my children and I love her."

He said he'd changed his mind, picked up the revolver and started fiddling with it, turning it over in his hands. He looked at the doctor and saw the terror that had seized him. "It looks like you're afraid of guns."

Karim had no idea what happened next. Did he just imagine that the man cried? Or had Matrouk's tears really fallen onto his cheeks, so that he had to wipe them off with a napkin that was on the table and then blow his nose at length before saying he'd decided to kill her lover?

"What do you say, Doctor? I thought I'd kill the man and get some relief. I oiled the gun, loaded it and said to myself, 'The second I see his face, I'll empty six bullets into his head and get some relief.'"

Had the man come to torture him psychologically before killing him? Karim didn't know where he found the courage but he picked up his glass and decided to drink it all at one go before telling Matrouk, "Get it over with then and kill me. You don't have to cry for me before shooting me. Shoot me and leave me alone." But he didn't say it. And at the instant that he began drinking, Matrouk brought his fist down on the table and started to shake.

He stood up, picked up the revolver, tucked it once more into his belt, and started walking about in the kitchen, talking. It came to Karim that he wasn't the person accused. The man whom Ghazala loved, and on whose account she'd threatened to kill herself should her husband do him any harm, was some other man – a youth of twenty-five, a member of the Amal Movement militia. "Some runt of a kid five years younger than her. I don't know what she sees in him, he's an ugly little shit not worth a damn."

He said he'd discovered her unfaithfulness because he'd sensed it. "It makes me embarrassed to tell you, Doctor. I could see she was all rosy and happy and getting more beautiful all the time. I just had to get near her and I could feel she was hot as fire. She'd come back from seeing him all warmed up and rosy. Then, you know what I found out? Really, it makes me embarrassed, Doctor. I found out she was giving him money and gold. I work like a donkey and the money just disappears, and when I found the gold ring wrapped up in a bit of cloth and stuffed at the bottom of the drawer I started to get it. I decided to follow her. I followed her. She got on the bus and set off for a shack in Shayyah, and before she could knock on the door of his house I grabbed her by the shoulder and told her, 'I know you're going to see someone. Give me the handkerchief you've wrapped the ring in.' I pulled the handkerchief out of her hand and heard the sound of the ring as it fell on the ground. She knelt down, picked it up and said, 'I got this with my money. It's none of your business.'"

Matrouk said at that very moment the door of the shack opened and a short, thin young man appeared. His black beard covered his face and he was carrying a Kalashnikov. "He looked at me, the fury flashing in his eyes, gestured with his machine gun, and I released her shoulders. She slipped from my hands and bent her head to pass beneath his gun and enter the house."

Matrouk had found himself returning the way he'd come. He reached his flat and smashed the plates and glasses. "In the evening she came home. I'd thought she wasn't coming back but she came back like nothing had happened, like she'd been to see my mother. Her face was rosy and her eyes drowsy. She entered the house like normal and ran to the kitchen to make dinner. When she saw the plates broken and thrown on the floor, instead of behaving like someone who's done something wrong she began screaming at me for breaking the plates. She's the one who did something wrong, Doctor, isn't that right? What had I done? I should have cut her throat at the door to the house like a real man. She started wailing and the neighbours came. You know how Mar Elias Hollow has people from all over – Sri Lankans, Egyptians, Ethiopians, and Syrians like us. The woman whose shame had been exposed exposed me to shame and everyone started telling me, 'Shame on you, Matrouk! What kind of person beats his wife these days?' Even the children stood in front of her legs and started cursing me."

Matrouk said she'd cried and made her children cry and the neighbours had tried to make peace between the couple. "The metropolitan came. You must have heard of the metropolitan, his real name is Ramzi, and people in the Hollow would do anything for him. He's Druze like us, from a village called Maasir el-Shouf. They call him the metropolitan because after the massacre in the village he went to the church and put on priest's clothes and started walking around the village square singing in Syriac. He said he'd learned Syriac at the nuns' school. He talked about stuff that happened in the war that no-one should talk about, Doctor, but I don't know why, everybody loves him. The point is the metropolitan honoured us with a visit and when he arrived everyone shut up. He looked at Ghazala and told her, 'Clean the house quick!' and she ran into the kitchen and set to work and then he looked at me and said, 'Go and kiss your wife's head, your wife's an excellent woman.'"

Matrouk said that once all was quiet again and the children asleep, Ghazala had told him she wanted him to know she hadn't stolen money to buy the gold ring for Azab. "The ring was a present from Dr Karim and you can ask him if you don't believe me."

When Matrouk answered her by saying he was going to kill the short ugly fellow called Azab she replied that she'd kill herself. "If you kill him I'll pour paraffin over myself and set myself on fire."

Matrouk sat back down on his chair. He looked into the doctor's astonished eyes and asked him if what Ghazala had said was true. "Tell me you gave her the ring, Doctor, and set my mind at rest."

Karim didn't know how to answer. He felt sympathy for Matrouk, as they had in common the fact that they'd both been made fools of. He felt like raising his glass and drinking a toast to betrayal, but the man's confused glances and wandering eyes decided him against it and he contented himself with nodding yes.

The man looked as though a load had been taken off his mind, said he hadn't told anyone else what had happened, and asked him to keep it a secret.

"So are you going to kill Azab?" asked Karim.

"Honestly, I don't know," answered Matrouk. "I love her and she told me she'd given it up once and for all and that it had been like she was possessed by some demon but now she was free of it and that Azab hadn't done anything bad. He'd fallen in love with her and then 'when he saw you with me and lifted the Kalashnikov to protect me from you he told me, "Go back, woman, to your house and children!"'"

"Thank you, Doctor!" said Matrouk, "You've reassured me but I still don't know what to do. Whenever I try to sleep with her it feels like knives in my heart and bits of glass in my throat. What do you think I should do?"

"Ask the metropolitan," said Karim, and he stood up and began carrying the dishes to the sink.

"That won't do at all, Doctor – leave it to me," said Matrouk as he washed up.

After Matrouk left Karim sat alone in the living room. He closed his eyes in the hope of summoning up the drowsiness of a siesta. He felt he was the real dupe in the affair. "I was like the goose that laid the golden eggs for Azab and Ghazala's passion for him. I'm just like the Yoyo. The Yoyo killed himself because the woman he loved was unfaithful to him but what am I supposed to do?"

Karim hadn't been in love with Ghazala. Even if he had been and had told her some of his stories, all the love had flown away when he came face to face with Matrouk's revolver and felt the terror it sent through his limbs.

How though could the husband have swallowed her infidelity?

Karim believed males couldn't take infidelity, and that the least Matrouk should have done was divorce his wife. Naturally, a man such as Karim could not in any way support people killing their wives, or what were technically known as "honour killings". All the same, he secretly wished someone would kill Ghazala. Jealousy cries out for murder. When the woman you love betrays you you both obsess over her more and hate her more. Only death can extinguish the flames burning in your breast. Death extinguishes everything, because death is the moment that lays the foundation for a space where everything is clear.

Karim was amazed at the attitude of the deceived husband and never questioned himself or his own views. He contented himself with supposing he'd never loved Ghazala, that his relationship with her had been purely sexual, and that Matrouk's visit had been enough to erase the story from his emotional world.

This wasn't, however, the truth. The truth was that Karim's affair with Muna had been an attempt to escape the impact Ghazala had had on him; he'd found himself getting more and more immersed in his relationship with this woman who wanted no attachments and who had in fact wanted her affair with Karim to be like one between passing travellers. "You're leaving now and I'm leaving in a little while so let's keep it light. Please, I don't like things to get heavy," Muna had told him when he found himself raving about "the love that grants one the capacity to hover in the heavens of the soul". At such moments he was recalling Ghazala as she jumped up and ran into the kitchen, as though flying. He spoke to Muna of hovering and before his eyes he saw Ghazala, but it was Muna who, unawares, would later cast him into the inferno of Sinalcol in the alleyways of Tripoli, and who, by recounting the stories of her husband's father, made him remember the pain.

Ghazala remained a question mark and Muna couldn't hover. It fell to Karim to find a solution that would allow him to come to terms with his sense of humiliation. This was not due to Ghazala's betrayal. Her betrayal of him was logical, for she'd found in him a lover willing to accept anything because of his lust for her, an accessory to her great passion for the militia boy who'd stolen her heart with his gallantry, courage, and sad eyes. Karim's humiliation was the consequence of his having deceived himself.

She'd said her name was Ghazala.

She'd said she was from a village called Shuhba in Jabal el-Arab, or Jabal el-Durouz, in Syria.

She'd said she was the mother of two small children and didn't do houses but had said yes for Khawaja Nasim's sake.

She'd told him the story a number of times. After the ecstasy had raised her to the heights of love, she'd jump off the bed as though flying. She'd spread her arms like wings and leap away naked, and the brownness of her complexion would blaze out, giving the void of the room a lining of musk. She'd laugh as she took him by the hand and led him to the bathroom.

She'd told him he was like a woman: he liked to stay in bed all sticky with the glue of love while she, by contrast, found the ecstasy could only be maintained with water. "Water purifies and renews love and washes it in light." She'd asked him if he could see the light from the water and he'd smiled at her naïveté and told her water was like glass: it didn't give off light, it reflected it. She'd said she didn't understand scientific language but she knew her grandmother's stories, and that water was the swaddling of the soul; people were born of water, died in water, and transmigrated by means of water.

Ghazala was fascinated by her own body. Now that Karim was in a position to put his memories into order he realised the woman had never looked at his when he was naked. She'd kept her eyes closed the whole time and never opened them until she flew from the bed and stood naked in front of the mirror, contemplating her lust-inflamed breasts and smiling before turning on the cold shower and swaying and letting out oohs and aahs beneath the gushing water, which refracted the light and spread it over the eyes of the man as he stood, astonished, in front of the bathtub, waiting for a signal from the woman to show that she was ready to "bury" him in water.

He told her that water wasn't sand and one couldn't bury someone in it. She replied that everyone came from water and had to return to water.

And she told him the strangest story he'd ever heard.

"They called me Ghazala after my grandmother. Father worshipped his mother and whenever he described a beautiful woman he'd say 'like my mother Ghazala'. His wife, my mother, would look at him as though she couldn't believe her eyes. My mother was never my mother. My mother was my grandmother and since she died five years ago I don't know what happened, it's as though her soul has passed into me and lives with mine. When she was dying she sat me down beside her and told me she didn't want to go to anyone else, she only wanted to go to me and when she died I don't know what happened to me, it's as though her soul entered my body."

"You mean you have two souls?" Karim asked, smiling.

"I knew you wouldn't understand what I mean. Obviously you don't believe in the transmigration of souls. I don't know why I'm telling you."

Ghazala was sitting on the edge of the bed and Karim was lying on his back smoking and watching how, as she told her stories, the dark blue of evening fell and covered the room with the remnants of the light.

Ghazala's memory was devoid of any concept of the succession of events. Events went round in circles. A moment of terror, such as that created by the encounter with Matrouk over the glass of arak and the grilled chicken, had been needed to break the circle and unstring its components. After that, her memory could do nothing but pick up the broken pieces.

She said her grandmother had experienced a very strange marriage, because she'd married her own grandfather. "Can you imagine, Doctor? When my grandmother found out, she refused to sleep with her husband!"

He said he didn't believe in such superstitions but wanted to hear the rest of the story.

The story went that the grandmother found out about her husband when she gave birth to her son Anwar. The same day her husband told her they must leave their tumbledown village, and that without delay.

He said that at the very moment Anwar had seen the light, Arif Bey Elwan had been found shot dead.

"I don't know who killed him, but I do know the Elwan clan will attack us and kidnap the child. They will never accept that the sheikh's soul pass into a poor peasant family like ours."

The woman was confined to bed and couldn't be moved. Next to her sat her mother, who pleaded with the man to delay their departure by two days so the woman could regain her health. This forced the husband to come up with an amazing stratagem. He announced that his wife had given birth to a girl, and he refused to receive well-wishers, wreathing his face in a genuine scowl born of fear.

And after a week he escaped with his son to the village of Shuhba.

The story is not, however, about Anwar, who remembered his former life only intermittently. His parents suppressed his memories and he lived his early childhood under the terror both of that trauma and of finding himself in the poor household where he had been reincarnated.

The story is that of the grandmother, who'd been sceptical about transmigration until the day her husband told her that, when he was three years old, he had spoken and recalled his former life, only for his mother to discover, twenty years later, that he wanted to marry his own grand-daughter.

"I didn't recognise you because you were reborn five years after I died, but you're my daughter's daughter."

"You mean you went and asked for my hand from your daughter?"

"When I saw you I lost my heart and there was nothing to do but marry you."

"And you knew I was your daughter's daughter?"

"Certainly not. You speak when you're two or three and then you forget what you said and remember it only if your parents remind you. I'd forgotten, and by the time my mother told me my heart had been lost and there was nothing I could do. We had to get married or I would have gone mad. Love makes people mad and love of you made me mad."

Ghazala said her grandmother's body shrivelled up at the horror of what she heard. She had fever for a whole week, and when she got better she couldn't sleep with her husband anymore. Whenever he went near her she felt sharp pains in her belly and her body would tremble, as though the shock that had caused the fever still lurked within it – "and that, my girl, is why your father stayed an only child. Everyone told your grandfather to divorce me because I refused to have any more children, but your grandfather, God rest his soul, kept on loving me. He just used to beg me to let him come to me at night and sleep next to me and not do anything. He said he liked listening to my breathing because my breath was sweet."

Karim had no idea why Ghazala had told him this story, but he knew that a bed that brings two bodies together calls for talk, for sex matures only with speech. Perhaps Ghazala, finding the doctor dazzled by the arts of love she'd taught him, had wanted to dazzle him with words as well.

Karim wasn't dazzled at the time; he gave the impression of one listening to naïve superstitions. But after the terror with Matrouk's gun he became convinced that Ghazala was indeed inhabited by two souls, her own and her grandmother's, and as he recalled her description of the end of the world he was seized with panic.

12

Karim had decided there was no point staying any longer in Beirut. The work on the hospital was going slowly and the architect, Ahmad Dakiz, was only interested in following up on his Canadian immigration application even as he persisted in raving about "the new Beirut".

Karim felt lonely in the dust-covered city.

Beirut seemed grey and naked. The numerous pockmarks that had formed on the reinforced concrete made its forest of piled stone seem diseased.

Everything here is sick, the doctor had thought on his return from his French expatriation – and I too am sick and must escape before the city's smallpox spreads to my skin and my soul and I become stuck in the place, unable to leave, unwilling to stay.

He'd laughed long on reading an article by a Lebanese novelist in the newspaper *al-Nahar* in which the author said "the only moment of joy felt by the Lebanese is on the plane. In Beirut you feel you are choking, so you decide to go to Paris, and the moment you get on the plane you feel as happy as though you had been let out of prison. After a few days, though, you are overwhelmed by nostalgia for Beirut and feel as though you cannot bear to be away from it, so you get depressed and your depression only lifts on the plane that is taking you back to Lebanon. The Lebanese is a flying creature, happy only in the air."

Karim had laughed because he'd felt he was on the verge of falling into the Lebanese trap which cancels all relationship with place and makes one a stranger everywhere. He realised too that his amorous adventures with Ghazala and Muna, and his dumb passion for Hend, were symptoms of the same sickness which rendered him incapable of giving his emotions a fixed direction, just as they rendered him incapable of speech.

And in the end the eccentric architect – who phoned him daily claiming it was about work but who behaved like a bully, browbeating his listeners with incessant talk of how Beirut's old city would be redeveloped once it had been demolished – had finally come.

The thirty-something, who had told his wife he was of mysterious Frankish origins, was passionate about the Solidere project. Solidere is a property company founded by the billionaire Rafiq Hariri to redevelop central Beirut, which was smashed to pieces in the war. This was of course before Hariri became first prime minister and then, thanks to his barbaric assassination on 14 February, 2005, history.

Dakiz was head of Solidere's demolition unit. In other words, he was the engineer who drew up the plans for the demolition of all the buildings surrounding Place des Martyres. The destruction was preparatory to the driving through there of a street the breadth of Paris' Champs Elysées. This was intended to link the city centre with two skyscrapers occupying the sea front and called, in the city's master plan, the World Trade Towers – an optimistic salute to New York's famous twin towers that collapsed on 11 September, 2001 as the result of a suicide operation executed by al-Qaeda using commercial aircraft, one of which was flown by an Egyptian engineer named Mohamed Atta.

Karim would never forget how the architect's face had quivered with the joy of victory as he described the plan for the demolition of the Cinema Rivoli building, which blocked the view of the sea from the city centre. It had crossed his mind that day to phone Muna and tell her her husband was a criminal.

Muna – the woman who had lodged in Karim's memory as she emerged from the bathroom, the drops of water glistening on her shoulders as she wrapped her body in a white towel that covered her breasts and upper thighs – had told him that in Canada she would disappear and no-one would be able to find her. "Even my family will give up, because I want to disappear, like a photo that's been permanently deleted."

"I don't like memories and dragging up the past. My problem with Eduardo was that when I became convinced of his point of view and stopped feeling anything after his wife discovered what was happening, he went to pieces and started going on about love and trying to keep the whole thing alive."

"Tell me, please. Why are men like that?" she asked him.

"Like what?" he replied.

"Like weak. All a woman has to do is be strong and say it makes no difference to them, and they go to pieces and turn into wet rags."

He told her he wasn't that kind of man and wanted to tell her the story of Matrouk, but thought better of it at the last moment. What was he to say? Matrouk and he had both behaved like wet rags. Only Azab had been a man. Though why should we have to believe Ghazala when she said Azab had told her to go back to her husband and children because he didn't want problems?

Azab wasn't like that, Karim had wanted to say but didn't.

"If you were to find out tomorrow that your wife was being unfaithful, what would you do?"

"My wife could never be unfaithful," he said.

Muna had burst out laughing. "You all say that and then you turn into little kittens."

"And who's Eduardo?" he asked her.

"It doesn't matter," she said.

He wanted to tell her about his father and about the sexual conquests and the unkindness and the cruelty. He wanted to tell her that the only real man was Nasri but how could he boast of something that he'd considered all his life to be shameful and humiliating? And how could he forgive a man who'd etched himself on his memory as a despicable rapist?

Muna asked what was wrong, laughing, the drops of water scattering over her shoulders. She held out her hands to him but he felt he'd lost all desire.

He asked her again about Eduardo.

She sat on the edge of the couch and told him about a relationship she'd had with a married Italian who worked for the French press agency in Beirut. She said she didn't know what had attracted her to him, maybe his grey hair and broad shoulders. She said he was fifty – "meaning twenty-four years older than me. You could say he was my father's age. I'd gone to the agency because I'd thought at first I might work in journalism. 'Why not?' I thought. I know French and English and have a degree in French Literature. I didn't want to be a teacher. I met him there. He said he'd like to train me and began trying it on – you know how men jump up and down like monkeys when they're trying to get a girl. At the time I was in love with Ahmad and we were about to get married and I don't know what happened. In fact, nothing happened. He took me out to dinner once at an Armenian restaurant in Ashrafieh and then we walked and found ourselves in front of his building. He said he was inviting me in for a small glass of grappa. I smiled and told him, 'No, Monsieur Eduardo.'

"Then he started talking in Arabic, which I'd thought he didn't know. Suddenly his tongue was loosened and I thought, 'God, what a bind!' 'You're backward,' he said, 'like all Eastern girls. What do you think will happen if you come up to my place? Do you think I'm going to rape you?'

"He turned his back and went through the door to the building and I found myself following him and went up and drank grappa. 'Where's your wife?' I asked him. He said she'd gone to visit the children in Cinisello.

"I asked him where this 'Cinisello' was. To tell the truth, I thought he was making fun of me and that the flimflam had begun.

"In the end I told him it was he who was backward because when he tried it on and I didn't let him, he'd sat down on the couch like he was being punished."

"And then?"

"Then nothing happened. He got up and saw me home and when he tried to kiss me I gave him my cheek."

She said the story should have ended there because two weeks later she married Ahmad and they went to Italy for their honeymoon and there she discovered Eduardo hadn't been flimflamming her because, as she confirmed, there was a small town close to Milan called Cinisello.

She said three months later she'd gone back to the French press agency and met Eduardo. He'd behaved as though nothing had happened and she'd begun her attempts to seduce him.

"I don't know what came over me. As soon as he saw me he started talking to me in Arabic and said, 'How are you, child?'"

She said she'd felt slighted and made her decision, "and when a woman decides, it happens the way she wants."

Karim said her story was silly and meaningless.

"He made a fool of you twice, the first time with the grappa and the second with 'child'. But what did you want from him? Just married and starting as a teacher – what, you didn't love Ahmad?"

"Of course I loved him and I still do, but the war."

"What's it got to do with the war?"

"It's how war is," she said.

"What happened?"

"It happened just like I told you. When I become convinced it wasn't serious and that he had to wake up and stop behaving as though he was in love, he went to pieces and started chasing me from place to place."

"And Ahmad?"

"Ahmad knew but behaved like he didn't, or like he didn't want to know."

"And then?"

"It ended."

"And me?"

"What about you?"

"Has Ahmad found out anything about our relationship?"

"Of course not. Why, are we having a relationship?"

She laughed and threw herself on the bed.

Muna's laugh sounded in his ears as he listened to Ahmad Dakiz describing the Solidere redevelopment project. On a table in his office he'd put a model of the project as designed by the architect Henri Eddeh previous to the latter's services being dispensed with following differences with Hariri. In the model the city resembled a curious mixture of Dhahran, Houston, Paris, and an Italian seaside town. In the sea, a few dozen metres from the World Trade twin towers, was an artificial island fated never to see the light of day because it was located over a deep marine trough known to the people of Beirut as Dogs' Hole.

Dakiz spoke briefly about the project, then led his guest to the computer, on which he'd installed a programme resembling an electronic game. He turned on the computer and Beirut appeared – weeds and trees sprouting from the cracks in its walls – like a ghost town, or a setting for a war movie in a city anywhere in the world.

Maroun Baghdadi said that in his film *Circle of Deceit* the German director Volker Schlöndorff had discovered the amazing expressiveness of Beirut in ruins as a setting but the Lebanese had spoiled it with dozens of movies that had turned it from a storehouse of human savagery into banal visual clichés.

Karim said the scene would have made a good setting for the moment of resurrection and the end of the world. He was thinking of the terrifying description presented by Ghazala of the end, as her other grandmother had imagined it. Dakiz, however, appeared not to be listening. He was preoccupied with making adjustments to the programme before starting the game, which Karim would later describe to his brother as "demolishing the demolished".

"Behold what I shall wreak!" said Dakiz, and suddenly the buildings began to fall, one after another, each disappearing behind a mass of dust before collapsing, broken up into a heap of stones and sand. The architect took the buildings down systematically, starting with Debbas Square, where the Café Laronda and Cinema Dunya were demolished, then turning to Cinema Metropole, and thereafter burrowing off to the right to demolish the police building formerly called the Little Palace; then he entered Mutanabbi Street, where Karim noticed a neon sign on the second-floor balcony of a building apparently untouched by the war and read on it, in English letters, the name Mareeka. "No, don't you dare demolish Mareeka's building!" said Karim. But the architect didn't give him time to finish what he wanted to say, before, on screen, causing the beautiful Ottoman house to collapse.

"This is insane!" said Karim. "What kind of person demolishes his memory?"

"Hang on a second," said Dakiz, "Cinema Rivoli's about to come down. Why is the computer doing that, even though I put in enough explosives to bring down a city? That cinema's like a hooker, it blocks the sea. For some reason it doesn't want to come down."

"Enough!" said Karim.

"Wadi Abu Jamil."

"You're going to knock the Wadi down too?"

"To the ground."

"And the Tawileh market?"

"The Tawileh market?! What are those silly little markets good for? They're all in ruins and full of rubbish. It's all going. We want to build a modern city – malls, like in Saudi Arabia and Dubai and America."

"And the memories?"

"Memories! This is a country without a memory. What use is memory? Memories of crap and shit, *c'est fini*. The architect Adnan said this is the age of architecture by explosion and demolition and I was put in charge, and when Adnan took a look at the plan he almost fainted. He said we ought to have shown it to Rashed, God rest his soul, he would have gone ape with joy."

Karim gathered from Ahmad Dakiz that the architects Adnan and Rashed had been military functionaries during the war. Adnan had gone on to become a contractor and Solidere had managed to persuade him to work with them, and Rashed had died in the Battle of the Hotels in 1976. Dakiz had fought when he was nineteen with the Communist Action Organisation, then left it to join a Maoist organisation that viewed the civil war as an opportunity to bring about radical change in Lebanon and the region. And today he oversaw the demolition of whatever the war had failed to demolish.

"This is insanity," said Karim.

"No, Doctor. What you just watched was what's called an *illusion d'optique*. Everything's like that now, everything today is an optical illusion. The whole of Lebanon is no more than an optical illusion! And what do you think we're doing? We're doing now what we couldn't do in the war."

"But you're a communist, right?"

"Sure I'm a communist."

"And you're working on a capitalist project?"

"Please, none of that tricky talk. I want to make a little money, emigrate to Canada, and forget."

He said he wanted to forget and Karim couldn't think of how to answer him. He was right to forget, we all want to forget. However, Karim was convinced that the protection of memory was a condition of forgetting. Memory had to be preserved somewhere so we could forget it and turn a new page. When we demolished memory in that barbaric way, though, it meant we wanted memory to make its home in our unconscious. That way the war would renew itself every time we thought it had ended.

Karim said nothing. He too had fled Beirut in order to forget. He'd left his memory hanging from the demolished walls of his soul and left. And now he claimed to be taken aback by the architect, who was continuing the war in his own way, demolishing whatever the war hadn't been able to, so that things might be built in their place that could then be exposed once more to destruction?

Why though had he come back?

When Muna asked him why he'd returned and whether anyone in their right mind would return to a country plagued by wars he hadn't known what to say.

Muna said he'd convinced her of the truth of his idea about the war that would never end and asked him, as she sipped the last drops of coffee from her cup and then dipped her finger in it to pick up the residue at the bottom and lick it off, why he didn't write about the idea.

She said she thought his return was just a whim, an expression of what she called the mid-life crisis, and launched into a psychological analysis of the latter. Karim could feel the drowsiness creeping into his eyes.

He told her she spoke like a schoolmistress and that that kind of talk turned into a sort of pillow of drowsiness.

He spoke of drowsiness and felt he was imitating Nasim. Nasim had told him that the teachers' voices tickled his eyes. "I don't know why but as soon as I hear the teacher talking my eyes begin to close, like their words were covering me in a grey cloud, and I can't understand a word anymore and my mind wanders off."

Karim had tried to get out of Nasri's decision that he should take the high school exam in his brother's place. He decided to study with his brother in the hope that it would encourage him to take things seriously and save him the risk.

Nasim just couldn't, though. Probably he switched off because he was certain the high school certificate was in his pocket, and all his brother had to do was go to the exam and bring it back home.

Nasri couldn't credit that, on the day, Karim was afraid he might fail. The youth's fear was real all the same. Three days before the exam he started feeling mildly dizzy and nauseous. He lost his appetite and his mouth felt dry as tinder. He told his father he felt ill but the pharmacist, who wanted his second son to get into university at any cost, told Karim it was just nerves: "What are you afraid of, boy?" Karim said he hadn't prepared enough and had forgotten Arabic Philosophy and didn't know what he was to do in the exam.

"What will it take? Just leaf through the book and you'll remember everything."

He didn't dare tell his father that whenever he picked up the book he felt drowsy, and that no sooner did he decide to pretend to be Nasim than his brother's personality would possess him.

He said he'd try.

He tried and succeeded.

But he didn't tell his father that the nausea had got much worse in the early morning in the exam hall. He'd been obliged to ask the supervising lady teacher for permission to go to the bathroom because he felt he was going to be sick, and the teacher had taken pity on him: she had a cup of tea brought to him and told him to pull himself together because she couldn't give him permission to leave the exam hall.

He told Muna that his crisis wasn't mid-life, it was a weird mixture of his love for and hatred of the city, and that what he'd told her about his theory of the war that never ends was a precis of a cheaply produced book put out by an Islamist group in Tripoli.

"The Islamists talk like that? Strange. Anyhow I have to go home now. You know, Ahmad has started getting on my nerves. He barely gets home and has something to eat before he jumps up and goes to the computer and starts playing at demolition. I feel he revels in it, as though . . . I don't know how to put it, but it's as though I don't know him."

Karim hadn't been lying to Muna when he told her he'd read the text in a cheaply produced book put out by a small organisation calling itself the Organisation for Righteousness and Proselytisation set up by Khaled Nabulsi in the last phase of his life to replace the Resistance and Fury Organisation.

Nor had he told the whole truth. Danny had begun writing the text in French, then asked Karim to help him translate it into Arabic. In the end the two friends rewrote it as a full-length text under the title *Arms and the Lebanese Balance of Power* and published it under a pseudonym in the magazine *New Culture*. This was a monthly that came out intermittently, edited by a poet who'd left the Communist Party under the influence of the ideas of the New Left before holing up in his village in Blad Jbeil. The magazine had closed when he had a revelation: that to write during a time of war was absurd.

The story of the transformation of this Marxist text, which stressed the role of the working class in the civil war and the impossibility of the Lebanese conflagration coming to an end without a solution to the Palestinian problem, deserves to be "written with needles on the eyeballs of insight", as Scheherazade has taught us.

After Muna left, the memory of the blue exercise book that he'd put in the file that Khaled sent him and asked him to look after flashed through his mind. Khaled had said it included the texts Yahya had written before he was killed, and that they were very precious. He was afraid the Syrian army would seize them, which was why he wanted the book kept in a safe place.

Karim couldn't remember what he'd done with those particular texts. He'd taken one text only – Jamal's diaries – with him to France, unable to bring himself to burn the notebooks of the heroine of the suicide operation as he had the rest of his papers before leaving for Montpellier. But what had he done with Khaled's papers? Had he burned them? Impossible – Khaled held a special place in his memory and it was inconceivable that he would have burned valuable papers given him by the man for safekeeping.

He remembered he'd read the papers quickly. They consisted of texts written by Yahya, Khaled's uncle, who'd died in prison in 1974, six months after his arrest. The charge against Yahya, which he in no way denied, was that he had led an armed uprising of peasants against the feudal landlords of Akkar.

When Karim read the papers, written in a poor hand, he'd thought of Salma. He told Hend that the Abd el-Karim family had been forced, under pressure from the peasant insurgents, to quit the village of Kherbet el-Raheb and flee to Homs in Syria.

He said Yahya had written of Abd el-Karim's three sons that they were distinguished by the savagery with which they'd treated the peasants and by the inventiveness they'd shown in oppressing them. The spark that had ignited the revolution had been struck on their lands and the peasants had torched and plundered their houses, forcing the three brothers to quit the village forever.

"Strange," said Karim, "when your brothers' mother was a peasant. Strange how, when one denies one's origins, one turns into a monster."

He asked her what she thought and she said the matter didn't concern her.

"They're my mother's children, not my brothers. In any case, I don't give a damn about them."

"Tell your mother she can see her boys now. Your mother's husband was killed and his lands were burned, and she can get her children back now."

Rather than being happy, Hend was struck with gloom, and instead of hurrying to her mother to give her the good news she told Karim not to tell Salma.

"If you tell her you'll reopen her old wounds and she'll remember something she's decided to forget."

"But they're her children. Who can live without their children?"

The strange thing is that years later Hend would ask Nasim to help find her three half-brothers. Nasim found them in Homs, where they ran a shop making Arab pastries.

Karim recalled that, of all he remembered from the war, he'd preserved only two texts – Jamal's diaries, which had accompanied him to France, and the texts Khaled had inherited from his uncle Yahya, who called himself Abu Rabia and died in prison of torture, though the official statement claimed he'd died of a burst appendix.

Abu Rabia was a true legend. Danny had met him in the hinterlands of Akkar when the man was gathering young men in preparation for the launch of an armed uprising against the feudalists of the Abd el-Karim, Meraabe, and el-Ali clans.

"Akkar is the reservoir of the revolution," Abu Rabia told Danny as he explained to him his Guevarist theory of the revolutionary nucleus and the need to create a revolution within the revolution. The man had worked all his life in his father's bakery in the Qubbeh quarter of Tripoli. On inheriting it he turned it into a cell where the young semi-unemployed men of the quarter would meet and plan the building of the revolutionary nucleus that would initiate the armed struggle. In all probability the baker was influenced by the Guevarist experience and was striving to apply it in Lebanon.

In Abu Rabia, Danny saw revolutionary material in need of polishing. The man was no intellectual, his reading being limited to the *Communist Manifesto* and Régis Debray's *Revolution in the Revolution?*. Danny didn't like Debray's book or his theorising, which sprang from a petit bourgeois mentality and a volunteerism in which he saw an antithesis of the necessity for a vanguardist revolutionary organisation, without which the struggle could never be victorious. All the same, he dealt with Yahya in a positive fashion, seeing in his project for the launching of a peasant revolution in Akkar the spark that might set the whole Lebanese plain ablaze.

When the revolution got under way, Danny wasn't a player. Abu Rabia was convinced that no-one who didn't know how to work with his hands could be a true revolutionary. Khaled related that his uncle had said he despised intellectuals, likening them, in the way they lived off others, to the clergy. The best comment on an intellectual, he said, was a saying he'd read in a book about the clergy: "Listen to what they say, don't do as they do."

Abu Rabia had enjoyed listening to Danny and his analyses of the international situation and to reading the texts by Mao that Danny brought to the Tripoli cell. But when things got serious he made his decision and didn't bother to inform his supposed leader in the revolution.

Danny was taken aback by the uprising and made his annoyance at Abu Rabia's stupidity and haste plain. This didn't stop him writing an article glorifying it, following its collapse under the blows of the Lebanese army, in the magazine *al-Hurriya*.

Today no-one remembers the Akkar peasant uprising, thought Karim. This is a country of oblivion and lost memory. Perhaps Ahmad Dakiz is right: the demolitions are an extension of the culture of oblivion on which rests a nation whose deficiencies even the long civil war could not make good – as though this is a nation that can only be made complete through death.

Danny was free now to take credit for this forgotten revolution, or forget it. When Karim met him they hadn't spoken of Abu Rabia, nor revisited the story of Jean-Pierre and how Danny had refused, indirectly, to give the French scholar Abu Rabia's papers.

Danny had turned up suddenly at the door, accompanied by a Frenchman. He said he'd brought a French comrade and sociologist who was working on an academic study of fundamentalist movements in northern Lebanon and the cities of the Syrian interior, and that the sociologist, Jean-Pierre, was a friend of Khaled's; it was he who'd told him his uncle's papers were in the keeping of Dr Karim Shammas.

"Khaled told you? How strange!" said Karim.

Danny asked Karim to give the papers to the French comrade.

"But Khaled told me to keep the papers safe and that I shouldn't give them to anyone but his wife," said Karim.

"Khaled's dead now," said Danny. "It would be preferable if we were to give them to Comrade Jean-Pierre so that he may make use of them in his study of fundamentalist movements."

"But Abu Rabia wasn't an Islamist! Abu Rabia died a Marxist!"

"Khaled was an Islamist leader, as you well know," replied Danny, "and he was the heir to the organisation founded by his uncle."

At that moment Jean-Pierre intervened, saying he knew Abu Rabia was a Marxist and that made him all the more interested in the topic. "Khaled wasn't an Islamist either but he embraced Islam later on," said the Frenchman, "and I believe this is the coming evolutionary line in the revolutionary movement. Islam is the future of the revolution."

Karim had no idea what came over Danny when he heard Jean-Pierre's words. He said, "*Merde!*" looking at the Frenchman. He said he didn't like that kind of Orientalist talk, it reminded him of the obsession of some Westerners with the East and Islam. "Anyway, that obsession was a cover for colonialism. Look at what Lawrence did. When it comes down to it the leader of the Arab revolution was a British spy."

Jean-Pierre said he wasn't an Orientalist. "I was born in Tunisia and decided to become an Arab the day the French army shelled Bizerte. That day I saw injustice with my own eyes and decided to become an Arab. Do you understand?"

Jean-Pierre spoke with a clear Damascene accent. He must have studied Arabic at the French Institute in Damascus, thought Karim, feeling sympathy for this man who'd actually chosen to become an Arab. Karim didn't agree either that the dominant tendency would be Islamist in the future, seeing Khaled's Islam as the expression of a crisis that had struck the Left and was bound to end soon, allowing things to get back to normal. All the same, he felt some sympathy for the Frenchman, who spoke lovingly of Khaled and said he considered him a major landmark on the path of his own personal development, both intellectually and psychologically. He said he'd learned from Khaled the meaning of "the people". "Before I met him and his comrades in the Qubbeh district I didn't know the meaning of poverty, misery, and pain. With them, I learned, and I want to write an academic text in which I can give the phenomenon represented by Khaled its proper status, as a marker pointing towards the future."

When the man heard no response his voice rose in anger.

"You complain about the Syrian regime?" said Jean-Pierre. "Who, in your opinion, is going to change things there? You? Honestly, that's out of the question. There's only one power there and I'm going to be the first to write about it."

Karim was surprised to hear Danny telling his French friend that he could understand Karim's refusal to give him Abu Rabia's texts. "They are a sacred trust. Let's put it aside for the moment," he said as he took the Frenchman's arm and they left.

Karim had been on the verge of agreeing to photocopy the papers to give to the Frenchman but Danny's behaviour took him by surprise and he said nothing.

Karim followed the French media's coverage of the French sociologist Jean-Pierre Giroux, kidnapped by Islamists in Beirut. His name was added to the list of hostages whose tragedies were acted out on Beirut's stage following the Israeli invasion of Lebanon in 1982. There, in France, Karim realised that the destruction of the Palestinian presence and the smashing of the Lebanese leftist forces had opened up the field for Islamists to take control of the revolution, as Jean-Pierre had predicted in an article published in *Le Monde* four months before he was kidnapped.

When the news of Jean-Pierre's death was announced following the discovery of his remains in an area called Harj el-Qatil in the Beirut suburbs, Karim was overcome with depression and told his French wife that he didn't understand.

"They killed him because he was French," Bernadette said. "They're savages and have no mercy. You know that better than me."

He was astonished that she could utter the word "savages" and look at him, as though accusing him of killing a person who had only become French against his will and because of his death. He tried to tell her the story but discovered he couldn't, not because he was obliged to speak French with his wife but because there were no words that could explain the tragedy.

Karim only met Jean-Pierre on that one occasion when he'd visited him to ask for Abu Rabia's papers, but he got to know the man after his death because of the French media interest in him. Then he came across a piece Jean-Pierre had written on the Islamist movements: it was this piece that was the true reason for his death, sick with hepatitis, in an underground cell in Beirut's southern suburbs.

This man, who had decided to abandon his French identity and who lived in Damascus, who had married a Syrian woman with whom he had had three children, and who had then moved to Beirut to work for C.E.R.M.O.C., had found himself simultaneously a prisoner and a victim of the ideas he had embraced.

Karim told his wife, who seemed annoyed by the conversation and listened as though forced to, that the tragedy of Jean-Pierre was a part of the tragedy of Beirut, and he wasn't sure it was the Islamists who'd killed him. In those days, after the Israeli occupation had smashed Beirut and ripped it to pieces, darkness had wrapped the city in silence and fear. That was when Islamist groups started popping up like mushrooms and everyone got mixed up with everyone else – Leftists became Islamists, Leftists collapsed, Islamists moved from one place to another, and an entire people lost hope as it watched the harvest of its dreams turn into nightmare. That was when Jean-Pierre was seized at a flying checkpoint set up on the Beirut airport road and kidnapping groups passed him on from one to the other, until he ended up in the hands of one of the security apparatuses.

Karim said he didn't know who had killed Jean-Pierre or left him to die in that cruel way, writhing with sickness and despair, but he had read the story of his visit to his home in Ras el-Nabaa, as recounted by his Syrian wife, who had come with her children to live in Paris after despairing of any possibility of his release.

He told Bernadette that the words had been like needles stabbing at his eyes. He said his tears hadn't fallen out of pity or empathy but from the pain in his eyes. He said what he couldn't understand was why they'd allowed him that one visit to his home.

In an interview with the magazine *Le Nouvel Observateur* his wife said that, about two months after her husband had been kidnapped, she'd heard a gentle knocking on the door, followed by the turning of the key in the lock. It was about eleven at night, the city was swimming in a gelatinous darkness, and the July heat stuck to her body. "I felt afraid. I got out of bed half naked and instead of running to see where the sound was coming from, I ran to the children's room, switched on a torch, and stood by the door of the room to protect them with my body. Then suddenly I knew it was him. I smelled the smell of his sweat and heard his laboured breathing. I yelled, 'Jean-Pierre!' and heard his voice, which sounded somewhat hoarse. He told me to lower my voice or I'd wake the children. I went to the living room and saw him. He was standing next to this tall man, who smiled at me. I ran towards him and hugged him but instead of taking me in his arms he pushed me back a little. I couldn't understand what the strange man was doing with my husband who had returned after being away for two long months.

"Jean-Pierre told me in a whisper that he'd come home to get Ibn Khaldoun's *Introduction* and go back.

"'Go back? Where?'

"'I'm going back there.'

"I didn't understand. I said, 'I don't understand.' The man accompanying him explained that they'd allowed Jean-Pierre a quick visit to his home to get some books before taking him back in.

"Where's 'there'?" she asked.

"The man smiled and told me not to worry and to stop making a lot of fuss about my husband's kidnapping.

"'Your husband is in friendly hands,' he said, 'and soon he'll be home, fit as a fiddle, don't you worry, madam.'

"'And why can't he be at home now?'

"I took hold of Jean-Pierre and shook him. That was when I noticed how thin he was and saw the yellow spread over his face.

"He was bent over the books, looking for Ibn Khaldoun in the dark. It was then that I realised I hadn't turned on the gas lamp, which had come to substitute for the city's missing electricity. I lit the lamp and the flat filled with light. Jean-Pierre closed his eyes, as though he had become used to darkness. I heard him ask the other man to help because he couldn't find the book. That was how I found out that the other man's name was Abbas.

"Abbas bent down, picked out the book, and gave it to my husband.

"'Turn the light off, madam,' Abbas said in a low voice.

"And instead of screaming to bring a crowd and save my husband from the claws of that Abbas, it was like I'd been hypnotised. In his voice I heard an irresistible power, and I turned off the light and saw my husband standing like a ghost waiting for a signal from the strange man.

"I went towards him to embrace him and felt he was far away, as though he wasn't my husband, as though he'd become a small shadow of that other man, who took the copy of Ibn Khaldoun's *Introduction* in his hand and left, my husband in his wake. He opened the door and they vanished into the darkness of the stairway.

"What puzzles me is why my husband didn't turn round to say goodbye to me. Why didn't he go to see his sleeping children? Why did they make him go back? What kind of wild dogs were they to let him come back to his home for just a few minutes? And why Ibn Khaldoun? What use to him would Ibn Khaldoun be in the dark cell they'd thrown him into?

"I believe he caught hepatitis after he visited us. I'm sure of it. The darkness makes things look yellow. No, he wasn't really yellow. I think of him that way now because after his death I found out that he'd caught hepatitis and suffered a lot of pain and they'd done nothing to save him. They left him to die like a dog because he believed in the same things they did. I told him not to write about the Islamist tendencies but he was convinced they were the future. It's got nothing to do with us. He was French and I'm Greek Orthodox from Damascus, and we're secularists."

She said she thought her husband had been killed as part of a complex game among intelligence services. "I'm not certain it was the Islamists who killed him. Sure, they were the instrument that killed him but it was really the traditional stupidity of French Intelligence in their game with Iranian or Syrian Intelligence."

There in Beirut, after telling Muna about the famous text that had been transformed into the theoretical manual of Khaled Nabulsi's group, which had decided to maintain its political action because it had no choice – there Karim had tried to remember where he had hidden those papers of Abu Rabia's which he hadn't given Jean-Pierre. It was strange how his memory of the papers had been erased and only come to mind again when he was getting ready to go back to Beirut. He'd decided that the first thing he'd do would be to visit Khaled's grave and that of Hayat and her daughter Nabila to apologise to them, but he'd frittered away his time in Beirut among family memories, frivolous love affairs, and a hospital construction project. And all he'd seen of the hospital project had been optical illusions on the computer of an architect whose only interest was in knocking buildings down and pulling them up by their roots.

When he went to his room to sleep after that first night's dinner that Salma had made, he'd noticed that the room had remained exactly as he'd left it on his departure for France. But he'd paid no attention to the brown bedside table, or hadn't seen in it a window onto memories he'd left behind and decided to bury in oblivion. Nasri had told him once on the phone that nothing had changed. "Your room will still be your room even if you don't use it and the same for your brother's. The maid cleans both once a month and she's been told not to move anything. They're your rooms, son, and anytime the two of you decide to come back to the house you'll find the house waiting for you."

"But I'm married, Father, and I've got two daughters. What do I want with the room? Use it any way you want."

"And your brother's married too and it doesn't change anything as far as I'm concerned. I just pray God lets me live long enough to see the members of the Trinity back together again."

When Karim hurried to the room where he slept, the bedside table and its two drawers took him by surprise. Why hadn't he noticed it before, why hadn't he seen something the eye couldn't miss? He was sleeping on the same sheets, laying his head on the same ostrich-feather pillow his father had given him as a reward for passing the school-leaving exam. The see-through curtains were the same and so was the small brass ceiling lamp with four bulbs, the brown bedside table with two drawers, and on top of it the small transistor radio on which he used to listen to the midnight news from Radio Monte Carlo. He turned on the radio, which made a crackling sound, which then suddenly stopped. The batteries would have to be changed, thought Karim. He bent towards the bedside table, opened the first drawer, and was struck by the lightning bolt of memory. The first drawer was dedicated to Hend: pictures of her in her bathing suit, a picture of her next to him as they stood in front of the St George's beach swimming pool, letters from Hend to him, and his letters – a flood of emotions flowing over the pages in dry ink.

Why had Hend loved to write letters?

It came back to him how Hend, at the end of their daily meeting, would give him a letter in a closed envelope and ask him not to open it till he'd reached home, and to reply to her the next day in writing. Karim hadn't seen the point of it. He would read in her letters what he'd already heard from her the same day and was supposed to answer her with what he was going to say the next day. This epistolary relationship exhausted him. "It's tiring studying medicine," he'd tell her, "and it doesn't leave me time for writing." But Hend had refused his excuses and he was obliged to write her a few lines each night as he struggled to overcome his drowsiness. In this way their love became an enactment of what was in the letters and reading her letters became for him a form of memory exercise. But remembering is tiring. Karim stopped reading the letters. He'd open them, glance at them before throwing them in the drawer, and begin his suffering before the blank piece of paper. His surprise when he found letters he hadn't opened was enormous. He picked one of them up and tore open the envelope. His lips took on a stupid smile. He read about his hands: Hend had celebrated the tips of his long fingers and his finely formed thumb, saying she didn't like round bulgy thumbs because they were a sign that their owners where disloyal. He went on reading and discovered that she wanted to kiss his hands. "Please, when you put cologne on your chin after shaving, wash your hands very well with soap and water because those are what I want to smell when I kiss your hands tomorrow, not cologne." He tried to remember what had happened the following day, to discover what Hend had said when she kissed his hands and found out that he hadn't carried out her orders, but he couldn't.

The atmosphere created by the letters took him back to the evening when Hend gave him her last letter and said she was sad: she was going to stop writing letters because he no longer answered them. He tried to explain that he loved her without needing to write a daily letter and that they met every day anyway.

"I don't know what you think," she'd said, "but in my opinion love without words isn't love."

"But we meet every day and talk about everything," he'd answered.

"No, no. Talking is like air. The only thing that lasts is what's written down," she'd said. "But whatever you wish."

Karim didn't try to hide his joy at the ending of the torment of the letters and put Hend's last letter into the back pocket of his trousers. He ordered two glasses of beer so they could drink a toast to love.

"I'm sure you've thrown all my letters away," she said.

"Certainly not. I have them all, in the drawer in my room."

"Mind you don't let anyone read them."

"The drawer's locked and I have the key on me," he replied.

He hadn't been telling the truth: the drawer wasn't locked and it didn't have a key. He had no idea whether Nasri had read the letters and laughed at the naïveté of his son's love affairs, but Nasim had probably discovered them and read some of them. It was Nasim who'd discovered his father's secrets and then put everything back the way it was, so it was difficult to believe inquisitiveness hadn't led him to the drawer.

Why, though, had he not torn them up? Had his heart not burned with jealousy of his brother? Or had the jealousy had a different effect, the one Karim had felt when listening to Matrouk: the instant his fear of the revolver that the deceived husband had placed on the dining table close to the glass of arak vanished, his heart had ignited with jealousy and desire. He'd felt jealous of Azab and an animal desire for Ghazala, and he'd realised that Matrouk's love for his wife had caught fire precisely when he'd seen her bend to pass under Azab's rifle and enter his house.

Strange are the ways of the heart, for they resist understanding. Even a former lover cannot recall the idiocies of his heart without feeling embarrassed or confused, which is why people erase the stories of their loves that have ended: they don't dare remember them, and especially not the jealousy which not only wounds the heart but makes it captive twice over.

Only once had Nasri spoken on the subject with his sons. Karim was gathering up his things to return to his home on Abd el-Aziz Street near A.U.B., where he was studying medicine, while Nasim was struggling to understand why he'd failed the first year College of Pharmacy exams a second time – meaning that he would now have to vacate the halls of academe and start work with his father as assistant pharmacist. That day, which Nasri considered his farewell to the Trinity, the aged pharmacist had drunk an incalculable amount of wine and seemed sad and tired. He looked at Karim and said, "Never fall in love with a whore."

"What?"

"I know Hamra and Zeitouna are full of bars and you're young and it's what life owes you, and I don't mind, but never, my boy, fall in love with a whore because it's a love that has no bottom. She betrays you and you become more fiercely in love. She can't not sleep with other men because it's her job and you can't not be tormented because you love her."

Then he looked at Nasim and asked him for his thoughts on the subject.

"You know best," said Nasim, laughing.

"And your experience isn't all that negligible either," his father answered.

Nasim got up from the dining table and left. A silence reigned that Nasri broke when he stood up and said he had a headache and was going to his room to get some sleep.

When Karim heard what had happened with Ghazala he realised what it means to burn with jealousy for a lover. Earlier, when he saw the revolver and Matrouk's flushed face, he'd felt love recede, starting from the tips of his fingers, and that his relationship with Ghazala had always been meaningless. But when Matrouk had begun speaking of the militia boy whom Ghazala loved and on whom she'd lavished all the presents Karim had given her, jealousy flared up in his heart and he experienced the fire of which Nasri had spoken. Karim would never forget the sleepless nights he then spent – as though he'd fallen in love with Ghazala precisely at the moment he'd discovered her unfaithfulness. He'd wanted her to come to him one last time so he could quench the thirst that burned within him, but when she came the woman had changed and all she'd inspired in him was regret.

Nasim must have experienced similar feelings when he read Hend's letters to his brother, so why hadn't he destroyed the photos and the letters?

While Karim was drowning in the memories of his love for Hend that rose up before him in a flood of images, the phone rang.

Karim picked up and found that the person to whom he was talking claimed to be a Sheikh Radwan, speaking from Tripoli.

"Who?" asked Karim.

"Radwan! I'm Radwan! Danny told me you'd come back to Beirut and I want to see you. What do you say you come and spend a couple of days with me in the Fragrant City? I've got a surprise for you too."

"Radwan, Khaled's friend?" asked Karim, recalling a round stout young man with white face, bulging eyes and almost non-existent eyebrows who had followed Khaled around like a shadow.

"Is that really you, Radwan?" asked Karim.

"Sure, sure," answered the voice, which said that he'd become a sheikh after the killing of Khaled. He taught religious law at the Islamic University in the city and wanted to see Karim because he had a surprise.

Karim said he couldn't because he had to go back to France.

"But he wants to see you."

"Who does?" Karim asked, feeling a shiver run through his body because in the old days "he" had meant only one person – Khaled.

"Sinalcol. Sinalcol wants to see you," said Sheikh Radwan laughing.

"Sinalcol? Does he know me?"

"Come and see. It's a big surprise."

Karim was certain Sinalcol was dead, so where was Sheikh Radwan coming from with this story?

Khaled had taken the decision to kill him, Danny was enthusiastic, and Karim had shaken his head in disagreement even though he was "neither in the caravan nor on the raiding party", as they say. He had, however, been present at the meeting in Tripoli in May 1976 at which sentence of death had been passed on the thief who was bringing the revolution into disrepute in the city.

But Sinalcol had disappeared. He seemed to have found his way, once again, to the ancient Mamluke quarters of the city, which in 1973 had proclaimed themselves the Republic of the Wanted. Subsequently the army had invaded them, destroying the bizarre republic which had brought together thieves, criminals, and the unemployed under the leadership of a man called Ahmad Qaddour.

When the army invaded the city the only ones to escape had been Sinalcol, Ahmad Qaddour, the leader of the republic, and an odd type who had attached himself to it called Albert Helou. The three had crept along a tunnel under the markets and emerged at the bed of the Abu Ali River, from where they had gone up to Akkar, reaching Wadi Jehannam. There, where the security forces never set foot because of its rockiness and the impossibility of maintaining control over its innumerable tracks, they'd starved and hunger had forced the three back to Tripoli, where Qaddour and Helou had been arrested. Sinalcol though had managed to go into hiding.

During the first two years of the civil war Sinalcol had reappeared. No-one had seen him though because he had proclaimed himself "a ghost of the city" and had come to exemplify a new form of thievery based on non-appearance and invisibility.

Sinalcol was an invisible man. Even his real name was erased. Khaled had been convined that Ibrahim Tartousi, a member of the Republic of the Wanted, had assumed the name Sinalcol so that he could practise thievery– but how could that be true when everyone knew Tartousi had been given a funeral in Tripoli on Wednesday, 17 November, 1973, and then interred in the Strangers' Cemetery on a cold and rainy day, to the sound of his mother's loud keening?

Radwan said he'd be waiting for Karim at the Hallab pastry shop the following Friday. "I'll meet you after the prayer, we'll eat shmeiseh, visit Khaled's grave, and then, if you like, meet Sinalcol. Anyway, we have lots to talk about and I think I need you here for me to be able to arrange things clearly in my memory. I need to ask you a few questions related to the memoirs I'm writing."

"You're writing your memoirs?" Karim asked, amazed.

"I am indeed, Doctor. The time has come for the poor to write their memoirs, through the bounty of the Lord of the Worlds who has guided us. Not like in your day, when we used to feel dumb in front of you and all those books that you read in French. Islam is light, Doctor, may God guide you to the light of Islam! I'll be waiting for you in Tripoli."

Sheikh Radwan rang off before he could hear Karim's answer, as though the call were more a military order than a request for an appointment.

Karim had decided to postpone his decision about going to Tripoli, but Radwan's call brought him back from memories of his love for Hend to the real reason for his opening the bedside table drawer.

After replacing the photos and letters he closed the first drawer and opened the second.

Here he met with a surprise. In the drawer he saw a brown folder, and memory returned. In this folder, which he'd fastened with blue ribbon, Karim had placed Yahya Nabulsi's papers that had been sent him by his nephew Khaled. Karim recalled that he'd leafed through the papers and read a part of them but for some reason hadn't found it in himself to read them carefully. No-one had asked Karim thereafter why he'd neglected the papers and forgotten about them, and he hadn't even put himself to the trouble of reading them. The only people who knew of the existence of these texts were the Frenchman Jean-Pierre, who was dead, and Danny, who wanted to forget.

Karim was convinced he'd made a mistake in not giving the texts to Jean-Pierre: the French Arabist would have translated them into French and published them, and they would, in the end, have been preserved. Now, though, they were merely papers of no interest to anyone in Lebanon. Who was going to care about a betrayed revolution whose hero was just a semi-literate baker – even if the baker had taught himself to read and write, discovered Marxism and Che Guevara, and decided he was going to be Lebanon's Che?

Danny was severe in his evaluation of Yahya Nabulsi's experiment and of his Challenge Organisation, which had folded with the tragic death of the hero on a bed at Maqased Hospital in Beirut. "These are *lumpen* ideas held by the *lumpen* classes," he used to say. "It's leftist childishness, without any culture or faith in organisation." Naturally it never occurred to anyone, even Khaled, to retort that Yahya and his comrades were workers, and that the whole idea of Marxism was that the workers should be the vanguard of change.

Why hadn't it occurred to Karim to answer him on that occasion? Why hadn't he pointed out that Guevara was no worker, that Lenin and all the other revolutionary leaders were intellectuals who thought they were bringing consciousness to the workers? Why hadn't he pointed out that the result of the class consciousness that Khaled had adopted with such resolve and discipline had been a turning to Islam – in other words the opposite of what we'd trained him in?

Karim recalled a comrade who, with the coming of the Islamicist phase that had taken over everything following the victory of the Iranian revolution, had become so obsessively religious that he'd prayed regularly five times a day. He'd been called Abd el-Messih but had changed his name to Belal. This Belal was a member of A.U.B.'s Faculty of Medicine and a model of modesty and silent dedication. There was no-one who didn't love Dr Belal. For a time he'd moved about among the Fedayeen camps of South Lebanon and had, with the outbreak of the civil war, devoted all his time to opening clinics in the poor neighbourhoods of the Beirut suburbs, never failing the while to keep up his work as a teacher and a surgeon.

When Karim asked about Belal, Danny answered that Abd el-Messih had emigrated to America.

"America? That's incredible! What did he do with his new convictions?"

"It seems he took them with him," said Danny.

When Belal announced his conversion to Islam, all his comrades were astounded. True, conversion to Islam was the sole means available to Catholic Christians to divorce their wives, but Belal had taken it really seriously. In the beginning his friends had thought he wanted to get rid of his wife in preparation for marrying Fatma, a student in the mathematics department at the Lebanese University fifteen years his junior.

When Belal took a bullet in the stomach during a visit to the fighters' positions in the area of Aley, he'd found himself alone. His wife had refused to leave Jull el-Dib in East Beirut, and the only one there for him had been Fatma Shoeib, a mathematics student at the university who'd joined Fatah and found herself nursing Dr Belal.

Belal had made his conversion at the hands of Sayed Hadi Taher who, since the outbreak of the Islamic revolution in Iran, had been one of the theorists of the concept of the Guardianship of the Jurist to which Khomeini's revolution had given rise. Fatma took him to see the sheikh, who wore a black turban as a sign that he was a Sayed, or one of the People of the House. From that meeting a special relationship had developed between the university professor and the Shiite sheikh who had studied at the feet of Imam Muhammad Baqir Sadr in Noble Najaf, then returned to Lebanon to work within the Iraqi-originated el-Daawa el-Islami Party before adopting Khomeini's ideas and becoming a founder of what would later become known as Hezbollah.

Belal had a strange attitude towards Khaled and his comrades. He said he didn't recognise their Islamism because they followed Sunni law. He spoke a jurist's language that Karim found hard to understand – as though Belal had been born a Muslim, rather than being a Christian – or a Marxist – who had adopted Islam only a few months earlier.

Abd el-Messih had emigrated to America to work in a hospital in Houston. Karim told Danny that Khaled was right: even Belal, or Abd el-Messih, had found himself a way out of the endless Lebanese impasse, and for one reason only, which was that he was an intellectual and bourgeois, while Khaled had been left to face death alone.

Danny said Abd el-Messih had divorced Fatma, abandoned his son Hasan, and gone back to his first wife so he could go with their children to Texas.

Karim opened the folder lying in front of him with its yellow pages and its words, some of which had been erased or become difficult to read, and beheld the destinies of the Lebanese taking shape in the form of stories that intersected and divided at death's portal.

Khaled's assumption about the ability of intellectuals to escape their fates wasn't entirely correct, or what are we to make of the stories of the dozens of students killed fighting in the ranks of the National Movement and the Palestinian resistance? And what more wretched fate could there be than that of Malak Malak, who had disappeared behind the mask of death without dying, so that he'd died while still alive?

His girlfriend had never told anyone what Malak did after she fled from him and his new look following the cosmetic, or disfiguring, surgery that had been performed on him in East Germany. She'd spoken of how she'd left him standing on Hamra Street and run off, but the more important part of the story, the part that Malak hadn't been able to tell anyone, remained unknown and would stay so forever. The man had sentenced himself to silence. Did Malak Malak now live in Italy, as the Lebanese student called Talal claimed? Or had he disappeared and had all trace of him been erased, which is what the story ought to say? Talal said his brother had known Malak well because they were fellow students at A.U.B., and he knew Malak was married to a Sardinian woman and worked in the Italian olive oil trade.

Talal had suggested to Maroun Baghdadi that his film begin with the return of Malak Malak to Beirut, with his feeling of being a stranger in his own city and among his old friends. "The film starts at the moment of his return, then shifts to flashback for a confused memory of the crime at A.U.B. and of a war whose story cannot be narrated within any clear context." Maroun had given the idea some thought before saying no, on the grounds that the story was real and he didn't like reality in the cinema. It would also bring Lebanese violence back into the equation, endorsing it as heroic, while he was looking for a straightforward story that glorified tolerance and portrayed violence as despicable.

Karim had failed to mention on that occasion that he knew Malak. He'd felt he couldn't speak, that he too had been struck by a form of dumbness, and that his dumbness might well be more painful than Malak's since his assumption of another personality had involved a change in neither his appearance nor his name.

"It wasn't even me who returned when I returned," Karim had said to himself as he read the papers relating to the beginnings of the story of the death of Khaled Nabulsi as a tragic hero in a war that bore all the marks of melodrama.

His name was Yahya, a.k.a. Abu Rabia. Married to Hayat Saleh, no children. Died aged twenty-eight in the prison where he had spent three years. His body was returned to his family at 5.30 a.m., 16 June, 1974, twenty-four hours after the announcement of his death at Maqased Hospital in Beirut. The security men got the body, wrapped in a white cloth like a shroud, from the ambulance and knocked on the door. Hayat opened it and began weeping and wailing and the security men put the body down in the house. They said the burial had to take place that morning with no delay, and that they didn't want a lot of noise and demonstrations. They told the wife they would hold her responsible for any reckless acts committed in Qubbeh, Darb el-Tabbana, or anywhere else in Tripoli and the port. Then they got into the ambulance and left in a hurry. The neighbours rushed in and saw.

Khaled said it had been a day of tears.

"We have to wash him," said the mother.

"Yahya's a martyr," said Khaled.

"We have washed him in our tears," said Hayat, choking.

When, however, they stripped him preparatory to washing him, the truth drove them insane. The mother saw a long cut in the lower stomach. Khaled reached out to touch it only to find that the stitches were still clearly defined. He took hold of the thread and the belly opened and they discovered a terrible fact. All of Yahya's internal organs had been removed. They couldn't find a thing – no stomach, no lungs, no intestines.

"There is no god but God," said the mother.

Khaled ran to the phone and called Dr Belal in Beirut. Belal said it was strange: a post-mortem to ascertain cause of death required only that samples of the organs be taken. He concluded that the removal of the internal organs was a deliberate act performed to prevent the family from carrying out a post-mortem. That meant that Yahya had been murdered rather than having died as a result of blockage of the air passages subsequent to the bursting of his appendix, as claimed in the report issued by Lebanon's Ministry of Health.

They carried Yahya to his grave without his organs and five thousand men and women walked in his funeral procession, and there was sorrow and dismay.

"The first thing I did after he died was marry Hayat," said Khaled. "I was tired. A week before Abu Rabia's death, I'd taken part in my first Fedayeen operation. I was in the south with a group from the Popular Front. We assembled in the Adisa orchards and infiltrated Misgav Am and for me it was a baptism of fire and blood." Khaled said he'd sensed that the aura of invincibility surrounding the Israeli army had all of a sudden evaporated. He'd heard the soldiers shouting in panic as the Fedayeen opened fire, and had it not been for the intervention of the Israeli helicopter corps all the members of the group would have returned safely. "I got back on my own without injury, carrying over my shoulder a youth called Abu el-Feda who'd been hit in both legs. Not one of the six other members of the group made it back. Presumably they were martyred. I returned from death to find death in my own home and it was appalling to see an empty corpse, with no life and no internal organs, as though Yahya had died twice over."

After the funeral Khaled sat next to Hayat. He said he'd seen the spite in the eyes of her father and her brothers and sisters. He said he had at that moment taken the decision not to let his uncle's widow's family sell their daughter off yet again, and had married her after the required waiting period.

Khaled's marriage to Hayat was the major turning point in his life. He got into a battle with her family similar to the one Yahya had had to fight with them, but he didn't have his uncle's standing, so he married her secretly. Then he went to them with a Kalashnikov and forced her father and four brothers to submit to the fait accompli.

Yahya's marriage to Hayat was the stuff of legends. It was 1969, three months after Yahya had left prison, where he'd spent a year, for the first time. Just before his arrest, as he was returning from Akkar, he'd come in his reading across Régis Debray, *The Communist Manifesto*, and Ho Chi Minh, and had embraced Marxism.

When released he began writing articles, which he sent to *al-Safir* in Beirut, on the situation of the peasants in Akkar, and even though the Lebanese leftist paper published only three of them it was enough to change Yahya's position in Tripoli. It made him, in others' eyes and his own, no longer the baker who'd stirred up trouble and led a gang of unemployed men but an intellectual and a journalist whose name people might read at the bottom of long articles full of analysis, someone who used mysterious expressions such as "dialectic" and "class struggle". His new position enabled Yahya to rethink the situation of the group of young men he led and to transform it into a clandestine organisation, which he named the Socialist Popular Rally. At the same time it qualified him to work for a short period as a journalist on *Sada al-Shamal*, a regional newspaper published in Tripoli.

The story goes that, one morning, as Yahya was about to enter the newspaper's offices, a girl he didn't know stopped him and said she'd come to him for help with a problem.

The girl was holding a baguette with cheese. She wrapped the sandwich, put it in a paper bag, and followed along behind Yahya.

"Finish your sandwich and then we can talk."

He ordered two glasses of tea, sat down behind his metal desk, and watched the golden-skinned girl with the long black hair, who was wearing jeans and an orange blouse that revealed her long neck. The girl drank her tea, stealing glances at the man sitting opposite her.

"I want to tell you my story," she said.

"Finish your sandwich and then we can talk."

He occupied himself looking through the papers on his desk, picked up his pen, began crossing out certain phrases and writing notes in the margins. Then suddenly the girl stood up in front of him and gave him a piece of the sandwich.

He smiled as he ate the Akkawi cheese and tomato.

"That's a nice sandwich you've got there," he said. "Tell me the story."

"I need your help," said the girl, and she recounted what was going on between her and her father, who was determined to marry her off.

"We're two girls and four boys. Somehow or other they came up with a husband for my older sister, a Saudi man of about sixty. Father came and said he was going with her to Saudi Arabia to perform the betrothal ceremony. My poor sister said nothing and when they got there she was taken aback to find that the intended groom was older than Father. They'd sold her. I can't tell you, Mr Yahya, what her life is like. She's had to drink olive juice, and now Father wants to sell me off too. I don't know how much he'll get for me but he says he's come to an agreement with Sheikh Mazyoud and I have to get ready to travel to Ras el-Kheima. Please, save me. I have no-one. My brothers all agree with Father and I'm thinking of killing myself but I thought before I did I'd come to you."

"Really, please don't call me 'Mr'. I'm just plain Yahya. If you like you can call me Abu Rabia."

"You're married?" she asked.

"No," he answered, "that's my name in the movement."

He told her he was ordering her not to commit suicide. "Anyone who comes to Abu Rabia has to be ready to do what they're told," he said. "Are you ready?"

She nodded and a lock of hair fell over her eyes. She wiped her eyes and raised her head.

"I don't know what kind of person your father is but I'll take care of it. The main thing is you mustn't kill yourself. Now be off with you."

The girl left and Yahya was left with an image of her which refused to go away.

That evening Yahya told his mother he wanted the girl as his wife.

"Let's find out who she is and about her morals and her family first," said his mother.

"My heart tells me it's her. I want you to ask for her hand tomorrow, before they marry her to someone else."

The mother hesitated and looked at her son in surprise. Then he said he'd fallen in love with the girl.

"You must have met her before and been holding out on us."

Yahya didn't tell his mother he'd met her only a few hours earlier. In fact, he let them think he'd been in a secret romance with her.

Once Hayat had gone back to wherever she'd come from he felt her eyes had buried themselves in his heart and that he couldn't not marry her. After they were married, when they were drinking arak at the Mar Sergius Spring restaurant in Ehden, he'd tell her that when she left his office he'd felt his heart plunge. "I suddenly understood Mohamed Abd el-Wahhab's song, the one that says, 'I plunged and was done for.' 'I plunged' means 'I fell in love' and also 'I fell down'. Me too, I fell in love and I fell down and you had to be mine."

"You're gallant and noble," said Hayat. "From now on I'm going to call you Nabil instead of Yahya."

"The only reason I married you was that I'd fallen in love with you," he said.

"Fallen in love with me!"

"I fell in love with you the moment I saw you."

"Impossible. Well, you know best why you fell in love with me. Perhaps you fell in love with me because you loved my love for you."

"You mean you were in love with me?"

"I came to see you because I was in love with you. I thought it's either him, or I'll kill myself."

When Yahya's mother went to call on Hayat's family the next day, her father showed his astonishment at the unexpected visit. Naturally, Nouri Saleh – such was the father's name – knew Yahya's mother from the bakery and had known her late husband. But he'd never dreamed she would ask for his daughter.

"Give us time to think it over."

"Think all you like, Abu Tareq, but you know Yahya. Yahya loves the girl and if he doesn't get her, God alone knows what he'll do."

"Our daughters don't know anything about love and we don't have any truck with that kind of stuff," he answered.

"God be my witness that I warned you. We await your answer," she said as she rose to go.

"Are you threatening me, neighbour? We don't give our daughters to layabouts and prison graduates."

"I'll inform Yahya of your answer, and God protect us," she said, and left without looking back.

Before the mother could find an opportunity to tell her son he'd been refused, Imm Tareq, Hayat's mother, came to Yahya's house. She didn't enter but stood at the door, panting. She said they'd set the date for Hayat's betrothal to Yahya for three days from then.

Yahya's mother had no idea what had happened to make them change their minds in less than two hours but the woman went to the offices of *Sada al-Shamal* to tell her son the good news.

"I knew it!" he said. "Get yourself ready, mother of the groom!"

Khaled's story was different in every way. He was an orphan, his father having died when he was three. He'd been raised in his grandmother's house and had become like a younger brother to his uncle Yahya. All the same, he never joined the organisation that his uncle founded. He went to the south and joined the Popular Front and there read Marxist thought and learned the importance of building a vanguard party, and took a serious military course in the forest of Qammoua on the heights of Akkar. Khaled only worked at the bakery after his uncle's death, when he told his grandmother, "You've worked enough. I'll take care of things." It was with the bakery, which they renamed the People's Bakery, that the story of a new death, more tragic yet than the first, would begin.

Had Khaled known that with his decision to marry Hayat he had sentenced himself to the fate that he would meet?

His grandmother said it wouldn't do. "It's not as though your uncle has children and you have to feel obliged to marry his wife. Forget it, son. The woman's older than you and it's not how things are done."

However, Khaled insisted, and was obliged to use force to make her family agree to him becoming her husband.

The torment began once they took up residence under one roof. Hayat told him she respected his decision and his noble intentions but she couldn't belong to another man.

"I still love Nabil," she said, "and I can't."

"Who's Nabil?" he asked her.

So she told him her whole story and said she'd loved his uncle Yahya, whom she called Nabil because he was noble.

"You mean that story about getting married to the sheikh was something you made up, and had no basis in truth?"

Hayat smiled and said nothing.

"So you lied to my uncle?"

"No, I didn't lie. My sister's story was true and I felt my turn was coming and I'd meet the same fate. Plus I was in love with Nabil."

"Don't call him Nabil! His name's Yahya."

"You can call him what you like but as far as I'm concerned he's 'the noble one'."

She said she released him from any obligation towards her but was sure that if he divorced her, her family would sell her, as then she'd be both a widow and a divorcee; still, he could divorce her and she wouldn't hold it against him.

At first Khaled had believed that by marrying his uncle's widow he was fulfilling his moral duty to the memory of his uncle, whom he'd only really got to know after his death, when he found himself gradually changing into a shadow of the dead man. Yahya's mother was the first to notice what was going on but said nothing. She could see her young grandson gradually turning into another person. Even his voice began to take on a new rhythm. She told him once, as she was leaving the kitchen, that she'd heard Yahya's voice. "God protect us, it was just like his. Pull yourself together, son. We don't need another martyr in this house."

Khaled was patient with Hayat as no other man could have been. She slept next to him in bed for two whole years without him touching her.

His love for her burned in his heart. He'd tried but she'd put him off, inventing all kinds of pretexts. But from the night she told him she couldn't give herself to another man, he decided not to touch her. She cooked, cleaned, and behaved in front of other people like any ordinary wife, but when night came she'd put pyjamas on under her nightdress and curl up on one side of the bed, covering her whole body and putting the pillow over her head and falling asleep. For sex with this eccentric woman Khaled substituted dreams. His nights were hot and moist with the water of life. He'd wake from his dreams, rush to the bathroom to wash himself off, then go back to sleep. Yahya had no idea whether Hayat was aware of what was happening to him because she wouldn't move. He'd get up from the bed, look towards her, and see her slumbering on her right side, her long hair spread over the pillow that had fallen off her face. He'd come back from the bathroom and find the same scene, as though the woman had neither felt him leap from the bed nor heard the water running in the bathroom.

Yahya spent two years between nights full of dreams and days in the bakery. His day began at 3 a.m., when he'd rise to the sound of the alarm clock, take a cold shower, make a cup of coffee into which he put a little orange blossom water, and smoke his first cigarette in front of the open living room window because Hayat disliked the smell of tobacco. Then he'd leave and not get back until 6 p.m., when he had dinner with his wife and told her stories about the customers. After that he sat in his corner in the living room and read a little before leaving the house again to go to his meetings with the boys, and when he came back at ten at night Hayat would have put on her pyjamas and nightdress and be waiting for him. She'd make two glasses of aniseed and they'd drink them in silence, then go to bed.

Over those two years, during which Khaled traversed the desert of the heart, he reorganised the ranks of the young men who had hovered around his uncle, forced them to attend the weekly meetings regularly, and discovered in Radwan Ali, a student at the Arabic Literature department of the Lebanese University, an intellectual on whom he could rely.

It was Radwan who suggested to Khaled that he meet Dr Othman. The Egyptian communist doctor, who had joined Fatah in Jordan and taken part in the battles of September 1970 that came to be known by the name of Black September, had come to Lebanon and begun working with young men of the Lebanese Left eager to take part in the armed Palestinian struggle.

Khaled met Dr Othman three times at the bakery and the forty-something man, who wore spectacles and smoked Egyptian Cleopatra cigarettes, aroused his curiosity and admiration. Dr Othman spoke as one with full command of the language, clear ideas, a simplicity derived from deep culture, and a vision indicating he had profound human and political experience stored within him.

It was Dr Othman who brought Danny back into the picture. At their third meeting he told Khaled and Radwan that he would organise a meeting for them with Fatah's representative in Tripoli and that Brother Danny, who had been a close confidant of the martyr Abu Rabia, would handle the follow-up with them.

Thus it was that, under Danny's direct and daily supervision, the Socialist Popular Rally was reorganised, to become later a coherent political organisation with a military wing whose influence extended not only to Qubbeh but to the districts of Bab el-Tabbana, the old city, and the port. The group would also play a major role in the civil war that broke out in 1975, while Khaled would be transformed into a political leader of the entire northern region.

Khaled and Radwan were preoccupied with the idea that the mistakes that had accompanied Yahya's experiment with the Challenge Organisation should not be repeated. They worked hard to educate the semi-employed youth who had joined the organisation in scientific socialist thought and helped many to find permanent jobs. "We're the organisation of the working class," Khaled told them, "not of the layabouts."

The work took up all of Khaled's time but he refused Danny's offer of a full-time position with Fatah and decided to keep on working at the bakery. Like his uncle, he disliked the chaos of Fatah with its blocs linked to the founding fathers. In fact he went even further in his position on this because he'd been raised in the Popular Front and had learned the necessity of iron discipline from the pupils of Dr George Habash. Still, he found something irresistibly attractive in Dr Othman's eloquence and Danny's culture and therefore decided to amalgamate his organisation with their Fatah-affiliated group, unaware that it was closely linked to Abu Jihad – was, in fact, his leftist arm within that forest of diverse ideological arms that this leader knew how to exploit for a variety of functions, creating a breath-taking concord out of their ideological contradictions.

Khaled made no attempt to destroy the legend of his uncle the martyr. He had his reservations about the chaotic, off-the-cuff methods used by the hero of the Qubbeh district in leading his boys and was critical, especially, of the 15 October uprising against the increase in electricity charges which had led to his uncle's imprisonment and death. The rebellion had indicated a naïve faith in the spontaneity of the masses, for while Yahya had been directing, from his hiding place in a flat in Qubbeh, the groups of young men who threw explosive devices in the streets and in front of the Qadisha power station, he was also waiting for the people to rise and assume power in the city. But the people, instead of going out onto the streets, were terrified by the explosions and hid in their houses, so that in the end Yahya found himself besieged in his hideout. He tried to shoot his way out but was wounded in the stomach, taken captive, and condemned to death, a sentence subsequently reduced to ten years. He died in prison three years after his arrest.

Abu Rabia had wanted to make 15 October, 1971, a turning point in the history of the city. The Akkar peasants' revolution had evaporated following the intervention of the Syrian-controlled Sa'iqa organisation at the point when the peasants' anti-feudalist struggle had appeared to be in danger of taking on a sectarian dimension, as though it were between Sunnis and Alawites. This had forced Yahya to withdraw from the area in which he'd believed he could establish the nucleus for a Guevarist revolution. He'd returned to Qubbeh, where he succeeded in restoring his image as a popular hero when a cholera epidemic broke out in the city. The Ministry of Health, whose duty it was to vaccinate all inhabitants free of charge, started distributing the vaccine to clients and supporters of the minister, who sold it on the black market. Faced with a worsening situation, Abu Rabia and a group of his boys took to making armed break-ins into pharmacies and the Ministry of Health headquarters and distributing the vaccine free to clinics. And Abu Rabia turned the bakery he'd inherited from his father into a vaccination centre, to which people came in droves.

Following this experience, Yahya put on a display of political strength in the city, exploiting a festival held in honour of the anniversary of the death of Egyptian president Abd el-Nasser. He brought in tractor-loads of his peasant supporters from Akkar chanting slogans against capitalism and feudalism and threatening a workers' and peasants' revolution.

In the wake of these two experiences, Yahya had become convinced that the time was ripe to proclaim the revolution. He wrote in his memoirs of "the necessity of depending on the principal of the Guevarist nucleus and of linking it to the factory workers' struggle" via the Socialist Popular Rally. Yahya's understanding was that the strike against the Qadisha Electrical Company would make it possible for the revolutionary nucleus to work in the city, and so he decided to proclaim the popular uprising.

In the event, however, things went in the opposite direction. "Authority can be overturned only through the building of a parallel authority; so Lenin taught us, and that was the reason for the failure of the uprising," said Danny.

Khaled didn't ask how a parallel authority was to be built or who would build it, or whether this new authority would be less repressive than its predecessor. Khaled was content to listen to Danny theorising and drawing up plans, while vehemently refusing organisational interference by anyone.

"Khaled is like his uncle," Danny wrote in a report he submitted to Dr Othman, "but more aware and disciplined, and will probably meet with the same end."

When Yahya went to prison with a bullet in his stomach he believed his time there would be an opportunity to take some rest. He was therefore overjoyed to meet Dr Sadeq Jalal Azm, a Syrian Marxist intellectual living in Lebanon who'd been put in prison because of his book *A Critique of Religious Thought*.

In a letter to his wife Hayat, Yahya wrote, "Yesterday, after being transferred to Ramal prison in Beirut, I met Dr Sadeq Azm in the dispensary and we had the following dialogue:

"'You're Dr Sadeq Azm, author of *Self-Criticism after the Defeat*, aren't you?'

"'Yes, I'm Sadeq Azm. How did you know who I was?'

"'I read your book.'

"'You read my book? What's your name?'

"'I'm Yahya Nabulsi from Tripoli, leader of the Qubbeh uprising.'

"I was astonished to find that he knew a lot about me and was sympathetic to our movement but said we had to join a revolutionary party that could lead our struggle.

"I told him there weren't any revolutionary parties in Lebanon or the region. He nodded and then asked me to read about the experiences of the workers' and peasants' soviets that had been founded by the Democratic Front in the city of Irbid in Jordan in 1970.

"I said the experiment had been a failure. He agreed with me and then asked if I'd read his book and when I told him I'd read it three times because it was the most important book to come out after the June defeat, I felt it made him happy. Then he asked me what had got me into prison and said he was charged with attacking religion and exciting sectarian tensions because of his book on the critique of religious thought.

"Meeting him, Hayat, was incredible. What a great man! An intellectual who's gone to prison for his ideas. I told him when I got out of prison I'd like to invite him to visit us in Qubbeh. He asked how long my sentence was and I told him ten years, but I'd be getting out sooner than that. I asked how long his was and he said he hadn't been referred for trial yet but was expecting a sentence no shorter than mine.

"I kept thinking to myself, what is this world? What is the value of thought in this society? Nothing! What does it mean that Sadeq Azm is sent to prison for publishing his book *A Critique of Religious Thought*? They talk of blasphemy? Of atheism? The coming revolution will not forgive the reactionaries who exploit innocent souls in the name of religion."

Sadeq Azm's book had caused a major fuss in Beirut at the time. The attack had focused on the Syrian writer for his authorship of an essay included in the book and entitled "The Devil's Tragedy". In this he had supposed, as a way of buttressing his deconstruction of religious texts, that the Devil, in refusing to obey God's command to bow down to Adam, was carrying out God's hidden purpose and that he had agreed to be the rebel and take the consequences out of extreme obedience. The Muslim men of religion had considered this mockery and sarcasm, while their Christian counterparts had joined the campaign against him because of another study in the same book in which he mocked the Virgin's appearances in Egypt, describing them as a naïve compensation mechanism for the June 1967 defeat.

The *al-Nahar* Supplement had set the match to the tinder when it published a picture of Azm on its cover over the caption, "The Infidel from Damascus".

Azm was in Ramal prison for only a few days, after which he was tried and found innocent. It was said that pressure brought to bear on the authorities by Kamal Jumblatt, leader of the Progressive Socialist Party, lay behind the judgement.

Yahya never had the chance to meet the Syrian thinker again. He was transferred from one prison to another and treated brutally, despite his wounds never having healed. He spent most of his time in solitary confinement and took to eating only the almonds and honey that were brought him once a week by Hayat, who was obliged to bribe the officer in charge to be sure they reached her husband, who suffered agonising pains in his stomach.

Things got to the point that in the end his gaolers put a viper in his cell.

The prisoners at Roumieh prison would never forget the shouting that erupted from Yahyah's cell that early morning. The man woke to a strange movement and found a snake at the edge of his bedding. Yahya knew, from his experience in the villages of Akkar, that you must not provoke a snake, so he got up stealthily from the mat that he slept on and stood at the iron bars, calling in a loud voice, "They've put a snake in my bed because they want to kill me!" At this, shouting arose from all the cells, the gaolers heard the cry "Shake the bars!", the bars of the cells started to shake violently, and pandemonium broke out. The duty officer ran to see what was going on. Yahya told him to open the door to his cell or he'd hold him responsible for his death by snakebite.

The confrontation ended when Yahya's cell was opened and two of the security personnel riddled the snake with bullets.

Yahya was convinced they'd wanted to kill him. He wrote to his wife that he could feel his time drawing near and said he regretted not having had a son (whom they'd decided to call Nabil) with her.

At the funeral, while the bier was borne aloft on people's hands, the cry went up, "Shake the bars!" People forgot all the political slogans and five thousand men and women walked behind the bier like prisoners shaking the bars of their plundered freedom.

The funeral ended with Khaled inheriting a story in which he had previously participated only from a distance. Khaled had certainly admired his uncle and the aura that Yahya had succeeded in creating around himself, but his admiration was diluted by his rejection of the path the man had taken to his death, seemingly fashioning his end of his own free will. Khaled, who had got as far as the school-leaving certificate class at Qubbeh's government secondary school for boys before deciding that the time had come for him to join the Palestinian Fedayeen, couldn't blame his uncle for anything he'd done. Yahya had been the son of a poor baker who'd been obliged to leave school during fifth primary, when his father had died, to work at the bakery. He was the offspring of the phase of populist leftist ferment that had followed the 5 June defeat. Khaled couldn't understand how his uncle had had dealings with Ahmad Qaddour and his men, who were just a group of murderers and thieves interested in nothing but thuggery and pillage. The greatest paradox that Khaled had faced, however, was embodied in the person of a young man to whom the name "Fan-it" had become so firmly attached that people had forgotten his real one. Fan-it was twenty-four years old, carefully brilliantined his hair, and took on all sorts of dirty jobs that no-one else would think of doing. Most likely the name Fan-it came from the youth's work at Abu Riyad's butcher's shop, where it was his task to grill skewers of meat; in other words, it was his role to keep the burning charcoal glowing, using a feather fan.

But Fan-it's real skills began to manifest themselves when he worked with Sinalcol on the gambling tables Qaddour used to run in Tripoli. The three-card trick and games of put-five-take-twenty-five, thimble, and seven-eleven were organised on small tables scattered around the inner quarters. These called for both adroitness and strong-arm tactics – adroitness to cheat customers and strong-arm tactics to keep winners from stopping playing: they had to go on till they'd lost everything they'd won or else Fan-it would beat them till the blood flowed down their faces and they put everything they possessed on the table. Fan-it was able to make such a go of running these games that he rebelled against Qaddour, split off from him, and ended up with his own tables and boys. At the same time, he never left his original job at Abu Riyad's butcher's shop, where he loved to breathe in the smell of the grilled meat and enjoyed watching the customers' lips drooling in anticipation of the hot skewers with which he'd present them.

When Khaled began reconstructing his uncle's by then disintegrated group he was surprised by Fan-it's arrival at the bakery with the announcement that he'd been Yahya's right-hand man and wanted to continue the struggle. It was Radwan's opinion that Khaled shouldn't antagonise Fan-it and his type but come up with a way of integrating him. However, Khaled couldn't contain himself and informed Fan-it that he couldn't include gamblers in the ranks of his organisation.

"We have to provide a good example to the masses and you're a gambler. What will people think of us? Drop the gambling and come back."

Fan-it refused to give up his little gambling empire but kept in regular touch with the boys and joined them at the road blocks they set up during the civil war. When Khaled was killed he knelt before the blood-spattered body, dipped his finger in the martyr's blood, and traced a circle of blood around his neck. Then he disappeared.

Sheikh Radwan told Karim that Fan-it had emigrated to West Germany along with innumerable waves of Lebanese and Palestinian youths seeking political asylum there. He said he thought Fan-it had had dealings with Syrian Intelligence to protect himself, but hadn't informed on or plotted against the boys.

In the end Fan-it did find a way to work with Khaled's boys, after they'd found Islam, by joining an Islamist group at the port whose emir was Sheikh Salim Muadhen. This sheikh also had contacts with Intelligence but claimed to be an Islamic fundamentalist, partnering Khaled and his comrades in leading the Islamist political action in Tripoli.

Khaled rid the group of the unemployed and of thieves. He embarked on his personal path as defender of the poor of the Qubbeh and surrounding quarters, and as a Marxist activist within the leftist current of the Fatah movement.

But fate turned everything upside down. The Syrian army entered Lebanon in 1976, taking particularly tight control of Tripoli. At the same time the Palestinians pulled back, understanding, especially after the assassination of Kamal Jumblatt, leader of the Lebanese National Movement, and the collapse of the Lebanese Left, that the goal of the Syrian presence in Lebanon was to force it into submission and make it their tool.

A new Palestinian strategy now evolved whose watchword was withdrawal from the Lebanese civil war, regrouping in the south, and ignition of the front with Israel. This strategy reached its climax with the suicide mission led by Jamal and eventually brought about the occupation of southern Lebanon.

Khaled wasn't convinced by the new strategy and he understood from Danny's gradual withdrawal that Danny didn't agree either. But when he went to visit Danny in Beirut he found the Fatah official had no answers to Khaled's questions, had given up political work, and had decided to take a job as an archivist at *al-Nahar*.

Khaled tried to adapt to the new situation. With a group of his comrades from Tripoli he joined the Jerusalem Martyrs' Brigade, which had taken Shaqif Castle in the south as its base. But he felt a terrible homesickness. He couldn't bear to be far from Qubbeh and the smell of lemon blossom in Tripoli, and he didn't see how the revolution could live in military bases far from its natural environment of the masses. What Khaled didn't say out loud, Radwan did. Radwan said he felt like a stranger there, announcing as he did so his call for a withdrawal from Shaqif Castle and a return to the Fragrant City. Khaled was surprised to find every comrade – forty young men in all – agreeing with Radwan and telling Khaled they felt the same but would leave the decision to him.

Khaled was tired. True, he missed his city but in establishing a base at Shaqif he'd found a way to escape from the house. His heart had been broken every night as he watched Hayat cover herself in pyjamas and flee into her body – two years lived in thirst and the pain of love. Khaled didn't think he could love like the Udhris and be content with the simultaneous presence and absence of the beloved and her never-fulfilled promises. Many times, when he leapt from the bed moist with the dream that had spread itself beneath his eyelids, he would decide to take a second wife; he'd tell Hayat he couldn't go on any longer and was prepared to continue supporting her if she preferred that to facing her family, but that he had to get another wife. When he got back in the evenings, though, exhausted from working at the bakery, even the glimmer of a smile of tenderness from her, bearing what seemed an obscure promise, would suffice to make him forget his decision and feel that even just to sit at the dinner table with her was to own the world.

When he told her he was going with the boys to the south because political conditions so demanded, she lowered her eyes with obvious sadness and said, "As you wish, but please take care of yourself and don't die, for my sake don't die."

She smiled and said she'd miss him, "but don't you worry, I'll go to the bakery and help out Imm Yahya."

He said he preferred to close the bakery while he was away.

"And how will we live?" she asked.

"I'll send you money from the south."

"No, Nabil. We don't get paid by the revolution. We give to the revolution."

She bit her lower lip and said she was sorry she'd said his name wrong.

He said she was right and the bakery must keep on working and he'd never take a penny from anyone.

"I depend on you," he said.

On his journey to the south Khaled took with him Hayat's smile, the tremor in her voice as she used the name she'd given his uncle, and her decision to keep an eye on the bakery while he was away.

At Shaqif Castle, before the rocky, plunging canyon where the wind buffeted the bodies of the men scattered through its stone-hewn passageways and vestibules – there, where one felt oneself alone before the gods of war and death and as though one were just one more block of stone left behind by the succession of wars that the castle had witnessed since it was first built, Khaled felt a mysterious freedom, mixed with a pain in his heart. He felt he had been liberated from Hayat, her blue nights filled with the sleeplessness of longing and the strain of a desire buried deep in the soul. His restless dreams, with Hayat at their centre, came to an end. Khaled had never dreamed of his wife naked, even though her upward thrusting breasts gleamed under her nightdress, spreading the colours of distant clouds through his eyes. His sleep was blue and his sleeplessness was blue and all he ever dreamed of was moving closer to her and looking into her face, which he would see either as covered by her hair, which spread over the pillow, or in profile, her lips touching the edges of the coverlet. He'd move closer to her, but the moment he felt her breath lightly fan his face he'd find himself jerking about on the far side of the bed, rise like one stung by the lust spurting from him, and leap out. He never got close to her in his dreams. He never touched her body with its armour of pyjama bottoms and socks that covered her lower legs, and which she always wore, winter and summer alike.

There, before the wind that ululated through the valleys and battered the walls of a castle resembling the vault of heaven, Hayat disappeared from his sleeping dreams to reappear in his waking dreams. He would sit behind the barricade, guard the stars, and see her. He'd cup her face in his hands and kiss her. Khaled had never kissed Hayat in the past – or at least he'd hugged her and kissed her on each cheek when his uncle had died but then she hadn't been his Hayat; she'd been, rather, the widow of the martyr. He didn't recall the feel of her cheeks on his lips but did remember the wetness of her tears. He told himself he'd kissed not her but her tears. Then, when it was time to say goodbye, when she'd smiled as she wiped away a tear suspended in the corner of her eyelid, she'd moved closer to him and kissed him on the cheek, but the surprise had so overwhelmed him that he'd felt the kiss only after he left the house. Here, though, on his own, before the gods of night that spread their shadows over Mount Amel, Golan, and the Sea of Tiberias, he discovered the kiss, and the nuances of its diverse flavours. Hayat would take possession of him with her lips that opened to reveal white teeth, saliva, and the sweet taste of her tongue. He would kiss her on her closed lips, on her upper lip, her lower lip. He would kiss her quickly, or with tender slowness, or with a lust that made him reach for all the flavours of her tongue. He would kiss her on her eyes and on her smile. He kissed her neck and moved down to her shoulders with quick little kisses and deep lingering kisses. He bit her lips and felt her teeth biting into his lower lip, heard the moan of the kiss and became drunk on her lips. He was alone with the blue of the night, a mouth that held the secrets of the world, and lips burning with talk of love that evolved into a sensation fashioned by the miniatures of the night.

There Khaled felt the pleasure of love, mixed with a pain in his heart. It was there that he came to understand that longing is another name for the pain that dwells in the soul. His pain was great but it was mute. To whom should he complain and what might he say? Even Radwan, who clung to him like his shadow, never learned the story. How could he explain to him the fact that he'd never touched the woman who was ever present in his heart, his house, and his bed? And who would believe him? Even she, even Hayat, didn't believe the story of his love for her, and how it had taken the form of a pain which was a synonym for waiting.

The stay in Shaqif Castle, known to the Franks as Belfort or Beaufort, was a moment of contemplation and an exercise in the recovery of love. The castle stored away in its stony walls the secret meaning of the absurdity of the present. For when the present bears witness in such a miraculous way to the layers and legends of the past, it too is in danger of being transformed into a part of the story of the place. *Shaqif* is a Syriac word meaning "towering rock". The castle is located at a distance of five kilometres from the city of Nabatiyeh and overlooks the fortresses of Hounein, Tebnine, and Baniyas, as well as the heights of Lebanon, Mount Amel, Mount Harmoun, the Golan, the hills of Safad, the Jordan Valley, and the Syrian coast all the way to Beirut in the north and Acre in the south. It is also known as Arnoun Castle with reference to the Lebanese village at its foot. The castle's foundations are entirely carved out of the rock and no-one knows the date of its construction. Some historians believe that Arnoun is a distortion of Renaud, the name of the Crusader lord of Sidon within whose domain it fell; to Arab historians it is known as Irnat.

Their residence in the castle was, however, merely for purposes of guard duty, for after the Israeli incursion into the south and the arrival of U.N. peacekeeping forces the Palestinian leadership had decided to observe the ceasefire.

At the organisation's general assembly Radwan said he could see no reason to stay there. "We're outsiders and we don't fight. We guard empty space and have to deal with an unfamiliar environment. We'd do better to go back to Qubbeh and resume our struggle there."

Khaled couldn't think of a convincing answer. He too yearned to get back but was aware of the difficulties. He knew that to return would be to expose themselves to a confrontation with the vast apparatus of repression that the Syrian regime had come to control in the city. The regime had allied itself with the city's traditional leaders and built up a large network of agents, most of whom were drawn from the hoodlums of the various quarters, people who had in the past submitted to the greater power of the Palestine Liberation Organisation and the forces of the Lebanese Left.

Despite this he accepted their argument and they returned.

When Khaled entered his house in the Mahalleh area of Qubbeh at 6 p.m. on Tuesday, 18 December, 1977, tired from the long journey and from walking through valleys and forests to avoid the checkpoints that were everywhere on the roads, he found her waiting for him. She was standing at the door with her long black hair hanging down about her neck, from which arose the smell of laurel-scented soap, the light smiling on her eyes. She was wearing the sky-blue nightdress that he knew so well but her legs were, for the first time, free and naked.

"I knew you'd come today. The water's hot. Go and take a bath. I've made the most delicious dinner."

When he removed his mud-caked clothes and tried to put them in the laundry basket, she took them from him, saying, "Give them to me. They're all going into the rubbish. Everything – the shoes, the socks, the sweater, the trousers, the underwear – goes in the rubbish."

She took everything from him from behind the half-closed bathroom door and left him alone and naked before the hot water and the soap. Later Khaled would think of that as the moment of his birth. When he reappeared from the bathroom wearing clean yellow pyjamas, he told her that he now understood what baptism meant to their Christian brothers – a feeling of being reborn, of being free and freed.

She smiled and led him to the dining table, which was groaning under delicious appetisers, kibbeh nayyeh, sambousek, vine leaves in oil, wheat kernels seethed in hot milk, cheese pasties, labneh with garlic, aubergine with yoghurt, shankaleesh, and, in the middle, local arak mixed with water gleaming in a glass jug set in a container filled to the brim with ice cubes.

"When did you cook all this?" he asked.

She said she'd sensed he would return that day. When she opened her eyes in the morning, she'd been seized by a mysterious feeling that he'd be home that night. "That's why I came back from the bakery at three and began getting ready, and when I'd finished the cooking I took a bath and waited, and before I heard your footsteps on the stairs I was standing at the door waiting for you. I've missed you."

She poured two glasses of arak, raised her glass, and said, "To you, hero!" Then she drank, sucking at the arak with her eyes closed.

Khaled had never before drunk alcohol in the house and he hadn't dared to invite her to a drinking party. When he drank of an evening with his comrades he'd return to the house feeling embarrassed, take the cup of aniseed from her hand, swallow it down quickly, feel the hot liquid burn, and go up to bed.

He looked at her. She didn't look like the wife he'd lived with for two years but like the woman from Shaqif Castle, the woman of fantasies and kisses after whom he thirsted more with every sip he drank. She reached for the kibbeh nayyeh, made a bite-sized morsel dipped in olive oil, placed a sprig of mint and a piece of white onion on top of it, and held it out to him. He held out his hand to take it from her but she refused to give it to him, saying, "Close your eyes and open your mouth." He closed his eyes and she put the morsel in his mouth and he tasted her fingers.

"I'm drunk," he said.

"Drunk! You haven't drunk anything or eaten anything yet," she said as she chewed the kibbeh nayyeh, saying she hadn't had it for ages.

He drank but ate only a little.

"You don't seem to like the appetisers," she said.

"Quite the opposite. Your food's very good but . . ."

"You're tired after the long journey, I know, but you have to eat."

"I'm not tired, I . . ."

"You're what?"

"I love you."

She moved closer to him and placed her hand on his shoulder, and he saw how the nakedness of her wrist gleamed in his eyes. She moved closer still, and he looked into her eyes, then dropped his and felt he wanted to cry. He took hold of himself, felt as though he was choking, pulled back a little to take a gulp of air into his lungs, and heard her speak a sentence that made him feel that this was the night of his transfiguration. At Sha-qif Castle, alone on the night watch, he'd felt he saw God, or made contact with His presence; but when he heard her say "I am your lawful wedded wife" the horizon opened and the universe lit up with the lamps of transfiguration.

"I am your lawful wedded wife," she said.

That night he drank her lips and sucked on them and became drunk on the sides of her long neck. He kissed her just as he had dreamed of doing – so much so that he would stop in the middle of a kiss, pull back, close his eyes, and then open them to make sure that what he was experiencing wasn't a fantasy or an illusion.

When his masculinity awoke to the rhythm of her femininity and the smell of desire spread, he felt he was both the woman's master and her slave. Instead of his tongue being released, love took him back to the language of childhood and he started making noises and grunts and speaking half-formed words.

After two years of waiting he had found her and after two years of sorrow and guilt she had found him, and they were as though they'd discovered a secret they could divulge to no-one – the secret people call love but which resists all names.

In their new relationship, which lasted eighteen months, they would only rarely speak. They communicated with one another through a minimum of words and experienced every potential that life has to offer. Even the strange transformation that led Hayat to don the Islamist headscarf passed quietly and without any of the long discussions with which Lebanese and Palestinian leftist circles resounded following the stunning success achieved by the Iranian revolution.

When her belly grew round and butterflies of joy spread their wings around her eyes, they disagreed over the name of the child. They were sure it was going to be a boy, though Khaled secretly wanted a daughter who looked like her mother. He didn't dare announce his hopes or his expectations in the face of the insistence of his wife and grandmother that the child would be a boy.

She told him her mother-in-law had no doubt that the boy's name would be Yahya. "She didn't discuss it with me. She looked at my round belly and called him Yahya. What do you think?"

It was the first time since his marriage to Hayat that the martyr's name had been pronounced in their house.

He told her his grandmother's suggestion made sense and he couldn't not share it.

"But I want to call him Nabil," she said. "Nabil is the name and the boy has to be noble. What do you think?"

"Whatever you want goes, Imm Nabil."

She smiled and asked him to tell his grandmother. "I don't have the heart to break her heart. You tell her please."

Hayat had no idea what Khaled told his grandmother but she noticed a change in the woman's behaviour: suddenly she aged. Imm Yahya no longer bent over the belly that was rounding out with new life so as to croon to the baby and call out to it "Yahya! Yahya, Granny's darling!" A hidden sorrow possessed her and limned itself in the creases of old age that had formed around her eyes following her son's death. But she didn't object, for she was a woman and knew how powerful a woman's authority can be, and she could see how Khaled had become two mutually contradictory men. At work and with the young men of the quarter he was a leader whose requests could not be refused, while at home he was a lover at the beck and call of the wife who had bewitched his heart.

Imm Yahya didn't ask what had happened. In the past, when she'd asked Khaled about his wife or hinted she was tired of waiting for the child that didn't come, she'd see Khaled's thick eyebrows knit and his face darken, and understand that he would never answer her questions. After he came back from the crusader castle in south Lebanon, though, Hayat's name was forever on his lips and it was he who had given her the good news that his wife was pregnant. She noticed, however, that the name Abu Rabia no longer crossed his lips or those of his comrades, who would come to the bakery to confer and meet while all the burden of work fell on his wife's shoulders.

"Your wife's pregnant and she should rest at home and not tire herself with the bakery. If you like I can go and take her place at work."

"You?!"

"Yes, me. I used to run the whole bakery in your father's day and your grandfather's! You think the work started when Nouri Saleh's daughter came along?"

"Your word is my command, but she doesn't want to stop working."

"Doesn't want to? Since when did women have anything to say about it? A woman obeys her husband. 'Men are the managers of the affairs of women.'"

"Managers, true, but not of Hayat. Hayat, Grandmother, is different."

"Different?! Didn't you say you'd become a proper Muslim, God guide you? And now your wife's expecting any day. In Islam there's no-one who's 'different.'"

"So when are you going to start covering your hair, Grandmother, and get me a heavenly reward for guiding you to the straight path?"

"All I need is lessons in Islam from an atheistical communist like you! I was a Muslim before they came up with all that nonsense."

"But the veil is the path of the Prophet, Imm Yahya."

"The veil is the light of the Beloved Prophet that covers the soul, not a bit of cloth we put on our heads. Get out of here, boy, God guide you and that wife of yours and your son whose new name I keep forgetting. Really! Who goes around giving their children names and then changing them before they're born?"

On his return to Tripoli Khaled rebuilt the organisation single-handed.

He knew that the Palestinian Fedayeen, whose hold over the Nahr el-Bared and Baddawi camps had been shaken, would be no help to him in a tough face-off in his city, which was now under the absolute control of the Syrian military. He lived in an atmosphere in which overt and covert action blended and which rendered movement through Tripoli's inner quarters extremely difficult for him as he was vulnerable to arrest at any moment. His relationship with Danny had been severed because Danny had stopped visiting the north, having retreated into his new work. He'd informed Dr Othman that he wanted to take a long holiday from organisational work to be free to write a long study on the Lebanese civil war. The objective was going to be to demonstrate the erroneousness of the sect/class discourse that had prevailed in some leftist circles as a justification for the sectarian language that dominated the civil war (the Shia being the deprived sect/class in question).

"This kind of Marxism has become the opium of the Lebanese Left," declared Danny.

Dr Othman, who was the main promoter of this discourse, was taken aback.

"How can you say that? That theory's one we came up with ourselves and you agreed with it. Heavens above! Did you think we were joking?"

Danny said he was in the process of writing a self-criticism that would pave the way for the refutation of the idea; he believed there was "a fundamental error in our orientation".

Dr Othman never reached an understanding of what the fundamental error might be. He was preoccupied with the intensification of work in the south and saw the class/sect discourse as a point of entry for the construction of a relationship with men of the Shia militia. The militia was starting to gain strength in the south thanks to intervention by the Syrians, who were preparing it to act as a substitute for an armed Palestinian presence.

Danny cut himself off from the world and Karim broke contact with the Fatah student cells in order to avoid the sharp ideological divisions that shook them. The only link that continued to tie him to political action was Jamal's diaries, which he'd been supposed to turn into a literary-political pamphlet but which had overwhelmed him with questions about the meaning of life and love and changed the taste of his relationship with Hend.

In his loneliness, and with the horizon closing in, Khaled thought of giving up political action, of devoting himself full-time to matters of the heart and paying more attention to the bakery.

However, following the assassination of four of his comrades close to a security checkpoint and the spread of an atmosphere of pursuit and siege – the objective of which was to break up and dissolve the group – he found himself in a tight spot.

Khaled had discovered he couldn't go back. The blood of his comrades had been spilled, the destiny of the boys of the Qubbeh quarter was unknown, and he was on his own. His only support was Radwan, in whose life and behaviour signs of change had begun to appear.

First, Radwan stopped drinking alcohol: he said it hurt his stomach. Then he started making use in conversation of verses from the Koran and the Prophetic Traditions, ascribing this to his study of Arab literature with Sheikh Subhi Saleh, an outstanding scholar of Arab philology and letters later assassinated in Beirut in mysterious circumstances.

New winds were blowing and the walls of the cities became covered with the slogan "Islam is the solution". Under the influence of groups of young Syrian members of the Muslim Brotherhood who had taken refuge in the city to escape repression, a new Islamicist language of struggle was spreading and had begun to dominate the minds of young men in the various quarters. Then suddenly Sheikh Ramadan Esawi proclaimed himself emir of the city and appointed Sheikh Salim Muadhen emir of the port. At the same time, he announced that the process of appointing emirs for each of the quarters of Tripoli had begun and requested Muslims to declare their allegiance to them.

Khaled had no idea how things had come to take on the form of armed confrontation in the Qubbeh quarter. It was twelve noon and he was working as usual in the bakery when the boys began pouring in with their weapons, announcing that they'd never let the army enter the area. Khaled picked up his machine gun, tucked his revolver into his waistband, and left the bakery followed by a group of more than sixty young men. In front of the Qubbeh roundabout he saw tracked vehicles entering the district's winding lanes, so he fired into the air in warning and they shot at him in retaliation. Radwan was injured immediately in the thigh. Khaled gave orders for him to be taken to the hospital and distributed his groups around the crossroads, and the clashes, which ended with the withdrawal of the military vehicles from the area, began.

Khaled noted that the cry "God is great!" had issued spontaneously from the boys firing the B7 grenade launchers and found himself shouting along with them, intoxicated with his first real victory in his own city among his own people.

The clashes had been preceded by heated discussions at the bakery on the subject of Islam and the emirs who had begun sprouting up everywhere in the quarters of the city. The discussions took on a more serious tone following the battle, when Khaled announced he had no choice but to ally himself with the Islamists.

"But we're all Muslims," said Radwan.

"True. All the same . . ." said Khaled.

"All the same" emerged hesitantly and falteringly from his lips. He was thinking there was no other way: joining the rising Islamic movement was the only way out if the organisation was to continue and preserve the boys' fighting spirit.

The next morning an envoy arrived from Sheikh Ramadan Esawi to announce that Khaled had been appointed emir of Qubbeh and asking him to come and meet the sheikh at the mosque. Khaled went – to object to his new title.

"I don't like the title 'emir'," he said. "I've spent my whole life in struggle against emirs and feudalists." The sheikh looked him in the eye and gave him to understand that the title of emir didn't mean belonging to a noble line. "In Islam, 'emir' derives from *imra*, meaning 'authority', and you now have authority over Qubbeh. Whatever you wish, though. We can call you whatever you like," said the sheikh.

"My name will be Abu Nabil," said Khaled, "and my boys will have full control over Qubbeh and Bab el-Tabbana."

Khaled returned from his meeting with the sheikh at ten at night to find the boys waiting for him at the bakery. He informed them of what had been agreed upon and said nothing would change. The organisation was the organisation and the work was the same work. "We were the army of the poor and we shall remain so, and it's revolution until victory. That was our slogan in Fatah and will remain our slogan until death."

"No," said Radwan. "One thing has changed. Perform your ablutions, boys, so that we can pray."

"But I don't know how to pray," said Khaled.

"Of course you know," said Radwan. "Islam is the religion that needs no teacher."

The boys formed rows behind Radwan, who led the prayer, and Khaled found himself with them, praying the way they prayed and believing what they believed.

Radwan stood after the prayer was finished, turned to Khaled, and said in a loud voice that all could hear, "You are now our emir and I pledge to you my allegiance." Then he held out his hand, shook Khaled's, and kissed him on the shoulder. The young men stood in a single line behind Radwan, each waiting his turn to ask Khaled to hold out his hand and accept his allegiance.

Khaled reached home at midnight. Hayat was waiting for him. He patted her belly, rounded with pregnancy, and said he was tired.

They drank aniseed. Khaled cleared his throat and said he wanted to tell her something.

"Before you tell me, let me tell you. I've decided to cover my hair and tomorrow I'll be another woman."

Khaled had come to visit Karim twice before his death. The first time he said he'd gone to Danny's flat in Tall el-Khayyat but hadn't found him so he'd come to Karim. The second time he came to Karim to give him the news of his impending death.

It was 6 p.m. Karim opened the door in surprised welcome. It was the first time Khaled had come to see him at home.

Khaled entered carrying three packages containing an assortment of sweet pastries of the kind in which Tripoli specialises.

"So those are for Danny, not me? I'll get them to him, don't worry."

"No, they're for you and Danny," said Khaled.

"What will you drink?" asked Karim. "I have a bottle of village arak that came to me yesterday from Douar, great stuff. Shall I set up a small one?"

"Still playing the bad boy?"

"We're your students, Boss. You taught us everything we know."

Khaled said he'd prefer a glass of tea.

Karim made the tea in the kitchen. He carried it into the living room and found Khaled gazing at the floor and smoking avidly, his mind so far away he failed to notice when his host entered.

Karim sat, poured the tea, lit a hand-rolled cigarette, and looked at his friend. Khaled, however, neither raised his head nor reached for the tea.

Karim cleared his throat and said, "Welcome."

Khaled looked up, rubbed his face as though he'd just woken up, and asked Karim about Danny.

"I haven't seen him for a long time," said Karim. "It seems he's busy organising the paper's archives. Last time I met him, which was about three weeks ago, he told me he was organising the archive on the civil war and writing a book evaluating what happened."

"But the war isn't over," said Khaled.

"Come on!" said Karim. "It's finished. The Syrians have taken over the country, the boys in Fatah have decided to go back to the theory of 'All guns against the enemy' and gone to the south, and the subject's closed."

"And us?" asked Khaled.

"You and we and everybody else have to look at things again and think about what to do."

"But we're still fighting," said Khaled, and he recounted in detail the battle for Qubbeh that he'd waged with the boys. He spoke of the agitation everywhere, from Tripoli to Homs and Hama, and said the revolution had started to reshape itself.

Karim said he wasn't convinced that kind of agitation could make a revolution, and he was tired of revolutions anyway. He told him of his project to write a book about Jamal.

"So you and Comrade Danny are still writing books and leaving us to die like dogs. No, Karim, we aren't done and we won't be till we've squared the books with you."

Then Khaled smiled and said, "In fact, though, your writings have their uses."

From his pocket he took two blue cheaply produced copies of a book and said he'd come especially from Tripoli, in spite of all the dangers, to give them to their authors – "you and Danny".

Karim flipped through one of the copies, then went back to the blue cover, where he read the words "Organisation for Righteousness and Proselytisation", and the title *Arms and the Lebanese Balance of Power*.

"We wrote a book that's been put out by the Islamists? You've got to be joking!"

"Anything goes in this war, as Danny used to say."

"But we're atheists, and everyone thinks we're Christians!"

Khaled took the book from Karim's hand, opened it at one of the pages, and said he'd put "Islam" for "the working class" and "socialism" wherever they occurred, "and it worked fine."

"What! Islam! You too, Khaled? And what are you going to do with the memory of Yahya, who died a Marxist and struggled for socialism?"

"Don't bring Yahya up. I know what you and Danny thought of him. You thought he was vulgar and self-taught and Danny used that French word which makes my skin crawl every time I hear it. What was it – 'lummen'? That's it – lummen."

"Lumpen," said Karim.

"Lummen, lumpen. Rubbish anyway. You had a very low opinion of Yahya, so spare me, don't ask me what he would have thought. If my uncle were still alive he'd have done what we're doing now."

There was silence and all that could be heard was the sipping of tea.

"You, Comrades, can give up, but not me. What would I do with the boys? Leave them to split up and go back to being neighbourhood hoodlums and working for Intelligence and taking drugs? We're poor, we live in the low-class neighbourhoods, we don't have flats in Hamra and Tall el-Khayyat like other people, and without an idea to bring us together we split up. Without Islam everything will fall apart."

Karim wanted to say that Khaled's new choices were wrong but he didn't. What was he supposed to say? It was true, the war hadn't ended and perhaps never would, but this phase was over. When those who had struggled started writing their memoirs, it meant they were finished and it was time for them to withdraw.

A deep silence reigned which Khaled broke by getting up to open the boxes of pastries from Hallab's he'd brought with him.

"I bet you brought feisaliyeh," said Karim.

"To tell you the truth I completely forgot about feisaliyeh. Anyway it's silly stuff – burma shaped into triangles that the people in Tripoli came up with to put one over King Feisal I, the one who was friends with a British spy called Lawrence and who turned tail and ran as soon as the first sound of a bullet was heard at Maysaloun. Why would you bother with feisaliyeh? Look and see what I did bring."

Khaled opened the three boxes and said they were the best sweet pastries in the world: "Pastries and revolutionaries are all that Tripoli produces."

"The girls are pretty too, and don't forget the scent of bitter-orange blossom," said Karim.

Khaled explained the three kinds of pastry, which bore unusual names.

"These are Hookers, these are Angel's Balls, and these are Bear's Turds."

"See what a vulgarian you still are?" said Karim. "And yet you come here this evening to teach us how to behave!"

"No, I swear. Those are their real names!" He showed him the names written on the coloured paper in which the three boxes were wrapped.

The two friends laughed as they ate the nammoura, which the people of Tripoli call Bear's Turds, the shmeisa, which they call Angel's Balls, and the basma stuffed with Aleppo pistachios that they call Hookers. Karim asked about the origins of the names but Khaled shrugged his shoulders indifferently. "How should I know, Brother Karim? That's what everyone calls them in Tripoli. Now you must have realised why I can't give up – who could leave behind these gorgeous Hookers and come to Beirut to be unemployed?"

Khaled asked for bread so he could eat the pastries, explaining that ever since he was a child he'd always eaten pastries wrapped in hot bread that his uncle fetched from the bakery. "I used to think it was because we were poor but then I discovered that the poor were right, they taste better like that and they fill you up."

They ate the pastries with bread and drank the tea and Khaled told Karim his wife was expecting a child and that Hayat was the greatest woman in the world because she understood him without him having to say anything.

He told him of his experience at Shaqif Castle: when he was there he'd kept thinking of Tripoli with its crusader castle of Saint-Gilles, which overlooked the city and topped the cliff above the Abu Ali River, and he said he'd had no choice but to return.

"I know what I did with your essays wasn't right, but honestly, Doctor, it fitted. If ideas are to stick together they need glue. We took off the Marxist glue, put on a new glue, and they stuck. Maybe Islam's better, because it's stronger. Anyway that's how I found rest and the boys found rest, and I wish you could see how happy the people of Qubbeh are. Now people aren't pleased with us just because we're tough guys and defend their rights, they feel we're part of them. Now, at last, we're like the fish in the sea."

"But Khaled . . ."

"Just say you were with us before and you're sticking with us. Isn't this guide to Islamic action your book?"

"But I don't want to become a Muslim like you!"

"Why not? Take Abd el-Messih, he became a Muslim and a Shiite and his Christian wife refused to let him divorce her. He told her, 'It doesn't matter. I'll go on supporting you and I'll marry my sweetheart', and so he had two."

"And are you going to take another wife alongside Hayat?"

"God forbid! One only: 'And if you fear you will not be equitable, then only one'!"

Karim said Abd el-Messih had been wrong. He thought the man had become a Muslim so he could live with the woman he loved, which wasn't a problem, but he'd pushed it too far, which was. What did it mean for a Christian intellectual to become a Muslim in these times? It was a covert invitation to kill Christians, and that was insanity, especially in a multi-sectarian society such as Lebanon's.

"God forbid!" said Khaled. "You Christians have been placed under the protection of the Muslims."

The conversation devoured the evening without their realising it. It was close to one when Karim said he had to sleep because his shift at the hospital started at six the next morning.

"You go and sleep in the bedroom and I'll sleep here in the living room. I'll heat water early in the morning if there's electricity. Don't forget to turn it off before you go or the pump will burn out."

"There won't be electricity tomorrow. Don't worry about it. You sleep in your room and I'll sleep here."

Karim spread a sheet on the living-room couch, placed a cushion on it and covered it, and went into his room. But he came out again wearing pyjamas to find Khaled in his underclothes, preparing to get under the covers.

"What's up?" asked Khaled.

"Nothing. I came to say good night, and that tonight you're under *my* protection."

"We all need the protection of the good guys," answered Khaled, laughing, and he turned out the light.

Now Karim understood why the veiled woman who had come to visit him a week after Khaled's murder had said she was "under his protection".

Hayat had come wearing a long black chador that covered her from head to toe and carrying her baby, Nabila, who was four months old, in her arms.

When he opened the door she said she was Hayat, Khaled's wife.

"Please come in, sister. This house is your house."

She came in but didn't sit down. She said Khaled had told her to go to Danny. "He said, 'If anything happens, go to Danny. Danny's like a brother to me and more, and he's married and has a little girl. You can have a nice talk with his wife while things are being sorted out.' I went to Danny and stood three hours in front of the door. I rang the bell and heard movements and felt someone was watching me through the peephole but he didn't open the door. I thought maybe he hadn't recognised me because I'm wearing a chador. I don't usually dress like this, our kind of veil is different, but I thought this way no-one would know me. We're in great danger. I took the chador off my head and I rang the bell and said, 'I'm Hayat, Khaled's wife.' I heard the same movements and felt the same eye but no-one opened the door. I covered my head again and thought, 'Be patient, girl, there's no-one inside because it's not possible Danny won't open the door. Danny slept at our house about ten times, he can't have forgotten us.' I sat down and waited on the steps and then I got so desperate I came to you. God is my sufficiency and the best of those on whom to depend. Do you know where Danny is?"

This was the first time Karim had met Hayat. She was indeed "the woman of light", as Danny had called her – an inner beauty manifested itself in honey-coloured almond-shaped eyes, slightly raised cheeks, eyebrows that seemed to have been drawn with a fine pen to overarch the eyes and contain the light that radiated from them.

Karim said he didn't know where Danny was.

"I'm under your protection, Brother Karim. I spent an hour looking for your house. Khaled, God rest his soul, described to me where it was and I didn't like to ask anyone so as not to raise suspicions. I have to find Danny today."

Karim's assessment was that Danny hadn't opened the door because he didn't want to see anyone. The man had gone into seclusion and even stopped answering the phone since hearing of his wife's decision not to go back to him. But he thought it a strange paradox: Hayat said her life was threatened and she'd decided to leave Tripoli, and Danny knew that. Why then hadn't he opened the door?

Karim felt embarrassed with the woman standing there hesitating. He told her he knew nothing about Danny but he could leave the flat to her and go somewhere. That was the only solution.

Hayat noticed the terror that had overtaken Karim. His hands were trembling and the words came out jerkily from between his lips, as though he was stuttering. She realised his invitation wasn't heartfelt and was made worse by the fact that she was looking not for refuge but for psychological and moral support.

"You mean we won't be able to find Danny today?"

"I think you should give me a moment and I'll leave the flat, if you want."

"What am I do to now?" she asked.

"I don't know," Karim answered.

The woman turned and left without a word.

Khaled's second visit to Karim's home took place six months after the earlier one. News of the doings of the Islamists in Tripoli was filling columns in the Lebanese press and Khaled's name was much mentioned as one of the leaders of the city. As usual he came without an appointment. He was exhausted, his hair a mess, his face marked with gloom and anxiety.

Khaled said he was on his way back from a visit to Damascus, to which he'd gone in the company of Sheikh Salim and a group of leaders of the Islamist movement with the objective of reaching an agreement to reduce the tensions in the city resulting from the armed clashes that broke out there nightly.

Khaled said he'd met the General. "I won't tell you his name because it would put your life in danger." He spoke of the discussions that had taken place between the two sides and of the General's low voice that you had to lean forward to hear. "But the discussions don't matter," said Khaled. "What matters is that I saw my death in his eyes."

He spoke of the death he'd seen in the man's eyes and fell silent.

Karim didn't ask him exactly what he'd seen when he saw his death, or how death could take shape in the killer's eyes as he gazed on his victim.

Khaled asked for a glass of cold water. "Death dries your mouth, you know. That's why everyone dies thirsty."

The man drank the glass of water at one go and said he didn't know what had happened to him there. He said he'd felt an unquenchable thirst, as though he had diabetes, then had noticed the General focusing his gaze on him, and that when he himself, the dead man, had raised his eyes to meet those staring at him he had felt his death. "It was like sparks of fire coming out of his eyes and then the whites of his eyes began to disappear. I don't know how to describe it – it was as though they had no whites left and I felt death and understood why I was thirsty."

The first time Khaled said the whites of the eyes had disappeared and the second time that they had filled the man's eyes. He stuttered as he told his story but said he wasn't afraid of death. "When all's said and done I knew the life I'd chosen would bring me to this point. I just hadn't realised I'd get here so fast."

Karim suggested that he not go back to the Fragrant City. "Stay in Beirut."

"It makes no difference," answered Khaled. "Anyone who can kill you in Tripoli can kill you in Beirut."

"Why don't you go abroad? Lots of young men get themselves smuggled into West Berlin and are given political asylum."

"You want me to become a political refugee in the ice camps of Germany? Out of the question!"

Khaled said he'd send him Abu Rabia's papers the next day with Radwan. "They're for you to keep safe. I don't have anywhere to hide them except with you. At first I thought of Danny but Danny's very confused. Please, once this all dies down I'll get them back from you, if I'm alive. If not, give them to Hayat, no-one else."

The papers were with him now but Karim, instead of reading them, sank into memories of the crime. He saw Khaled as they shot at him. He was driving his car and about twenty metres after he passed the checkpoint there was a hail of bullets. Sixty bullets ripped through his body and left him dead and alone. No-one dared approach the popular leader's body, and when Hayat picked up his shredded remains in her arms she looked like a mother cradling her child and walking through a desert of faces and silence.

Hayat came to Beirut two weeks after Khaled's killing and returned to her house the same day. She decided to go back to her work at the bakery. She would leave the baby with her grandmother and go to work alone in a bakery that was now empty of all the boys, some of whom had fled to the Ain Helweh camp in the south and the rest of whom had been arrested. Radwan led the flight to Ain Helweh, disappeared there for nine years, and when he returned to Tripoli did so in the shape of a beturbaned sheikh.

On the night of 9 June, 1980, six months after Khaled's murder, Hayat and her daughter Nabila were found with their throats cut in their home in Tripoli's Qubbeh district.

Ever since Karim had heard Radwan's voice on the phone inviting him to Tripoli he'd felt the tingling of fear, like a sudden resurgence of the same emotion that had made him tremble before Hayat when she came to him wearing the chador. Fear can't be remembered; it's like a smell we're able to recall only when we smell it again.

Karim recalled that it was Radwan who had brought him Yahya's papers.

Danny aside, Radwan was the only living person who knew of their existence.

Karim decided not to accept the invitation and forget about going to Tripoli to meet Sheikh Radwan.

He took off his clothes, bathed, got into bed, and closed his eyes.

13

He'd never seen Salma as sad as she was that day. He'd gone to his brother's flat for Nasim's thirty-ninth birthday, only to discover that Nasim had revived and incorporated into the celebration all their father's old rituals. To the original Sunday rites, however, he had added going to the Church of the Lady in Ghazaliyeh Street in the Siyoufi district, where he'd take his three children to attend 9 a.m. mass. After this they'd go to Jull el-Dib to buy a platter of kenafeh-with-cheese before returning to the flat.

Hend refused to go to church with her husband. Salma was a neutral party in the struggle over religion between husband and wife because she felt that it didn't matter what she said as she had no right to speak. She was from a Muslim family, and despite the fact that she'd married the second time in church and accepted the sacrament of baptism she continued to belong, in the eyes of her son-in-law, to "our Muslim brethren". Anything she said on the subject was likely to be unwelcome to Nasim, who had decided to make no concessions to his wife in the matter of his new-found religious beliefs or of the necessity of raising his children in the religion of their fathers and grandfathers.

That day, while Nasim was getting the grill ready, mixing the tabbouleh, and diluting the arak with water, Salma was sitting silently on the end of the couch like an unwanted guest, unresponsive to the larking about of the boys, who considered her visits to their house, like theirs to hers, an occasion for celebration.

"What's up with you, Mother, sitting there like an owl and not answering the boys?" Hend asked, as she came and went bearing the food her husband had made. "I always thought you adored them."

The conversation between the two women flew in all directions and was made up of incomplete sentences that followed the rhythm of Hend's comings and goings to and from the kitchen. As a result Karim understood nothing. The only thing that stuck in his mind was the phrase "the three moons" and he thought the women must be discussing the school of that name located in Nazlet el-Akkawi, a semi-free school founded by the Greek Orthodox diocese of Beirut for the poor children of the community. He surmised Hend had decided to move her boys from the Lycée to the school.

"How come? The Three Moons isn't an S.K.S. barracks any longer?" he said, referring to the Phalangist military police.

Hend explained that the diocese had recovered the school from the Phalanges party and appointed a new headmaster, a graduate of the Greek Orthodox Balamand Monastery called Father Eliyya, "but we weren't talking about the school, we were talking about something else."

Karim recalled the story of Salma's three sons by her first marriage in the Akkar district whom Hend had called "the three moons". He wanted to ask Hend why she hadn't told her mother that the three brothers had fled their village after the peasants burned their houses during the revolution led by Yahya Nabulsi. But he thought the subject too sensitive and that it would cast a shadow over the feast his brother was preparing, so decided to drop it. He spoke of the children's problems at school and said a solution could be found for that of Nasri, his brother's second son, who was seven: the boy was no worse than his father and his inability to write was a minor issue, especially with the development of modern pedagogical methods. There was no need to ruin the boys' future by transferring them from the school they were in to another of below-average standard.

He looked at Salma and said, "I'm sure Mrs Salma would agree with me."

But Salma didn't answer. She looked at him with vacant eyes and said she was sorry but she hadn't been paying attention.

Karim fled the stifling atmosphere of the dining room, preferring to go to the kitchen to help his brother.

In the kitchen he beheld an extraordinary sight: Nasim, sleeves rolled up, was threading pieces of meat onto the skewers, giving strict orders to his wife, mincing the parsley, then discovering that he'd forgotten the bulgur, shouting for a bowl, then starting to chop the aubergine preparatory to threading it on the skewers next to the meat, yelling, then laughing, then pouring himself a glass of arak and sipping it. He noticed his brother in the kitchen. "What's wrong with you, standing around doing nothing? Pour yourself a glass of arak and come and help me."

"What's this shambles?" said Karim.

"It's a shambles and worse than a shambles," said Hend. "I swear, every Sunday he comes back from church all hot and bothered and see what happens. He calls himself a chef! He gets everything dirty, strews bulgur and parsley all over the floor and stinks up the sink with the meat and the fat, and then it's, 'Go to it, Hend, and clean up!'"

"If I were all hot and bothered like you say, I'd have screwed you on the bed, madam!"

"I've told you a hundred times I hate that kind of talk, especially in front of other people."

"Why? Where are the other people? My brother's 'other people' now?"

Nasim looked at his brother and said his wife was crazy. "We begged her to let us get her a maid and she kicked up a terrible fuss, saying she couldn't bring herself to exploit people. Ghazala came. I told her, 'This is Matrouk's wife and Matrouk's my friend. Let her come and help you with the flat.' Then when Ghazala was here she'd sit with her in the living room and treat her like a lady and they'd drink coffee and at the end she'd give her some money – and now she comes and starts going on about the housework. Sunday's the one day when I can enjoy myself. I like cooking and getting drunk with my family, and every Sunday, swear to God, it's the same. Even on my birthday she wants to spoil my mood. But, with the arak in place, morale is high! Cheers!"

Karim went to the table and began threading meat with his brother and the laughter – of a childhood recovered in the shape of two grown men drinking arak and making food – rose high.

"If only you could be with us, Nasri!" said Karim.

"What made you think of the departed in the middle of all this?" asked Nasim.

Karim said that ever since his return to Beirut he'd felt a strange yearning for the man. "You know, we didn't give him his due and caused him a lot of grief at the end of his life. All the poor man had eyes for in this world was his Trinity and by the time we came together again and started working he was dead. Damn it, life's cruel! If he could just have been in on the hospital project with us, it would have been the happiest time of his life."

Nasim nodded in agreement and said he'd discovered he grew more like his father the older he got. "Even those rituals of his that I used to hate I now perform with my children without realising it. Strange how people change."

They were the twins whom Nasri Shammas had wanted, complementing each other so they could become him. "I have to mix you into one another so you can become like me. There must have been some kind of technical slip-up and instead of the genetic components sticking together in one egg so that you could come out as one boy they got divided between two and you became two, one my brainy half and the other my canny half. It's all your late mother's fault. Her body couldn't gather enough strength together to push, so she divided the genes into two, God rest her soul – she was sick and her body was weak."

It was talk like this that had made the blood of the two small boys run cold with fear and made them feel permanently inferior.

"But he was very hard on us, God rest his soul, and gave us no room to breathe," said Nasim.

"But the poor man lived a long life alone," said Karim. "Twice we prevented him from marrying. He used to say, 'All the women in the world aren't worth one of my boys' legs!'"

"Don't forget there was nothing lousy he didn't take a shot at. Why should he marry again when he could get any woman he wanted? I'm sure Father was a dirtier dog than us. He was in macho mode the whole time and had a roving eye till the day he died," Nasim said.

In this dialogue, which took place to the clatter of pots and plates, what wasn't said was more important than what was. Nasim would have liked to tell his brother that the sympathy Karim felt for Nasri now was a result of the fact that he hadn't lived with him; he'd run away to France and left the entire burden on his brother's shoulders. Plus he'd been the indulged child while the whole weight of repression had fallen on his younger brother. Karim for his part would have liked to say that all the disasters started when his brother had run away from home. Nasri had changed radically that day and become underhand and full of bitterness. He would have liked to ask his brother if he'd ever felt the need to apologise to his father and acknowledge his mistakes.

For his part, Nasim hadn't been able to understand his brother's behaviour in Beirut. "Who gets up to that kind of stuff with the maid? Damn, he must be repressed! He comes all the way from France, the land of sexual freedom, to make scandals for us?! If God hadn't kept the lid on it and Matrouk hadn't turned out to be a fool, there would have been a crime in the family. And why does he make sheep's eyes every time he sees Muna? Doesn't he know she's my friend's wife? Though for sure he didn't do anything with her anyway. If she'd wanted any she would have come to me. Karim's off his rocker. Father used to think he was smart – God, how wrong he was!"

Nasim said nothing – he was wallowing in the pleasure of preparing the feast like his father, who believed that making Sunday dinner was more fun than eating it. Nasri would pour himself a glass of arak and go off into the kitchen alone because he didn't like people helping. He would reappear bearing the dishes, drunk and staggering, and put on a song by Abd el-Wahhab or Umm Kulthoum, turning his feast into a moment of fun with the family, and this he thought the greatest pleasure life had to offer.

They drank and worked in the kitchen like one man divided in two and listened to Hend's voice as she shouted at her mother to change the subject.

Nasim opened the kitchen door and yelled, "Food's ready!"

Hend came bearing dishes and the boys sat at their places at the table. Salma sat at the head and they started hearing snatches of Umm Kulthoum's song "You Are My Life" emerging from Nasim's throat as he gave the final touches to the food.

Suddenly Hend shouted, "No!", shut the kitchen door, and told her husband in a low voice that it wouldn't do. "I told her about it yesterday, and now she's in a terrible state. We can't put the cheese pastry you got from Homs on the table. Mother will break down."

He said she was being silly; they had either to eat the cheese pastry that day or throw it away "because it doesn't last".

He said he hadn't bought the usual platter of kenafeh because there was nothing to beat the cheese pastry made in Homs, and instead of thanking him for having gone to Syria, which had been a major undertaking, she was giving him the usual hard time "because Madam is never happy".

"Please, you're the only one who can convince him," she said to Karim.

"But I don't know what you're talking about," said Karim.

"Tell him no cheese pastry, if you have any regard for me."

"Forget it, Nasim. Let's do it another time."

"As you wish, madam."

Nasim poured four glasses of arak. Then he poured three glasses of what he called "kids' arak" and handed them round to the boys. He raised his glass and drank a toast to life.

Salma raised her glass and drank a toast to Bernadette, Nadine, and Lara. "Your children should meet and the whole family should get together. God give you better days than mine."

Things were going smoothly. Nasim kept up a constant stream of jokes, passing little morsels of food to the boys, and asking everyone if they liked the kibbeh nayyeh that he'd made with his own hands.

Salma said life had changed a lot. "In the past we used to pound the meat in the mortar till it was smooth and all mixed together. That was the difficult bit. The trick was getting the onion into the fibre of the meat before we mixed it with the bulgur. These days kibbeh isn't kibbeh anymore. The butcher grinds it up with the onion in the blender so it never really mixes. Never mind though, we all do it that way and we've got used to it."

Nasim said he was the one who used to pound the meat at home and to this day he felt a numbness in his right hand every Sunday morning.

"I'm the one who used to pound the kibbeh!" said Karim. "You used to stay in bed and pretend to be ill."

"Me? How can you say such a thing? All I can remember is me pounding away at the meat and you standing next to Father and the two of you giving me orders."

"Now the lies begin," said Karim, addressing the boys. "Your father's like that, he can't say a true word to save his life."

"By the Virgin I swear I'm not lying! You're the liar!"

At this point Hend intervened to give them a lecture on memory. She said the most curious thing was to hear two people who'd been present at some event in the past recount their memories. "Each remembers things differently but that doesn't mean they're lying. It just shows the limitations of memory and that it's always mixed up with the imagination."

"So who's right in this case?" asked Nasim.

"You're both right," said Hend.

"You mean memory is an *illusion*?" said Karim, using the French word.

"A *wahm*, Uncle. *Illusion* in Arabic is *wahm*," said Nadim, Nasim's eldest son. "I hear you speaking French a lot. Does that mean you don't know Arabic?"

"And in France I speak Arabic, because memory, as your mother said, is a *wahm*."

Suddenly the atmosphere became electric. Nasim leapt to the kitchen, staggering drunk. His wife ran after him and everyone heard them quarrel. Then Nasim came back bearing a square cardboard box wrapped in shiny green paper on which was written "Raheb Pastries – Homs". He opened the box and said he'd brought them the best pastries in the world, that in Homs they made the best cheese pastry, and that when he tasted it he'd discovered that the secret of Arabic pastry making was a one hundred per cent Homs thing.

Salma looked at him as though she couldn't believe her eyes, her lower lip trembled, and a cold sweat started from her forehead.

Hend took hold of the pastries and said she was going to throw them in the rubbish.

"You, shut up and sit down!" said Salma, who then looked straight at Nasim and asked in a trembling voice, "That's the boys' pastry, isn't it?"

Nasim nodded. "Mokhtar was on his own in the shop when I went in. He gave me a warm welcome and I could feel how tender-hearted the boy was. He refused to take money and like I told you, Mother-in-law, he said he was very anxious to get to know his mother, and then I don't know what happened. The atmosphere changed. Two men arrived and I gathered that one of them was called Deyab."

"He's the eldest," said Salma.

"When Deyab saw me and heard my first few words, he held up his hand, pointed to the door, and said, 'Out! We don't have a mother.'"

Salma's face started to flush red and shadows described themselves over her eyes.

"Tell me more," she said.

"I told you yesterday, Mother. Damn this whole business!" said Hend.

Salma's face grew more flushed and she tried to get up from her chair, steadying herself against the table, but fell back into a sitting position saying she felt giddy.

Hend ran to the kitchen and came back with a big head of garlic. Nadim jumped up, got a knife and began quickly peeling the garlic and giving the raw cloves to his grandmother, who devoured them, an expression of disgust on her face.

"What are you doing?" asked Karim.

"Her blood pressure's gone up," answered Nasim. "Her blood pressure's started to scare us it goes up so fast."

"But why the garlic? Don't you have any medicine? Adizem's the best. Run to the pharmacy, Nadim, and buy your grandmother medicine instead of this silly nonsense."

"I don't like medicines," said Salma, catching her breath and licking her lips with a tongue that burned with thirst.

Hend said the best medicine for blood pressure was raw garlic; it was something her mother had learned from the late Nasri. "Anyway this garlic doesn't have chemicals. We buy it from Jalal Turmus."

"Don't talk to me about garlic and all that nonsense! What a farrago! I'm a doctor, my dear Mrs Salma, and at your age everyone should take medicine for blood pressure."

Hend continued to give her son cloves of garlic which the boy would peel and feed to his grandmother and the smell spread everywhere, blending with that of the sugar syrup – the scene was bizarre. Facing this comedy Karim felt he was about to burst out laughing so he got up and went to the bathroom, where his laughter faded into a half-smile. He

371

washed his hands and face and when he got back Salma's expression had begun to relax. She had stopped eating garlic and said she must go home. Hend got up and said she'd drive her mother. The two women left and the boys disappeared into the living room to sit in front of the television.

The brothers found themselves alone at the table with its cheese pastries – into which the smells of sweat, sugar syrup, and garlic had been infused – like the heroes of a comedy set in an atmosphere of fake tragedy.

Karim looked at his brother and said it was his fault.

"Your wife told you to forget the dessert. Why did you put it on the table?" he asked.

"Damned drink!" said Nasim. "Shit, the woman could have died in front of us and then we'd never have heard the end of it, with Mrs Hend accusing me of having killed her mother."

Nasim said the story had begun eight months earlier. Hend had asked him to look for her half-brothers. She'd said she was sure they were in Homs and that Karim had told her how they'd fled from Kherbet el-Raheb during the peasant uprising in Akkar and migrated to the Syrian city closest to their village.

Hend had decided to forget the story, which Karim had told her a long time before, believing the reappearance of the three brothers would only cause her mother pain. But when her mother, who suffered from diabetes, started to show symptoms of high blood pressure, she'd felt she didn't have the right not to tell her the truth before she died. All Hend knew of the story was what Karim had told her, based on Yahya Nabulsi's memoirs, written in prison before his death. Also, Karim was abroad and she didn't want to phone him because she'd decided to forget him; Hend believed forgetting was a decision that had to be taken if life was to go on. When she overheard fragments of the heated discussion between Karim and Ahmad Dakiz about the memory of Beirut, she'd wanted to say the discussion had no meaning – we have to forget if we are to go on living. This was Beirut's greatness – it was the opposite of all the other cities of the Levant because it was built on the idea of forgetting and drew its vitality from this fact. As for Karim's words to the effect that forgetting was why the civil war had repeated itself several times over during a single century, that was meaningless too. The war kept repeating itself because they were a small people surrounded by greedy neighbours. They were at the crossroads of a disturbed region incapable of solving its problems. That, not memory, was the reason for the war.

When Karim returned to Beirut, he'd questioned Salma repeatedly on her health. He told Hend that he'd noted as a doctor that the woman needed to undergo a full medical examination because her high facial colour and bleary eyes indicated a problem.

Hend had wanted to ask him what information he had on "the three moons", and whether he'd be able to help her find them. But she did not. She was sure Karim too had decided to forget, and that after his long sojourn in France he wouldn't want to speak of the past – how else was she supposed to interpret his agreement to return to work in a hospital to be built in East Beirut, stronghold of the Phalangists, against whom he'd fought during the war?

Hend told her husband she didn't want to get Karim involved in the matter. "You know everybody and you can fix it."

"But it's difficult for someone like me to make a trip to Syria. You know I was with the Lebanese Forces and the Syrians don't like us."

"I know, but I'm sure you can if you want to."

He'd returned from Homs two days before that wretched Sunday. He told his wife the brothers didn't want to see their mother and recounted what had happened when he met them. The same evening his wife begged him to go with her to Salma's, who wanted to hear the story from him in person. He went and summarised it for her with a single sentence: "The boys don't want to see you, Mother-in-law." Salma asked no questions. She coughed a lot, her tears flowed, and she curled herself into a ball, repeating over and over again, "I bear witness that there is no god but God and I bear witness that Muhammad is the Prophet of God." She said it five times. She kept drinking water from a glass placed next to her and repeating the twofold profession of faith, leading Nasim to suppose she wanted to die.

On their way home Nasim told his wife they had to start looking for a solution then and there; the woman's death shouldn't take them by surprise or they'd have to tie themselves in knots trying to find a way to bury her in an Islamic cemetery.

"Don't be so pessimistic! What a way to talk! This isn't the time. The poor thing couldn't ask you a single question, but when I told her the news this morning she drove me round the bend asking about how they looked and their health and whether they were married and how many children they had."

Nasim told his brother as he poured two new glasses of arak that he couldn't understand why Salma had behaved as though it was a surprise to her – "She'd already heard what happened two days before!" He said he'd gone to a lot of trouble to arrange the business of his visit to Homs "and then we came out of it looking like fools. I ought to have taken you with me so you could see the results of what you did, you and the Tripoli boys. Now the sons of the feudalists look just like the heroes who led the peasants in that stupid revolution – afterwards both sides turned into fanatical Muslims and their women covered their hair, and you came out of it with nothing."

As usual, Nasim was't telling the whole truth: he hadn't had to go to any great trouble to get to Homs, he'd simply fixed it with Mustafa Najjar. This Mustafa had been leader of the Syrian Baath party in Lebanon and, in all probability, now worked for Syrian Intelligence. He was an old colleague of Nasim's from his drug smuggling days who had also given up his former business, in favour of running one that imported Sri Lankan and Ethiopian maids.

Nasim had phoned his old friend, who'd fixed it. Waiting for him in front of the Syrian–Lebanese border post he'd found the man Mustafa had sent for him. The fellow got into the car next to him and they crossed the border on a military road usually used by Intelligence and not subject to inspections. The escort had stayed with him until they arrived in front of the Hotel Safir in Homs.

The man got out with him and fetched the key to Room 877, sparing Nasim the trouble of having to take out his passport for formalities at the reception desk. The fellow told him he'd be waiting for him the next day at 4 p.m. in the lobby of the hotel to take him back to Beirut and gave him a phone number, saying if he needed anything he should ask for Abu Ahmad and he'd be with him in minutes.

Nasim concluded he was supposed to have nothing to do with the hotel management as his account had been settled in advance, and he was free to wander around Homs as he wished.

Mustafa hadn't been able to come up with residential addresses for the three brothers or their phone numbers but he'd provided the address of the Raheb pastry shop on Shukri Quwatli Street. "Ask anyone in Homs for Shukri Quwatli Street and they'll show you, but the three most important things in the city are the Dik al-Jinn restaurant on the River Asi, the grave of Khaled ibn al-Walid, and the Nouri mosque."

"You think I'm going for the tourism?"

"Don't you need to eat? Go eat on the Asi, best tabbouleh in the world. And I know you like churches. There are two you have to visit – the Saint Mary Church of the Holy Belt and the Church of Mar Elian."

Nasim arrived at the Hotel Safir in Homs at twelve noon and, deciding not to waste time, took a taxi from in front of the hotel and asked to go to Shukri Quwatli Street. He made the taxi stop at the entrance to the crowded street and decided to walk. He ate a shawarma sandwich he bought from one of the cheap restaurants situated at intervals along the street and strolled. He was amazed by the old city – a mixture of Mamluke, Ottoman, and modern – and the aromas which filled the air from shops selling herbs and spices. He walked slowly, reading the names of the shops that ran along either side of the street. Suddenly, he read the name "Raheb Pastries" over a low wooden door. He bent his head and entered, finding himself in a vaulted space gleaming with the black-and-white stone that distinguishes the buildings of Homs. The floor was of white marble, there was a smell of orange-blossom water, and a coolness that emanated from a little pool in the centre of the place.

It was crowded with customers. A group of men, their heads covered with white caps, were standing behind the pastry platters taking orders. He didn't know what to do. He went forward, stood with everyone else, ordered a plate of cheese pastry, and sat down at one of the tables.

In a few minutes a tall man with a white face, grey eyes, and light brown hair came bearing a small tray with a plate of cheese pastry, a glass of water, and a small flask of orange-blossom water.

He placed the tray in front of Nasim and said, "You're from Lebanon, aren't you?"

"How did you know?" asked Nasim, who noted that the man wasn't wearing a white cap like the rest of the workers and that his sideburns were greying.

"The boys told me. Welcome, Lebanon, and the scents of Lebanon!"

Nasim took the spoon to eat but noticed there was a question in the man's eyes.

"Can I ask you a question?" said Nasim.

"Of course," answered the man.

"The fact is I came from Lebanon specially, because I have a message for the owner of the shop."

"All's well, I hope," said the man and sat down.

Nasim said he carried a message to the three brothers from their mother in Beirut. He said he was married to her daughter Hend, that the woman had one foot in the grave, and that her last wish before she died was to see her children, whom she called "the three moons", and hold them to her breast.

"Salma!" said the man.

Nasim said he understood their position and that of their father, "but to forgive is noble, and Salma is a mother who was deprived of her children."

The man stood up, then sat down again. He lit a cigarette while Nasim devoted himself to devouring the pastry in front of him.

"What a cheese pastry! You should be proud," said Nasim, adding that he'd buy two kilos to take back to Beirut.

The man waved to one of the workers, and in minutes Nasim found the table before him covered with three sorts of pastry that he'd never seen before.

"This is bashmeeneh," said the man. "Layers of wheat baked with country butter between which we put a mixture of sugar syrup and natef. It's made only in Homs. And this is khubziyeh and this is simsimiyeh. Eat and praise God, as the Beirutis say. Come here, Shukri. Fetch me three kilos of cheese pastry for the gentleman. Put the clotted cream on its own in a cold pack because the gentleman's travelling to Lebanon. And we'll need a box of bashmeeneh too."

The man rested his head on his hand, looked at Nasim for a long time, and then said he was Mokhtar, Salma's third son. He said he didn't remember his mother because she'd left them when he was very little. He'd been raised to hate and despise her; he'd never married because he loathed women – all because of her. Yet he too had been waiting for this moment. He said he'd never seen a picture of his mother, which was why he didn't remember her, but he'd seen her in his dreams and was sure that the phantom which had for so long visited him in them looked like her. When he saw her he'd know her without her having to be pointed out. "I know my mother's very pretty and cute."

The story of the three brothers in their exile can excite only pity. They'd spent their childhood without a mother and with their cruel paternal grandfather, who despised his son Qasem because he'd been cuckolded. Their father had been stricken with depression and taken to the bottle. When their grandfather died and authority passed to the drunkard son, he began behaving like the feudal lords of Mamluke times. His cruelty and the savagery of his behaviour towards the peasants were on every tongue. The peasants of Kherbet el-Raheb and the seven villages had never suffered oppression as they did with this man. He seemed to have become a different person. His haughtiness, drunkenness, and depression were replaced by viciousness. He imposed compulsory labour on the peasants, roaming through the farms with a group of rifle-bearing guards. The crack of a whip heralded his coming and people would pray God to protect them from the Devil. He'd even wanted to revive an ancient custom no longer widely practised, the *droit du seigneur*, and his appetite for food and women knew no bounds.

The people of Kherbet el-Raheb could never forget the savagery with which he treated Salma's father, Abu Salah. Sheikh Deyab Abd el-Karim had refused to allow Abu Salah to leave his land and prevented him from moving about the village, but when Qasem inherited he took possession of the land that Abu Salah had farmed and threw him out of his house. He allowed his daughters to take their mother in but Abu Salah was forced to remain alone, without shelter or work. He died homeless. He told his wife to go to her eldest daughter Daad and remained alone in the open, then vanished. Presumably he died, though no-one found his body to wash and bury.

Mokhtar said the peasants' revolution that had burned down their house and killed their father was the last chapter in the tragedy of their life with that savage man, "though there was no call for them to drag our father's body through the streets of the village. That was wrong and indecent." He recounted how his eldest brother Deyab had hidden gold liras in the waistband of his trousers and taken the decision to migrate to Homs.

"And why didn't you go back after things had calmed down?"

"We thought about returning but the civil war had begun. 'Where are we going to go?' we said. 'The land has been left unsown and here we have a pastry shop which is doing well, thank God,' and then Deyab and Ahmad married sisters from the Atassi family, which is a very respected Homs family, and I'm now about to marry a girl from Tartous and we're doing fine, thank God."

Mokhtar said he wanted Nasim to give his mother and Hend his greetings and that he didn't think he could arrange a meeting between Salma and her children. "That Deyab, God protect us! Like his father, arrogant and without a trace of tenderness. He certainly won't agree to let Salma come here, but thank God, three years ago God gave him guidance and he stopped drinking arak, his wife started covering her hair, and even his daughter Salwa, who's fifteen, covers her hair. This year the three of us are going to make the pilgrimage. May you do so too, God willing, brother-in-law."

"His eldest daughter's called Salma?" asked Nasim.

"Salwa, not Salma, and forgive me: you're one of our Christian brethren, right?"

"Right," said Nasim.

"No problem – 'May you do so too' because God guides to the Truth whomsoever He pleases."

Mokhtar started to laugh but his laughter was choked off in his throat, his face darkened, and he started fidgeting in his chair. Then he rose and looked in the direction of two men who had entered the premises.

He spoke with them in a low voice, pointing at Nasim. The men, on whose foreheads could be seen the dark mark made by frequent prayer, approached him.

"I'm Deyab," said one of them who, from the grey of his sideburns, seemed to be the eldest.

Nasim stood up and extended his hand in welcome, but the other man's hand wasn't extended to meet it so Nasim withdrew his and said, tripping over his words, that he brought a message to Deyab, Ahmad, and Mokhtar from Beirut.

"But we don't have anybody in Beirut," said Ahmad.

"The message is from your mother Salma. I'm the husband of her daughter Hend and she wants to ask for forgiveness from her three sons before she dies and to see them."

As soon as Deyab heard the first words he raised his hand and pointed towards the door. "Out!" he said. "We don't have a mother."

Nasim rose and began walking backwards, feeling it could be dangerous to turn his back and leave. He saw Mokhtar coming towards him carrying the two boxes of pastries.

"Leave them here," shouted Deyab. "We don't want to sell."

"But the man paid and they're his," said Mokhtar, giving the pastries to Nasim.

Nasim tried to say he hadn't paid and wanted nothing but he saw something like supplication in Mokhtar's eyes, as though he were pleading with him to take the pastries to his mother and tell her, "These are from your youngest son, Mokhtar."

Hend told him her mother had diabetes and shouldn't be given the pastries. "Even now when she sees the children eating chocolate I don't know what comes over her. It seems she can't resist anything sweet because when you have diabetes you can't resist your cravings."

Karim said the story was depressing and he didn't know why Nasim had gone there. "There's no pain worse than that. How terrible life is! But maybe it's her fault. Now she's paying for the mistake she made."

"You're calling love a mistake? If love's a mistake what's right?" responded Nasim.

"Everything's a mistake," thought Karim as he sat in the back seat of the Volvo driven by Ahmad Dakiz, his wife Muna next to him. Karim felt sure it was Muna who'd arranged things. When she phoned him he'd explained he was in two minds about going to Tripoli. He'd said he was supposed to go on the Friday morning to visit an old friend but wasn't sure. He was exhausted by lack of work. "An idle mind fills with devils," he said.

He'd decided against going because he felt Radwan was hiding something. His commanding tone and reference to the code name Sinalcol in a conversation that combined blackmail with jocularity had made him feel absolved of the need to carry out his promise to visit Khaled's grave.

Muna had made him give in. After her last visit to him she'd phoned to say that their journey to Canada had been postponed because of complicated immigration procedures. When he asked if he could see her she refused and said their relationship had come to an end at his flat, when they'd made love while she was still wet from the shower. She'd said she couldn't do a repeat of the farewell scene but she would like to talk to him on the phone, if he didn't mind. "Why should I mind?" he said. "But I swear I don't understand anyone anymore and no-one understands me anymore." Then he told her about his delayed Tripoli project.

Karim was taken aback by a phone call from Ahmad Dakiz inviting him to Tripoli. "Muna tells me you're a specialist in the Franks and crusaders so I'm inviting you to see something incredible."

How had Muna found out about his old article on the Franks and his interest in their castles and what had become of them? He couldn't remember telling her, and besides he'd never pretended to be a specialist in crusader history. All it came down to was that as a young man he'd written an article, lacking historical accuracy, on the topic, Abu Jihad had liked the article, and so on and so forth . . .

He couldn't remember telling Muna. The only woman he had spoken of it to was Bernadette, at the beginning of their relationship, and he hadn't said much even to her because he didn't know much. He might have told Muna in bed without realising it, or perhaps he got things mixed up in Beirut as much as in Montpellier. But he was sure he hadn't committed here the error that he had in France when he'd called himself Sinalcol.

Ahmad said he was going to go with his wife to see his father before they migrated to Canada. "I suggest you come with us. We'll have lunch and get back the same day. You'll see something incredible. We're not going to show you a castle or stones and ruins. You're going to meet crusaders in the flesh."

The trip was set up, with Ahmad Dakiz deciding that he'd drive Karim to his appointment at noon. They'd be waiting for him at two-thirty at the Silver Shore restaurant in the port, where he'd introduce him to his father.

Karim phoned Radwan and told him he was coming to Tripoli the next day.

"Then I'll be waiting for you at Hallab's after the noon prayer."

Ahmad Dakiz decided he'd take the old Tripoli road and avoid the motorway, which was full of lorries and pollution, and that would be an opportunity for the doctor to see the beauty of the Lebanese coast. In fact the doctor saw nothing, neither the sea which hugged the mountains, nor the magical sweep of blue undulating with white.

Karim had found the best solution: going with Ahmad and Muna gave him an illusory feeling of security, despite which he had no desire to listen to the stories of Ahmad's father, whom Muna had characterised as senile but sweet. Karim felt his heart had become like a vessel filled with stories and tales, and that he could listen to no more. For the first time, he thought of Montpellier with longing. There he would close his eyes, block his ears to the hubbub of Lebanon, cast into oblivion all these stories that had reclaimed him and begin his life over again. He would return to his two girls, whose existence he had almost begun to forget, and restore his relationship with Bernadette.

Instead of seeing the Lebanese coast stretching on beyond the horizon, he imagined the beach at Palavas with its firm sand and gusting wind, and saw himself carrying Nadine and Lara and making them fly, and Bernadette running behind them, stumbling over her ballooning skirt.

He longed for the quiet of his home, for his cup of *café au lait* at the Grand Café on the Place de la Comédie, for the films at the Cinéma

Diagonale, and the tobacco-stained moustache of Monsieur Roger who used to come to see him at the hospital to beg off him the price of a bottle of wine and remind Karim of the days when they were friends, when the Lebanese medical student had stayed at the Le Ponant hostel on Avenue Palavas, far from the university, because he hadn't been able to find university housing during his first year. Monsieur Roger, the hostel concierge, had been his guide to the secrets of the small city and the tales of its women.

Instead of drawing up a detailed plan for his visit to Tripoli and what he wanted to see and do there, in the City of a Thousand Libraries, he curled up on the back seat of the car, giving his imagination free rein to summon up the French city as a lost paradise.

He felt his affection flowing out and covering the small fine-featured face of his French wife. The love that he'd secreted away revived and he saw himself surrounded by a loving smile that described itself on the white-skinned woman's lips. He realised he was on the verge of losing his great love for the woman to whom he'd said, when proposing to her, that she was the love of his life. Would it be possible to begin his life over again with her, the woman who'd been his refuge during hard times? Paternal feelings for his daughters swept over him and he pulled out his wallet to contemplate his photo of them with their mother.

Ahmad and his wife thought Karim was asleep on the back seat and, not wanting to disturb him, decided to forget about stopping at the Patisserie Helmi in Batroun to drink the frothy Batroun lemonade.

When they got to Abd el-Hamid Karami Square at the entrance to the city – now called God's Square because the Islamicists had replaced Karami's statue with a stone monument composed of the words that form His many names – Muna turned around and shook Karim's shoulder to wake him and the photo fell to the floor of the car.

"Show me the picture," said Muna, who, as soon as she looked at it, declared his wife beautiful and said the girls were to die for.

"You never told us the names of your wife and daughters," said Muna.

He put the picture back in his wallet, got out of the car, and walked sluggishly to Hallab's, hearing Ahmad's voice saying, "You'll be taking a taxi to the Silver Shore restaurant in the port. Don't be late."

He found a young man waiting for him at the door to the shop. "Are you Dr Karim, sir?" he asked. Karim nodded. "This way," said the young man. "Mawlana is waiting for you on the second floor." The young man walked ahead, Karim followed in his wake. They climbed a flight of stairs leading to a second dining salon. Karim scanned the people there but the young man kept on going, so Karim followed him and they emerged from the large salon to find themselves in front of a closed door. The young man knocked three times and they entered.

"Welcome, welcome, Doctor!" said the sheikh, who got up, his arms open in greeting.

The young man left the room, closing the door behind him. Karim approached the man, who was wearing a grey mantle that failed to hide his belly; he had a large white turban on his head. They embraced, to the accompaniment of the sheikh's astonished exclamations that Karim hadn't changed a bit.

"It looks as though France agrees with you, Brother Sinalcol. Heavens be praised, you're just the same as ever. No paunch, no grey hair, not like us, God help us."

The conversation had got off on the wrong foot but Karim made no comment on his being "sinalcolised". He swallowed the name and behaved as though he'd heard nothing.

Soon a waiter arrived with dishes of meat cooked in pastry, stuffed lamb, and salads. The sheikh rolled up his sleeves and removed his turban, exposing his bald pate. "In the name of God the Merciful, the Compassionate," he said, reaching for the food and inviting Karim to join him. The waiter came back carrying a jug of chilled ayran. The sheikh poured two glasses, raised his, and said, "Cheers!"

Karim was too embarrassed to say he couldn't eat because he was invited to lunch at the Silver Shore, so he reached out and ate a few mouthfuls while drinking the ayran and listening to the sheikh's requests.

Sheikh Radwan wanted Yahya's papers from Karim. He said he remembered very well that Khaled had sent him, Radwan, to Karim with the papers and he wanted nothing else from him. "You're far from the country and the struggle now and I have need of the papers for two reasons, the first being my memoirs – the revolutionary movement that we created here must be documented and I am currently engaged in that very process – and the second is that I am thinking of publishing them as an appendix to my book so that all may see how we were guided to God's religion through our commitment to the defence of the impoverished."

Karim was surprised at the classical tone of the sheikh's Arabic. He had abandoned the aesthetics of the dialect of Tripoli and the people of the north who changed the glottal stop into a *w*. He listened to the sheikh recounting how he'd taken the decision to wear the turban during his long stay in Ain Helweh camp, how he'd worked with Palestinian brothers engaged in jihad, and how now he'd come back to Tripoli convinced that education and cadre-building had to come before jihad and the bearing of arms.

Karim nodded and told the sheikh he respected his choices, and that he'd loved Khaled and had respected his choices too, even though he wasn't convinced by them. True, Marxism no longer attracted him and the repressive excesses of China's Cultural Revolution had made him rethink it all. All the same he was still a secularist and a believer in social-ism who thought the struggle for Palestine was the shortest path to the liberation of the Arab individual.

The sheikh cleared his throat before saying, "Thou guidest not whom thou likest, but God guides whom He wills."

The sheikh's questions focused on the Arab and Islamic communities in France, especially in Marseille, and on the great renaissance that these communities were experiencing – he predicted a major role for them in the future.

The conversation continued along the same lines, Sheikh Radwan not asking again about Yahya's papers, a topic Karim also avoided. Instead he spoke about living abroad, saying he understood the thirst of second- and third-generation immigrants for an identity. He spoke of his experi-ences with patients from Maghrebi communities who suffered from the identity disease, which had now replaced the nostalgia so widespread among those of the first generation.

Karim continued by saying he thought that the death of nostalgia for one's homeland and a sense of the impossibility of return lay behind all the identity-based turmoil. It was further fed by European racism, which had begun to target Muslims more and more. "The Muslims and Arabs seem to have become the Jews of Europe now. Strange, how people are put together. Capitalist societies seem to need anti-Semitism to release their inner complexes. The Arabs and Muslims are becoming the Jews of Europe and the Palestinians have become the Jews of the Jews. It's bewildering."

Sheikh Radwan said he wasn't surprised by these developments. "Verily, the Europeans have ceased not to be crusaders in their heart of hearts and their hatred of Muslims will continue to grow as they weaken and collapse, God willing."

"What are you talking about, Mawlana? First of all, the Arabs called them Franks, not crusaders, and besides what crusaders are you talking about? The crusaders were over long ago and modern colonialism has nothing to do with crusader times. Have you forgotten Lenin's maxim that 'imperialism is the highest stage of capitalism'?"

"Lenin too was a crusader."

"What?! It looks like we have nothing left to talk about, Sheikh Radwan."

"Talk? We can talk as much as you want! The hegemony of this imported culture is, however, no longer viable. The age of 'sinalcolised' culture is at an end, my dear Brother Sinalcol."

Karim swallowed the slight and there was silence.

"Why do you not eat? In a minute they will bring the kenafeh with clotted cream and other comestibles," said the sheikh.

Karim looked at his watch and saw the hands were pointing to a quarter to two. He told Radwan he was in a hurry because he had an appointment with some friends at the port and thanked him for the meeting.

The plates of pastries arrived. Karim ate kenafeh with clotted cream, which had been his favourite when he'd been in Tripoli with Danny. Then he drank from the glass of water in front of him, and said he had to leave.

"When willst thou send me the papers?" asked Radwan.

Karim said he was sorry, they'd been placed in his safe keeping. "You're the one who brought the papers to my flat in Beirut and I'm sure you remember Khaled's message that they were only ever to be given to one person – Hayat."

The sheikh said Hayat was now in the keeping of God, Great and Glorious, and that he himself had issued a ruling that Karim was released from his promise to Khaled. So, as the promise was no longer valid, Karim could give him the papers because he, Radwan, was now the person closest to the martyr.

Karim was at a loss as to how to reply. He felt he ought to hand over the papers to no-one, especially not to Radwan. He was sure Radwan would omit sections and insert words, which was what Khaled and Radwan had done previously with the text that they'd turned into their blue book.

"Do you still use the blue book?" Karim asked.

The sheikh replied in decisive tones. The book was no longer of any value since its secularist ideas were no longer valid and their Islamic approach could not be grafted onto it. "We derive our culture now from the works of the religious jurists, and above all those of Ibn Taimiya."

Karim got up to leave but the sheikh grasped him by the arm, forcing him to sit again.

The sheikh said his request for the papers reflected the wishes of Khaled's grandmother. "Imm Yahya has expressed a desire for the papers and I am of the view that that is her right as the sole legal heir to both martyrs. She wishes me to publish them so that the memory of the two men be not consigned to oblivion."

Karim stood up, twisting his lower lip, as though not accepting what had been said.

"Where are you rushing off to? What, you don't want to see Sinalcol?" said the sheikh.

"As far as I am aware Sinalcol is dead," said Karim.

"True, but who says we can't see the dead?" responded Radwan. "Nothing could be easier, sweetie pie, than to arrange for you to meet your namesake there in Hell. Do not imagine you can refuse me the papers. If I want them, I'll damn well get them, whether thou likest it or not."

Sheikh Radwan raised his finger threateningly and Karim, who sensed danger, began to prevaricate. He sat down again and told Radwan that he ought not to use threatening language with him. "You threaten to kill me when you know that 'whoso slays a soul . . . shall be as though he had slain mankind altogether'?"

"God be praised, you have committed the Noble Koran to memory!" said Sheikh Radwan.

"If it's Imm Yahya who's asking for them, I'm willing to give her the papers but I have to hear the words from her, not because I don't believe you, God forbid, but because they are a sacred trust and I care about these things, if you understand what I mean."

The meeting ended with Karim in a fix. Sheikh Radwan said that that was Karim's right and he'd send a car to the Silver Shore at five-thirty so they could visit Imm Yahya together at her house in Qubbeh, and there Karim could hear her request with his own ears.

Karim arrived at the restaurant at three to find a fish banquet spread out and waiting for him, at its centre a sea bream grilled in the Tripoli style which they call "hot fish". Ahmad got up to welcome him saying they'd forgotten all about him because he was late and he should excuse them for having started eating.

And at the restaurant Karim heard the strangest of stories.

At the start he was sullen and incapable of responding to the jolly atmosphere imposed by Ahmad's father, with his overbearing presence, his way of drinking arak straight without water, and his theory of how water spoiled the arak's purity. Abd el-Malek Dakiz reminded him of his own father in his movements, his domination of the table, and his theories about food. He was a man of seventy-five with snow-white hair unblemished by a single strand of black. His bearing was erect with no sign of a stoop, he had a smile that never left his thin lips, a lean brown face, and a long nose. Abu Ahmad's hands and the black liver spots that dotted them were everywhere at the table, whether pouring arak or distributing morsels to those seated around. The dilemma of having to meet Yahya's mother at five-thirty prevented Karim from joining in, but Muna deftly seized the thread of the elderly man's conversation to tell him Dr Karim had written a study on the crusaders and was interested in tracing the destinies of their descendants in Lebanon. "Tell us, Uncle, about your family's crusader roots."

"Our family, Muna? It's your family too!" he responded.

"How come? Are you a Christian, Abu Ahmad?" asked Karim.

"I'm a Muslim, and praise be to God," he replied. Then he pointed to the minaret of the mosque that could be seen through the restaurant's rain-spotted window. "That's the Dakiz mosque. When my father returned from the pilgrimage, he sold a lot of the family's property to build this mosque, and you ask me if we're Christians!"

"Tell us the story of the French passport," said Muna.

The man sat up straight, took a draught from his glass, and said he hated the French colonialist mentality. "Can you imagine, the French consul's only concern was whether I was Francophone? I told him, 'I know French but *je suis arabophone*,' and I pronounced the *a* with a guttural consonant before it the way we say it. He didn't like that, though. Maybe he believed in the myth of bilingualism that some Jesuit came up with but it doesn't matter. What matters, Dr Karim, is that we are originally from the house of De Guise – we say Dakiz in Arabic to make things easier – and I have correspondence with members of our family in France, particularly Count Bernard de Guise, who wrote to me that it would be an honour for them to become acquainted with their cousins of the line of the knights who had occupied the East and liberated Jerusalem, but what can one say?"

Abd el-Malek Dakiz spoke of how, at the beginning of the war and at the insistence of Muna, whose only dream was to emigrate, he'd gone to the French consulate in Tripoli, where he'd met the consul, Monsieur Gérard, told him about his family origins, and sought to reclaim his French nationality. The French consul had looked at him as though he didn't believe him, so Abd el-Malek Dakiz had shown him his correspondence with the French side of the family, stressing the fact that his was the sole family with scientifically proven Crusader-Frankish roots, though the Bardawil family might perhaps share that status since the Arabic historical sources did refer to King Baudouin as Bardawil.

The French consul had thought he was in the presence of a madman.

However, faced with Abd el-Malek's insistence on his right to French nationality, he said the matter was not in his hands and the decision had to come from the French foreign ministry; he gave the crusader a nationality claim form to fill.

"It was murder. Endless forms to fill," said Abd el-Malek, "and documents and financial instruments and birth certificates for me and my father and my mother and my grandfather and my grandmother. The important thing, my dear sir, and so as not to bore you is we went back to the consulate and submitted them all to the consul. This time, though, I didn't like the way he behaved. He treated me as though I were a madman who'd escaped from the lunatic asylum. It made no difference to me. The truth was clear as daylight and I felt sure that French nationality was in my pocket."

He said he'd waited three long months before getting back in touch and they'd given him an appointment for three weeks from then.

"He asked me why I wanted French nationality. I answered, 'because of the war.' He said he sympathised with my motives but was sorry to inform me that my application had been rejected."

"Why?"

"At that point, gentlemen, the man said something no mind can fathom or logic accept. He said my family might have Frankish origins but that the Franks weren't French: they were *des francs pas des français*. Heavens above, what kind of rubbish is that? He said the French state hadn't existed at the time of the crusades, which meant that the crusaders were Franks and not French. I roared with laughter and asked him if he could fix me up with a crusader passport."

When Abd el-Malek heard the justification offered by the French consul, first he laughed as though listening to a joke, then he grew furious. He said if that was how things were, why had the French General Gouraud stood in front of the tomb of Saladin in the Umayad mosque in Damascus and told the Arab leader, "Saladin, we're back!"

"No, no," said the consul, "that is a widespread historical misunderstanding. General Gouraud had nothing to do with the matter. The founder of the State of Greater Lebanon had no interest in the past. Those were the words of General Goybet, commander of the Syrian campaign and Gouraud's deputy. You're right, there was no call for such words, but you know the warrior mentality and the *folie de grandeur* to which they're prone."

"And why did General Allenby say 'Today the crusades have ended' when the British occupied Jerusalem on 9 December, 1918?"

"It seems you know your history well, Monsieur De Guise," said the consul.

Dakiz had left the French consulate cursing the hour that Muna had got him involved in the absurd project. "Damnation! The French and the English can claim they're crusaders whenever it suits them but the original crusaders have to shut up and die in the civil war."

Abd el-Malek said he'd been so angry he'd phoned his only son Ahmad and asked him to divorce his wife because she was "a discord in the land".

"Me, a discord in the land, Uncle?" asked Muna, laughing.

"God damn passports and the day they were invented! Now you, your husband, and your children are going to get Canadian passports when Canada wasn't even on the map at the time of the crusades."

Karim felt as though he had been transported to an unreal world. The man truly believed he was descended from the crusaders even though all his forefathers were Tripolitanians, he was a Sunni Muslim, and his family had built a mosque in the city! What caught his attention was the pleasure Ahmad took in what his father was saying. The whole family were either telling the truth or believed that they were. Abu Ahmad claimed he still spoke the language of his crusader ancestors and was sorry his son had refused to learn it and that the only person who could speak it now was his father's uncle's daughter, who was eighty-seven years old and lived alone in her house opposite the mosque.

When Karim heard the story of the crusader language, he too was sucked in and found himself inside the imaginary world fashioned by Abu Ahmad's words, for it had never before entered his mind that the crusaders spoke a language all their own, different from those of the countries from which they came.

He asked about the language and got an answer from Muna that obviated the question. "It's called *lingua franca*, Uncle, not 'the language of the crusaders', and it wasn't a language, it was a mixture of numerous dialects, including Arabic."

"All languages are mixtures," said Ahmad.

"Fine, so why did you become Muslims?" asked Karim.

"The story of our forefathers is a truly strange one," said Abd el-Malek. "Everyone around them were Muslims. You've heard of the terrible massacre committed by the Mamluke Baybars when he occupied the Fragrant City?"

"I have," said Karim, "but I know too about the savage massacre committed by the crusaders when they occupied the city."

"History is nothing but massacres," said Abu Ahmad, "but that's not the point. Our forefathers became Muslims because they had no other option. If you come to the house with me I'll show you the family tree and how we started mixing with Muslims a long time ago and intermarried with them long before the Mamluke conquest of the city. I deduce that our forefathers became Muslims in order to fit in with their environment. Not me, though. I'm a Muslim by conviction. I studied philosophy at the university and worked as a philosophy teacher at the Mar Elias School and I've studied the matter in depth and thought about becoming a Christian again like my forefathers, especially as I love the Byzantine hymns. When you listen to Dimitri Coutya chanting you'd think it was a voice to open the Gates of Heaven. But I discovered that Muhammad was the true prophet."

The man then expounded his theory on religions. He said Muhammad was the only prophet in the three divinely revealed religions who had died a member of his own religion because he had personally supervised it. Moses wasn't a Jew and Jesus wasn't a Christian because the Jewish and Christian religions took shape long after them and it wasn't certain they would recognise themselves in them. Only Muhammad had died a Muslim and in accordance with the religion that was the vehicle of his message. In this way God had rendered Islam superior to all other religions. This was why Abu Ahmad Dakiz had chosen Islam as a religion; however, he had also adopted the theory of the Sufi Ibn Arabi and become a Muslim "following in the path of Jesus, son of Mary".

The clock said five. Ahmad looked at his wife and said, "We have to go."

"Stay the night at my place," said Abu Ahmad.

"I wish we could," said Ahmad, "but things aren't looking good. The atmosphere in the country's bad and everyone's afraid the fighting will start up again."

Karim asked if he'd be able to find a taxi at seven or seven-thirty. He estimated that the meeting with Imm Yahya would take a while and so he'd make use of his visit to her to go in Radwan's car and visit Khaled's grave.

Ahmad said he doubted he would be able to, given that the clouds of war were gathering.

"I'll work it out," said Karim.

"Why? Aren't you going back with us?" asked Muna.

He told them his friend would be sending him a car at five-thirty so that they could go together and visit the mother of one of their friends who had died.

"We'll wait for you at Uncle Abd el-Malek's," said Muna.

Karim noticed Ahmad's doubtful glances and said they didn't have to wait because he could manage on his own.

"At my place. You'll sleep at my place," said Abu Ahmad. "My house is opposite the mosque. In any case, you'll find me there, at the Ash'ash café, smoking a narghile and waiting for you."

"It's an idea," said Ahmad, apologising that they had to go back because the Philippine maid couldn't stay with the children after seven.

"Why not?" said Karim, thinking that to stay the night at Abu Ahmad's would give him more time to think of a way of getting around Sheikh Radwan's request.

There followed a strange Tripolitanian night during which Karim discovered the relationship between the dissolution of memory and the disintegration of the present: two women, an elderly man who had found a second youth in the past, and a city dominated by a concrete arch whose significance and the reason for whose construction no-one could recall.

Karim got into the car sent for him by Sheikh Radwan at five-thirty.

A young man in jeans and a black shirt, his eyes covered by thick sunglasses, arrived and made a sign to Karim from a distance. The doctor rose, said goodbye to his hosts, and confirmed to Abu Ahmad that he'd meet him at the Ash'ash café.

The black Mercedes reached the Exhibition district. The young man looked back and said apologetically, "One moment. I just have to go up and get Mawlana." Karim deduced that "Mawlana" had moved from Qubbeh to live in the Exhibition neighbourhood, a new residential district built opposite the land that had been set aside for the Tripoli International Exhibition grounds. At its centre stood a concrete arch built by the Brazilian architect Oscar Niemeyer to provide the city – dominated by the crusader castle of Saint-Gilles – with a modern symbol to clash with its old one.

Sheikh Radwan sat next to the driver and the car set off enveloped in the silence of the two men, who had nothing more to say to one another. The journey from Exhibition to Qubbeh took about forty minutes because of the traffic. Karim would think of it later as "the thirsty journey". His mouth felt dry and his thirst was so desperate that he asked the driver to stop so he could buy a bottle of mineral water. But it seemed the driver didn't hear him, or the sheikh's security requirements prevented him.

Each of the protagonists in the story of what would happen at Imm Yahya's house was supposed to know the part he had to play. The sheikh would clear his throat before knocking on the door. Imm Yayha, swathed in black, would open the door to find before her Karim, bent over to kiss her hand, his eyes flooded with tears. The woman would pull her hand away with an exclamation of "I seek refuge with God!". Sheikh Radwan would say Karim was an old friend who had kept the late Yahya's papers safe and in trust, for which he was to be thanked. The woman would nod her head and say, "May God be pleased with you! You are like my sons." And in the end Karim would say that the papers would be sent to Sheikh Radwan in accordance with Imm Yahya's request. Probably Imm Yahya would make them tea and offer them her famous almond-and-sugar flaky pastry rounds, which were one of the notable reasons for the success of the bakery she ran.

In the event, an unexpected element would enter the script, overturn the set piece, and mess up the precisely calibrated formula that Sheikh Radwan had drawn up for this meeting, which he had planned to be very short "because the woman is not well, is very old, passes all her time in prayer, and does not receive visitors".

They got out of the car into the crowded street, the sheikh looking right and left and greeting people, his escort sticking close by him. They found themselves in front of a flat located on the ground floor of an old four-storey building. The young man hung back, the sheikh gestured to Karim to go ahead, and they stood in front of the door. The sheikh cleared his throat and then knocked, saying in a loud voice, "Open the door, Imm Yahya. It's Sheikh Radwan."

No-one opened the door. Karim heard what might have been foot-steps. "The woman's got very old," said the sheikh, "and she doesn't hear well." He knocked again and when no-one opened he pushed on the door using his shoulder and, saying "With your permission!", entered, signalling to Karim to follow. Immediately, however, he recoiled, knocking into Karim.

Imm Yahya was standing behind the door, her back bent with the years of her life, her head covered with a white headscarf, like a ghost swaying in the darkness.

"Why don't you turn on the light?" said Radwan, moving restlessly where he stood because the woman was blocking the entrance.

"I'm blind, son," she said in a low quavering voice, "and anyway the electricity's always being cut off in this town. They steal everything here, son. We're just a bunch of paupers."

"I'm Sheikh Radwan, Hajja, and I have Dr Karim, a friend of the late Khaled, with me."

"Who's Khaled?" she asked.

"Your grandson Khaled, Imm Yahya, and I'm Radwan."

"Who?"

"I'm the sheikh. I came to see you this afternoon and we talked about Yahya's papers."

"Honestly, son, I'm a poor woman and I don't have anything to give you. Go away, and may God find you others to give."

Radwan looked at Karim and said she thought they were beggars. "Dear God, help us out here!"

"Come on! Have you forgotten, Hajja?"

She said she didn't know a Sheikh Radwan or any other sheikhs. A slight smile appeared on her lips before she closed the door, and the two men heard the sound of the key turning in the lock.

"I seek refuge with God from lapidated Satan! God's curse on women and their wiles! I came and saw her at three o'clock this afternoon and she was sharper than you or me and told me she'd be waiting for me at home at six this evening. I seek refuge with God! People can really make one sick! She understands, then she fades out and can't even remember her children, so how's she supposed to remember me or you? Let's go," said Sheikh Radwan. "But as we agreed, Doctor."

"What did we agree?" asked Karim.

"We agreed about the papers. When are you going to give them to us?"

"That's not what we agreed. We agreed I'd give them to you based on Imm Yahya's request and you saw what happened," said Karim.

Sheikh Radwan put his hand on Karim's shoulder. "Don't play with me, Sinalcol. I'm not joking."

"And I'm not joking either," replied Karim, though when he saw Sheikh Radwan's face turn red with anger he started talking again, saying, "Just give the order, Mawlana, but the fact is I don't know where the papers are. I'll have to look for them. Don't worry, though, I believe you, and the papers will get to you."

"When?"

"That I don't know."

"You have to know."

"Let's say next Friday. I'll come to Tripoli, same day next week. We can meet at Hallab's at noon and then go together and visit Khaled's grave."

"You're a gentleman, Doctor. God bless you."

Karim turned to leave but Sheikh Radwan stopped him and told him that his companion would take him to el-Tall Square where he'd find the taxis for Beirut. Karim explained that he would be spending the night in Tripoli at a friend's house.

"If you're sleeping the night in Tripoli you must stay with me, and most welcome."

Karim explained he'd promised Abd el-Malek Dakiz that he'd spend the night at his place and the man was waiting for him in the café at the port.

The sheikh suggested he take him there in his car and on the way warned him against Abu Ahmad. "He's a madman. I swear if it hadn't been for me the boys would have killed him. During the war he used to climb up on the morning of the Eid to the Castle of Saint-Gilles, wash down the tombs of the crusaders and beg mercy on their souls. 'These are our ancestors,' he'd say. A hundred times I told him, 'They were polytheists and it won't do,' and he'd answer me that they weren't infidels, they were our Christian brethren and he was doing his duty towards the souls of his ancestors."

Karim tried to explain that Abu Ahmad's view might well be correct because the name of the Dakiz family did indicate it might be of crusader origin and the man was just following his conscience. "But they are infidels," said Radwan, going on to say he was sorry if his words upset Karim as one their Christian brethren. "It's Khaled's fault. When we took over the castle it was my opinion that we should demolish the tombs but Khaled refused. He said we couldn't act aggressively towards the graves of People of the Book. God rest your soul, Khaled, what a noble spirit you were! Now, though, there aren't any more tombs, of course. I don't know who removed them. You know there are none of us left in the castle. Our Syrian brothers are sitting up there."

Sheikh Radwan recounted that a fit of insane fury had overcome Abd el-Malek when he saw what had happened to the tombs. He'd cursed Islam and the Muslims in the courtyard of the Dakiz mosque "and if I hadn't intervened, the boys would have beaten him to death with their shoes."

The sheikh said he was free to phone him at any hour of the night if he felt in any way upset with Abu Ahmad: he'd be standing by to send him his car whenever he wished and to save him from the predicament he'd got himself into.

*

Sheikh Radwan was right: the night with Dakiz turned out to be a predicament and more, but there was no reason for fear. The elderly man was peaceable and kind. All one had to do was listen endlessly to the same stories and put up with his theories of the ins and outs of religion, the meaning of life, and the meaninglessness of history.

Abd el-Malek Dakiz was a philosopher – that was how the man introduced himself. He'd completed a huge work in three parts on the crusades but hadn't been able to find a publisher. People told him Amin Maalouf had beaten him to it with his story of those wars and that after his book *The Crusades through Arab Eyes* no-one was going to be interested in Abd el-Malek's work. Abd el-Malek was convinced there was a conspiracy to prevent him publishing his book. When he asked his son Ahmad to get him an appointment with Rafiq Hariri so he could try to get a subsidy to help him publish it, his son had wormed his way out of it using various excuses. "The worst thing is feeling that your own son is embarrassed by you," said Abu Ahmad as he explained to Karim that his book was different from all the others because it dealt with history only as a point of entry to a discussion of life; he'd discovered from studying the history of his family that there was a mismatch between history and life. Daily life was full of noble qualities but history was frivolous, repetitious, bloody, and mad.

Karim had arrived at the Ash'ash café to find the elderly man sitting there waiting for him, smoking a narghile. It had occurred to Karim that his prevarications with Sheikh Radwan had been a mistake. He would have done better to agree to what he wanted from the start and avoid the visit to Imm Yahya and the pain that he'd felt when he saw the woman in such a state. Karim felt his every limb was hurting and found the torment of memory unendurable. Why was he going to spend the night here in the home of this madman whom he didn't know? And could his soul find room for yet more stories?

At the same time, but from a different perspective, he felt, with a vehemence he found difficult to explain, that he should refuse to give the papers to Sheikh Radwan. The papers were just like Jamal's. They had become his personal memory and no longer had any general significance, so why should he let Sheikh Radwan distort them? Jamal's papers were still with him. True, because of the chaos that had overwhelmed Fatah following Abu Jihad's assassination, no-one had asked him for them. But what if someone were to ask him for them today so they could be published, and supposing they were modified and their contents played around with and her picture put on the cover with her hair – which, the last time he'd seen it, in her posters, had been flying in the wind – hidden from sight by an Islamic headscarf and a frown in place of her laughing eyes, would he then hand over her papers?

What should he do with the papers? Should he leave them to turn yellow and disintegrate in the drawer? Did the Islamists, now the rising power, not have as much right to take control of their past as the Leftists had had in their day when they'd made a turbaned sheikh and warrior such as Izz el-Din Qassam an icon of the class struggle?

Though he had stolen nothing, Karim felt as frightened as a thief. True, Khaled had placed his trust in one who didn't deserve it, but that was Khaled's fault not Karim's and he wasn't about to give the papers to Radwan now, whatever the cost, even if they killed him. He would give them nothing. He would preserve them and let them disintegrate and disappear in silence into the frivolousness and meaninglessness of history of which Ahmad's father had spoken.

Karim came to his decision as he sat in the café drinking lemonade and smoking a narghile next to the elderly man, who kept up an unstoppable flow of stories, none of which Karim heard.

He decided he'd pretend he hadn't been able to find the papers. He'd phone Sheikh Radwan on Thursday morning and postpone the appointment because he hadn't been able to locate them – and then let whatever happened happen.

The decision was made.

Karim became aware that Abd el-Malek Dakiz was shaking him by the shoulder as though waking him from a coma and saying Gloria was waiting for them.

"Who's Gloria?" asked Karim.

"I've been telling you about her for the past hour. What? Were you asleep? She's the daughter of my father's paternal uncle who knows the crusader language. We'll go and see her for quarter of an hour and then we can go to my place. I've ordered a little grilled meat to go with the drink."

"I'm stuffed. I couldn't eat more."

"Up with you, man. 'The key to the belly is a morsel of food', as they say. The woman is waiting for us."

Karim had never imagined that his night in Tripoli would be spent between two women, the first senile, or pretending to be so to escape Sheikh Radwan and his demands, the second insane and believing herself to be the last guardian of a language that had never existed.

"I'm tired, Uncle. Let's put Gloria off till tomorrow."

Abd el-Malek explained that the woman was waiting for them, had phoned the café a few minutes before to say the tea was hot, and that he'd promised.

Karim rose sluggishly and went to the flat, which exuded the smell of all closed flats. The woman never opened the windows or the thick green curtains because she hated the sun. She told Karim her body had never been able to stand the sun and that even though all her life she'd worn long dresses closed at the neck with sleeves that covered her arms, the sun still burned her and left red spots on her skin, "and now the allergy has spread to my eyes. I can't see at all in the daylight and I use only night lights in the flat."

Abd el-Malek explained to her that his guest was a specialist in the crusader period and was interested in finding out about the language of the crusaders.

Gloria, who attached much importance to the title "Mademoiselle", poured the tea, saying her memory wasn't of much use to her now. She looked at Abu Ahmad and said he was responsible for the loss of the language because he'd promised her lots of times he'd come and record the words she knew and publish them as a special appendix to his book on the crusaders. "You, Abu Ahmad, are afflicted with the family disease, whose name is sloth!"

Abu Ahmad looked at her and said, "*Cando mi intrate fi beit abusch, falso.*"

Mademoiselle Gloria answered him, laughing, "*I barra fuor casa mio.*"

Then he said, "*Gramerze cater ala cairech.*"

"Did you understand what we were saying?" asked Abu Ahmad.

"I understood a few words. It sounds like Latin with Spanish and Italian," said Karim.

"And Arabic. The most important part is the Arabic. This is the language of our ancestors. I know a few words but Gloria speaks it like a songbird. What a waste of the woman! She has a talent for languages. I have to get back to my work on the book because without me she's *mamamouchi.* I swear, my boy, I don't know how to thank you. You've made me feel alive again with your interest in culture. You should have been my son instead of Ahmad. Ahmad doesn't have time for anything. All he wants to do is emigrate so he can make money."

At his flat Abu Ahmad prepared two glasses of local arak, saying it was much better than the commercial arak they'd drunk at the restaurant. "This is triple-distilled home-made arak."

Karim did not eat any of the food – he could feel a slight pain in his stomach – but he couldn't not join Abu Ahmad in drinking the arak because he didn't want to upset him.

Silence reigned, as though the elderly man had emptied his quiver with the effort he'd expended in trying to speak a strange language. Karim guessed it wasn't a proper language but the remnants of spoken dialects that had formed a primitive means of communication among the hordes of Frankish warriors arriving from various parts of the world on the one hand, and the original Arab inhabitants of the land on the other.

To fill the silence Karim asked Abu Ahmad whether what Radwan had told him about his visiting the tombs at the Castle of Saint-Gilles, cleaning them, and placing flowers on them was true.

"It's both true and untrue," answered Abu Ahmad. He recounted that it had started with curiosity. He'd visited the tombs looking for the names of the slain and to confirm the hypothesis that his was a real crusader family. But he hadn't found what he was looking for: the names were almost completely erased and the tombs themselves had been nearly effaced. After three days of searching Abu Ahmad had seen what seemed to him to be something like letters forming the name of his family. He said he couldn't be sure but he "had his suspicions" and was very excited. On the morning of Eid el-Fitr, after he'd visited the tombs of his grandfather, father, and mother, he'd climbed up to the castle. "I didn't wash down all the tombs, just the tomb of my grandsire, and I asked the Lord of the Worlds for mercy on his soul and forgiveness for his sins and those of his descendants."

"But they're Christians, Abu Ahmad, and Islamic law doesn't allow that!" said Ahmad, borrowing Radwan's logic.

"So what if they're Christians? I'm a Christian too."

"You're a Christian? A little while ago you told me you were a Muslim, not to mention that Christians believe Christ is the son of God."

"And so do I."

"What?!"

"Jesus is from God's spirit. It says so in the Koran."

"But Christians say he was crucified, while you Muslims say 'they did not slay him, neither crucified him, only a likeness of that was shown to them'."

"Correct."

"What's correct? You've lost me."

"'A likeness of that was shown to them', meaning they did mean to crucify him and the one they actually crucified looked so like him that his mother, Our Lady Mary, thought the crucified man was her son. Do you really think there's a mother in the world who wouldn't know her son? Do you get it now?"

"I get it and I don't get it," said Karim. "Anyway, what difference does it make to know if one's forebears were crusaders or Arabs or Turkmen? In the end they're all the same."

"Right!" said Abu Ahmad. "But for one to be a descendant of the crusader hordes who occupied this land for two hundred years, and who left behind them only a few castles and a few descendants, most of whom have become Muslims – now that's a lesson to learn from. I, my boy, am the last witness. The meaninglessness of history is engraved on my forehead. Everyone should read my forehead to understand what a criminal history is, and how trivial."

With this, Abu Ahmad raised his glass and started declaiming something that sounded like poetry:

O la Zerbitana retica!
il parlar ch'ella mi dicia!
Per tutto lo mondo fendoto
e barra fuor casa mia.
O i Zerbitana retica
come ti volare parlare?
se per li capelli prendoto
come ti voler conciare!
cadalzi e pugne moscoto
quanti to voler donare!
e cosi voler conciare
tutte le votre ginoie.

"What's that?" asked Karim.

"*Tareez! Tareez!*" responded Abu Ahmad. "*Tareez* means 'Silence!'. It's poetry. Don't ask me what the poem means because I don't know. Olga knows. My father, God rest his soul, used to declaim it when he was drinking and made me learn the whole thing by heart."

Abu Ahmad said he usually got up early and wanted to take Karim on a morning tour of the Castle of Saint-Gilles "so you can smell your country's history".

Karim's sleep was close to sleeplessness – a restless night in which dreams intersected with the black visions of insomnia. The pain in his stomach was worse but he didn't get out of bed to make a cup of "white coffee", as Abu Ahmad had suggested to him before going to his room – Karim had refused for fear of finding himself caught up once more in a web of words. He dreamed of the orange-blossom essence mixed with hot water that the Lebanese call "white coffee" and whose heart-breaking smell they love to inhale. He spent what was left of the night stretched out on this bed of drowsiness and sleeplessness, listening throughout to Abu Ahmad's footsteps thumping through his head.

The image of Imm Yahya, covered in darkness, blended with the ghostly lights that had made shadows on Gloria's face as she received them at her flat. Two women living in darkness, the first blind, the second afraid of light, together embodying the memory of oblivion that time had built. Two women occupied his night. He dreamed as though awake and lay awake as though dreaming.

The pain in his stomach mixed with the pain in his soul and Hayat was there. He saw her, her head covered with a headscarf, carrying her daughter and standing at his door while the phantom of death formed haloes above her. And he saw her unveiled, love spreading out around her, her long black hair flying in the wind. He saw Hayat's hair covering Jamal's eyes while Hend tugged at his hand to make him go with her.

He would open his eyes and hear the man's footfalls, then close them again and see two small sharp eyes staring into Khaled's face – eyes with something yellow in their whites that cut through the darkness of death. He saw death coming out of the small eyes like a pale thread of vanishing light and heard shooting and saw Khaled shaken by the convulsing of the soul as it left his lacerated body.

Karim had no idea what had been dream and what apparition; he woke at six in the morning to the smell of coffee spreading through his room. He opened his eyes, felt skewers of light piercing his drowsiness and saw Abu Ahmad standing in front of him holding a coffee pot.

He closed his eyes again but Abu Ahmad's voice called him to get up because it was already six and they had to go to the castle before he set off for Beirut.

He had begun to get out of bed when he found Abu Ahmad sitting on the edge of it, pouring two cups of coffee, and saying, "There's nothing nicer than to drink your coffee in bed in the morning!"

Karim said he'd visited the castle many times before and there was no need to climb up again this morning as he had to go back to Beirut; but Abu Ahmad insisted. "It won't take more than two hours. I'll show you the tombs and then we can go down together to the Mahatra quarter and I'll show you Mamluke Tripoli, an architectural gem, though people call it Old Tripoli, which is wrong. Old Tripoli is the port – that was the city of the Banu Ammar and the crusader city – and then we can have beans for breakfast at Akar's and I'll take you to el-Tall."

"Please, don't talk to me about food!" said Karim rubbing his stomach, which still hurt.

Abu Ahmad was as good as his word. The visit to the Castle of Saint-Gilles took no more than two hours. They'd climbed up to it by 7 a.m. and at 9.15 were shaking hands in farewell at el-Tall in front of the long-distance taxis to Beirut. The man talked the whole time; even when they were eating their breakfast beans, Abu Ahmad found a way to talk and chew simultaneously. His words were filled with the clangour of history. He spoke of the genius of Raymond de Saint-Gilles who had built the castle to prepare the way for the taking of the city. In this he was unique in his day because castles were usually built for defence; this, however, had been built for attack. He spoke of the effaced graves and the prisons that the Ottomans had built. He pointed out the church, which had been converted in Mamluke times into a mosque. He knew the castle inch by inch, as though he'd been born there, and he knew how the crusaders had built the only residential quarter that surrounded it. He said Tripoli had been the port and the soldiers in the castle had built the Mahatra quarter to serve their needs. "Don't believe anyone who says they're of crusader origin and lives here. They were Arab and Turkmen servants and if they have crusader blood it's because of *droit du seigneur*. The Dakiz clan is the only crusader family in Tripoli because after the massacre we fled into the surrounding fields and lived in Bahsas before returning to the port. We refused to live in the Mamluke city, which was just an extension of the servants' quarter."

He said the restoration had been carried out in part by the Germans, in Khan el-Khayatin and Souq el-Haraj, then the Lebanese architect Jad Thabet had completed it in Souq el-Bazarkhan, making the Mamluke city once more a gem. But the Tripolitanians didn't love their city. He said he could think of nothing more beautiful than the mosque of Sayed Abd el-Wahed, built by Abd el-Wahed el-Maknasi in 1305, which had been a Frankish caravanserai before the latter had converted it into a mosque; or the Ajamiyeh madrasa, founded in 1365. "A wonderful city," said Abu Ahmad. "All its quarters, not just Mahatra, bear witness to the beauty and magic of Mamluke architecture, especially the Great Mosque of Umar."

They sat in the café in Souq el-Haraj, where they had breakfast, then made their way through the Old City, where the white restored walls were already starting to peel, until they reached the Mosque of Tinal and the Ramal cemetery. They entered the cemetery and Abu Ahmad went over to one of the tombs. He fetched water and washed it while Karim searched for but failed to find Khaled's grave.

"Thank you, Abu Ahmad, for this lovely tour," said Karim as they said goodbye.

"*Pissonyu!*" said Abu Ahmad.

Karim was wondering how to respond to this insult when Abu Ahmad quickly allayed his confusion. "That's *la cerise sur le gâteau*, as the French say. I've been keeping this expression from the crusader language for the end. It's really '*pas un mot*'. Now you'll never forget our language."

As Karim was getting into the taxi he felt a hand touch his shoulder. He turned to find Sheikh Radwan's companion, who said he'd just happened to be passing, and asked if Karim needed anything.

"No thanks," said Karim, "and give my greetings to Sheikh Radwan."

"We'll be waiting for you on Friday, God willing," the young man said as he left.

Karim got into the front seat next to the driver. His eyes were heavy with sleep and he'd begun to surrender to its dominion when he started, as though stung. He was overcome by the strange idea that the sheikh's companion was following him, that he'd fallen into the trap.

Every time he caught sight of a black car travelling behind the taxi he'd slide lower in his seat as though trying to hide.

This hellish thought accompanied Karim throughout the last week of his Beirut sojourn; throughout, he found himself prisoner to a mysterious fear, always turning right and left, looking, panic-stricken, behind him, then continuing on his way as fast as he could.

The last week Karim spent in Beirut was a kind of maelstrom. He'd returned from Tripoli on 30 December, 1989, in a state of exhaustion, to find that his brother had invited him to spend New Year's Eve with him at his flat. Karim got out of it by saying he was invited to a party at the home of one of his old university friends.

He was lying and regretted having to spend the night alone in his flat. He'd tried to phone his wife in Montpellier, as he had done on Christmas Eve, but the lines were impossible. The ghosts of Tripoli, which had brought his old fears back, haunted him. He had to find a way out of his predicament with Sheikh Radwan. At the same time, he had to take a final decision regarding his family. He had to persuade Bernadette of the viability of the hospital project and he had to find a way to be absent from his job in France for six months a year.

On the morning of Monday, 1 January, 1990, to the intermittent sound of shells whistling through the city's skies, his brother and his wife came bearing the traditional New Year's breakfast of kenafeh-with-cheese and manaqish with thyme. It had been the only religious festival that Nasri had celebrated. His celebration had been limited to an early morning breakfast consisting entirely of kenafeh-with-cheese so that the year would be as white as the Akkawi cheese that oozed from beneath the pale golden kenafeh.

Nasim reported that the boys preferred to celebrate the New Year's breakfast with their grandmother Salma and so hadn't come. He said the situation was deteriorating fast, he felt the winds of war had begun to blow once more. He gave a protracted explanation of the situation in the Christian areas after the failure of parliament to elect a new president of the republic following the end of Amin Gemayel's term and the formation of a military government under the presidency of General Michel Aoun.

Nasim said the general was going to proclaim a war of liberation against Syria and the Ta'if Agreement sponsored by Saudi Arabia, America, and Syria, because the agreement had stripped the Maronite president of the republic of his prerogatives, and only the general could change the formula.

Nasim spoke of the general, who occupied a special position in

Lebanese politics, as though he was the heir to Bashir and said he expected him to restore confidence among the Christians.

"More war? That's insane!" said Karim. "No, please. I don't want to get stuck in Lebanon."

Nasim reassured his brother: he didn't think the war would be serious. "A little manoeuvring as usual and then they'll go back to the negotiating table."

Their breakfast was interrupted halfway through, however, by that mysterious phone call and Nasim left in a hurry, leaving his wife with his brother. From that moment, Karim's time in Beirut was in ferment.

Hend told him the truth about his father's death, leaving him with the overwhelming sense that a crime had been committed. At the same time, relations between Hend and her husband grew tense enough to drive her to leave home and live at her mother Salma's. The next day Karim tried to mediate to solve the disagreement. He phoned his brother, who told him he'd been coming to see him anyway to give him some news of extreme importance. Instead of talking about the need for a reconciliation between husband and wife, Karim heard from his brother of the catastrophe that had befallen the family. The Cypriot cargo ship *Acropol*, carrying a shipment of oil paid for by Nasim, had gone up in flames at the Port of Beirut's Dock Five as a result of being hit by a 155mm cannon shell, before unloading its cargo. Nasim said he'd found himself obliged to review his accounts as he'd taken on huge debts and placed all his hopes on the deal. He'd wagered his shirt on it and now found himself obliged to change all his plans.

He said he was obliged to sell the land for the hospital and asked Karim to sign a general power of attorney that would allow him to sell their father's flat and the pharmacy and a plot of land in Brumanna on which Nasri had hoped to build a summer house.

He said he'd booked him a ticket back to France but hadn't been able to find a seat before the morning of Thursday, 5 January. "I hope the airport will be open and the road safe."

He'd said this didn't mean he was abandoning the hospital project, "but we have to wait till things are clearer."

When Karim broached the subject of Hend and the need for a

reconciliation, his brother looked at him, eyes burning, tried to say something, but instead ground his teeth and said nothing.

"It won't do, brother. She's your wife and the mother of your children."

Nasim denied there was a problem. "She came back home this morning. I brought her and instead of apologising to me I was forced to apologise. Salma took her by the hand and she came home with us. I have this catastrophe to deal with and she's upset because in a moment of anger I called her names! If you could just see her now, making faces and scowling!"

Karim signed the papers, took his plane ticket, and suddenly felt as though a huge burden had been lifted off his shoulders. He felt lighter than he had done throughout the six months he'd spent in Beirut, as though he'd been saved from a predicament whose significance he was only now comprehending. He didn't ask his brother what would happen to his shares in the flat, the pharmacy, and the land because he realised Nasim would take them and there was nothing he could do about it.

His brother left. Karim felt returning to France was the only means he had to escape Radwan. He decided he wouldn't leave Yahya's papers at home in Beirut but take them with him to his new country, hide them, and never part with them.

He decided to visit Salma to say goodbye and thought of phoning Hend but felt the time for talking to her was over. What would he say and what would talking mean after everything that had happened?

Karim didn't leave home that day. He had only a little time left to pack his bags, and besides the smell of war had spread through the city, forcing him, like everyone else, to stay indoors.

At nine at night Karim heard a loud knock on the door of the flat. He opened the door hesitantly and saw by the flickering light of the candle the face of Ahmad Dakiz.

"You scared me, old man. What brings you out on such a night?"

Ahmad said he apologised for dropping in at that late hour of the evening without phoning. He'd brought the complete plans for the hospital because he'd be leaving the following morning with his wife and two children for Canada.

"They called us from the Canadian Embassy in Damascus. We leave tomorrow morning early, pick up the visa, and fly from there to Canada."

He said Nasim had asked him to give the plans to the doctor.

Ahmad opened a folder he was carrying and began explaining the plans he'd drawn up. "I think it's going to be the best hospital in the Middle East as far as architectural design goes. I wish you success and hope this round ends without mishap so you can start work."

"What's it got to do with me?" asked Karim. "You have to give them to Nasim."

"What do you mean, what's it got to do with you? You're the director of the hospital! Nasim doesn't understand these things. All he understands is how to siphon off the money. Your brother's smart. I have no idea how he managed to make all that money and become a millionaire."

Ahmad asked about his night in Tripoli and Karim said it had been excellent. "For the first time I saw how beautiful Tripoli is, and I learned a new language too."

"You mean you believed my father's ravings?"

"I believed and I didn't, it doesn't matter, but there's something I forgot to ask him about. I forgot to ask him if 'Sinalcol' comes from the *lingua franca* of the crusaders."

Ahmad laughed and said it was the name of a fizzy drink once made in Lebanon. Its name was Sinalco, not Sinalcol, and it had been manufactured by a German company; the company still owned a factory in Hasaka, in Syria's Jezira region.

"German! Damn, what a bind! I don't want a German name sticking to me," said Karim.

"Why? You don't like Germans?"

. . .

"And what have you got to do with Sinalco?"

"I am Sinalcol," said Karim, though when he saw the frown on Ahmad's face he corrected himself and said he was joking.

Ahmad left Karim's flat convinced by his wife's theory that the war had sent the Lebanese mad, and that they had to get out of Beirut or the children would end up paying the price for the collective hysteria.

Karim put the plans back in the brown binder, which he placed carefully in the drawer next to Hend's letters. He closed the drawer and shut his eyes, waiting for time, which had become sticky and slow, to pass before he found himself on the road to the plane that would carry him back to Montpellier.

14

On 4 January, 1990, Karim reached the age he had feared ever since learning the meaning of the words "fear" and "age". The man completed forty
years to the sound of his father's voice whispering that a man's body is his
coffin.

All Karim could remember of his dream on his last but one Beirut
night was his father's whispery voice muttering indistinguishable words,
as though the sounds of the city had vanished, to be transformed into
mysterious raspings that conveyed no meaning.

"A man's body is his coffin." From where had Nasri got that terrifying
metaphor? Why had his tongue wagged on before his sons with this talk
of forty being the beginning of the end, even as he boasted of his sexual
prowess to his comrades in the Qazzaz café in Gemmeizeh, saying he had
no fear of age?

"What remains cannot be more than what has passed," Nasri would
say, grinding his teeth, which he regarded as a true miracle – "Forty years
old, and not a rotten tooth in my head!" The pharmacist would repeat
into his young sons' ears the story of the slope down which one slips
when one reaches forty. "Suddenly, time starts to pass quickly and we
discover that what's behind us is more than what's ahead and we begin to
make a mess of everything."

Nasri stayed forty for many long years. He refused to quit the age and
with each new year his forty years became more firmly entrenched; the
boys grew older and he still insisted he hadn't passed forty, for he knew
that one additional day would mean the beginning of the slide into the
abyss.

Nasri turned grey and his forty years turned grey but then suddenly
he declined to sixty. He jumped twenty years at one go and no-one knew
the reason. Salma alone knew but refused to explain.

"Poor thing, he was still young. He died at sixty," said Salma.

Nasim looked at her in amazement and said his father was seventy-six when he died. "Where do you get this story about him being sixty, Mother-in-law?" – but then he exploded with laughter before saying, "He was stuck all his life at forty. He turned grey and grew old and we grew up but his age never changed. Then we stopped knowing how his relationship to his age had evolved. We got sick of him and his age."

"But the last time he came to see me and told me about his eyes, he said he was sixty-five," she said.

"And you believed him?" he asked her.

"I'm the only one in the world who used to believe, but the pity of it is that I didn't when he needed me to. That's life – a big trap we all fall into."

Forty was too far away for the two boys to grasp. When they were told someone was forty they would see a coffin suspended in the sky, and the image of their father, with his slight stoop, would trace itself over their eyes.

In Beirut Karim would discover that what had been far was now close. Instead of celebrating his birthday at home with his wife and daughters, he'd found himself stuck, hoping the next twenty-four hours would pass without incident so he could leave the following morning for Montpellier via Paris.

His fortieth birthday arrived without fanfare. He didn't feel he'd entered the age of fear or that turning point at which the course of his life would be determined. He didn't feel he had only to look back to discover that the "to come" he'd been looking forward to had become a part of the "once" that had gone, as Nasri used to say.

Karim decided not to look back because all he'd find would be a vacuum. His life had passed in a state of indecision. He'd gone to France twenty years before out of an instinct for survival. When he'd decided to decide and had agreed to the hospital project, he'd discovered he'd decided nothing because he'd cast himself into an illusion.

Karim had awoken at six in the morning. He'd slept badly because of the sound of shells bursting all around. His brother phoned at eight to reassure him that a ceasefire had been announced half an hour earlier; Beirut airport was still open and there was no call to be anxious. Nasim apologised for not being able to come and say goodbye to his brother properly; he was very busy because of the oil tanker catastrophe; he would have liked to invite his brother to dinner "but, you know, the atmosphere's very tense. It's true, Hend's come home, but she's not herself so I'd rather forget about the dinner."

Karim told him the architect had come the night before and left the plans for the hospital with him, and that he'd put them in the drawer.

"It doesn't matter," said Nasim.

He drank a whole pot of unsugared coffee, heated water on the paraffin stove because the electricity was cut, bathed, shaved, phoned Hend, said he was sorry for everything, and decided to visit Salma.

It wasn't necessary, now that Hend had gone back home, but he hadn't known what to do with his day, so a visit to Salma suggested itself. He thought everything was wrong and the woman deserved at least a condolence visit.

Nasri had died, or been killed, and no-one had paid her any attention. Nasim and Hend had been preoccupied with covering up the story. They'd failed to notice the melancholy into which the white-skinned woman had sunk, and which had made her revert to wearing black nylon stockings as a sign of mourning for a man who through his stupidities had lost any possibility of love.

He walked alone along the deserted street. In the twinkling of an eye, the city had emptied itself of people. It was enough for people to sense the stirrings of war for the city to be transformed into a wasteland, the few who ventured out to turn into mere phantoms, and all sound to disappear.

He reached the entrance to the small two-storey building, distinguished by its semi-circular balcony, where he'd sat with Hend for long hours watching the stars that in those days could still find room for themselves in the Beirut sky.

He walked, seeing Hend ahead of him, feeling himself clinging to her fine-boned little body, bending over her long brown neck, and breathing her in with the air.

No, it wasn't love – when love goes it doesn't return – but a longing to breathe in the woman from her neck and bury himself in the folds of her long hair.

No, it wasn't love – Karim hadn't come back to Beirut because of Hend. Hend was over. Even talking to her had become difficult if not impossible, in addition to which his romantic escapades with Ghazala had left no room for the past. Even Muna, to whom he'd once said she was tasty as an orange, could find no room for herself in his heart. Admittedly, her shudders, the shivering of her cheeks, and her suppressed sighs had made him want more, but Ghazala's infidelities and stories had taken him captive, making of him a lover deceived – as it is meet all lovers should be. That was how Nasri had characterised lovers, and he was right, even if Karim had learned that deception was meet for lovers alone only when he was on the verge of forty, when he'd had to swallow two deceptions at one go.

Muna hadn't liked his comparisons or his talk of love, perhaps because she'd felt his words weren't addressed to her, were a kind of delirious speech with which he filled the gaps in his soul. When he'd likened her to an orange she'd burst out laughing and said she hated the smell of oranges because it clung to her hands and wouldn't go away.

"I don't like that romantic stuff. You only have to talk that way and my mood's spoiled. I like love without words," she said.

"So you love me," he said.

"I'm talking about making love. That's what the French, being a refined people, call it. They don't use the word the way you Lebanese do. That makes me cringe."

"But in French you say *baiser* too, and it means 'fuck.'"

"*Stop!*" she said.

Everything here told him "*Stop!*" Even the encounter in Tripoli, which he'd wanted to be an occasion to honour the memory of his friend Khaled – the only one who deserved to be called a hero – Radwan had come along and destroyed, reviving the atmosphere of fear and threat that had driven Karim to flee to France.

Karim would go back to France the next day because it had become impossible to remain in Beirut and because, once at least, he had to confront his fate, not go on fleeing it – his fate of living as a stranger and dying as a stranger. He walked, declaiming the two verses that he'd known by heart ever since he'd learned to memorise, because his father had always repeated them:

> *We walked them as steps written for us*
> > *And he for whom steps are written will walk them*
> *And he whose end lies in one land*
> > *Will not meet his with death in another.*

He stopped beneath the semi-circular balcony, looked at the small white building with its flaking paint and, noticing that the flowerpots had been thrown into the street, felt a sudden fear. The earthenware pots that Salma tended were smashed, the small flowering plants shredded. He bent over the star jasmine, Damascus rose, lily, Arabian jasmine, and gardenia; for a second he thought Salma's balcony must have been hit by a stray shell. Looking up, he could see no sign of damage but the parapet of the balcony was devoid of plants. He climbed the stairs at a run, knocked, panting, on the door, and waited a long while before the woman, cloaked in the darkness of that flat of closed curtains, opened it.

"What happened to the plants?" he asked.

She gestured for him to enter. She sat on the edge of the couch, he sat facing her. He asked again what had happened but she didn't reply. She left him alone in the living room, then returned carrying the coffee pot and two cups. They drank the coffee in silence and when she spoke she seemed to have lost her voice, her words emerging covered in silence – a low sound, whispers, and a kind of rattle.

Darkness and whispers, and a woman sitting on the edge of a couch drinking coffee.

He told her she was right. The war would never end because it was inside them.

She said she hated the war and hated herself. "Everything was wrong through and through, son. What do you want from us here? Go back to your wife and daughters."

He told her he'd spoken with Nasim and that things were back to normal between him and Hend. She replied that nothing was normal but it was better that way.

She said Hend hadn't been wrong to tell him the truth of his father's death because he had to know, but Nasim suffered from the same touch of madness that afflicted Nasri.

"I told her he was a man to be loved because he was a real man, not like the doctor, who was present and not present, kind and unkind. 'Take care, daughter, you don't make my mistake. I discovered I loved Nasri after he died. Take care you don't kill Nasim too and then regret it, the way I now live with regret.'"

She spoke about the doctor in a voice wrapped in cotton wool. Karim, seated opposite her, had to lean forward a little to catch the meanings of her words, but he made no comment. He said only that he believed Hend was innocent of his father's blood; he wasn't sure his brother was.

"Neither of you is innocent," said Salma. Suddenly the woman recovered her voice, which emerged over the whispering. "You and your brother are both criminals, but your brother has a good heart and behaves like a man, while you're something to be scared of."

"Me?"

"You know, so why ask? The truth is you killed your father ten years before he died. You turned your back and went and left your father alone with the war."

"But my brother was here."

"Your brother was always fighting, he was a champion. But what are you? You're nothing."

"I too was . . ." Karim stopped without finishing his sentence. What difference would it make if he told her who he was and why he'd fled Lebanon? Maybe the woman was right. But why had she thrown the plants off the balcony?

When she told him about the plants, her voice fell low again. He wasn't sure he'd heard her say what she had, or whether he'd just imagined she'd said that her plants were simply an illusory form of life; like everything else there, they gave the impression of living but had no life, which was why it was better to throw them into the street and leave them to rot, as had the bodies of so many in that city.

He left wishing he hadn't made the visit. He'd been ready for anything, but it had never crossed his mind that Salma would bring an end to the story of his return to Beirut with such a dismal scene – a woman of sixty-five out at night on her balcony, throwing her flowerpots onto the street; the falling flowerpots sounding like shells exploding, but not one of the neighbours daring to stick his head out of the window to find out what was going on. The city, having donned the raiment of fear, had curled up into itself, retreating into a shell of stupor resembling death. Everything in it had been transformed into a silence interspersed with hoarse sounds, the symptoms of an endless demise.

Like one sinking towards his death – such now was Karim Shammas as he bent to lift his suitcase out of the boot of the black Mercedes taxi that had been taking him to Beirut airport en route back to Montpellier.

His watch said 5.30 a.m., and the Beirut dawn was tinted with darkness and dust.

It had rained the day before. Beirut's spring had arrived, carried on the sound of thunder, the thunder blending in turn into the sound of the intermittent shelling that roamed aimlessly around the city.

The man, who had just completed forty years, had found it impossible to sleep. He had sat on the couch in the living room, yawned, and waited for dawn to the rhythm of the thunder and the rain.

He sat there alone in the darkness of his soul and decided to rewrite his story. He poured a glass of whisky, placed a plate of roasted salted almonds before him, and darkness enveloped him. The electricity was cut, the light of the candle shuddered, turning objects into ghosts, and Karim drank the whisky without ice, feeling his stomach burn.

"It's like the end of the world," Karim said out loud, addressing the dark.

Ghazala had told him that her grandmother, Ghazala, had once described to her the Last Day. The end of the world wouldn't take the form of volcanoes and earthquakes, it would be calm and full of mirrors.

Ghazala the grandmother lived in constant awareness of the Ghazalas who had been and would be her, but her sorrow at not having been reincarnated in her beautiful grand-daughter, in whom she had seen her own longed-for mirror, was great.

The grandmother had lived in that distant village to the rhythm of the meaning of death and the infinite possibilities of recurrence. She'd said that she remembered nothing of her previous life, and that she hadn't spoken of it because she'd died a natural death. "For the soul to remember a person, that person must die violently." She'd told her grand-daughter Ghazala that she hoped she would die a violent death, for those who die that way, when reborn, speak during childhood of their former life. Then they become absorbed into their new lives, take on new roles, and their memories are erased.

"People forget all the time, which is why they're able to start over again and become someone else. In each of us, my daughter, there is someone else. That's why a person is himself and not himself, the one he is he forgets, and the one he isn't becomes him. Woe to us, though, on the Last Day! On that day, my daughter, on that day, a person discovers his true self."

The grandmother said Sheikh Rateb had told her a secret that his grandfather had told him. She said the sheikh had chosen her: "He told me he'd chosen me and I didn't understand what he said. He was talking proper Arabic, the way he did. When he was talking about religion he'd talk in that special tongue. He said proper Arabic was the language of the soul and when we want to talk about the soul we should speak the chaste language. I can't repeat what I heard the way I heard it but what I can say, my daughter, is God save us from that hour, because everyone will see before him all the human forms that he has taken and remember everything. Each will have a thousand and one memories and all of them will be present, and every one of them will be in the head of each of the persons his soul wore on its way to that terrible day, and each person will become a thousand persons and no longer know who he is."

The grandmother said that after hearing this story from Sheikh Rateb she'd no longer set much store by life. "He was sitting in front of me the way you're sitting in front of me now and suddenly I felt he was drowning. The water started flowing around and about him. 'What's happening to you, man?' I said. He said to me, 'You still have much to see.' I told him it wasn't right, 'You're sweating too much.' He told me, 'That's the sign. When one comes close to the secret, the secret swallows you up and you melt into it. This is what I've been waiting for for a long time,' and he started, my dear, I can't say how, to melt. He seemed to get smaller and then he closed his eyes. I went closer to him. He was white and cold and the sweat that had covered him had dried, or disappeared."

The grandmother said that from that day on she had trembled in panic at the thought of the resurrection. "Reincarnation is a fact, my daughter. It's the way life is. A person takes off one garment to put on another in its place. The body is the garment and the soul forgets and only at that instant remembers, and then the person becomes all the people through whom his soul has passed. Imagine yourself, daughter: you're young and old, high-born lady and peasant woman, pretty and ugly, brown and white, sighted and blind, in good health and sick, sound and lame, decent and a whore, lover and beloved, coddled child and orphan, sad and happy, a mother and her daughter. Imagine yourself at that instant. You'll see yourself and discover you are all these, and that the one has been divided and must now be united once more, and then suddenly that one sees before him a thousand individuals and each individual is he and he can no longer tell who he is and where the truth lies. At that instant the one truth is made manifest, the one that doesn't change and is never exchanged, and the person discovers that all of him is false. That's how the resurrection is and that's how a person's story with his story comes to an end."

Ghazala said her grandmother was sweating as she spoke, the sweat pouring from her face, eyes, neck, and head. Her white hair, tied in a bun at the back, was dripping water, as though she had bathed in herself without water. She said she couldn't distinguish between her grandmother's sweat and her tears. "I told her, 'It's not right, Grandmother. You're sweating too much.' 'Me?' she asked. I felt her face, hands, and hair and she began to tremble. 'It's the Hour,' she said; she said she was afraid and didn't want to die. And she started, I can't say how, to melt. She seemed to get smaller and then she closed her eyes. I went closer to her. She was white and cold and the sweat that had covered her had dried, or disappeared."

Ghazala said her grandmother had died in front of her, and whenever she thought of her death her saliva dried up and she developed a fever.

They were sitting naked in bed when she told him her grandmother's story. She'd looked at him with sad eyes and said she felt she'd begun to sweat, the water was covering her, and she was going to die. Karim burst out laughing and said she was lively as a monkey and nothing was going to happen to her.

"I shouldn't have told you what I did. I know you don't believe in these things and you're going to laugh at me. I don't know what came over me to make me tell you. It's the secret of life. You've made me betray myself and my secrets. Damn me, what an ass I am!"

She put on her clothes and left, then disappeared behind the story of her love for Azab, and so on and so forth . . .

On his last Beirut night, in the middle of the darkness and fear, Karim believed that semi-literate woman who had told him her secret.

Karim hadn't had to wait for the resurrection to meet the human incarnations that he'd worn. The months he'd spent in his city had been enough to reveal Beirut's secret, which was that the city was made up of mirrors, and that the individual was not one but a collection of individuals who had made from their misery mirrors for their souls.

"It's misery," said Karim, addressing the dark. He discovered that his voice was vanishing, as though his throat had become hoarse without shouting. He saw all his stories wrapped in silence and discovered he hadn't been speaking when he spoke. He heard his voice drop to a rattle and the cotton wool blocked his ears. He saw how everyone had melted into silence and the universe had fallen still.

His whole story was without words. Speaking of it revealed nothing, for it was written in silence. What he had heard in Beirut and what he heard on that strange night was the sound of silence. Silence has a sound, it can even roar, but it is the roar of a whisper, the rattling of a language that has disintegrated and turned into letters whose wounds will not knit.

He felt his life had been transformed into a shattered mirror. He was enveloped by the sounds of the city, which seemed poised to fall into the valley of darkness – that was how the words had traced themselves in front of him. He saw the city on the brink of the valley and felt everything was sliding into the abyss. Nasim had reported that the ship had caught fire; he'd lost all his wealth in one fell swoop, and the hospital project was over because he was obliged to sell it, and the flat, to pay off a part of his debts. Karim hadn't needed the news about the oil tanker to know that the project had fallen apart and that he would have to bury his story in this city, in silence.

Karim Shammas bent to lift his suitcase out of the boot of the black Mercedes taxi that had been taking him to Beirut airport en route back to Montpellier. All at once the sky lit up and the whistling started. The driver ducked to protect himself from the mortar shells that had begun to fall on the airport road. Suddenly the car turned. Karim heard the screeching of tyres and felt everything shake. He closed his eyes and prepared for death. He heard the driver shout that he was going back to Beirut. He opened his eyes and asked him to keep going and get him to the airport. All at once the car stopped and he heard the driver's voice say through the screeching of the tyres that he couldn't. "If you want to go on, sir, find yourself another car. I've got children and I want to go home."

Karim had a vision of himself as another person. He got out of the car, bent over the boot, lifted out his suitcase, set off down the middle of the dusty, garbage-strewn road, and thought that he'd reached the end of the world.

This was how his Beirut adventure ended, with a ringing in his ears and a feeling that he was supporting himself on his shadow. When he caught sight of the Beirut airport building, with its ruined façade, he looked back and wept.

He entered the check-in area. It was cold and empty, with shards of window glass lying on the tiles. He had to tread on the glass to get to the check-in desk for the plane to Paris.

He could hear the glass crunching under his shoes as he went forward in the direction of the stewardess. She had covered her hair in a blue cap and looked at him with silent, astonished eyes. Suddenly the airport concourses began to shake. It was a soundless bombardment, or so it seemed to Karim, who found himself a seat in a corner, far from the shattered windows. The shelling was like a roaring so hoarse no-one could hear it. At that moment he felt a desire to write a long letter to his twin in which he would apologise to him for everything and tell their story from the beginning.

In his pocket he found the piece of paper on which he'd written the phone numbers of Radwan and Abd el-Malek and on which he'd drawn a plan of the Castle of Saint-Gilles, though he'd placed it at the edge of a steep valley, like those of the south that are overlooked by Shaqif Castle. He turned the piece of paper over onto its blank side and began writing. He wrote a number of lines, read them several times, and discovered that they weren't right for the beginning of a letter that would be worthy of his story with his brother.

The shelling didn't stop. Flashes traversed the city's empty sky, which was covered with a dust resembling fog – a soundless bombardment that seemed to penetrate the walls, the windows, and the body. He wrote to his brother that he had listened at the airport to a new kind of shelling that no-one had ever heard before, that he was tired, and that he wanted to sleep.

He looked at the lines he'd written and found the words were piling up on top of one another, and that the language in which he'd written them no longer served to carry their meanings. He tore the letter up and threw it on the ground, among the scattered fragments of crushed glass. Then he closed his eyes, sat in the darkness of his soul, and decided that to embrace the darkness in a city like Beirut led to death. And such a death, he thought, would be a fitting end to a novel written by Elias Khoury.

Author's Note

Part of this novel was written in Beirut and New York between 2008 and 2010. It was completed in June 2011 in Berlin, where I spent the 2010–11 academic year as a visiting fellow at the Wissenschaftkolleg zu Berlin.

Glossary

The aim of this glossary is to provide the minimum amount of additional information needed to orient the reader. Terms not addressed here are sufficiently explained within the text or may be understood from their contexts. I am greatly indebted to Jim Muir for providing much of the information on recent Lebanese history below. Unattributed translations from the Koran are my own.

Proper names are listed under their first element. English and Arabic definite and indefinite articles are ignored.

Abd el-Hamid Karami (1890–1950): a Sunni Muslim religious figure from Tripoli and a leader of the movement for the independence of Lebanon from France (obtained 1943); Karami served as prime minister and finance minister of Lebanon from 10 January, 1945 to 20 August, 1945.

Abd el-Nasser: Gamal Abd el-Nasser (1918–79), Egyptian army officer, leader of the 1952 revolution that overthrew the monarchy, president from 1954.

Abd el-Rahman Munif (1933–2004): Saudi Arabian novelist; *East of the Mediterranean* (1975) deals with the torture of political prisoners in Iraq.

Abd el-Wahhab: see Mohamed Abd el-Wahhab.

Abu: literally "Father of" and traditionally used, with the name of his eldest son, as a respectful form of address and reference to a married man.

Abu Iyad (1933–91): organisational name of Salah Mesbah Khalaf, deputy chief and head of intelligence for the Palestine Liberation Organisation, and Fatah's second most senior official after Yasser Arafat.

Abu Jihad (1935–88): organisational name of Khalil Ibrahim el-Wazir, Palestinian leader, co-founder of Fatah, and eventually commander of its military wing; assassinated by Israeli commandos in Tunis.

"the adornment of this present life": cf. Koran, al-Kahf (18:46) "Wealth and sons are the adornment of this present life".

al-Akhtal al-Saghir: pen-name of Bishara Abd Allah el-Khouri (1890–1968), Lebanese poet of the Romantic school.

Akkawi cheese: a white brine cheese originating in Acre (Akka) in Palestine.

'ala rasi: literally, "on my head", meaning "I will do what you ask with the greatest of pleasure".

Amal Movement: Lebanese political party founded in 1974, most of whose followers are Shiites; the name Amal ("Hope") derives from the acronym of the party militia, Afwaj al-Muqawama al-Lubnaniyya ("The Lebanese Resistance Detachments").

American University of Beirut: a private English-medium university located in West Beirut; founded as the Syrian Protestant College in 1866, it assumed its present name in 1920 and is often referred to as "A.U.B.".

Amin Gemayel (born 1942): son of Pierre Gemayel (founder of the Phalanges party), brother of Bashir Gemayel (leader of the Lebanese Forces), and twelfth president of Lebanon (1982–8).

Amioun: large Greek Orthodox town in northern Lebanon's Koura district.

"And if you fear you will not be equitable, then only one": Koran, al-Nisa' (4:3).

Anis Freiha (1903–93): Lebanese author who wrote extensively on traditional village life.

arak: a distilled spirit made from grapes and flavoured with aniseed.

Ashrafieh: an old, largely Christian, district of East Beirut.

A.U.B.: i.e. the American University of Beirut (q.v.).

B7 grenade launchers: a term used in Lebanon for the RPG-7, a portable, unguided, shoulder-launched, anti-tank, rocket-propelled grenade launcher.

Bahsas: a neighbourhood of Tripoli.

Baissour: a village in the Aley district of Mount Lebanon, near Souq el-Gharb.

Banu Ammar: Muslim rulers of Tripoli previous to its conquest by crusaders in 1109.

"The Bash": nickname of Bashir Gemayel (q.v.) used by his followers.

Bashir Gemayel (1947–82): Lebanese politician and military commander, son of Pierre Gemayel, founder of the Phalanges; co-founder of the Lebanese Front and supreme commander of its military arm, the Lebanese Forces; president-elect from 23 August, 1982, until his assassination on 14 September, 1982; often referred to as Sheikh Bashir by his followers.

Batroun: a town on the northern Lebanese coast approximately halfway between Beirut and Tripoli, famous for its citrus groves.

Battle of the Hotels: a subconflict during the 1975–77 phase of the Lebanese Civil War which occurred in the Minet el-Hosn hotel district of downtown Beirut; it constituted the first large-scale confrontation between the Christian right-wing Lebanese Front and the leftist Lebanese National Movement militias in alliance with Palestinian fighters and was fought for control of high-rise buildings, access to which permitted or prevented the shelling of nearby Christian districts.

Baybars: Baybars I, Mamluke sultan of Egypt from 1260 to 1277 and vanquisher of the Mongols, who besieged Tripoli in 1271 during his campaign against the crusaders.

Beqaa: a fertile valley about thirty kilometres east of Beirut.

Bey: an Ottoman title awarded to notables such as landowners.

B.G. Squad: the Bashir Gemayel Squad, a military formation within the Phalanges (q.v.) led by Bashir Gemayel (q.v.).

Bhamdoun: a town in Mount Lebanon twenty-three kilometres from Beirut on the road to Damascus, scene of a battle between incoming Syrian forces and retreating Palestinian fighters in 1976.

Bizerte: a city on the Tunisian coast sixty-six kilometres north of Tunis.

Black September: i.e. September, 1971 which saw the opening phase of the war between the Jordanian Army and the Palestine Liberation Organisation that ended in June 1972 with the expulsion of the P.L.O. from Jordan; also the name of a Palestinian armed group that carried out attacks against Israeli and other targets outside the Middle East, the most famous of which was the killing of eleven Israeli athletes and officials and a West German policeman during the 1972 Summer Olympics in Munich.

Brummana: a town in the Matn district of Mount Lebanon overlooking Beirut and the Mediterranean.

Burj el-Barajneh: a southern suburb of Beirut and adjacent Palestinian refugee camp.

el-Burj Square: central Beirut's main square.

burma: a pastry made of shredded filo dough fried, stuffed with pistachios, and soaked in syrup.

Butrus Bustani: educator and writer of textbooks on classical Arabic poetry whose lectures at the Lebanese University were well received by students; sometimes referred to as Master (Muallem) Butrus Bustani; not to be confused with his earlier namesake the philologist (1819–1883).

Camille Chamoun (1900–87): Maronite leader and politician, president of Lebanon 1952–8, founder of the National Liberal Party and its militia, the Tigers, and co-founder of the Lebanese Front.

Carmel: mountain on the Mediterranean coast near Haifa.

CERMOC: Centre d'Études et de Recherche sur le Moyen-Orient Contemporain (Centre for Study and Research on the Contemporary Middle East), a French government-supported centre for social science research established in Lebanon in 1977.

Charles Malek (1906–87): Lebanese philosopher and diplomat, co-founder during the civil war, with Bashir Gemayel and Camille Chamoun, of the Lebanese Front.

Communist Action Organisation: Marxist-Leninist political party and militia group with its roots in the Lebanese branch of the pan-Arab Arab Nationalist Movement.

concours internat: French entrance examination for hospital work.

el-Daawa el-Islami Party (*Hizb el-Daawa el-Islami*): a Lebanese twin of the Iraqi party of the same name that promotes a resurgent Shiite Islam.

Deir Yassin Group: the Deir Yassin groups consisted of young Fedayeen fighters within el-Asifa, Fatah's military wing; one such group, led by Dalal el-Mughrabi, carried out the 1978 Kamal Adwan Operation (q.v.).

Dhahran: a city on Saudi Arabia's Gulf coast that serves as a major administrative centre for the oil industry.

Dhour el-Choueir: a mountain town thirty kilometres east of Beirut, just north of the Beirut–Damascus highway.

Dik al-Jinn (778–*c.*850): Abbasid poet, born in Homs.

Dimitri Coutya: Tripoli-born Greek Orthodox interpreter of Byzantine chant.

"a discord in the land": Koran, al-Anfal (8:73) (trans. Ahmed Ali).

Djamila Bouhired (born 1935): heroine of Algerian resistance to French colonial rule who allegedly placed a bomb in an Algiers café in July 1957 killing eleven people.

"Dr Dahesh"/Daheshism: see Salim Moussa Ashi.

Druze: followers of a monotheistic religion with historic ties to Ismaili Shiite Islam but reflecting also influences from other philosophical and religious systems, one of the most important of which is belief in the transmigration of souls; the largest concentrations of Druze are to be found in Syria, Lebanon, and Palestine.

East Beirut: the mainly Christian side of the city, divided during the civil war from mainly Muslim West Beirut by a confrontation line that ran through the devastated city centre.

Eid el-Fitr: the three-day feast celebrated by Muslims at the end of the fasting month of Ramadan.

Elissa the Phoenician: another name for Dido, legendary Queen of Carthage; some trace the origins of the Lebanese people to the Phoenicians of Tyre, of which Carthage (in today's Tunisia) was originally an outpost.

Emir: a title used in a secular context in a way similar to "prince" and in the Islamic context to denote a district commander, either appointed by a religious leader or self-appointed.

Fairouz: professional name of Nouhad Haddad (born 1935), pre-eminent Lebanese female singer.

Falouja: a Palestinian village thirty kilometres north-east of Gaza City allocated to Arab territory under the 1947 U.N. Partition plan; the Egyptian Army entered the area but were besieged there by Israeli forces from October 1948 to February 1949, after which they withdrew under an international agreement.

Farid el-Atrash (1910–74): a Syrian-Egyptian composer, singer, virtuoso oud (Arab lute) player, and actor.

Fatah: reverse acronym formed from the Arabic name (Harakat al-Tahrir al-Filastini) of the Palestinian Liberation Movement, the major political grouping within the Palestinian Liberation Organisation; historically Fatah has sponsored several armed groups.

fattet makdous: layers of crisped flatbread with tomato sauce, pine nuts, deep-fried eggplants stuffed with meat, yoghurt, and garlic.

Feast of the Cross: one of the twelve major yearly festivals of the Eastern Orthodox Church, celebrated on 14 September to commemorate the rescue of the true cross from the Persians by the Byzantines on that day in 628 AD.

Fedayeen: Palestinian guerrilla fighters against Israel.

Feisal I (1885–1933): Hashemite prince, King of Syria for four months in 1920 until the defeat of his forces at Maysaloun (q.v.); later appointed King of Iraq by the British.

Fragrant City: epithet of Tripoli, in northern Lebanon (Arabic, el-Fayha').

George Habash (1926–2008): Palestinian physician and founder, in 1967, of the Popular Front for the Liberation of Palestine, a break-away from the Palestine Liberation Organisation that opposed a two-state solution to the Palestine question.

Georges Wassouf (born 1961): Syrian singer.

Ghassan Kanafani (1936–1972): Palestinian writer and spokesman of the Popular Front for the Liberation of Palestine, assassinated in Beirut by Israeli secret service agents.

Great Southern River (el-Nahr el-Kabir el-Janoubi): a river that starts in Syria and flows into the Mediterranean Sea forming the border between Syria and Lebanon.

the Greek Orthodox hospital: the popular name of what is officially called St George's Hospital.

Guardianship of the Jurist: a theory in Shia Islam which holds that, in the age following the occultation (temporary disappearance from the world) of the messianic leader descended from the Prophet Muhammad, Islam gives a *faqih* (Islamic jurist) custodianship over believers; since its 1979 revolution, Iran has been ruled according to this concept.

Haganah: a Jewish paramilitary organisation in British Mandate Palestine which later formed the core of the Israel army.

Hajj/Hajja: "Pilgrim" – an honorific form of address and reference used for men/women who have performed the pilgrimage to Mecca (if Muslims) or Jerusalem (if Christians).

Hallab: pastry shop close to el-Tall Square in Tripoli.

Hammana: a town in Mount Lebanon, twenty-six kilometres east of Beirut.

Hamra: a major shopping street in Ras Beirut (West Beirut) and the surrounding district.

Hate nothing – it may be better for you: echoes the words of the Koran: "... it may happen that you will hate a thing which is better for you" (Koran 2:216, trans. A. J. Arberry).

Herzliya: a city on Israel's central coast north of Tel Aviv.

Hezbollah: a Shiite Islamist militant group and political party based in Lebanon.

"his eye was white": he had a roving eye.

Homs: a city in Syria, close to Lebanon's northern border.

Houran: a volcanic plateau in south-western Syria famous for its fertile soils and rain-fed agriculture.

Hundred Days War: a sub-conflict in the Lebanese civil war that pitched Christian Lebanese Forces members against Syrian troops and lasted from February to April 1978.

Ibn Arabi (1165–1240): an exponent of metaphysical Sufism.

Ibn Khaldoun (1332–1406): historian and historiographer, best known for his *Introduction* (to his universal history), in which he elaborated theories of history, society, and economics.

Ibn Taimiya (1263–1328): a conservative Muslim theologian whose views have been widely adopted by modern Islamists.

Imam: (literally, "prayer leader") title accorded Muslim leaders and thinkers; also a proper name.

Imm: literally "Mother of" and traditionally used, followed by the name of her eldest son, as a respectful form of address and reference to a married woman.

Izz el-Din Qassam (1878–1935): Syrian-born Muslim preacher who was a leader in the fight against British, French, and Zionist organisations in the Levant in the 1920s and 1930s; he died in Palestine in a violent confrontation with British authorities.

Jabal el-Arab ("the Mountain of the Arabs"): volcanic highlands in southern Syria with a predominantly Druze population; also known as Jabal el-Durouz ("the Mountain of the Druze").

Jalal Turmus: a Lebanese organic products farm and company.

Jbeil: a city (ancient Byblos) on the Lebanese coast about forty-two kilometres north of Beirut.

Jeha: a "wise fool", the hero of numerous popular anecdotes.

Jerusalem Martyrs' brigade: a fictitious group.

"the Jesuit university": i.e., the Université Saint-Joseph, a private French-medium Catholic university founded by Jesuits in 1875.

jihad: "struggle", whether in the sense of armed action for the expansion or the defence of Islam or of the Muslim's effort towards moral and religious perfection; also a proper name.

Jihad Muqaddas Brigades: (literally, "the Sacred Struggle Brigades"), a Palestinian irregular force in the 1947–48 Palestinian–Israeli war, led by Abd el-Qadir el-Husayni and Hasan Salama.

Joint Forces: military force comprising members of the Lebanese National Movement (a coalition of leftist and Arab Nationalist organisations led by Druze leader Kamal Jumblatt) and Palestinian fighters that was active in the Lebanese civil war from its start in 1975 up to the Israeli invasion in 1982 and constituted during those years the main military opposition to the Lebanese Forces.

Jounieh: largely Christian city on the Lebanese coast about sixteen kilometres north of Beirut.

June 5 defeat: the defeat by Israel of the armed forces of Egypt, Jordan, and Syria in the Six-Day War, fought between 5 and 10 June, 1967.

Kamal Adwan Operation: an attack carried out on 11 March, 1978 by guerrilla fighters of the Palestine Liberation Organisation's Fatah organisation led by Dalal el-Mughrabi that involved the hijacking of a public bus on Israel's coastal highway; the operation was named after the P.L.O. chief of operations killed in an Israeli commando raid on Beirut in April 1973.

Kamal Jumblatt (1917–77): the main leader of the Lebanese Druze and founder in 1949 of the Progressive Socialist Party, which, as an armed force, became the backbone of the Lebanese National Movement (q.v.) during the civil war; Jumblatt's assassination by gunmen in the Shouf mountains was widely blamed on the Syrian regime.

kenafeh: a kind of pastry soaked in sugar syrup, often prepared over a layer of melted cheese.

Khaled ibn al-Walid (born in Mecca in 592, died in Homs in 642): leader of the Muslim armies under the Prophet Muhammad and his immediate successors.

Khalil el-Wazir: see Abu Jihad.

Khalil Hawi (1919–82): Lebanese symbolist poet.

Khawaja: title accorded Christians of substance.

kibbeh labaniyyeh: meat balls prepared with strained yoghurt.

kibbeh nayyeh: minced raw lamb mixed with fine bulgur, onions, and spices.

kufta: balls of minced meat, prepared in a variety of ways.

labneh: strained yoghurt.

Land Day: 30 March, the annual day of commemoration of the 1976 general strike and protests by Palestinians in Israel against an Israeli plan to expropriate thousands of acres of Palestinian land for security and settlement purposes.

Lebanese Forces: the military arm, created in 1976, of the Lebanese Front, a coalition of right-wing Christian parties; commanded until his assassination in 1982 by Bashir Gemayel.

Lebanese Front: coalition of Christian right-wing parties formed in 1976 by Camille Chamoun, Pierre Gemayel (father of Bashir), and Suleiman Frangieh, as a counterbalance to the Lebanese National Movement.

Lebanese National Movement: coalition of left-wing and secular parties formed in the 1970s and led by Kamal Jumblatt.

the Lebanese University: a public Arabic-medium university founded in 1951.

madrasa: medieval building for the teaching of Islamic law.

Maghdousheh: town fifty kilometres south of Beirut famed for its agricultural produce.

Mahmoud Darwish (1941–2008): Palestinian poet and prose writer.

Mamluke: pertaining to either of two dynasties of slave soldiers who ruled Egypt and Syria from Cairo between 1250 and 1517; a member of either dynasty.

manaqish: flat rounds of dough baked in the oven and topped with thyme, cheese, or other ingredients.

Mandate: i.e. the mandate for the temporary government of Lebanon granted by the League of Nations to the French, in force from 1923 to 1943.

Mar: saint.

Maronite: pertaining to, or a member of, a Christian sect in communion with Rome whose members form a majority in the Mount Lebanon area of Lebanon and up to 22 per cent of the population of the country as a whole; according to an unwritten agreement, the president of Lebanon must be a Maronite. The name derives from an early leader of the Church called Maroun.

Mawlana: "Our Master", a title accorded certain Muslim religious leaders.

Maysaloun: a town in Syria about twelve kilometres west of Damascus where French forces defeated those of the short-lived Arab Kingdom of Syria on 23 July, 1920.

"Men are the managers of the affairs of women": Koran, al-Nisa' (4:36) (trans. A.J. Arberry).

mezze: assortment of small dishes served as a prelude to the main course or as a meal in themselves.

Michel Aoun (born 1933): Lebanese general and one of two rival prime ministers from 1988 to 1990.

Misgav Am: kibbutz in the Upper Galilee in northern Israel close to the border with Lebanon, attacked by Palestinian guerrillas on 7 April, 1980.

Mohamed Abd el-Wahhab (1902–91): prominent Egyptian composer and singer, a pioneer in the development of modern Arabic music.

Muhammad Baqir el-Sadr (1935–80): Najaf-based Iraqi Shiite cleric, writer, and Islamic theorist, ideological founder of el-Daawa el-Islami Party (q.v.).

Mu'in Bseiso (1926–84): Palestinian poet from Gaza.

Museum crossing: one of the main crossing points between West and East Beirut during the Lebanese civil war, in front of the National Museum.

al-Mutanabbi (*c.*915–65): Abbasid poet.

al-Nahar: an influential Lebanese daily newspaper (founded 1933) with a weekly cultural supplement.

Nahr el-Bared Camp: a Palestinian refugee camp about sixteen kilometres north of Tripoli in northern Lebanon. Clashes with the Lebanese Army broke out there and in other camps in 1969 as part of a wider crisis over the presence of Palestinian guerrillas' in the country. These clashes led to a secret agreement signed in Cairo in November regulating the Palestinian presence, under which they were given security control inside the camps.

Najaf: city in Iraq, about 160 kilometres south of Baghdad, burial place of the fourth caliph Ali ibn Abi Taleb, nephew and son-in-law of the Prophet Muhammad and, according to Shiites, his rightful successor; a major centre of Shiite pilgrimage and learning.

Nasri: male personal name meaning "My Victory" (hence the decision of a character to name her French son Victor after Nasri Shammas).

natef: cream used in pastries made from tahini, syrup, and a certain plant.

Nazim Hikmet (1902–63): Turkish radical poet, novelist, and playwright;

Nevsky Prospekt: the main street of St Petersburg, laid out by Peter the Great.

"no compulsion in religion": Koran, al-Baqara (2:256).

Normandie: the Hotel Normandie on the once fashionable Avenue des Français; the latter became covered with landfill during the civil war.

Nouri mosque: large mosque in Homs, Syria; in antiquity a pagan temple that was later converted into a church.

Palavas (-les-Flots): a seaside village and resort about six kilometres south of Montpellier.

the Palestine Catastrophe: the dispossession of the Palestinians of their homeland in 1948 at the hands of Zionist forces and through the establishment of the State of Israel.

Palestine Liberation Organisation: organisation created in 1964 with the purpose of creating an independent Palestine.

People of the Book: members of religions other than Islam with revealed scriptures (i.e. Christians, Sabians, and Jews) whom Muslims are bidden in the Koran to protect.

People of the House: descendants of the Prophet Muhammad.

Phalanges (the Lebanese Phalanges Party): a right-wing Maronite Christian political party founded in 1936 as a paramilitary youth movement by Pierre Gemayel and others in conscious imitation of the Spanish Falange and Italian Fascist parties; with its military wing, the Kataeb Regulatory Forces, commanded for much of the period by Pierre Gemayel's son Bashir, the Phalanges constituted the largest component of the Lebanese Forces coalition.

Popular Front for the Liberation of Palestine: Palestinian Marxist-Leninist group founded in 1967 by George Habash; the P.F.L.P. broke away from the Palestine Liberation Organisation in 1974 in opposition to the P.L.O.'s adoption of a two-state solution to the Palestine question.

Progressive Socialist Party: founded in 1949 by Kamal Jumblatt with a secularist, pro-Arab Nationalist, and pro-Palestinian stance; the backbone of the leftist Lebanese National Movement during Lebanon's civil war.

Prophetic Traditions: accounts of the words or deeds of the Prophet Muhammad.

qarqashalli: a dry biscuit often dipped in tea for breakfast.

Rafiq Hariri (1944–2005): Lebanese business tycoon, twice prime minister (1992–8 and 2002–4); assassinated 14 February 2005.

Ramallah: a city in Palestine, in the West Bank.

Ras el-Kheima: one of the seven emirates constituting the United Arab Emirates.

Rawsheh: an upscale district of Beirut, well known for a rock formation in the sea close to the coastline and known as Rawsheh Rock or Pigeons' Grotto.

Régis Debray (born 1940): French leftist intellectual and activist; his book *Revolution in the Revolution?* (1967) analysed the tactical and strategic doctrines then prevalent among militant socialist movements in Latin America and acted as a handbook for guerrilla warfare that supplemented Che Guevara's manual on the subject.

Renaud, the Crusader lord of Sidon: Renaud (or Reynald or Reginald) de Grenier, ruled 1171–84.

Ricard: i.e. Ricard Pastis, an aniseed-flavoured liqueur produced by the French company Pernod Ricard.

sablé: a kind of biscuit.

Sadeq Jalal Azm (born 1934): Syrian philosopher and human rights advocate; his book *A Critique of Religious Thought*, a collection of his essays, uses a Marxist-materialist approach to analyse the exploitation by Arab governments of the religious sentiments of their populations as a cover for their own incompetence and responsibility for the 1967 defeat; accused of stirring up religious conflict with the book, Azm was imprisoned in Lebanon in January 1970 and released the same month after being acquitted of all charges.

al-Safir: a Lebanese daily newspaper.

Safra: village on the Lebanese coast north of Jounieh, whose Safra Marina resort was the scene of the massacre in 1980 of Dany Chamoun's Tigers Militia by the Phalangist militia of Chamoun's erstwhile ally Bashir Gemayel (q.v.).

Said Aql (born 1911 or 1912): Lebanese poet writing in both classical Arabic and Lebanese colloquial and an ideologue of Lebanese linguistic, cultural, and political particularism.

Sa'iqa: a Palestinian Baathist political and military faction created and controlled by Syria.

Saint-Gilles, Castle of: fortress built, starting in 1103, by crusader Raymond de Saint-Gilles overlooking Tripoli, Lebanon, to lay siege to the city.

Salim Moussa Ashi (1909–84): founder of the religion of Daheshism (in reference to his self-bestowed sobriquet of "Dr Dahesh", meaning "Dr Amazing").

Sannine: second highest peak in the Mount Lebanon range, visible from Beirut.

shankaleesh: balls of dried cow or sheep milk cheese, usually dusted with thyme or other spices; a common mezze dish.

Shaqif Castle: twelfth-century crusader fortress in southern Lebanon close to the village of Arnoun; from 1976 it was a Palestine Liberation Organisation stronghold and was frequently attacked by Israeli forces, which finally took control of the castle in 1982 during the Israeli invasion.

Shatila and Sabra: Palestinian refugee camp and neighbouring district in Beirut, scene of a massacre of between 750 and 3,500 civilians, mostly Palestinians and Lebanese Shiites, carried out between 16 and 18 September, 1982, by Phalangist fighters led by Elie Hobeika with the knowledge and indirect assistance of the Israeli army.

shawarma: meat or chicken grilled on a vertical spit from which portions are shaved, often to be served wrapped in bread as a sandwich.

Shayyah: a south-eastern suburb of Beirut, with a mixed Christian and Shiite population.

Sheikh Imam (1918–95): Imam Mohammad Ahmad Issa, an Egyptian leftist composer and singer, styled "Sheikh" because of his early training at the religious university of al-Azhar.

shmeiseh: a kind of sweet pastry made in Tripoli.

S.K.S.: acronym of the Section Kataeb de Sécurité.

the Socialist Revolution Movement: a fictitious organisation.

Sofiel: neighbourhood in the Beirut district of Ashrafieh.

the Souk, the General Souk: the commercial area of downtown Beirut; also, euphemistically, the nearby red light district.

tabbouleh: salad typically made of bulgur, tomatoes, finely chopped parsley, mint, and onion, seasoned with olive oil, lemon juice, and salt.

Ta'if Agreement: signed 22 October, 1989, in Ta'if, Saudi Arabia, by members of Lebanon's last parliament (that of 1972) and designed to put an end to the civil war; among other things, it strengthened the powers of the Sunni Muslim prime minister *vis-à-vis* the Maronite Christian president.

Tall el-Zaatar: Palestinian refugee camp in Beirut, up to 1,500 of whose residents were massacred on 12 August, 1974 by right-wing Christian forces as the denouement of a seven-month siege during which many hundred more Palestinian civilians also died.

tarnib: a popular card game.

"they did not slay him, neither crucified him, only a likeness of that was shown to them": Koran, al-Nisa' (4:157) (trans. A.J. Arberry).

"Thou guidest not whom thou likest, but God guides whom He wills": Koran, al-Qasas (28:56) (trans. A.J. Arberry, *The Koran Interpreted*).

Tripoli: a city in northern Lebanon, the second largest in the country.

tuk-tuk: passenger-carrying motorised tricycle.

Udhris: members of the Banu Udhra tribe of Bedouins of the Hejaz during the Umayyad period (seventh/eighth centuries A.D.), famed for their poetry celebrating chaste love.

Umm Kulthoum (1904?–71): Egyptian singer.

Uncle Sam's: a restaurant close to the main gate of the American University of Beirut on Bliss Street.

Ustaz Wahid: name of the romantic lead character played by Farid el-Atrash (q.v.) in a number of films (literally, "Mr Lonely").

Volker Schlöndorff (born 1939): German filmmaker; his film *Circle of Deceit* (*Fälschung*, released 1981; based on a novel by Nicholas Born) concerns a German journalist sent to Beirut to report on the civil war.

War of 1860: series of largely Druze–Maronite conflicts that resulted in the deaths of many thousands of Lebanese and culminated in a massacre of Christians by Druze in Damascus.

West Beirut: the mainly Muslim side of the city, divided during the civil war from mainly Christian East Beirut by a confrontation line that ran through the devastated city centre.

the White Sea: i.e. the Mediterranean Sea.

"whoso slays a soul . . . shall be as though he had slain mankind altogether": Koran, al-Ma'ida (5:32) (trans. A.J. Arberry).

yalla: Arabic: "Get a move on!" or "Let's go!"

Yehoshua (born 1936): Abraham B. Yehoshua, Israeli novelist, essayist, and playwright.

zaatar: breakfast staple consisting of a mixture of thyme, sesame, and sumac eaten with bread and olive oil.

Zakariya Ahmad (1896–1961): Egyptian musician and composer.

Zeryab: nickname (literally, "blackbird") of Ali ibn Nafi' (789–857), a musician born in Iraq who spent much of his life in Cordoba.

zimmi: member of the People of the Book (q.v.) (literary Arabic *dhimmi*).

Author Biographies

ELIAS KHOURY is the author of thirteen novels, four volumes of literary criticism and three plays. He was editor-in-chief of the cultural supplement of Beirut's daily newspaper, *An-Nahar*, and is Global Distinguished Professor of Middle Eastern and Islamic Studies at New York University.

HUMPHREY DAVIES has been twice awarded the Banipal Prize for his translation of novels by Elias Khoury, in 2006 for *Gate of the Sun* and in 2010 for *Yalo*. His translation of Alaa Al Aswany's *The Yacoubian Building* was voted Best Translation of 2007 by the Society of Authors.